TO DIE ON SKOPELOS

TO DIE ON SKOPELOS

CADEN ST. CLAIRE

ISBN: 978-1-7365524-3-8

A NOTE TO MY READERS

In my research for Skopelos, I discovered the national bird of Greece is the Phoenix (a bird who dies in a blaze of glory and is reborn from the ashes) which fit perfectly. (Greg Rupel, my formatter, splashed it beautifully across Chapter One!) I also unearthed Greek sayings and proverbs suited to each chapter along with the fact that in the Greek language, unlike the English, there many different definitions of love. I found this fascinating, as did my main character...

The motifs located below each Chapter heading are called "meanders" in the Greek and are found on statues, page borders, and antique vases. The word originated from a reference to the River Meander mentioned in "The Illiad" by Homer; he described a river that twisted and turned as it wandered through the countryside. But it also symbolized an eternal flowing of friendship, love, and devotion—as well as actual waves like the constantly moving ocean. A Greek saying, "the sea never dies," very nearly became the title of my book for reasons I shall leave you to discover...

Finally, being slightly agoraphobic (from the Greek "fear of the open marketplace"), I begin Layna's story with "Do not disturb my circles" because it reminded me of inmates in mental wards who walk in circles to keep their world in balance (an interesting concept I discovered in "I Never Promised You a Rose Garden" by Hannah Green about a young girl who goes quite mad) — which pretty much says it all, about the rest of us…

Caden St. Claire

To Demetra Giannopoulos Mustafaoglu
who taught me to bellydance and inspired me to be all I could be
with her grace, her humor, her unselfish befriending of
others, and her incredible singing voice.

Thank you for introducing me to
moussaka, spanakopita, feta cheese, koefte, çaçok, the
hasapiko, and all things Greek and more,
for allowing me to envision a world of
whitewashed buildings trimmed in blue
beside a cerulean sea.

Opa!

CHΛPTΣR OΠΣ

μὴ μοῦ τοὺς κύκλους τάραττε.

DO NOT DISTURB MY CIRCLES.

She clawed her way to consciousness and collapsed against the pillows, her lungs begging for air.

Breathe in. Breathe out.

Her chest shuddered, then rose and fell.

A high ceiling soared upward to a chandelier, bronze and ornate, swaying in a gentle breeze that filled the room—while an unfamiliar bed cradled her body and held her captive.

Sounds invaded the silence. The cry of gulls from nearby. Then, farther out, a boat sounded, low and mournful. Music beckoned from a distance in strange, hypnotic rhythms that gave substance to the burgeoning certainty she was somewhere in the Mediterranean.

But why? And why was it important?

Turning her head brought sudden pain. She waited for the dizziness to pass.

Where was she?

White ceiling-to-floor drapes caught each breeze, undulating in and out, equally spaced between window openings three feet across and six feet tall, as if carved out of stone in a high castle. But there were no panes of glass. Only openings. She wondered what they did about mosquitoes.

And burglars.

When the dizziness passed, she held onto a bedpost and pulled herself up. Halting steps took her across polished wooden floors to the closest window, where sea air filled her senses. The aroma of sunshine on water helped her breathe; even the smell of dead fish seemed a new and unexpected sensation.

Her head pounded. She grabbed the wall to steady herself. Wooden floors felt cool to her bare feet, the simple nightgown foreign to her body. And images swirled in her brain, battling one another for dominance.

There was a dream. A horrible dream. A car crash. A collision.

Pain seared the left side of her brain.

Something about a ring.

And water.

She halted, one hand against the wall. It occurred to her this might also be a dream. And yet, she saw every detail in the room, felt the coolness of wood and the warmth of sun, smelled the sea, heard hypnotic music that sounded familiar.

Disjointed scenes from the nightmare began to surface.

She glanced at Jack behind the wheel of her aunt's car. So cool, so carefree. Then, she looked down at the diamond ring on her third finger. It was the ring she'd always wanted. Strange, it seemed out-of-place against faded jeans and a sweatshirt. Besides, Jack would never have spent that much money on her. Twenty minutes in front of a judge—that's all it had taken to sign her life away. So, this was the honeymoon? In a beat-up Chevy cruising down the highway at breakneck speed when we had all the time in the world?

Road signs zipped past the car with a whizzing sound that said too fast, too fast, too fast. Everything, moving too fast. She could feel his eyes on her. If only he would watch the road.

"So, how's it feel, being married?"

"I suppose it's too late to change my mind," she mumbled. The half-teasing tone she was trying for didn't come out right. It seldom did.

He laughed.

"Do I have to—"

"Don't worry about a thing," he said. "I'll get you drunk and you'll never know what hit you." His lopsided grin almost made it palatable. Jack always knew just what to say.

She tried to smile, but her mind kept screaming if only, if only, if only, if only.

Morning sun broke through the clouds and covered her more completely than Jack could ever hope to. She closed her eyes to the raw heat while her husband reached over to fumble in the glove compartment for his sunglasses, cursing beneath his breath.

The squeal of tires.

A sensation of flight.

A sickening thud.

A place of darkness where even the sun couldn't find her.

And then, she drowned.

Eyes opened wide, she sucked in her breath, swiping at a billowing drape that brushed her cheek like a cobweb. The brightness of the sky and sea, so welcoming a moment ago, assaulted her. Cupping her hands to shield her eyes, she scanned the horizon, where picturesque cliffs climbed upward. She leaned over and looked down, instinctively fighting a fear of heights.

A narrow balcony below the windows ran the length of the building. At the end of the balcony, stone steps led down and disappeared into a walled-in garden, ending at a gate that stood slightly ajar.

A gardener, surrounded by potted flowers, hand-tilled the soil. He was crouching down to plant a fuchsia-colored bougainvillea.

She frowned. Once it attained its true height and width, the bougainvillea would completely block the walkway. And they could never be cut back, not that drastically. How stupid.

The gardener looked up, his olive complexion half-hidden in the shadow of a straw hat. For a moment, she imagined another face beneath the gardening hat, that of an older woman smiling up at her. She smiled in return, but the friendly face melted into a man's dark eyes staring up at her. He stood and backed away, stumbling like a servant. Then, for no apparent reason, he turned and hurried through the gate into an alley.

A breeze scattered her hair, bringing a corresponding chill between her shoulder blades up into her neck. Something was wrong. And not just with the gardener.

People don't dream in color. Where had she read that, that if you dream in color, it comes true? The dream about Jack and the car wreck had been in black and white. But here, roses hung from trellises in shades of deep crimson and bashful pink. Violets burst forth from the soil. Orange-red geraniums in clay pots basked in the sun. Explosions of color, everywhere she looked. A perfect picture postcard from the Greek Isles.

Fabric from the curtain slipped through her fingers—a fine cotton, expensive and unbelievably soft, draped from wooden rods set into the stone wall. They fluttered along the window-like openings that spanned the room on three sides. Like the nightgown she wore, it all spoke of a simplistic elegance her spirit longed to embrace. Yet again, she looked around the room where she'd been reborn. Was it a prison, or a sanctuary? Or both?

The fragrance of flowers wafted through the room as she made her way back to the bed, running her fingers along the polished wood of the bedpost in hopes of remembering how she got there. That's when she saw the diamond ring, the same as the one in the dream, sparkling in sunlight that danced through the window and illuminated her nails, long and manicured, but unpolished.

Holding lightly to the walls, she made her way to the four matching windows on the far side of the room, drawing the curtains back to capture another glimpse of her world. Fishing boats of blue, orange, and white dotted the sea, whitewashed homes mounted on stone steps honeycombed the hills, and the sounds of an open market hummed in the street below. Windows flanked by blue shutters complemented matching rooftops. Dogs barked in the distance, competing with the gulls for attention. Housewives bartered with vendors in a strange, rhythmic language. The aroma of olive oil and pungent garlic wafted up from the streets below, mingling with the odor of dead fish.

She looked back the way she'd come. Without knowing it, she'd made a kind of circle. Hadn't she read about a young girl in a mental institute where crazy people walked in circles to keep the world in balance?

The door opened, but she ignored the intrusion—as long as she focused on philosophical issues, reality had nowhere to go. The pounding in her head had diminished, but she could feel it biding its time like a dormant volcano; she feared awakening what lay beneath.

"Layna?"

The voice was husky, masculine, gentle.

Her spine stiffened. The name meant nothing, but the voice that called to her sounded familiar. Too familiar. Curiosity demanded she face whatever may come. Dreams are like that.

The man looked to be in his mid-thirties, possibly older, but handsome and solidly built. His casual clothes looked like they'd cost a fortune. His hair was dark, just beginning to get distinguished streaks of gray at the sides, and longer than...what?

He stared at her, his body language as hesitant as her own, as though waiting to see which one would make the first move.

She had no idea what that move should be. Her senses, coupled with his unannounced entry, told her this was his bedroom. So, what was she doing here?

He walked toward her, self-confident with a hint of an unpretentious swagger, yet cautious. Can a person smile and frown at the same time?

She backed way, heart pounding.

He stopped where he was.

"I cannot believe—awake at last," he said, his voice thick with a beautiful accent. "I was think maybe you sleep forever."

His eyes flickered, as though he'd said the wrong thing. A breeze teased her with a scent of musk, reminding her of woods in autumn, an aroma that deepened as he approached another step, then another. His strength and bearing pulled at a memory deep inside her; otherwise, he stayed a stranger.

She watched as he drew close enough to search her face for answers, though he'd asked no questions. For a moment, the sun pierced through the curtains, shining life into dark, brown eyes blessed with thick, dark lashes any woman would kill to possess. The sunlight caused tiny golden specks to dance inside the pools of liquid brown. The curtain billowed back against the window in a silken flow, and she wondered how it felt to run her fingers through his hair.

A deep breath separated her; she stepped back, holding steady against the inclination to sway. Better to deal from a position of strength. She'd heard that somewhere.

He smiled in approval. Not knowing why, she could only wait, stupefied, while her ridiculous heart broke its steady rhythm at the sight of his mouth, full-lipped and sensual.

"You are back," he whispered. "How do you feel?"

His hand reached out to touch her cheek. She recoiled.

Back from where?

Horrified, she realized his gaze had settled on her mouth, like he wanted to kiss her. Like he already had.

"Where's Jack?" she asked. Her throat hurt. "What have you done with him?"

"Jack? Layna, what is it? Did you have the bad dreams again? I am sorry. I do not mean frighten you. You have been ill. Are you hungry? Do you need anything?"

Too many questions. Broken English.

"Where's Jack?" she asked again, her voice still hoarse.

A look of disappointment flickered across the man's face.

Okay, if it's a dream, it's time to wake up.

But the harder she tried to disassociate herself, the more the reality of her here-and-now collided with the nightmare about Jack. It ended in a blinding pain that streaked across the left side of her head. She pressed the palm of her hand there, blinking against the sudden throbbing.

"Layna?" He moved as if to comfort her.

She drew back, knowing he'd comforted her before, gasping at the questions such knowledge called forth in her heart and mind.

He stepped closer with a half-hearted gesture of kindness, but fear backed her against the wall. Her heart hammering, she ran her hand over the rough ridges of plaster on the stippled wall, pricking her finger. She brought the hand forward and stared at the dot of blood, then at him, praying she'd wake up now. Nothing happened.

"Oh God, it's real," she whispered.

He made as if to reach for her hand. She blinked against the throbbing in her head.

"It is all the right," he whispered. "No one will harm you. You've been ill. I call the doctor. Things are fine, I promise."

Too many words.

He stopped, his dark eyes shadowed and confused as he turned to leave.

When the door closed with an ominous click, she closed her eyes and leaned her forehead against the coolness of the stuccoed wall, recalling one of the things he'd said.

Did you have the bad dreams again? Why did he say that? How many had she had? Were they all the same?

Her brain swam, and she tasted bile. Mucus rose in her throat as the volcano came to life and moved in her stomach like an angry tiger, threatening to erupt at any moment.

"Oh, God," she moaned, stumbling to a small hallway, praying it led to a bathroom. But she faced a wall-to-wall closet and another hallway. Careening through the maze, she sped onward like a determined mouse and reached her destination as a bout of heaving claimed her. Nothing else mattered for a long while, except the quiet that followed.

After taking care of other needs almost as pressing, she made her way to the sink and splashed water in her face until she felt somewhat human. Maybe she'd gotten rid of whatever drugs they'd given her. Steadying herself at the sink to pour a glass of water, she looked up and stared into the eyes of a madwoman—a thin, frightened creature with dark, matted hair that smelled funny and haunted eyes that looked back at her from another time and place.

It was all wrong. But one question erupted from both sets of eyes.

Who's Layna?

CHAPTΣR TWO

Απο μικρό και απο κουζουλό μαθαίνεις την αλήθεια.

FROM A CHILD AND A CRAZY PERSON, YOU LEARN THE TRUTH.

Her hands shook. Water sloshed over the rim of the glass.

The madwoman in the mirror looked like she belonged in Ward D. The one where what's left of their bodies scuttle across the tiles and end up against the wall, holding themselves and nodding for no reason.

Her heart started pounding again.

Wait. He'd said something about a doctor, calling the doctor. Maybe she really *had* been sick. Maybe she still was! Even if she'd been in a sanitarium, she was okay now, right? She was awake, which apparently she hadn't been for quite a while. Was she okay now, or was he just running out of drugs? She checked her arms. There was a strange bruise on top of her right hand, a tiny reddish dot, and the imprint of a bandage.

That's it. I'm out of here.

She glanced at her nightgown. A little fancy for Ward D. Anyway, the aftertaste from throwing up took precedence. A brief rummage of drawers resulted in a toothbrush, toothpaste, and mouthwash, though the latter two carried strange names and forced her to trust the picture and the minty taste alone. She refilled the glass with water and carried it into the endless closet, setting it on top of a built-in dresser.

Finding street clothes wasn't that simple. She opened all the cabinets and drawers in the line of built-ins, searching for anything that looked familiar while she tried to remember how she'd gotten there. But last night and the night before, and the night before that were a blank. Or was it just the horrendous headache that came in receding waves whenever she tried to think?

The clothes were wrong, like everything else, though there were choices enough to fill a small department store. She ran her fingers down hangers filled with silks and rayons, most of them in bold, garish colors. Italian leather sandals caught her eye in the row of shoes, while the extravagance astounded her. Designer clothes, designer man, designer house.

She grabbed things and tried them on. Everything was in European sizes that made no sense, especially when she had no idea what size she wore to begin with. The black slacks were too big and a little short—a belt would help. She yanked one off a belt rack. The Italian sandals were too large as well. The bra proved far too voluptuous for her average-sized blessings; she opted to do without, hating the fact that she was small enough to do so. A simple black blouse all but engulfed her, but with a second belt to hide the fact, the outfit was complete.

Okay, maybe a scarf or hat to hide her awful hair, and sunglasses for the dark circles beneath her eyes. When she reached for the glass of water, the perfect scarf in just the right colors spilled out of a black patent purse and slid off the dresser. She reached to catch it. A long sheet of embossed paper followed the scarf and floated to the floor, landing beside it. Wrapping the scarf around her hair, she used the paper as a catch-all for the contents of the purse and dumped everything on top of it.

There wasn't much. No wallet. No identification. No keys. Some foreign paper money, coins, makeup in all the wrong colors, and a hairbrush. She had money now, even if she wasn't sure if it was drachmas or euros. It looked like euros, so maybe she hadn't slept through a decade or two. Whatever it was, surely it was enough to make it to the American Embassy, and from there, home to Jack. She froze, but it wasn't the thought of Jack that held her attention.

Laying the paper money down, she pushed the makeup and coins slowly to one side and studied the document, some of it printed in English as well as what—Greek? Even in another language, it would still have resembled a marriage certificate in black and white. Or in this case, beige paper with fancy, black print. *Théora Elayna Giannopoulos to Endréus Leonidas Amratsis. Married in Nicosia, on the Isle of Cyprus.*

The date bothered her, only because it held no significance. She realized she had no idea what today's date was, or yesterday's date, so the date on the paper meant nothing, but the name roiled through her brain. *Layna. Elayna. Layna.* That's what he'd called her. Was this supposed to be her? But she was already married, to Jack.

She sat down in a chair to keep the room from spinning, and squeezed her eyes against the pain that came with remembering. *Don't pass out, not now, not here.*

Breathe in. Breathe out. She retrieved the glass of water and drank slowly until the dizziness abated, wishing it was something a bit stronger than water. Her stomach rumbled. Food. How long had it been? No matter. She had to get out, and now!

As if to underline her resolve, muffled shouting filtered up from downstairs.

Her stomach growled even louder. Maybe she could grab something in the kitchen, wherever that was, and make it out the back door, wherever that was. But for now, she needed to find out what was happening.

Easing the bedroom door open, she stepped out into a long hallway that stretched all the way to a door at the opposite end of the run. A second bedroom? Her bare feet stepped onto a luxurious

Persian rug that ran the length of the hall and covered most of the wood. At the center of the open hallway, a wide staircase led downstairs to a grand foyer and a front door of olive wood with an ornate, raised carving of an olive tree. Which told her it was either Greece or Israel.

The open foyer boasted a spectacular chandelier, but it was the unattended front door that held her attention, and not because of any expensive or artistic merits. She calculated her odds of making a run for it. Her hand reached automatically for the wall. Okay, her odds weren't that great, considering she was too weak to run.

From her vantage point upstairs, she gazed down into parts of rooms that made up the ground floor. A portion of a long, polished dining table gleamed in the room to her right, while the room to the left revealed bookcases and half of a swivel chair. Okay. A dining room and an office. A brief flash of a man pacing back and forth in front of the bookcase confirmed it as the source of the argument. There weren't doors to the rooms, just extremely wide openings, curved at the corners.

The men yelled at each other in what sounded like Greek—if foreign movies and strange names were anything to go by. Lines creased her forehead as an image of Anthony Quinn passed through her mind vaults. She shook it aside and slid her hand along the bannister, crossing to the other side and hiding behind one of the two columns that flanked the balustrade. The voices rose, angry and emotional, then everything stopped. There was a solid sound like someone's fist hitting a piece of wood. Someone made a loud, grunting noise. Then a door slammed—a door leading outside?—followed by the sound of breaking glass.

Her calculations for escaping out the front door were put on hold when it fractured into pieces and three men with guns burst in, flattening themselves against the foyer wall. She shrank even farther behind the column and against the wall. Two of the men lifted their weapons and rushed into the room with the bookcases.

Gun shots! The third man hesitated in the foyer, glanced around, then headed for the stairs, and her! She caught her breath. More shots rang out in the office, and the man abandoned the stairs to follow the same pattern as the previous two. Once he disappeared into the office, she quickly retraced her steps to the bedroom, locked the door, and propped a chair up against the doorknob, fairly certain it wouldn't stop anyone from breaking in. Especially one of the thugs from downstairs.

She yanked a jacket off a hanger and threw everything, including the document, into a Gucci bag, then stumbled to the window. After a deep breath, she drew the drape aside and scouted the garden area. The gardener was still MIA. Excellent.

Easing out onto the balcony, she scooted along its surface on her behind as far as she could, then hobbled down the stone steps and headed for the gate. Just as she reached the gate and turned the corner, a slight ping hit the stone wall beside her right ear, shattering her nerves completely. Muttering something very American, she made for the marketplace and people.

Sounds of a real world engulfed her as she stumbled down cobblestone streets into the main plaza. Tent roofs of all sizes, colors, and shapes pulled in and disgorged a multitude of people, filling the plaza with incredible sounds and smells equating to a sensory overload. She hyperventilated, using her purse for a paper bag until she could breathe again.

Vendors argued with buyers, and buyers argued back. The flower stalls made her queasy; the food stalls made her hungry. In headscarf and sunglasses, she hoped to pass for just another tourist in a crowd of fishermen, tradesmen, and housewives. She tried to blend in, zigzagging between eggplants and tomatoes to the other side of the marketplace. Holding onto whitewashed walls and ambling down side streets, she reached a thoroughfare and waved down a taxi.

The driver spoke little English, but seemed to understand "embassy" enough to get her there the fastest way possible, or maybe it was the terrified look on her face that moved him to action. The car swerved in and out of near-collisions. Strangers shouted obvious obscenities in their wake, judging by their tactile embellishments. She took the document from her purse and folded it, then slipped it into her jacket pocket.

The taxi screamed to a halt. It threw her forward against the back of the front seat and brought renewed pain to her head and neck area. She shoved money at the driver, who smiled and nodded, letting her know she had grossly overpaid him.

Flags unfurled in the morning breeze. She walked quickly and confidently through the beautiful wrought-iron gates beneath them, and exhaled. Home free. If something called *Ploutarchou Street* could be called home.

"May I help you?" the man at the desk asked, a nice man with glasses and a tailored shirt. Not American, but close, his accent decidedly British. Hadn't the British ruled in Greece once upon a time and, as usual, overstayed their welcome?

She took a deep breath, but the strange sound that came out was shaky and raspy. It took a moment to clear her throat. She tried again.

"Yes, please," she said. "I'm an American, you see, and I need to talk to the person in charge. I may have just witnessed a murder. And I've been kidnapped. There were these men shooting at each other—"

All in all, the man took the news rather well. A raised eyebrow was his first response, followed by a look of confused determination.

"I see. Well, we shall certainly do what we can," he said with a condescending smile. He whipped out a form and picked up his pen. "Your name, please?"

Name. Name. The name game. Charlie, Charlie, Bo-Barlie, Banana-Fanna, Fo-Farlie, Fee, Fie, Mo-Marlie. Charlie. Simple enough. Pick a name, any name. She was losing it. Somewhere inside her throbbing brain, a thought swam in murky water, trying to make it to the surface. Fear took root instead, and closed in, choking whatever brackish thought was struggling to be heard. The side of her head ached from the effort.

Her eyes watered. Her mouth went dry.

"Miss? Your name?"

Somebody's name. I'm not a Layna. But if not a Layna, who?

"Miss, we must have your name, some means of identification if we're to help you. It could be a passport, a birth certificate, even a driving license."

The man was getting impatient. Her mind raced to find answers it didn't have. She fiddled with a ring on the third finger of her left hand, the same ring as the one in the dream. The first one. The one about Jack, where she was who she was supposed to be, before she woke up and wasn't anymore.

Because she was someone else now, somewhere in the Mediterranean. Wait a minute. How could she know *where* she was, and not know *who* she was? She wasn't the lady in the mirror, and she sure wasn't the wife of the man who touched her face in the dream before she woke up to the nightmare. Confusion took over. The man's face began to blur.

"Miss? Miss? Are you unwell?"

"Please, I'm hungry and scared," she begged. "I'm afraid that, what I mean to say is—"

The world heaved and turned upside down. She felt herself being pulled into that murky place where today, yesterday, and tomorrow all swam together like barracudas in dark places.

Dreams and reality merged and gurgled like a toilet.

She went under, sliding down the side of the nice man's desk and collapsing outward like a gutted fish on the floor beneath.

CHAPTER THREE

Το καλό το παλικάρι ξέρει κι άλλο μονοπάτι.

THE WISE MAN ALWAYS KEEPS IN MIND AN ALTERNATE PATH.

Leo Amratsis sat at his desk working on a shipping manifest in a feeble attempt to accomplish something before breakfast, but it was no use. The way she had regarded him, the fear in her eyes. But she was awake! The time when she had floated through life, half-cognizant of her surroundings, oblivious to thought or feeling—what had the specialist called it? No matter. It was over. She was alive, awake, responsive. Now, if she could only remember!

He scowled, recalling how she'd pulled away from him as if he were a disease, or worse— the enemy. She finally had a chance at living a life, and part of him was happy for her. But now the second half of the nightmare began. He had neglected his business, his personal life, everything. And she did not even know him. Which was as it should be. After all, she owed him nothing. He tossed meaningless papers aside, not caring that they floated to the floor.

There was a knock at the front door. It took a second knocking to remind him that this was the housekeeper's day off. He pushed his chair back and went into the foyer, looking through the keyhole and muttering an expletive when he saw who it was. Still, he opened the door to a man in a grey suit with a black shirt and tie, a man who barged past him with no word of greeting. Leo closed the door with a scowl and led the way into his study, inviting his guest to sit as well in the hopes of reaching an understanding of some sort. The first words out of the man's mouth let him know this was not to be.

"So! The bitch is awake!" he yelled in Greek. "Now you can give us what we want!"

"Lower the voice." Leo rose from his chair, deadly calm. "She is resting."

"Resting! Resting! You do not understand who these people are! I come to you as a friend, to warn you to hand over the girl, and you say she is resting?!"

"Your threats mean nothing to me, Boiko, or the threats of your *people*."

"My people? They are not my people!"

"Then why you obey them, like little boy?"

"You would do well to obey them as I do," the man warned. "They have the money, the power. I am a wealthy man because I will deal with them, do the business with them, ship what they want where they want. A customer is a customer. You of all people should know that!"

"Not when you risk everything! Not when you cannot sleep at night from the fear! Not when you have sold to them your soul!"

"My soul is my own!" The man's nostrils flared with rage. "You should look to your life, my friend, and the life of your cousin, Petras."

"Your threats do not scare me, Boiko," Leo responded. "I thought we discuss like gentlemen, but you do not wish. Now, will you leave, or do I throw you out?"

"I am here as your friend, Amratsis," the man pleaded, trying a quieter approach. "You must give me the girl."

"So, you do not have what you are after," Leo said with a taunting grin. "You cannot think I turn her over when you snap the fingers. It is not enough what you have already done?"

"It is nothing to what *they will do*," Boiko continued. "They can get information from anyone. You know that! Why risk your life, your business? Unless maybe you have the hots for the girl, eh? I hear she is very pretty. Maybe, while she was *resting* —"

Leo smashed his fist into Boiko's face. The man cursed, grabbed his nose with both hands, and backed up to the French doors as Leo advanced, fists clenched, face flushed.

Somehow, Boiko managed to get the door open with one hand. He whirled and ran out, slamming it so hard the glass shattered. Leo listened to the retreating footsteps, but a splintering crash at the front entry seemed a repeat of Boiko's exit in reverse with only minutes to spare.

"Damn!"

In two steps, he crossed to the desk drawer and retrieved his gun. In the reflective glass of the armoire at the opposite end of the room, he counted three men in the foyer, their guns out. They saw him. Two of them headed his way.

He heaved the desk over in a single move and dropped down while papers flew everywhere. They must have been waiting outside for Boiko's signal.

Where the hell was Petras?

When shots rang out, he was too busy to worry about his cousin or anyone else. The first shot blasted what little glass was left in the French doors that led to the garden. The second one went through the desk and into his left arm, like someone had stuck a hot iron through his flesh.

He gasped and rolled away from the desk, knocking both chairs over with his feet, trying to forge some means of protection. Coming up on his elbow, he fired twice. The first bullet got one of the men in the stomach. When he fired again, the second man grabbed his temple and leaped to one side. Another gun went off somewhere, and the third man crumpled to the floor. The man who had been grazed along his temple looked around in panic and leaped through what was left of the French doors, rolling and running while Leo watched in amazement. He looked at his rescuer, a man in his late twenties in black slacks, t-shirt, and jacket.

"You are late," Leo said. He tried to grin through the searing pain in his arm. Petras was his cousin, his friend, his extra gun, his *rock*. How many times had they saved each other's life? There was no need to count. He raised himself up. Together, they surveyed the damage.

"Thurman will not be pleased," Petras said quietly. He holstered his gun.

"He will be angry we did not call him first, eh?"

They both laughed, but Leo grabbed his arm as the throbbing began. His friend moved to help him out of his shirt.

"Petras," Leo said, stopping him, "the girl—quick. This could be the diversion."

Petras nodded, pulled his gun from the shoulder holster and made his way, quickly and quietly, up the stairs.

He leaned against the bedroom wall and listened. Hearing nothing, he tried the knob. Something was holding the door closed. He rammed his way through, stepping over the remains of the chair to search for the girl.

Nothing in the bedroom.

Nothing in the bathroom.

No sign of a struggle.

He saw the open window and the scrapes along the sill.

He checked Leo's bedroom and bath at the opposite end of the hall to be sure she wasn't there, then grinned and shook his head. God knows what she must have thought about the gunfire. Smart girl. Or maybe just *scared girl*.

He grabbed bandages and two small bottles from Leo's bathroom, a clean shirt from the closet, and headed downstairs to the kitchen. They always bandaged wounds at the kitchen table. Not very appetizing, just a long-standing tradition.

"She's gone. Out the window." Petras rolled out the cotton gauze and examined the wound. "It's not so deep, I think. Liatos can fix you up, no problem."

"First the girl," Leo muttered. "We must find her before they do. If you were in a foreign country, where would you go?"

"American Embassy," Petras replied without hesitating.

"Exactly. If she can find it. She has no money. She does not speak the language." Leo gasped as Petras unceremoniously cleaned the wound with alcohol and added iodine.

Petras frowned in response. "We'll find her, cousin, but not now. Do I need to tell you to get the bullet out as quickly as possible? These pissy little bandages won't stop the bleeding."

"No, you do not need. Do what you can."

Leo's heart and mind raced. He tried to exercise some kind of control, but his cousin took forever with what gauze they had. Time was the enemy. If he knew to check the embassy, they would know as well.

Finally, it was done. Petras helped him into a clean shirt. Neither of them mentioned the obvious bullet hole in the very expensive jacket that he put back on.

Returning to his office, Leo wondered if it would ever be as it once was. He ran his fingers over the dents and gashes in his father's magnificent mahogany desk. Then stepped over a body and shoved a lifeless leg to the side in order to retrieve his laptop and salvage any papers he didn't want lying around. The unimportant ones remained as they were. He called Thurman.

"Thurman?" he said, "We had visitors."

"How bad?" Thurman asked.

"One room wrecked, three doors smashed, bullet in my left arm. And...the girl is gone."

"Gone? They took her?"

"I do not think so. The shooting starts, and when we check upstairs, she is gone."

"Is she still out of it?"

"Out of it? Oh, I see. No." Leo's voice assumed a more intimate tone. "In fact, she woke up this morning. I mean *really woke up*."

"What! Does she remember?"

"No, I do not think so. She asked for Jack."

"Damn. Who was involved in the shooting?"

"Boiko showed up first. Warned me cooperate. I convince him to leave. A few minutes later, his men come in with guns. Three of them. We will need the cleanup crew. Should we involve the police?"

"What's the body count?"

"Two dead, one gone, not counting the girl."

"We'll take care of it. I'll head off any locals. Do you need help locating the girl?"

"No. I think we can do it. We are leaving now." Leo ended the call and nodded to Petras. They needed to find the girl and a doctor, hopefully in that order.

His phone rang. He listened and nodded.

"Yes, I understand," he said. "Thank you."

He turned to Petras and grinned.

"We have her!"

CHAPTΣR FOUR

Από την πόλη έρχομαι, και στην κορφή κανέλα.

I'M COMING FROM TOWN, AND ON THE MOUNTAIN-TOP, CINNAMON. (NOTHING SEEMS CONNECTED TO ANYTHING ELSE.)

"Mrs. Amratsis? Mrs. Amratsis? Are you unwell?"

She longed to stay inside her current world, where it was nice and dark. A cold washcloth shocked her into the light. The voice pulled at her, and she responded more to the voice than the words. Such a kind, British accent.

The nice young man from the Embassy removed the washcloth and helped her into a seated position. She looked around and discovered she'd been laid out on a plastic lounge—a cheap, orange thing with no back or armrests. Still, better than the floor. She smiled when he handed her a bottled water, nice and cold from the fridge.

"Have you recovered then?"

"Yes, better," she said. "I'm sorry. I didn't mean to pass out on you like that, Mr.—?"

"Tarkington. William Tarkington. Perhaps you're diabetic? Do you require a doctor? Is it hypoglycemia? My sister had that; she had to spend a full week in hospital—"

"No, no, I don't need a doctor. But thank you. I—skipped breakfast this morning."

"I see. I know it's not much, but one of the girls extracted these crackers from the vending machine. Perhaps it will help. I must say, you *sound* like an American."

"I *am* an American. I think."

"When you became unwell, I took the liberty of looking through your things, as a means of identifying you."

"You what? How dare you!"

"Miss, we are an embassy, and as such, we are responsible."

"I want to speak to your supervisor!"

"That's what I was getting to. I say, do you mind terribly, waiting here while I go and get her? Her name is Mrs. Scofield. The girl covering my desk isn't allowed to leave it unattended, you see. And, this *is* the ladies' facility. It's the only one with a lounge."

She nodded. It gave her time to finish the crackers and water so she could lean back against the wall and close her eyes. The supervisor would come, the mess would be resolved, and she could go home, wherever that was. She made sure that what little she had to call her own was still in her possession, even if none of what she called her own was actually hers. Her stomach rumbled. The crackers and water helped, though she was fairly certain she could put away a nice, seven-course meal. Maybe a Greek salad with black olives and feta cheese. She froze as words and phrases flooded her mind—moussaka, efcharistó, spanakopita, opa! Opa?

She flinched as the handsome face of the Greek she'd just escaped from flashed across her mind and heart. The restroom door opened, and she jerked back to the present. A lady in her 50's with pink glasses and white hair peeked in.

"Mrs. Amratsis?" She came in and seated herself in the chair beside the lounge. "Are you quite recovered?"

"I feel a little better, but I'm not Mrs. Amratsis."

"I see," Mrs. Scofield replied in a tone which said plainly she did not, "and do you feel up to conversing?"

"Of course. Believe me, I'm anxious to get home."

"No doubt. However, there are a few things that need clarification."

"Clarification? Oh, you mean the name thing!"

"Actually, Mrs. Amratsis, I was wondering what exactly you're doing here."

"I'm here because I need your help. You're the American Embassy. I'm an American."

"Yes, yes, I believe you. But do you not see that therein lies the problem?"

"Problem?"

"One of them, yes. You see, even overlooking the fact that the only documentation you have in your possession upholds your Greek citizenship, a fact we must never overlook—"

"Of course, but you see—"

"And not to mention your allegations of kidnapping and murder, which are of course matters for the local police —"

"So you say, but don't you see that—"

"Which leads us to the larger problem of propriety, if indeed you are, as you say, an American citizen."

"But I am! No, I am! I'm sure of it! Why won't you people believe me?"

"Yes, quite," Mrs. Scofield concluded, not a bit ruffled after my self-argument over my country of origin. "Still, I've taken the liberty of notifying the local authorities. You see, this is, in point of fact, the *British* Embassy on Ploutarchou Street. I believe you want the *American* Embassy on Vassilisis Sophias Avenue."

"What?"

"Yes, my dear. I'm afraid you've come to the wrong embassy."

CHAPTΣR FIVΣ

Βοήθα με να σε βοηθώ ν› ανεβούμε το βουνό.

HELP ME, SO THAT I CAN HELP YOU, SO THAT WE CAN CLIMB THE MOUNTAIN.

She reached for her purse with a sigh of the purest boredom and laid a fistful of money on the lounge seat. Mrs. Scofield immediately rose to her feet.

"I beg your pardon," she whispered, her voice as icy as the North Sea. "Are you attempting to bribe a British subject on foreign soil?"

"What?" Raising her eyes up to Mrs. Scofield's proper height, it took her a moment to understand the bizarre accusation.

"Nonononono. I'm looking for something to write with. I'd appreciate it if you could point me in the right direction for the American Embassy. Look, I don't even know where this money came from, or how much there is, or how much it is in dollars or pounds sterling or whatever the British call it these days. So how could I possibly try to bribe you or anyone else? I don't even know if you're still using euros or if the EU has gone bottoms up, or if Brexit is still an issue. Don't you see? I just want to go home."

"Quite. Yes, well." Mrs. Scofield reseated herself with the utmost care, not quite so close to the crazy lady. "Then, if you've recovered, might I suggest you wait in the front foyer for your husband? He can drive you."

"My husband?"

"Forgive me, Mrs. Amratsis," she said, "but your husband, being who he is, well, we felt sure he could lend some explanation, some direction to—"

"My husband's dead. He's been dead for some time. There was this car crash—"

"Dead? Oh no, you're quite mistaken." Mrs. Scofield's penciled-in eyebrows appeared permanently raised. "Why, I just spoke to him on the phone."

"Tell me you didn't."

"Oh, but I did. It's only proper."

When she stormed out of the ladies room, Mrs. Scofield followed, waited patiently while the crazy American lady took a wrong turn at top speed and ran into a wall. She was there when that same lady aka Mrs. Amratsis came back in defeat to face Britain's obviously-higher morality, whereupon Mrs. Amratsis thought a moment, then stared Mrs. Scofield full in the face.

"Look, I'm escaping an abusive relationship. My husband beats me, okay? Is there a back door to this place?"

"Oh, my. Well, yes. The other hall and to the left." Mrs. Scofield's voice yielded slightly, like a custard tarte. "I'll ring you out so the alarm doesn't sound, though it's frightfully irregular. Mrs. Amratsis, if I may, surely the other matters you spoke of earlier to Mr. Tarkington—i.e., the kidnapping, a murder—surely those are matters best left to the local police?"

Thankfully, it was at this point a young woman named Elayna escaped the confines of Great Britain into the open air of the Greek Isles, without directions to the right embassy, which would have to wait.

She felt lightheaded. The sidewalk tilted under her. She needed a place to hide, but first she needed food. Her body followed the aroma of garlic and roasted lamb that wafted down the alleyways.

A huge bus zoomed by advertising tours of the Parthenon. Athens seemed a safe bet as to her present location—a city large enough for an embassy or two. She was lost all right. And she needed to get even more lost, before her so-called *husband* showed up, which meant getting as far away from the British Embassy as possible.

Her nose brought her to a side street, and she wandered down a block or two until she discovered a small, crowded, out-of-the-way restaurant with an unoccupied corner table. A far cry from fancy, which made it perfect. She could see out and no one could see in, unless they really knew where to look.

Grizzle-bearded men in wrinkled clothes played backgammon at front tables next to huge windows. Tables and chairs were carved from wood worn smooth by time. The smell of moussaka filled the room. It's what she ordered, salivating when it finally arrived with a glass of Retsina wine. She ate slowly, savoring every morsel, determined to keep it down.

Halfway through the meal, a waiter appeared. With a heavy sigh, she pulled a wad of paper money from her purse, fairly certain she would once again overpay.

A familiar voice behind the waiter mumbled something in Greek. The waiter stiffened, frowned, then smiled politely in her general direction and handed all of the money back. All of it. He then faded away, replaced by the face of her husband.

Not the dead one.

The Greek one.

Leo sat down rather stiffly with a brief nod, offering a passing recognition to others as he glanced around the room. So much for thinking she would be any safer in an out-of-the-way Greek restaurant than in an embassy full of idiots or a house where people shot each other. She saw how the other customers regarded him in a strange, respectful way, then whispered among themselves. Like maybe he was related to Onassis.

"What do you think you are doing?" he whispered from clenched teeth. A droplet of perspiration trickled down the left side of his face. That's when she noticed he was sweating more than the moderate climate warranted. And he winced when he used his left arm to spread a napkin on his lap. Nice manners, but until she knew who he was and what was going on, she refused to feel anything for him.

"I don't know who you are," she whispered back, waving her butter knife in his face, "but whoever you are, I'm not your wife, and you're not my husband. What are you doing here? Did you follow me from the embassy?"

"My name is Leo Amratsis," he said, "and no, I did not follow you. The woman, she tell me you are passing out from hunger. A crowded restaurant is a good place to hide if you are hungry. Would you not agree, Layna?"

"Don't call me that."

"Then, what shall I call you?"

A delicious softness in his voice made her pause a moment. His broken English was kind of cute, but she let it pass and changed the subject. "Is this something to do with those guys with guns? And shouldn't you be dead? There were three of them! How could they have missed?"

When he half-smiled, it scrunched the corners of his eyes. But it wasn't the sadness in those dark eyes that froze her in place. It was a familiarity, the knowledge that she'd seen those eyes before, up close and personal. A shock went through her when she realized he was looking at her the same way.

"You maybe lower the knife, I think," he said.

She glanced at the knife, unaware she was still holding it in a threatening position; she nestled it quietly next to her fork beside her plate.

The man sitting opposite her seemed to let out a sigh of relief, though why, she couldn't say. She was the least threatening person she knew, as far as she could remember.

"You will be overjoyed to learn all of the guys with the guns, as you say, did not miss," Leo said, indicating his left shoulder. "I have been shot. And be assured—it *hurts like hell.*"

"I applaud your knowledge of American westerns," she said, giving her kidnapper an appraising glance. "I bet you're very good at what*ever* you do."

"I am. However, I do not like the way you say. Come. We need to leave. I have not the time for idle talk."

"I don't know who you are, but I know you can't force me to go with you," she said. "I'm an American citizen."

Leo closed his eyes and took a deep breath. He glanced down at his hand resting on the table. She did the same, and watched the blood seep slowly onto the light blue cuff of his long-sleeve shirt just beyond where the jacket ended.

"Like I say, I have not the time," he repeated, noting the same thing. "I need the doctor, and you must come. It is unsafe for you alone. You must trust me, as you have before."

She fought the urge to push him up against the brick wall of the restaurant, but kept her voice as close to a whisper as anger allowed. "Trust you? I woke up this morning with no memory of who I am or how I ended up in your *bedroom*. For all I know, you kidnapped me or drugged me. Why should I be concerned if people are trying to kill you?"

"You do not know what you are talking. For one thing, it is not my bedroom. And there was no kidnapping. I would not do. You were there to protect you. The drugs were for saving the life. If you look for answers, I have none. You do."

"That makes no sense. I can't remember what day it is, and I sure don't want to get involved with the police over all those dead bodies. I just want to go home."

"What dead bodies?" Leo asked. Suddenly, a spasm of pain whipped across his face. He looked down and made a sound like when someone rips a sticky bandage off their arm.

She looked at him, dumbfounded. He really *was* in pain. "The bodies on the floor of your study," she said quietly.

"We are not in your country," he said in a semi-vicious whisper. "Do you think the American Embassy will believe you any more than the British Embassy did? That marriage license, fake or not, is your only identification, your only means of protection."

"There you go again. Is it fake or isn't it? And protection from what?"

He lowered his head and, again, half-grunted in pain. A muscle clenched in his jaw. He raised his eyes. "From the men who broke my door down. Layna, please. We need to go."

He watched her face for a reaction. She continued to stare at him while her mind raced down a darkened street directly into a brick wall.

Damn it, he was right. She had no means of identification, no memory, very little money.

She delayed answering by looking out the window, then slowly around the restaurant. The backgammon players were gone. In fact, the clientele had mysteriously disappeared. She wondered if the restaurant was closing. The waiter was nowhere in sight. Where did everybody go? There was a bad feeling in her gut, and it wasn't the food.

Leo followed her trajectory and looked around, but said nothing.

"I want to go home." She said with a sigh, and regarded her empty wine glass.

"As do I," he said, working against the pain in his shoulder. "You must come with me now. Where else can you go? You need passport, the driving license, a certificate of birth. If you just trust me a little while longer—"

"Trust you? I told you, I don't even *know* you."

His eyes flickered. Golden fire sparked from a place deep inside those rich brown eyes, and he looked like she'd slapped him in the face. When he spoke, his voice sounded close to defeat.

"Then I tell you the facts. You are alone in a foreign country with a wedding certificate that identifies you as married Greek woman. And those guys with the guns? They were not looking to kill *me.* I am just in the way. My bodyguard earned his euros today. You should thank him for saving your life. His name is Petras. He waits for us now."

"You have a *bodyguard?*"

"My business requires it," he said, his voice matter-of-fact as he struggled to rise from the table, "but Petras is more than bodyguard—much more." He leaned into his fist on top of the table. "I am a wealthy man who requires doctor," he said. "So unless you want me to pass out in front of you and leave you to explain things to police, then come. You cannot go home if you are in the jail. I am well-known. You are not."

"Like Onassis," she muttered beneath her breath.

He held out his hand and said no more. His ring bore the face of a lion in gold, with two small diamonds for the eyes. Just as she reached for his hand, it was withdrawn to answer his phone. With a quick glance out the front window, he grabbed her and dragged her from the chair onto the wooden floor. They landed together, seconds before gunshots rang out and glass shattered around them.

"Is there a back door to this place?" she whispered, glancing from the floor into the kitchen, where even the cook had disappeared.

"Back door is first place they look. They are there now, waiting. We go out front."

His breathing sounded labored, and pain flashed in his eyes. She realized he'd come down hard on his left side. She tried not to think what the fall had done to his wound. His eyelids flickered, and he groaned as she helped him to his feet.

"Don't you *dare* pass out on me," she threatened, then slung her purse over one shoulder and used her other one to help support Mr. Leo Amratsis out the front door of the restaurant, leaving the place in a state of upheaval. One window sported two bullet holes; other windows had been completely shattered. One of the wine glasses at the backgammon table had fallen; the other still stood. She hadn't trusted his backward logic about all the bad guys waiting for them at the back door, and she wasn't sure how long she could support his weight. But right or wrong, they had only one option left.

Just as they cleared the door, a black car pulled up outside. Leo, looking like he could crater at any moment, nodded her in that direction. The driver jumped out and ran towards, yanking a gun from his shoulder holster.

CHAPTER SIX

Ο θεός βλέπει βουνά και ρίχνει χιόνι.

GOD SEES MOUNTAINS AND THROWS SNOW ON THEM.
(WHEN YOU DO WHAT YOU CAN,
YOU DO WHAT YOU MUST.)

A bullet pinged against the side of the doorway just as Leo nodded in the direction of the car. A shard of wood grazed his temple, but by the time he cried out, Petras was there with a gun, returning fire. With his cover shots, they managed to reach the car and get inside. Layna tried not to think about being shot at in broad daylight on a busy street in a foreign country, but something had become patently clear. Like Dorothy in *The Wizard of Oz*, she wasn't in Kansas anymore.

With a queasy feeling in the pit of her stomach, she recalled what Leo had said in the restaurant—that the guys with the guns weren't after him. The inference of what he hadn't said convinced her that in case he really had taken a bullet meant for her, or even because of her, then maybe letting him call her Layna wasn't so much to ask. Since she didn't know her real name, it was good as any—for now.

While Leo struggled to stay conscious and coherent in the back seat, Layna helped him off with his jacket. Apparently not all of the guys with guns had decided to wait for them at the back door, but now wasn't the time for gloating. She tried to catch a glimpse of the driver, the infamous bodyguard-and-so-much-more, but it proved impossible as long as he took every corner on two wheels, rocking the car back and forth.

"How far away is the doctor?"

Petras responded to her question by tossing her a box of tissue, which she emptied and handed to Leo. He took the whole wad and pressed it inside his shirt to soak up the blood.

Layna checked behind them at every stoplight, scared they were being followed without knowing why they were being chased to begin with. She watched Petras in the rearview mirror, his eyes intent on the road while obviously concerned about his friend.

Leo groaned and roused himself. He looked around and motioned to the left with his free hand. Petras nodded, zipping quietly onto a side street where he stopped. He reached in and pulled Leo out of the car, refusing Layna's offer to help. Only when Leo muttered something to him in Greek did Petras turn and motion for her to come with them.

Petras took Leo to a nondescript back door of a building resembling all the other stucco buildings along the cobblestoned alleyway. After knocking rather loudly, they were admitted by a woman in a nurse's uniform who took Leo's other side as though bullet wounds were an everyday occurrence. Layna watched as Leo was maneuvered into an adjacent room, leaving her alone in a small, sterile hall that reminded her of a hospital corridor.

She'd dismissed the "trust me" deal Leo had proposed in the restaurant. Objectivity's hard enough without a man bleeding all over the car seat. But now, even in a doctor's office, she waited for men with guns to burst through the door, grateful when the nurse appeared and showed her into the room where Leo lay on an examining table, half-naked.

The doctor turned and appeared startled for a moment, like he'd recognized her. Before she could say anything, he pointed to a sink behind a semi-circular curtain. "You wash, please. You help."

Layna looked around, frantic. Why? Was it the weekend? Were they short of staff? She saw the one nurse busy preparing a blood transfusion. So, it looked like just the three of them. Layna took a deep breath, and she washed. The nurse wrapped her in a white smock, then handed her a pair of latex gloves, which gave her the distinct feeling she wasn't going to like whatever came next.

Sure enough, the doctor motioned for her to come and help him with the patient. She castigated herself for keeping him at the restaurant so long with all of her stupid questions while he was hurt and bleeding. So far, he'd been kind to her, which was even more perplexing. She forced herself to look at him. On his back, unconscious, pale. Either the doctor had given him something to knock him out, or he'd passed out on his own. The doctor motioned her closer as he explained what he needed her to do.

"Turn on side, like this," he said. "Then, hold."

Nodding, Layna helped him roll Leo onto his side and held him steady while the doctor wiped away the remaining blood on his side and back, then swabbed the area with alcohol. She tried to turn away when he picked up the scalpel, but the good doctor wouldn't hear of it.

"You must watch," he said, his voice stern, considering they were strangers. "Keep still. Do not move. Use this if he wakes up." He pointed to a wad of cotton wad and a small bottle on a side table.

Chloroform? Wonderful.

The doctor looked at her, really looked at her, and looked away again.

Layna tried to swallow with a throat gone dry. She was sure the doctor recognized her, but how, when? After the car crash? Leo seemed settled onto his side, but she slipped her left hand into his to catch him if he should turn over for some reason. She rested her other hand along the back of his neck despite a curious glance from the doctor. The rhythm of Leo's breathing pulsed through her fingers entwined in his. She tried not to notice his thick, soft hair, the perfect curve of his mouth, his beautifully muscled body, or the two-inch scar on his lower back. Another bullet wound? What business was he in? Drugs?

The doctor made his first incision. Leo's muscles twitched in response. She squeezed his hand and tightened her hold on his neck. *Hold and roll. Hold and roll.*

Okay, where did that come from?

The blood brought her mind back to the business at hand, and she found herself willing him to live and not understanding why. The doctor extracted a misshapen, bloody bullet and laid it on a wad of cotton, then disinfected the wound before stitching the torn flesh together, beginning with the deepest layer. Layna closed her eyes and bit her lip with every in-and-out sucking sound, feeling the thread being pulled through her own flesh. For some inexplicable reason, she clenched her pelvic muscles.

Just when she thought the worst was over, the doctor held up a hypodermic needle. She gasped and looked away, hating it when he chuckled at her fear of needles.

The nurse finally pried her fingers from Leo's in order to start the blood transfusion. Layna noted that while Leo's eyes remained closed, his color had changed for the better. The doctor motioned her into an adjoining room where he handed her the bullet inside a plastic bag. Was she supposed to keep it for a souvenir? How strange. Once they were alone, she laid her hand on the doctor's arm until he looked her full in the face.

"You recognize me," she said, making it a statement rather than a question.

He stopped and glanced around, then made doubly sure the door was closed. He shifted his 5'9" frame and regarded her with dark, worried eyes. She wondered how many late night surgeries he had performed on Leo, or Petras, or both.

"Please," she pleaded.

"You...remember?" he asked.

"Some," she said. "Bits and pieces, like a dream."

"Ah. I have wondered."

"Then you do know me. Who am I?"

"I cannot say." He shrugged his shoulders and glanced away.

Did that mean he couldn't say, or wouldn't say? Had Leo sworn him to secrecy? She felt her hopes sink to the bottom of the Aegean Sea.

"Please," she repeated, her hand gripping his flesh while Leo slept.

"You hit your head," he said," pointing to his left temple. "Sleep a long time."

"Concussion?"

"Yes. That is right."

"But what about the headaches? The amnesia?"

"Aamanezeea!" the doctor exclaimed, nodding like he had discovered gold. "I make the apology; it is not my expertise."

"Forget the amnesia. What happened? How did I get here?"

"He find, his cousin."

"He found his cousin?"

The doctor frowned and tried again.

"No find his cousin," he explained. "His cousin find *you*."

"His cousin?"

"Yes. He find you."

"You mean, Petras? He's Leo's cousin?"

"Yes. No. I am not sure."

"Wait, where did he find me?"

"Skopelos," the doctor answered with a common shrug, as if everyone knew.

"Skopelos?" Layna repeated in an incredulous voice.

"SKOPELOS." The voice boomed from the open doorway and echoed in the room.

Layna jumped and turned to face him, her hand at her throat.

Leo stood in the doorway, looking like he had stumbled in from a battlefield. He was on his feet, holding onto the door, just barely, and giving the doctor a look as dark as thunder.

"We need to go," he said. "We are here too long."

The doctor tried to exit as best he could, but Leo stopped him. They spoke in Greek, quietly at first, then heatedly, then quietly again, as if they'd reached an understanding.

Finally, Leo laid his hand on the doctor's shoulder as a friend would, said something in obvious gratitude, retrieved a wad of money from his pants pocket, and placed it in the doctor's hand. The doctor appeared embarrassed, but thankful. Layna had a feeling the same scene had been reenacted many times before.

Leo turned to her in watchful silence. She wondered how much he'd had to fork over when Petras or somebody's cousin had found her half-dead. Would he ever get his money back? She turned away, hiding once again behind her designer sunglasses.

With the plastic bag still in her hand, she argued with herself. If this Leo character thought she owed him, he needed to rethink the issue. She was married to Jack. She had the ring to prove it. She was Mrs. Whatever-his-last-name-was, damn it. When she looked up in defiance, Leo's eyes showed cold reserve. She wondered how he could still tell what she was thinking, even behind sunglasses.

Petras limped through the door. He had changed into black slacks and black shirt. Leo turned to speak to him. Seeing the two side by side, Layna noted how muscled Petras was, though Leo was slightly taller. Petras pointed to his thigh and measured something with his thumb and forefinger, then made silly reenactments of smashing into furniture. Apparently, he'd been injured in a fight, but not directly and not by a bullet. The two men laughed while Petras helped Leo with his jacket. Though a little unsteady, they managed it. After all, they were both in excellent shape. Having seen Leo with his shirt off and Petras in a snug-fitting shirt, Layna could definitely testify to that fact.

The doctor handed Petras a bottle of pills and spoke hurriedly in Greek. Petras listened and nodded, then glanced at Layna when he felt her watching him. The laugh wrinkles around his eyes and the look of acceptance surprised her. Confused, she decided now would be a good time to answer nature's call. The nurse showed her to the restroom.

Once inside and surrounded by four walls, Layna contemplated what she'd have done if there'd been a window. Would she have crawled through it? What if Boiko's men were waiting outside? No, Leo was right. Where else could she go until she knew who she was? Even if she eventually found the right embassy, she still had no answer for what they were sure to ask. *Who was she?* Her best bet for finding answers lay with these two strangers who were her only means of protection, even if they knew who she was and weren't talking. She finished, washed up, and returned to her captors.

Petras reminded her to remove her purse off the couch in the waiting room. His eyes admonished her as if to say, *"We musn't leave any evidence of our visit, now must we?"*

Layna gave him a cryptic half-smile in return, uncertain what role he'd played in saving her life, then or now. She looked around for the doctor to thank him, but he'd disappeared.

It's not polite to ask questions and bother people.

The credo came unbidden from her past as she entered the car. It was all she could do to keep from straightening back up so she could *look* at it. A second admonition came on the heels of the first. *Sit up straight.*

Words to live by? Mementos from her childhood? The thought flitted through her mind like those little birds by the ocean. The ones that leave their prints in the sand, only to have the ocean wash them away with the tide.

Silence filled the car, along with the smell of a doctor's office Leo still carried with him. Layna noted their car had metamorphosed into an American-made Chevrolet, an old Lumina that looked like it had seen too many repair shops. She glanced at Petras, but he responded in much the same way as Leo. They seemed to think it perfectly normal to arrive in a Bentley and leave in a Chevy.

God, I'm tired.

She leaned back against the headrest, a little woozy. Here she was in a getaway car headed God knows where, when all she wanted was a soft bed in a darkened room and no gunfire till morning.

Leo's eyes were closed. She smiled, thinking he probably wished for the same thing.

His hand lay open on the seat between them. She had an uncontrollable urge to reach over and cover it with her own. Where did *that* come from? And why should she care, beyond his role in saving her life? In any event, she was married to Jack, who'd died in a car crash. So, why wasn't she heartbroken? Why hadn't she cried? Did it have something to do with having amnesia? Had she forgotten she loved him?

Her life wasn't her own. The purse she clutched wasn't even hers. In fact, nothing had anything to do with her or her life except the people trying to kill her. And a marriage license in someone else's name. Elayna Giannopoulos, lately married to one Leonidas Amratsis. There was nothing she could point to and say, that's mine. Nothing to prove her existence.

Her reflection flashed by in the car window—a pale, unfamiliar lady in a scarf, no makeup, a puzzled expression creased across her face. She didn't recall having dark, stringy hair. Then again, she didn't recall.

She took her sunglasses off and closed her eyes. A memory shot through her brain like wildfire zipping up a dead tree. Unconnected thoughts licked at her mind. *Somewhere hot. The sun blinded her, someone held her, begged her to do something. Do what? No! Let go! No! No!*

A scream raked through her throat. Her soul shut down. She choked, then gasped. Her eyes jerked open. It was like being hit in the head, but from the inside. Her hand instinctively reached for Leo's, then hesitated when she found him awake and watching. The fiery fragments of memory turned to embers, then vanished.

"I am here, Layna."

He took her hand, entwined their fingers, and winced. He'd used his left hand.

She stared at their hands together, then up at him.

Acceptance replaced concern on the face of Leo Amratsis. He gave her a weak smile, leaned back, and closed his eyes. The wound needed time to heal. They all needed time to heal. He had turned away, yet his fingers remained interwoven with hers. How could she disentangle them without appearing rude? Why should she care about being rude to a stranger?

She studied his face a moment longer, then lowered her eyes and looked away. Because he wasn't a stranger. He never had been.

I am here, Layna.

The words he'd spoken seemed frighteningly familiar. A voice, not of a stranger, but one she'd heard before, speaking those very same words. In bed.

A friend?

A lover?

The enemy?

Lights streaked by in the evening sky as they left Athens behind.

CHAPTER SEVEN

Το ‹να χέρι νήβει τ› άλλο, και τα δυο το πρόσωπο.

THE ONE HAND WASHES THE OTHER, AND TOGETHER THEY WASH THE FACE.

The car had stopped moving. Heavy citrus permeated the air. Sitting up, Layna discovered Petras had parked the car between two trees heavy with oranges.

How long had she slept? What time was it?

Voices reached her in the night air. Leo and Petras, speaking in whispers, in Greek.

Layna opened the car door, noting the absence of an interior light as well as a clock, but with a full moon in the night sky and both men standing no more than five feet away, she had little difficulty seeing Petras put his finger to his lips in warning. She nodded and closed the car door as quietly as she could. There was no way she was going to be left behind. And she needed a ladies' room again.

"*Where are we?*" she whispered to Leo.

"A block or two from the house. We need to make sure it's okay before we go in."

"Into the house where people tried to kill you? Why don't we just get a hotel room?"

"This is Athens!" he whispered angrily, *"I am known everywhere!"*

"Like Onassis?" She heard Petras chuckle. *"I just want to know what we're doing here standing around whispering. Why don't we just drive up to the house and go inside? It's your house isn't it?"*

Leo leaned against the car and shook his head, then looked at Petras. *"You tell her,"* he said in a weary voice.

"It is a crime scene," Petras explained, *"and the last place they'll look."*

"You speak English." She gasped, instantly embarrassed and glad it was dark so he couldn't see her face.

"Better than I do," Leo muttered.

Then Petras' words sank in, and she turned to Leo.

"Crime scene! I thought you got rid of the bodies!"

"What bodies?" The remark came from Petras.

"I missed one," Leo whispered, with a shrug that he regretted. "A *man I hired to watch the back."*

"You mean the gardener who knew nothing about gardening?"

"The gardener?" Petras asked, leaning into the conversation.

"He was planting a bougainvillea in the wrong place," Layna explained. *"When he looked up and saw me—"*

"He saw you?" Leo's question was accusatory, like it was her fault.

"In the window, when I first woke up."

"What did he do?" Leo asked.

"He looked surprised, or scared. I couldn't tell. Then he backed out through the gate and ran. Why? Who was he?"

"He didn't make it." Leo said, exchanging a glance with Petras.

"He was not as loyal as we were led to believe," Petras muttered.

"You killed the gardener?!"

"Shhh. There are people watching the house." Leo's voice was gruff. *"Until we know how many and where they are, we must be quiet."* He looked into her eyes as he spoke. *"I'll go first. You follow, then Petras. If I stop, you stop. Understand?"*

"I thought you paid them off!" Layna said, shaking off Leo's hand.

"Paid who off?" Petras asked.

"The police!"

"Layna," Leo hissed, *"stop arguing! I'm not concerned with the police!"*

"Then who?" she asked. A knot of fear grew in her stomach.

"People you don't pay off," Petras whispered from somewhere behind her.

They stayed in the shadows and approached the back gate.

"Layna!"

Leo pulled her into the cover of a Cypress tree. Petras had disappeared.

"My name's not Layna!" she whispered, aware of being pressed against his lean frame. His cologne washed over her, a gentle cascade.

"It will do until you find another," he responded.

His sarcasm killed the moment. Together, they watched and waited. Up close, she breathed in the scent of the sun and the sea that was Leo Amratsis.

Petras returned and indicated the front of the house was being watched. She thought them both quite mad when they made for the French doors that opened from the lawn directly into Leo's office, now boarded up with huge sheets of plywood and crisscrossed in crime scene tape. Leo stepped aside. Petras whipped out a knife.

Admirable, the way he maneuvered in, under, and around the tape, carefully removing each nail to keep it from squeaking. When he was done, he slid the sheet of plywood aside so they could enter. Fragments of shattered glass crunched beneath her feet. One of them punctured her sandal. Leo heard her gasp of pain, picked her up with his good arm, and carried her on his hip like a sack of potatoes and into his office.

"No lights," he said. *"You'll need to get the glass out yourself. Be careful."*

She took her sandal off, gently inching her fingers along the bottom of her foot, testing for the shard of glass. Once it had been removed and her sandal replaced, her attention turned to Leo's cousin.

Petras pulled a roll of crime scene tape from his jacket and looped it over his wrist. As she watched, he began replacing the plywood and blocking out what light they had.

Layna's eyes adjusted to the encroaching darkness and she realized that, when completed, Leo's friend would be stranded outside.

"What about Petras?"

"He will replace the nails," Leo said matter-of-factly. *"It will be as before."*

"No, how will he get inside?"

"He'll be fine."

The ingenuity of both men amazed her. With the extra tape, the illusion would be complete. *They'd done this before.*

Leo led her around a huge, upturned desk and created a path past chair legs, a tall plant that had been knocked over, and a swamp of papers across the floor. He swished them aside with his feet until he located his laptop, which he handed to her without comment.

She held it while he picked up an empty folder, pulled out a device from his pocket, and clicked open a hidden wall safe. He looked more like a burglar than a businessman, hurriedly dumping papers and stacks of money into the folder like in a movie. All that was missing was a dead body on the floor. Wait.

Leo closed the safe before wading through the remaining debris into the foyer. She noted crime scene tape covering the inside of the front door as well, and recalled with a shiver how the gunmen had smashed through.

"Keep to the walls," Leo whispered, nodding toward the huge, undraped dining room windows, where full moonlight poured in and illuminated everything. She nodded and followed him beneath the stairs into a large kitchen, where the laptop and overstuffed folder were deposited on the kitchen table. Leo regarded the window over the sink, pictured the shrubs that surrounded it just outside, and decided they needed what little light was coming in more than they needed to draw attention by closing the blinds. He checked the deadbolt lock on the back door and breathed a little easier, then crossed the room to a huge pantry and reached inside. She heard a click. A hidden door opened seamlessly to the outside, and there was Petras, waiting in the shadows. He and Leo whispered hurriedly in Greek.

With lunch in the fated restaurant only a memory, Layna sighed with relief when food appeared as the next order of business. Petras reached behind the fridge and unplugged it before he opened the door. With no illumination pouring forth, he foraged at will using the diffused light of his phone and delivered an assortment of cheese, bread, and wine. They ate quickly and quietly by the sparse moonlight coming through the kitchen window. She noted how Leo favored his arm and shoulder as he took the meds Petras counted out for him. Fever glistened on his forehead.

"Are we staying here?" she asked.

"No," Leo said in a haggard voice.

"Yes," Petras followed, his tone serious and unrelenting when he turned to his cousin.

"I got what I came for," Leo argued. "We're in danger here."

"You think they won't be watching the house as well? The boat, the docks? You need sleep, my friend. We all do. We'll leave before dawn tomorrow morning, the way we came. No one will know."

"I thought *this* was your house," Layna whispered.

Leo looked at her and closed his eyes, unable or unwilling to respond. He lowered his head, grabbed a dishcloth, and wiped the sweat from his forehead, leaning into the damp cloth for a moment, exhausted. Petras took over, keeping his voice barely above a whisper.

"No lights, no noise," he said. "There's a man watching the front of the house from across the street."

"And another in a parked car one block over," Leo added.

"And another in a parked car one block over," Petras repeated. "That's why we came through the side door—plenty of trees and shrubs. Stay away from the windows. In the morning, take only what can be carried in one bag."

Leo smothered a cough and got up from the table, guzzling bottled water and engaging Petras in a discussion that sounded more like an argument. She waited. Eventually, they reached an accord.

"It's decided," Petras said, throwing a dark glance in Leo's direction. "The wound must have time to heal. I will watch until morning. I ask that you stay with him as he sleeps. I do not know what the medication will do. Have you handled a gun before?"

"A Smith & Wesson '38," Layna said, nodding. She frowned. How did she know that? "But I've never shot anyone. That I know of."

Petras raised an eyebrow. Leo's mouth twitched in amusement. From the look that passed between them, Layna knew she wasn't about to get her hands on a weapon.

"Let's pray the need does not arise," Petras said. "Allow your eyes to adjust to the dark before you go into a room. No tub or shower—too much noise. If the faucet's too loud, trickle the water. Use a washcloth and wash in the sink. Do what else you must do, but do not flush! That is how it must be. Sleep until I wake you. I'll be downstairs if you need me, next to the front door. No lights, no noise. I'll let you know if something happens. Stay dressed and be ready to move at a moment's notice."

He handed her a small, round candle and a book of matches.

Layna nodded and made her way through the foyer, then up the stairs to the bedroom, feeling her way along the walls until she found the windowless bathroom. Once the hall door was closed, she lit her candle. After taking care of the first necessity, and when she could no longer avoid doing so, she looked in the mirror.

A war refugee. That's what she saw. An air of rebellion rose to the front. She'd obey Petras' orders, but for one night only. She might die by dawn, but come hell or high water, she'd face the firing squad with a clean body.

She washed up, probably not as quickly or as quietly as Petras would have wanted, and made a face as she redressed. No makeup, no gown. No light to enable her to rifle through the closet or the dresser drawers. She'd have to sleep in her borrowed, day-old clothes till morning? No way.

She blew out the candle then, feeling her way back down the

myriad of hangers, she found a shirt and some pants that would do for the night if she used her scarf as a belt.

When she stepped into the bedroom, moonlight poured through each of the tall windows, but there was no Leo in other-worldly beams asleep in her bed. Of course. He'd opted for his own bed in the master bedroom, against Petras' wishes. His idea of being a gentleman, or a simple wish to sleep undisturbed?

When she started to climb into bed, she instinctively knew the answer. Just the thought of sleeping in a bed where nightmares had haunted her sleep, scared her through and through. Too much history, even if it remained unknown. It was where she'd awakened not knowing who she was or where she was. If she slept in that same bed again, would she wake up as someone else in the morning? As she turned to go, something caught her attention. Even in the moonlight, her eyes picked up dark streaks on the white pillow, and a gasp escaped her. They were way too dark to be blood. Her hands went automatically to her hair. They'd dyed her hair? No wonder it looked all wrong! Why had they done that? What else had they done to her?

She couldn't breathe. She started hyperventilating and pulled her shirt up over her mouth, bending over till she could breathe again. It wasn't working. She stumbled to the window. Cotton drapes billowed with a night breeze that spelled salvation to her straining lungs. The deed was done with no forethought, the night air too inviting to resist. She lifted her eyes to the moon and held her hands at her sides, palms out, willing her body to that place of calm where she could finally draw a breath without shuddering. The task completed, her gaze fell upon the garden below, where a man stared up at her. He tipped his hat. She jerked back into the shadows.

Oh God, what had she done?

She scurried down the hall, sneaked down the stairs, and kept to the walls until she reached Petras next to the broken front door.

"What is it?" he asked, his voice quiet.

"I did something stupid without thinking," she said. "I couldn't breathe, and I was scared—"

"Just tell me what happened!"

"I saw someone, in the garden, out the window. And he saw me!"

"What did he do?"

"He tipped his hat," she said, "and then he just walked away. What should we do?"

"Tipped his—oh, that's Thurman. Go back to bed."

"Thurman?"

"Interpol," he said. "Go back to sleep. I'll explain in the morning."

Petras resumed his sleeping-sitting-up position next to the door and closed his eyes.

Bewildered, Layna retraced her steps upstairs, thinking every step of the way. Interpol? Interpol was watching Leo Amratsis' house? Why? And who wore a hat anymore? Was it a Greek thing?

At the head of the stairs, she paused, then turned to the right, walked a few feet down the carpeted hallway, and quietly opened the door to the master bedroom. She padded across the interior rug to a massive bed where moonlight bathed Leo in a soft, heavenly light. Staring down at him, something stirred in her heart, something she was unaccustomed to.

But these were the sleeping arrangements for the night, right? She lay down beside him, turned onto her side facing the windows, and breathed in the scents of the sea. She slipped her arm beneath a pillow to help cushion her face—the curse of every side-sleeper. That's when her fingers touched cold metal. A gun?

Her eyes flew open as she slid it out oh-so-carefully and held it up in the moonlight. It seemed so impersonal. She imagined herself having to shoot someone, in self-defense of course, and wondered if she could do it. Maybe not, before all this had happened. But now?

Damn straight.

She slid the gun back where she had found it, hoping she'd never be put to the test, and lowered her hand across the top of the pillow. How would she ever fall asleep like this? Should she put the gun somewhere else?

Leo suddenly shifted from lying on his back onto his side and

CHAPTER EIGHT

Χεστήκαμε και η βάρκα γέρνει.

WE SHIT OURSELVES, BUT THE BOAT'S STILL LEANING. (WE'VE DONE ALL WE CAN, BUT THERE'S STILL A PROBLEM.)

snuggled up against her back, then laid his arm across her as if by habit. A tiny grunt of pain told her he'd used the wounded arm to do so, but he didn't awaken. She stared wide-eyed into the dark and waited. His face moved closer to her own. His breathing deepened.

Exhausted but warm and nestled in her captor's arms, her body grew sleepy while her thoughts continued to explore the murky waters of circumstance, of people trying to kill her, of whatever had happened on Skopelos that had somehow led her to this place, and Athens.

There was a wounded man beside her, a gun beneath her pillow, and a stranger in the garden. But whatever it all meant, she was too tired to consider it.

She closed her eyes.

She woke up slowly and sweetly, feeling like she'd slept for two days instead of six hours. Still dark outside, but not for long. A quick look revealed an empty space next to her. In a way, she felt a sense of relief. No explanations needed, no assumptions made. She lifted the pillow; the gun was gone. Things to do.

No shower? No tub? No problem.

Filling the bathroom sink with hot water, she soaped every part of her body and scrubbed with a washcloth, then rinsed and dried off. Dental hygiene followed. Last of all, her awful hair, which reeked of dye. She recalled the stains on the pillow and knew it had to be temporary; just washing her face had revealed light brown eyebrows. Whoever had dyed her hair had used black eyebrow pencil on her eyebrows as well. The experience left her eager to discover what she really looked like, and to find out who'd done this to her so she could kill them.

It took two sinkfuls of hot water and frantic scrubbing with the strongest shampoo she could find, but she finally removed most of the black dye from her hair and scalp. After pat-drying her hair with a towel, she walked to the window for a quick glance to make sure Interpol was still on the job, but Thurman was nowhere in sight. A soft knock on the bedroom door brought her up short.

"*Layna*!" It was Petras, whispering rather loudly. "*Time to go*! *We are late*!"

She tiptoed to the door and leaned against it.

"*I'm not dressed! Ten minutes, I promise*!"

She scoured the bathroom, gathering what makeup she could find onto the counter next to the sink, mixing and matching bottles and tubes to come up with shades more forgiving than the brunette for whom they were originally intended. Then, wrapping her stolen articles in a towel, she grabbed a hand mirror and returned to the bedroom. Sitting on the mattress and holding the mirror in one hand, she captured enough light to quickly apply foundation, mascara, and lip balm—the basics. The eyebrow pencil and eyeliner were impossibly dark, and the tube of hideous, red lipstick would have left her looking like a hooker.

She held the mirror up and studied the results. It was amazing what sleep, soap, makeup, and five minutes of defiance can do. The awful shadows beneath her eyes were almost gone, and her natural hair, more blonde than brown, made her eyes a gray-green like the ocean.

Hurry! Hurry!

Bending over, she finished towel-drying her hair, then brushed and picked it out as best she could until it cascaded onto her shoulders, clean but somewhat tousled. The girl who looked back from the mirror was, well, maybe not runway material, but she would do, even if there was still no name to go with the face. She would have to be Layna a little while longer.

Next, the shelves and drawers in the clothes closets.

Quickly, quickly, quickly.

Surely she could find some casual, non-designer, everyday clothes. Grubby clothes couldn't be a purely American custom! At the back of the closet, neatly folded and stuffed in a Gucci shopping bag she discovered just what she needed and in a smaller size. *Odd.*

Fighting the huge sleeves on the bathrobe she'd *found*, she emptied the bag onto the bed where there was more light. Out fell a pair of low-cut jeans, white shorts, a pullover, a tank top, underwear, bra, straw hat, sunglasses — everything a tourist could possibly want for an overnight stay, and in a size 6, American. At the very bottom? A sketching pad and pencils, which she set aside.

Both the pullover and the shorts were covered in a faint brown stain. The shorts had been cut in two from the waist to the hem, straight down the front, like it had been cut off of a body.

The room moved out of focus and back again like a zoom lens. She took a second to allow the connection in her brain, but nothing more came concerning a camera. Whose camera? It meant something, but the link was gone. She turned back to the clothes.

Were they hers? She couldn't be certain. If they belonged to her, how on earth did they get here, and why were they hidden in the closet? Her breath caught in her throat. Maybe these were the clothes she was wearing when she got hit on the head and Petras took her to the doctor! Was the blood from the car crash? What about Jack's clothes?

She ran her fingers through her hair and stared at the bundle, knowing she had to go through it, even the blood-stained items.

Another urgent knock on the door. When she failed to answer, it opened and Leo's cousin peeked in. "*Now, Layna. It is —*"

He saw her hair, then the clothes on the bed. He threw her a nervous glance and closed the door. That's when she knew they were hers.

Some of the washed-out bloodstains were in spatters, big droplets in a kind of pattern all along the left side of both the pullover and the shorts. The rest consisted of smears and blotches, still on the left side, but darker, larger. As badly as she needed to remember, she felt only relief when nothing surfaced.

She threw the stained clothing back in the closet and slipped on the jeans and tank top, wrinkled but free of blood spatter. They fit, maybe a tad loose. Toiletries and everything else went into the kingsize Gucci shopping bag, along with the sketchpad and pencils and the contents of the ugly purse.

This is me, and it's now or never.

From the landing, she could see Leo and Petras downstairs in the foyer, talking. She got halfway down the stairs before they looked up. Petras stared, first in surprise, then with approval. Leo gazed at her in wide-eyed wonderment, taking it all in, from her dark blonde hair to her sandaled feet. She did the same, thinking how drop-dead gorgeous he was in a blue shirt and jeans, then chastising herself for thinking it. Then, his face changed from admiration to anger. He saw the bag, recognized it, swallowed hard, and came up for air. He forgot to whisper.

"Layna, what the hell have you done? Now everyone will know!"

Know what? She wasn't sure if his words were directed at the fact that she'd washed her hair, or the fact that she'd discovered her bloody clothes. In any event, he succeeded in turning a moment of freedom into one of mutual resentment.

She froze, halfway down the stairs, angry that he didn't approve and furious that it mattered. Before she could think of something tacky to say to him, a tiny noise at the front door drew everyone's attention. A long, skinny pair of scissors sliced carefully through the crime scene tape from the outside through a rent in the olive wood. This unfathomable action was followed by the sound of a key attempting to turn in the busted lock. Whoever it was, it was too late to run.

Leo took two quick steps, which placed him facing the door. He loosened the back of his shirt.

Layna saw the glint of the gun cradled against his back. He stood with his arms at his side, hands unclenched and ready.

Petras had already pulled a gun from his shoulder holster and was against the wall beside the door frame, waiting for it to open. Layna didn't move, but every muscle in her body grew tight. She felt perfectly able to scream the moment they came through the door, guns blazing.

Curiosity replaced their trepidation when the only thing assaulting their vision was a woman's ample buttocks forcing their way through the taped doorway backwards. Splintered olive wood competed with her many packages, her oversized Gucci canvas tote, and her rather ostentatious, wide-brimmed hat as she backed her way into the house. Layna's mouth fell open.

Turning around, the woman paused at the sight of Leo.

"Leonidas! What de hell goin' on?"

Layna couldn't see the woman's face clearly for the tilted hat that extended at least a foot in either direction, and apparently the woman couldn't see her. Still, she heard an exasperated sigh as the woman set her belongings down and placed bejeweled hands on her hips.

"I leave four weeks and all the hell breaks a-loose! Watch you doin' in Athens?"

The woman's accent was Mediterranean, and not. While Layna couldn't quite place its origin, she could definitely identify the designer clothes. They belonged on matching hangers, right beside all of the other garish clothes in the upstairs bedroom closet. This had to be the larger-sized, dark-haired Gucci lady in person, sporting a hideous shade of red lipstick. But who was she? If she was the housekeeper, she was grossly overdressed. And overpaid.

"Aleksandra," Leo said. "I could ask same thing. I thought you are in Cyprus."

Layna's eyebrows twitched. Cyprus? Wasn't that on the marriage certificate? A country populated by both Greeks and Turks, forever at war? Had she read that somewhere? And why didn't Leo go forward to greet the woman, or kiss her on both cheeks? An image flashed through a part of her brain, of two Arabs in flowing robes greeting one another in such a fashion. Then, it was gone. Okay. Maybe it was just an Arabian thing.

Even with mixed feelings and snapshots running through her mind, she could sense the tension between Leo and Aleksandra from where she stood on the stairs. Aleksandra turned slightly in her black sheath dress and ridiculously high heels to address the man waiting beside the door.

"Petras, you bring my things, no?"

Layna watched Petras ease his gun back in its shoulder holster and grit his teeth against being ordered around like a busboy. He cautiously stepped through the front door, looking both ways. Layna prayed he wouldn't be shot because of this rude, obnoxious woman.

"Yes, I see them. Two men in car. Eeze no importante," Aleksandra said with a sigh of boredom, looking around as she addressed Leo. "What kind of trouble you in dis time?"

Layna thought the woman's voice had an ugly, nasal quality, unlike the melodic Greek accents of both Leo and Petras. Hungarian? Wait. How could she know that?

Aleksandra made a minor production of removing the hatpin and lifting the hat from her head. Her hair was dark, almost black, professionally dyed, and coiled fashionably behind her head. Her earrings were dangling black sapphires. As her vision encompassed the rest of the foyer and ran up the staircase, she stopped the cursory inventory, her beady eyes resting on the intruder on the stairs.

"Who de hell is dat girlie?"

To Layna, the woman's calculating eyes gleamed even more wickedly than her jewels. She looked to be forty-something, a very well-kept, high-maintenance forty-something.

Petras, having completed his odious task, resumed his station next to the closed front door. He remained composed, but Layna caught the frown that didn't quite surface, a look that said this was bad timing on everyone's part.

"Who you are, and what you are doing in my house?" Aleksandra's eyes narrowed.

Layna cringed inside. So much for introductions and common courtesies.

"*Our house*, Aleksandra," Leo said through clenched teeth. Then he turned and gazed up at Layna. His demeanor changed completely, his dark, gleaming eyes pleading she play along, even if she didn't understand the game. Her first impulse was to do so only because he was still her best shot at finding out the truth. But something deep and wonderful passed between them, and Layna responded with a half-smile of complicity.

Leo's dark eyes gleamed with gratitude. He turned back to Aleksandra.

"You will be most happy to know the lady on the staircase is—my wife."

"Layna, come," he said in a gentle voice, as if it were what he wished more than anything in the world. She descended the stairs as gracefully as she could, wondering with each step how Leo could say it aloud like that in such a caring voice, when it was all a lie. She was Jack's wife, not his. Her journey completed, Layna set down her bag and took Leo's hand. He thanked her, again with his eyes. She gave him one of her better smiles. He kissed her on the cheek, as any loving husband would do.

"Layna," he said, bringing the two women face-to-face, "I like you to meet my stepmother, Aleksandra Papatia Roselli Amratsis." Layna thought he was going to choke on all the names, but he managed to finish with great decorum.

"Aleksandra," he said, "this is my wife, Théora Elayna Giannopoulos Amratsis."

The eyes that inspected Leo's young wife were the eyes of the enemy. Needless to say, no hands were offered in friendship on either side. Layna felt like Cinderella—before the ball. In fact, she had an overwhelming urge to go and sit in the fireplace, only there wasn't one. Leo squeezed her hand. Suddenly, she knew she could be anyone she wanted to be. You can do that when you don't know who the hell you are.

"You are not the Greek," Aleksandra said in a voice that dripped venom, as though she were listening in on Layna's thoughts.

"Neither are you," Layna replied quietly, playing a hunch and hoping like hell she was right. Her first instinct was to punch the woman in the face, but she required all of her energy just to keep her gaze steady, pushing the intimidation that threatened to overwhelm her deep down inside her, where her female organs were the only things clenched in terror at the moment.

Aleksandra's brown eyes flashed with resentment and a grudging respect.

"I am marrit to Mr. Amratsis, Leo father. I belong here. You do not."

"And yet, I'm here," Layna said. Aleksandra seemed confused by the non-answer.

"You sound like American."

"Because I am," Layna said, "on my mother's side. My father is Greek. I grew up in America." Layna couldn't believe this woman was so intimidating that she'd been thrown on the defensive, babbling away like an idiot and lying her ass off. She didn't have to defend herself to this bitch! Unless what she'd said was true?

"I don't believe. You lie. Say something Greek."

A study lined with books. People milling about. Someone quoting Aristotle. Another making a crude joke. A *very* crude joke. Her father laughing. *Her father?*

"Eínai oraía, í egó tha spásei báles sas."

Layna twitched, wondering where the alien words had come from. Petras coughed and almost choked to death. Leo pressed his lips together to maintain some sort of self-control. Layna had no idea what she'd said. Apparently, Aleksandra did. Her face turned dark red.

"You just try dat," she growled in reply, followed by something guttural in a native tongue, definitely not Greek. Then she went back on the offensive. "Where in America?"

"New York," Layna replied. "Ever been there?" It was the first big city that came to mind. At this point, she'd say anything to get the woman out of her face. Where was Leo, her so-called protector? She didn't dare turn in his direction, though she caught a wide grin from Petras, practically holding himself to keep from laughing. Thank God he was behind Aleksandra, next to the busted door.

"I do not approve this decadent Western culture," the woman was saying. Layna could swear Aleksandra's nostrils flared slightly when she said it, presumably for effect, but possibly because she actually meant it.

"Yes, I can see that from your Gucci bag." Layna replied with a lingering, measured glance at the woman's ensemble. A closet full of designer clothes from all over Europe testified to the fact that Aleksandra indulged herself in many aspects of Western culture. Just thinking it brought a sweet smile of revenge to Layna's face.

Aleksandra's eyes turned to slits. She dismissed Layna and focused instead on the destruction in Leo's office, taking in the overturned furniture, the broken glass, the plywood across the window. She turned to her stepson with upturned eyebrows, awaiting an explanation.

"Someone broke in," he said.

"I do not believe," Aleksandra said in her thick accent.

"You see damage."

"Not dat. I do not believe you marry to this girl."

Layna had had enough. She approached the hideous woman, retrieved the marriage certificate from her jeans pocket, and held it out.

Aleksandra yanked the paper from her hands and read it, then glared at Layna.

"You are pregnant?" she blurted out.

Layna felt herself blushing, horrified, as Leo stepped between them.

"Enough!" he growled. "Leave it alone."

"Oh, I leave alone, darlink, but I do not tink Turman leaves it alone."

"Thurman?"

"Michael Turman. Yes."

"How do you know him?" Leo asked.

"*He* come to *me*," she replied, "and not for so-call break-in."

There it was again. Thurman's name. As badly as Layna wanted to look over at Leo, she maintained eye contact with his stepmother and forced herself to remain composed. It was Aleksandra who spoke next, zeroing in on Layna as if she could read her thoughts.

"*Elayna*, if dat iss your name. Maybe you go back America where you belong. Your husband in deep shit. Did he not say you? I hope you learn swim where you come from, in dat New York City."

"No, Aleksandra," Leo said, squeezing Layna's hand, miraculously reconnected to his own. "It is you must go. Back to beloved Cyprus. Even better, Istanbul. It is best you stay until end of summer."

"You do not say me what I do! I not be driven from my house!"

"Our house," Leo said. "Think, Aleksandra. Both doors smashed, the office, it is destroyed, and the windows have boards. The house is not safe. It is open to anyone to come in. Government officials are not the only ones interested in our business, thanks to you. Take your bags and go, so you be safe."

CHAPTΣR NIПΣ

τὸ πεπρωμένον φυγεῖν ἀδύνατον.

IT'S IMPOSSIBLE TO ESCAPE FROM WHAT IS DESTINED.

"Not until I find what goes on. And what you mean *thanks to me*! If you mean what I think, you—"

"Yes, I am sure I can go to the hell," Leo said, completing her sentence. He threw up his hands. "Then stay! Confuse the men outside, along with Boiko and anyone else."

Alexsandra's gaze zeroed in on Leo like an owl on a field mouse. Layna watched and tried not to shudder. Who was Boiko?

"If you are still alive in year's time, and can prove me you are no involved in anything illegal," Leo said in a sarcastic tone, "I will sign over to you the house. It will be *your* house. But for now, I am leaving with my wife who is two months of pregnant."

Pregnant? Layna smiled her best, boastful, most-pregnant smile and took her marriage license from Aleksandra's hand while the hateful woman stared open-mouthed at them both.

Definitely time to leave.

"But where are we going?"

Layna held onto her Gucci bag, borrowed from Aleksandra the Great's bedroom closet, while Leo pulled her along, rattling away in Greek with Petras and totally ignoring her questions.

They headed into the kitchen, leaving Aleksandra standing speechless in the middle of the foyer.

In desperation, Layna yanked her hand away, or tried to. "What are we doing in the kitchen?"

"We can't just walk out of here," Petras said, opening the pantry and activating the secret panel he was more than familiar with. "Don't you remember what she said about the two men in the car? We're going to have to gun our way out of this mess."

"A gun?" Layna asked, hopeful she'd get her own this time. After all, she'd proven her bravery, right? Gone over and beyond and then some.

"A car," Petras explained. "Gunning a car—isn't that an American saying? Anyway, we'll get caught in the crossfire if we just leave. And we're bound to be followed. So the element of surprise is all we've got."

"Where did you learn to speak such perfect English? Even the slang words!"

Petras and Leo both stopped just short of the door leading outside and regarded Layna as though she were an alien. Leo put his finger to his lips while Petras whispered his answer.

"University, at first," he said, slightly embarrassed. *"Leo gave me all his books, and I took night classes, listened to audio tapes. Many, many audio tapes. In the car, in my sleep till I wanted to puke."* He grinned and blushed. *"Difficult language, all mixed together with other tongues and no rules—only exceptions. But finally I started liking it. Especially slang words."*

"No more questions," Leo said.

Still holding Layna's hand, he motioned to Petras. As soon as they exited into the garden, they stayed in the shrubbery. A man waited just outside the back gate, pacing, then pausing. Pacing, pausing. He wasn't wearing a hat. Boiko's man? Thurman's man? She couldn't tell.

Leo frowned and glanced at Petras, who nodded, crouched down, and made his way to the brick wall surrounding the house. After climbing a huge oak tree, he shimmied out onto a large branch, swung onto the top of the wall, and disappeared.

When Leo motioned to Layna, she followed him around the wall of the garden up to the gate. Leo had obviously timed their arrival to coincide with the man's pacing. As soon as the stranger turned and walked in the opposite direction, Leo motioned for her to cross to the other side, which she did.

She waited, shaking and trying to breathe as quietly and steadily as a racing pulse would allow. He motioned for her to lift the latch from the gate and swing it open at his signal. She looked at him like he was crazy. He grinned.

She heard Petras gunning the motor in the Chevy, then everything happened at once.

He whipped around the corner and brought the car to a screaming halt. Layna lifted the latch and pushed as hard as she could. The man jerked around, pulling a gun from behind his back. Leo came crashing through the gate, landing an elbow in the guy's jaw, and they all piled into the car. Even knowing the bullets were real, Layna was having so much fun, she had to remind herself not to grin—she never felt so *alive*! She wanted to ask them if shit like this happened every day, but she didn't dare.

"Stop looking around!" Leo pulled her down onto the car seat, her Gucci bag flew to the floorboard, and Petras peeled out. Two bullets pierced the back windshield, showering them with glass. Layna thought she heard answering shots. Thurman's guys?

As soon as they were out of danger, they regained their seating. Petras passed his handkerchief back to Layna. Leo retrieved his own from his pocket, with a grunt of pain for his effort. They proceeded to brush and pick glass from their clothes and hair as best they could while being thrown side to side in the Chevy. She thought how

Hollywood could use a good stunt man. Then she saw Leo favor his left arm again and wondered what it had cost him to punch the guy out with his elbow, even if it had been his good arm. Wouldn't hitting someone like that reverberate through your whole body?

The ridiculousness of the situation suddenly appealed to her American sense of humor, and she started laughing, leaning over to pick pieces of the windshield out of Leo's hair. It must have been contagious. Leo laughed aloud. Suddenly, he pulled her down on top of him and kissed her. In fun the first time. In earnest the second time. Definitely in earnest the third. Then, he pulled away and continued brushing glass from her shoulders, mumbling something about his arm and shoulder hurting, almost apologetic for what had happened.

Layna looked at him, but he wouldn't meet her eyes.

In the rearview mirror, Petras frowned as he careened down a narrow, cobblestone street, barely missing a girl on a bicycle.

Suddenly, a second car swerved, tires squealing, and tried to block them. Leo cursed and pulled Layna down again but in a protective mode, holding her as best he could through the impact of the Chevy wrenching the fender off, or at least that's what it sounded like. When she heard a gunshot—either that, or a blown tire—she buried her face in Leo's chest. His breathing was labored from being tossed side-to-side. Tires squealed as Petras cut down yet another side street, putting "the petal to the metal" and muttering things in Greek that she took to be oaths, curses, or prayers. It seemed a miracle that no one, like a pedestrian or two or three, died in the process. At one point, she could have sworn they were airborne.

It seemed a long time before they could sit back up, but the car finally came out onto a major highway where there was some semblance of normal traffic and no one shooting at them. Layna sighed with relief.

"Are you hurt?" Leo finally said, exhaling with difficulty.

"Aside from a few bruises, I seem to be okay. To think I was worried about you maybe punching out an Interpol agent!"

"Thurman?" Leo said in an astonished voice. "I would not do to Thurman. He is like family."

"Then who the hell has been chasing us all over Athens?"

"The people Thurman is watching," Leo said. "As you say—one of the bad guys."

"You mean one of the people who tried to kill you? I mean, me?"

"Not now," he said. "When we are on road—"

"But if that wasn't Thurman," Layna began, about to ask why he tipped his hat to her in the moonlight last night, but decided against it. She caught Petras' eye in the rearview mirror, confirming her decision.

"What?" Leo asked.

"Nothing," she said, trying to separate the good guys from the bad guys in her mind. Then another, totally unrelated thought broke in.

"What exactly did I say that was so funny?"

"To Aleksandra?"

"Yes. I'm not sure where it came from, or how I even remembered it. Something to do with my father and a library. It was weird. I don't speak any Greek that I know of. But both of you practically exploded with laughter. Aleksandra looked like she wanted to punch me in the face!"

"You want to know for sure?" Leo asked, his lips twitching.

"Yes," Layna said. "I think so."

Petras grinned at them from the front seat. "You told her to be nice, or you'd break her balls." He chuckled. "And you said it rather well," he added, nearly choking.

Layna's eyes grew wide. "*That's* what I said? But I'd never say anything like that!" She stared at the seat back in shock while Leo and Petras laughed at her expense. Eventually, Leo launched into a lengthy discussion with Petras in Greek, leaving Layna to brood in silence and check the car seat once more for pieces of glass. While she did so, she struggled to resurrect the memory of her father, but it was gone. A moment in time. There one second, gone the next. Her eyes misted over.

When Petras pulled into the parking lot of an ancient-looking church with stained–glass windows, she read a sign in English proclaiming it to be Greek Orthodox. Leo's sleek, black Bentley sat two parking spaces over. An old man waiting on the curb got up and ambled their way, tilting his head and rubbing his grizzled beard when he saw the Chevy's shattered windows, twisted fender, and assorted bullet holes.

They got out, and Petras put their belongings on the pavement. Leo handed the man what looked like enough money to buy another car, or two. The old man removed his knit cap, slipped the money inside it, placed the cap back on his head, and climbed into his demolished vehicle, a wealthier, happier man. Layna watched the Chevy amble slowly away.

"I'm amazed it still runs," she mumbled.

"He will buy another," Leo said, matter-of-factly. "It is how things are."

After transferring their bags to the Bentley, Petras slid into the driver's seat.

Though he glanced around with great satisfaction, Layna was fairly sure he missed burning rubber in a Chevy.

Leo got into the back seat, favoring his shoulder more so than before. She thought what a miracle it was that he hadn't opened the wound, the way they'd been thrown all over the car. But what about the kissing thing? Why had she done it? Why had he pulled away? Of course he'd pulled away—she was a married woman. So was it just part of the game, like what happened with Aleksandra? What if she learned who she was, what happened to Jack, and why Boiko's men wanted to kill her—and it wasn't anything to write home about, anything that made her feel even half as alive as she'd felt these last few days? What happens if you're hiding behind the door when destiny walks up or when love passes by?

Layna felt a little sore in several places, but that was physical. What worried her more was what she felt in her spirit. How could she have said such a gross thing, even to Aleksandra and in front of Leo? Was that person really her? Or was she just discovering the real her?

She didn't belong here. She should withdraw. *Where did that come from?* She struggled to locate the source, then tried to recreate her father's image again. The library. Anything. A feeling of abandonment came over her, and she couldn't stop thinking about kissing Leo or why she felt drawn to him. By the third kiss, she could've stayed in his arms for days, weeks, months, years. What the hell was she doing? Her husband was Jack, not Leo.

Petras waited for traffic, then pulled slowly away from the church parking area onto the major road. Leo settled into the luxury of the Bentley and turned his eyes to check on his passenger, tilting his head when he read something there he couldn't make out.

CHΛPTΣR TΣΠ

Τα πολλά λόγια είναι φτώχια.

TOO MANY WORDS CAN LEAD TO POVERTY.

"What is it, Layna?"

"I want to go home," she said quietly.

"We *are* going home," Leo said.

"Skopelos?" Petras asked from the front seat as he turned onto a highway.

"Skopelos," Leo replied, deep in thought.

"No. No more Skopelos," Layna said. "I'm done. You don't understand. I want to go home. To the United States of America."

They looked at her like she'd lost her mind.

Petras didn't slow down until they were well out of Athens. Layna noticed he regularly checked his rearview mirror and frowned a lot. Were they being followed? Or was he checking to make sure she didn't jump out of the car and make a run for it every time he slowed down.

"The mountains are beautiful," she commented, trying to commit the names of towns they passed into her broken memory banks in case she needed to find her way back to Athens and the embassy. The American one. Not the British one. After a while, she tried to wring information from Petras regarding landmarks. Names of mountains. Tourist attractions. Anything. A thought came unbidden from the gods.

"Will we pass by Mount Olympus?" she asked. *A well-known landmark.*

"Not from Athens," Petras replied. "If you come from Thessalonica, you go around it. This way is longer—three hours. Not so scenic. Less traffic."

She gave up. His answer was short and not what she needed. Restlessness plagued her body and soul. Highway signs passed them by, some in Greek, some in English, some in both for the tourists. She concluded that they were taking the long way on purpose, that *less traffic* translated into fewer people trying to kill them.

Leo stared out the window, resting his good elbow on the armrest as he continued thinking in silence. Something was wrong, and he didn't know how to fix it. He had to try. Perhaps he had been too decisive in turning her away, in keeping everything from her. Women needed conversation—if not with one another, then with any man fortunate to listen. Abruptly, as though remembering her presence, he turned and spoke.

"ευχαριστώ," he said. "Thank you, for earlier, with Aleksandra. I appreciate much what you did for me."

"Aleksandra was surprisingly hostile, for family," Layna replied.

He turned back to the window. "I never feel she is family. It is most unfortunate. She has never been friend. I am not sure we are enemies. I think maybe we are."

"Is she Greek?"

"No. She is many things. Polish, Turkish, some Armenian. Her uncle is Italian. I cannot be certain. She does not speak Greek well because she refuses to learn. My father spoke English enough. She was immigrant, one of thousands."

"You mean, like a refugee? She certainly understood what I said to her in Greek."

Leo chuckled. "She know street talk in several language."

"How did she meet your father?"

"She trains as nurse before. Or so she say. That is where my father first see her, in the hospital. When he requires a nurse at home, she asks for assignment. She is poor. My father has a great deal of money. He is lonely, a kind man. She does everything she can to—*accommodate* him? In my mind, he married stupidly, but I would never say such a thing to my father."

"Surely he loved her, to marry her I mean."

"I think not," Leo muttered, playing with a random thread on the car seat. "He loved my mother. But I tell you one thing. When my father dies, she does not mourn him as a woman mourns when she is in love. Perhaps it is because she is not Greek? No, I do not think so. I have seen Turkish men mourn the loss of goat with more compassion than she shows at the death of my father."

Layna thought a moment. "Why was she so angry when you told her I was your wife?

Leo looked out at the towns as they passed, pulling at the thread to keep from pulling at his brains. He wanted to rest, not talk. But she had the right to know such things.

"Here, men do not marry young if they wish to succeed," he said, "unless they have the money before. In the family, I mean. Family is everything. But the woman, she marries young."

Aware he hadn't answered her question, Layna didn't want to give up on learning more about her captor. "I'd imagine you'd have many women interested in you," she said quietly, "of any age." For some reason, she checked the rearview mirror and caught Petras' inquisitive glance. She ducked her head and looked out the window at yet another A1 road sign, yet another mountain. She feared reaching their destination and feared not being allowed to.

"Yes, there have been," Leo answered, adding a sad, howbeit boastful grin, "perhaps more interested in family's money than in me." He cast his eyes down. "There was someone," he began, his voice wistful, "when I left for university in America. I was gone long time. She did not wait. She married a man with good business and no wish to disappear to a foreign country. I did not become serious again, nor did I have the time to go in search of what I did not need."

"Do you have children?" Layna asked quietly.

"No."

"Neither do I," she said. "I mean, not that I know of."

"Then it is true? You have forgotten everything?"

She started to tell him about the flashes of insight now and then, but decided not to give him even that much information. Had he overheard all of her conversation with Dr. Liatos, or just the last part?

"I wait to marry," Leo continued. "I concentrate on university because I attend later than most. My father is modern—he leaves choice of a wife to me. He thinks it would be good thing if I spend time working on ships. Anyway, the Greek university is free, but after that, it is better somewhere like America. I go there until my father is ill and Aleksandra comes to take care of him. Suddenly, my father is no longer alive, and I am no longer young man."

"Is that why you told her I was pregnant?" Layna threw a glance in the rearview mirror at Petras, who's grinning. Why? Because she's busy making a fool of herself?

"No, I say you are pregnant to make Aleksandra angry," Leo explained. "As wife, Aleksandra inherits half of my father's wealth, or so she thinks. But she is given nothing in her own name, not for five years more."

"Five years?"

"It is complicate. My father gives me both houses—one in Athens, one in Skopelos where we go now. He left business and money to me with houses and something each month for Aleksandra. In the will, he says if I do not marry and produce heir in five years, by the time I am forty, then Aleksandra will get the house in Athens and half of business."

"Is that how it's done here? I mean, five years isn't very long." Layna looked at it from a different angle. "And forty isn't very old," she said. "Not for children. Not for the man at least."

Leo shifted his position and eased his arm with several slow shoulder rotations. He laughed. "Are we near end? You ask more questions than Interpol."

"You've been questioned by Interpol? By Thurman?"

Leo rolled his eyes and took up the threads of conversation, along with the threads of the unraveling car seat, but where Layna would not see evidence of his nervousness.

"Good. I will explain. For owners of ships, marriage is like merger with two families, much the same as my grandfather when he starts his business. Aleksandra is not happy with half anything. She want all. This is why she is angry towards you. There. It is done. Perhaps it was wrong to say you are pregnant. Still, I want to see the look on her face, the big disappointment."

"You used me to get revenge," Layna said.

"Only in a small way," Leo said. "Forgive, but ah, the look on her face! Eh, Petras?"

They chuckled. Layna was not amused. Rather, she was appalled that men still regarded a woman as an heir-producing, baby factory. And she found no humor in that knowledge.

"If you want to know marriage and children, ask Petras," Leo said, nodding to his cousin in the mirror. "He is married to lovely young wife and they have four children."

"Really? I'd think working for you would leave him little family time."

"She waits for me," Petras said matter-of-factly, "like any decent Greek wife would do. Σε περιμένω, eh?" he said, grinning, to Leo. The topic appeared to be closed.

"Ne. Se periméno," Leo translated, turning to Layna. "It means *I wait for you.*"

Something flickered in his eyes, like a bird's wing caught in a fierce wind, then it was gone, replaced by momentary sadness before he looked away.

Layna didn't care to begin a lengthy discussion of the dominant versus subservient roles of men and women in another culture, but there was one aspect she meant to explore while Leo was still open to discussing it.

"Before, when you were talking about Aleksandra, you said five years. I'm curious. When will the five years be up?"

"I do not know. Maybe one and a half years more?" He looked at her in an odd way and shook his head. "No, do not think it," he said. "There is nothing to worry. I will not hold you to it, the marriage I mean. In fact, I am thinking I give Aleksandra the house anyway, in hopes she will go away. Or that I will go away, live on Skopelos. Our marriage only done to protect. You know this, right? We have never made the marriage good, but, of course, if you wish me go out and impregnate first Greek woman I find—"

Petras laughed aloud from the front seat, and even Layna had to smile, though again, she didn't find the situation entirely humorous. And she still had no answers to what had happened.

"You said the marriage took place to protect me. Protect me from what?"

"You were hurt," Leo explained. "You were alone, with no memory. You were young, in foreign country. Many things to protect you from."

"No, that's not it." Her voice was so determined, Leo sat up straighter and prepared for whatever came next. With Layna, he could never say. Like now, with that blazing in her eyes while she struggled to judge the truth of something.

"Earlier," Layna began, "you referred to those men, the ones who broke into your house that morning. You said they weren't after *you*. Which means they were after *me.* And the men who shot out the windows in the restaurant. Were they after me as well? And if so, why? Why would anyone want to kill me? From all that you've told me, I can only assume it has something to do with your business. That seems to be your priority in everything you do. But how could I possibly be connected to whatever it is you do? By the way, what *do* you do?

"Shipping." Leo turned away for moment, appeared to have made a decision, and rejoined the conversation.

"For what you cannot remember," he said, "something hidden deep inside head. This is why they want to kill, okay? Do not look so. I do not know what it is. Only you know this."

CHAPTER ELEVEN

Αγάλι-αγάλι γίνεται η αγουρίδα μέλι.

A GREEN FRUIT RIPENS SLOWLY.

"No, I don't. I don't *know* what's buried in my head!"

Leo remained silent.

"Okay," Layna said. "What about the men at the restaurant?"

"Ah, now *those* men were after *me*."

"And the ones who chased us in the car all over Athens? Do we know which one of us *they* were after?"

"Both," he said, gazing out the window. "They were after both of us."

"Why?"

"As you have guessed, it is something to do with my business. It is not personal."

"So, the only reason you're protecting me is because of what's inside my head? And you're doing it for your business?"

Her words brought him back from his study of landscape.

"It is not like that. Do not be angry."

"Then what is it like? What happens if I can't remember? What do they want from me? What do *you* want from me?"

Leo let go with a heavy "puh!" sound and leaned his head back. "I am tired of the cat-and-mouse games," he said.

"So am I!" Layna said, equally exasperated. "Tired and hungry," she added, leaning forward in the seat.

"Petras, is that car still following us?"

"What?" Leo said, bolting upright. He turned to Layna in surprise, then Petras.

"Thurman," Petras confirmed from the front seat, "since Athens."

"Damn," Leo said with a growing smile. "Then perhaps by now he is hungry as well. Where is nearest town?"

"Atalanti, maybe half an hour," Petras replied. "I know a restaurant there."

"You always do," Leo said.

Petras grinned.

A mid-sized, gray sedan pulled up alongside the black Bentley at *The Desert Rose* on the main street of a town called Falaraki just outside of Atalanti. A man in a white shirt and black slacks, sporting a two-inch brimmed fedora, got out of his car and nonchalantly followed them into the restaurant. Layna took note that they were the only customers, possibly due to the odd hour of the afternoon.

A delighted proprietor showed Leo and his party to a table that seated four, and the man from the gray sedan joined them, uninvited. His refusal to remove his hat told Layna either he was all about making an entrance or he was totally lacking in manners. And even in a deserted restaurant, she noticed Leo and Petras still kept their voices low and quiet.

"Thurman?" Leo nodded.

"Amratsis?" Thurman acknowledged, nodding to Petras as well. "Savakis, good to see you alive. You drive a mean Chevy."

Petras grinned, and everyone turned to Layna, who focused on the menu. She'd already checked Thurman out during the stilted greetings. In the daylight, Interpol Agent Michael Thurman proved to be a tall African American, nice-looking, with kind eyes. She wasn't sure how Leo intended to handle the situation, but Thurman took the initiative, tipping his hat.

"Mrs. Taggart, awake at last," he said. Layna looked at him for a full five seconds while her mind raced across an endless desert littered with possibilities. *Taggart? Jack Taggart?*

"I'm sorry, my wife, Elayna Amratsis," Leo said. "Layna, J. Michael Thurman."

"Ms. Amratsis," Thurman said, with unwarranted emphasis. He finally removed his hat and set it down beside his plate. Leo shot daggers at him, while the Interpol Agent studied Layna like she was a painting in an art gallery in France.

Well aware of his attention, she kept her eyes on the menu.

"Shall I order for you?" Leo placed his hand firmly over hers. He interlaced her fingers with his as he spoke and pretended not to notice her hand trembling.

"Ευχαριστώ," she replied, hoping she put the right pronunciation on *thank you.*

His look of surprise washed over her like soft rain. He ordered a salad with black olives and feta cheese, Retsina wine, and souvlaki—lamb cooked on a spit with onions and tomatoes.

She felt Thurman's eyes on her during the conversation that followed and sipped her wine like a lady, all the while thinking how she'd kill for just one margarita. She salivated at the thought of lime and salt. Like the song said, Jose Cuervo was a friend of hers. *Whoa! Where did that come from? And who said tequila makes your clothes fall off?*

"So, has Leo told you how we first met?" Thurman was out to impress.

"No. It is too long in the telling." Leo spoke before Layna had a chance to—and with an underlying tone that said Thurman would be better off if he avoided the subject entirely, which only served to encourage him.

"It was Petras here," Thurman said, "a Greek of many talents."

Petras glared at Thurman over his moussaka.

"One of the best cat burglars I've ever had the privilege of arresting. Seems he made the mistake of trusting a pig like Hector "Defector" Houlis, a wizened, arthritic half-Armenian who begs for political asylum every time he's arrested, which is often. No brains, but some very important connections. It's all tied up in *family*, you see."

Layna tore off a piece of garlic bread, delighted with any and all information that might be forthcoming from this so-called friend of Leo's. Also, it kept her mind off the tequila. Yeah, right.

"Hector had a beautiful daughter named Demetra, who married the son of a man whose uncle was in the tobacco trade big-time. Lord, but these Greeks could roll some of the finest cigarettes you've ever tasted. Anyway, thanks to Hector's daughter's husband's father's uncle—have I lost you yet?—Hector moved up in the world. At first, he brought in premium tobacco from Turkey, then he added things like illegal refugees and a few kilos of heroin—"

"You don't know that for sure," Petras argued, then resumed eating.

Thurman continued, seemingly unaffected. "With business booming, Hector talked his new son-in-law into sharing the profits along with the danger. They bought a second boat for the new son-in-law, a boat subsequently captured coming out of Soma."

"That's enough, Thurman," Leo muttered.

"Oh, but I'm getting to the good part," Thurman replied. "That's when I first met a young man named Petras Savakis, Hector's son-in-law. And Petras' lovely wife, Demetra. And Petras' cousin, Leo Amratsis. I'll never forget the sight of this man walking confidently into my office in the middle of an interrogation, like he owned the joint."

Layna dipped her bread in olive oil. "Leo walked into Interpol?"

Thurman nodded. He smiled at Petras. "Can't tell you how badly I wanted the pleasure of that collar, but Demetra changed my mind. Beautiful, shy, no more than sixteen, and deeply in love with Petras here, who faced some serious prison time. But Leo Amratsis spoke with such compassion and honesty about youth and bad life choices, and the fact that Demetra and Petras were expecting their first child, well, he mesmerized an entire room of badass agents."

Layna glanced at Leo, who stared at the tabletop.

"Something was happening on my ships," Leo said with a growl, surprising Layna by stepping in. "I had traced what you call washing the money—"

"Money laundering," Thurman added.

"Yes, but also the word *terrorists* enters the conversation, does it not? The *Prometheus* and the *Golden Voyage*, my ships, named in certain documents difficult and costly to obtain—"

"So he called *me*," Thurman said. "Damnedest thing. Naturally, I arranged a meeting. And Leo showed up with Petras. Told me he suspected smuggling. Said the money was going somewhere, and he meant to find out. I've always believed it's better to work *with* someone instead of *against* them." Thurman paused and looked directly at Layna. She felt the tension rise at the table but wasn't sure why. "That's when Leo first mentioned—"

"Enough!"

Layna jumped at Leo's outburst. A glance around told her the waiter was equally alarmed. She saw Petras' eyes narrow, and even Thurman sat back in his chair, pretending to be shocked at the reaction he'd caused. At least, that's how she saw it. And she didn't care for his tactics or his manner.

Leo ordered coffee in a subdued voice, effectively closing the door on the past. Over coffee, the men returned to the business at hand.

"So, where are we headed?" Thurman asked. "Volos?"

Layna saw Petras glance at Leo over his coffee cup.

"I told my people one of us should go along with you folks," Thurman said. "You know, just to make sure nothing happens."

"I do not think it a good idea," Leo said.

"I do," Thurman said, "especially after Athens. It's still a good ways to Skopelos, even by hydrofoil. But hey, you've got a boat! That'll give us plenty of time to talk. By the way, Aleksandra sends greetings. I told her a hotel would be safer, but you know how she is."

"I do."

"I could always get one of my men to break the other window," Thurman said. "Maybe it would scare her into a hotel."

"Maybe it scares her so much she shoots him," Leo replied.

Thurman laughed. "I see what you mean. Well, my second idea would be to park the car in Volos and go with you folks to Skopelos. I could use a vacation."

"I don't recall inviting you." Leo said. His voice carried an undertone of friendly banter.

"I don't remember asking," Thurman countered.

Petras cleared his throat while Layna continued to listen, wondering what kind of strange friendship existed between the three men at the table.

"The lady could always go with me," Thurman said, "and you two could ride ahead."

"No." Leo said. "She stays with me. That is the agreement."

"And what agreement is that?" Layna gave the men her full attention.

"A *gentleman's* agreement," Leo replied, his voice hard like concrete.

Thurman raised his eyebrows at Leo's response, then let it go. Petras picked the car keys up off of the table while Leo slid several banknotes beneath the plate.

Lunch was over.

Everyone rose.

"My apologies, Ms. Taggart. I mean, Ms. Amratsis. Looks like this is where I say goodbye." Thurman gave a little bow and a mock wave of his hand.

"And the cowboy rides away," she said with a smile.

Thurman grinned.

Layna lowered her eyes in acknowledgment. Her ploy hadn't worked. Now what? If she screamed her head off, would anyone come to help, or would they look the other way because Amratsis was a man of importance? Everyone had their own agenda except her. Maybe there was a window in the ladies' room. Nodding to Thurman, she turned and headed for the unisex sign she'd seen over a door in the back. Leo rose to accompany her.

"Is there a back door to this place?" She grinned.

Leo panicked for a second, then remembered the other restaurant, where they'd ended up on the floor. He laughed.

Layna slipped into the ladies room and locked the door, only to find herself surrounding by four walls and no window. She took care of business and reemerged to find Thurman gone and Leo waiting for her by the entrance. Their little group got back in the car and headed for Volos. Layna sat in the front seat and Leo drove, allowing Petras some downtime in the back. Even with his eyes closed, Layna knew Leo's second-in-command would hear every word. She buckled her seatbelt and leaned back, letting questions circle like vultures until one of them landed.

"What is it I've forgotten that people want me to remember?"

"I-I don't know," Leo said, jarred from watching lines on the road.

"I'm supposed to believe that?"

"If I know the answer, there is no need for υπεκφυγή—Petras?"

"Subterfuge."

"Ah. Subterfuge. And you would have the life back, I would have the information I need to save my business, and Thurman could close his files and go out and find a woman of his own. No people trying to kill us. No nightmares. We could all sleep at night. Even Thurman."

Layna gave a small laugh. "I'd give a lot to sleep at night without these horrible dreams. In fact, I had the strangest dream about when Jack died in a car crash, only it was more like a nightmare, because I feel he's still alive somewhere."

Leo glanced at her, definitely interested. "Tell me this," he said. "I listen."

Layna quietly related the dream she'd had in the house in Athens—the sun in her eyes, the ring, what Jack said, the squeal of tires, the crash. "That's all I remember," she said, glancing at the third finger of her left hand, "except this—the most beautiful ring I've ever seen."

"Layna." Something in his voice broke through her reverie. "Jack did not die in car crash; he only fractured the arm," Leo said. "The car crashed a year or so before—before he comes to Greece. The ring I buy for the marriage. Since you are not there to pick out, I am flattered very much you adore it. I tell my jeweler he does the good job. I am sorry. You have no jewelry when you are found."

She sat up straight. "Not even a cheap, gold wedding band?" The thought brought tears to her eyes, but they weren't tears of joy or of sorrow—just tears. The fact triggered a feeling, but not the thought behind it. Besides, something was wrong. There had to be more. She stared at Leo, who stared at the road. "Then, I'm not married, and Jack isn't dead."

"I am sorry," Leo said in a quiet voice. "Jack is dead. That part is true. What is not the true is he did not die in car crash. He is killed."

"As in *murdered*? How?"

Leo was silent.

"On Skopelos? Is that why we're going there?"

"There, or another island close by," Leo said. "But is not the only reason. It is my home."

"I thought you lived in Athens."

"I have a house in Athens, this is true. My home is on Skopelos."

She saw the way Leo gripped the steering wheel, the sadness in his eyes, how his lips remained pressed together as though determined to see it through. See what through?

"No, there's more to it," she said. "Or is that what I'm supposed to remember, the rest of the story?" There was a thought, and she tried to follow it, but it was like holding on to a slippery fish. "You said you gave me the ring," she said, "so it couldn't have been in the dream about Jack. I don't understand why everything's mixed up. Unless you're purposefully leaving out pieces of the puzzle."

Leo drove a little farther until he came to a rest stop. He pulled off to the side of the road and kept his hands on the steering wheel. He left the motor running. When he spoke, he chose his words carefully, speaking slowly, his eyes burning in their intensity as he stared deep into her soul.

"There are things I cannot tell to you," he said. "Not only you would not believe, such information makes you worse maybe. Many hours I spend reading dis-so-cia-tive disorder, amnesia, concussion, trauma, all these things I am told could be what happen to you, what still happens to you maybe. If what I say can make you to remember a certain way, I am told you can throw back—no, is not correct—be thrown back to what you had when you are found. No one deserves this. This is what I have been told. I cannot be responsible for do such a thing."

Layna swallowed the parts she hadn't wanted to hear. It was a long speech, filled with more grammatical errors than usual, probably due to the deep emotion that ran beneath his words like a current. "That's why you stopped Thurman in the restaurant," she said. "He was about to tell me what really happened."

"You are most correct."

"Fine. Then you tell me. Or tell me what you can."

Leo exhaled and gripped the steering wheel, fixing his eyes on the road ahead. "What everyone wants is something your husband know, something he has in possession. No one is sure. Maybe he tell you something, give you something, say something. You are with him when he dies."

Layna digested words, meanings, possibilities. She stared at Leo, her eyes widening in comprehension. "You know how he died," she said. "This isn't some random fact someone told you. Why can't you tell me even that? Or what you're all looking for? I don't think it's asking too much!"

"Because, I explain to you. Like the ring, the car crash, you mix this with that and maybe come up with false truth. A doctor can explain more. I only say how important it is you come to the *real* truth that rests in your mind, in memory. You must find it on your own. You must awaken it yourself."

"Why is this so important to you? Where do you fit in? Is it your business? The money laundering?"

"Yes."

"How can something buried in my brain have anything to do with that?'

"That I cannot say." Leo took a deep breath and coughed. "It is nothing to you, this part of what is happened," he said matter-of-factly, "but I have only the two ships. If I lose them, *I lose everything.*"

Petras mumbled beneath his breath, opened the car door, slid out of the back seat, and walked over to switch places with Leo in the front. "He needs rest," Petras told her, "not this. I will tell you what I can. I'm rested now."

Layna nodded. Leo climbed into the back seat, leaned his head against the cushioned head rest, and closed his eyes.

Petras strapped in and pulled the beloved Bentley back on the road.

Layna felt a headache coming on. "Petras, I'm sorry. I have so many questions, I don't know where to start."

Petras shifted in his seat. "I'll start, then. You didn't go with Thurman because you didn't want to. You realized if you did, we could no longer protect you. Am I correct?"

"I think some of those books you studied were psychology books.

Petras laughed. "I learn from life more than from books. How about you?"

Layna looked out the window. "I don't know," she said. "I wish I did. I know there was a library in the house, so I must have read a few books, right?"

"I'm sorry," Petras said. "I should not have brought it up. Do you understand why we need Thurman and vice versa? We're both looking for answers. After Leo's father died, there were too many discrepancies to explain away—large sums missing after shipments to Larnaca in Cyprus, and again from Volos to Italy and Italy to Germany. Manifests altered, container weights miscalculated, personnel unaccounted for. And Aleksandra spending more money than she had. Do you understand?"

"I do. And international smuggling brought J. Michael Thurman and Interpol into the picture," Layna added. "Okay, so what happens if you can't get the evidence?"

"Then we are responsible," Petras said. "I do not wish to go to prison. My lovely wife Demetra would weep, and I could not see my children."

Layna watched the scenery fly by. It sounded more serious than she'd thought. "I don't think I want to know any more."

"But you are the one who *must* know more, who *does* know more," Petras said. "You are involved because of Jack and what he found. It was the last thing he said before he was killed."

"You saw him?"

"No. Leo spoke with him on the phone."

"Wait. If Leo knew Jack, then he—both of you—must have known Taggart was my last name as well," Layna said. "Why did you lie and say you didn't know me?"

"We did not lie," Petras said, gritting his teeth. "Surely you know this by now. We never knew your first name. When Jack spoke of you, he called you his wife, always. He showed us your picture the one time. It did not look like you look now. But he never said your first name. It would have done little good to call you Taggart if the other questions could not be answered."

"But Thurman knows, right? He has all the resources of Interpol!"

Petras said nothing.

"Give me *something*," Layna pleaded. "What did Jack do for a living? How did he and Leo first meet?"

"Those answers will have to wait until we get to Skopelos."

Layna turned to see if she could get any more information from Leo, but his eyes were closed. The discussion was at an end. But why?

Layna gripped the hand rest, sifting through the limited information Leo and Petras had divulged, wishing for a computer so she could read for herself what the effects and cures might be for amnesia coupled with dissociative-whatever, and worsened by trauma. Anger raced through her veins. The stripes on the highway merged into one long string of hypnotic lines that took her backward instead of forward. Suddenly, she was in the house in Athens, crying.

She couldn't stop sobbing. Leo took her in his arms and held her gently, lovingly. She buried her face in his chest, his all-too-familiar scent washing over her, drawing her in like the tide to the sand while waves of emotion crashed against a cliff. His fingers caressed her cheek, and she looked into his eyes, knowing he would be a part of her life forever. He bent down and kissed her, passionately. But he would go no farther. No farther. No matter how badly she—

"Leo," she whispered, unaware she was back in the present until

CHΛPTΣR TWΣLVΣ

Η θάλασσα δεν πεθαίνει ποτέ.

THE SEA NEVER DIES.

a truck's horn blasted the image away, even as she spoke his name. The deep bass of the horn grew as it passed their car, then diminished into the distance. She glanced at Petras, wondering if he'd heard. He seemed focused on the rearview mirror and on the highway ahead. On an impulse, Layna turned slowly around and looked longingly at the man asleep in the back of the Bentley, whose gleaming, half-closed eyes met hers head-on as if he knew only too well what this particular memory had been, and why.

Layna pleaded with him in silence, and he closed his eyes in reply. She slowly turned back around and leaned against the door, wondering what had really happened in the house in Athens before she'd awakened that morning, and why Leo kept raising a wall between them. Why did he act guilty? Was what happened so horrible she wouldn't be able to face the truth when she finally remembered? Shouldn't he be protecting her from remembering?

One moment, she'd give anything to know, to understand what had passed between them in Athens. The next moment, the whole thing frightened and confused her. She knew in her heart of hearts that Leo Amratsis would never take advantage of a woman not in her right mind. Even when they kissed in the back seat of a Chevy like giddy teenagers, he only allowed it to go so far before he stopped. She thought at the time, okay, I'm married. But he knew even then that Jack was dead.

Facts, not feelings.

Another invasion from the outside world. Or deep inside her mind?

Okay. His questionable business dealings. He'd proven himself a man of high morals the day he walked into Interpol. But what about his dealings with Jack? She couldn't face it if she found out he'd deceived her in any way. Better to fight the attraction like he did. He'd already admitted he was only protecting her in order to save his business. What more did she need?

He'd even taken a bullet for her when those men had broken down the door.

Or had he?

Early afternoon sun beat down on the town of Volos—according to Petras, the very port *Jason and the Argonauts* set out from when they left in search of the Golden Fleece. Layna could hear the pride apparent in his voice when he told her the story, but all she felt was anxiety.

When Leo stopped at a market to purchase bread, cheese, and wine, Layna noticed some of the shops were closing and asked why.

Petras explained. "Everyone takes a *siesta* from 2:00 to 5:00 in the afternoon. Then they open up again in the evening. Some restaurants serve meals as late as 10:00 at night."

"I thought siesta was Spanish."

"Everybody knows siesta," he said with a grin.

"By the time we arrive in Skopelos, most the shops will be closed," Leo said. "Nitsa, my housekeeper, she does not know we are coming. It is better we bring food with us."

Layna nodded, biting her lower lip as she wondered at his casual conversation. Was he sharing his life in detail to keep her from asking more questions, or to make up for his refusal to answer the important ones? She watched him argue with a vendor in animated Greek over the price of grape leaves stuffed with rice and meat, called *dolmades*. It was like a picture in a magazine—an open market in a foreign land, and two Greeks haggling over money. It fit with a perfect blue sky, whitewashed houses, and red geraniums.

Under other circumstances, she would delight in the people and colors all around her and savor every moment. But there was a ghost to lay to rest. A ghost trapped in her mind.

Leo finished with the vendor, each satisfied with the exchange. When they returned to the dock, Petras handed a man the keys to Leo's car. She watched, puzzled, as the Bentley was driven away. She turned to Leo.

"I leave the car on Volos," he said. "From here, we take my boat."

Since it seemed a commonplace routine, she walked with Leo and Petras down a plank to the end of a long pier. A short, older man in jeans and a plaid shirt waved to them. She didn't know much about boats, but this one looked somewhere between a rowboat and a small yacht. Maybe a cabin cruiser? It had to be 40 feet long, and as sleek as a model on a runway. Leo got in and assisted Layna while Petras hoisted the bags and baskets of food on board.

After introducing her to Erikos, the pilot, she was directed to one of two cushioned seats. Petras disappeared below and came back bearing bottled water, which she heartily accepted.

Leo sat beside her and leaned back, resting his good shoulder and arm behind her. Petras took a seat opposite them, promptly got his phone, and turned aside to make a call.

Layna turned her face to the sun and soaked in the calm of early afternoon, nervous about what she would find, or not find, on the island. Again, blue sky over whitewashed houses dotted the cliffs they passed. And beneath all the beauty, a layer of corruption and death.

She leaned toward Leo, raising her voice to be heard. "What do people do here for a living?"

"Fishing," he yelled back, "and the tourists."

"Then what was Jack doing here? You still haven't told me what he did for a living."

Leo frowned and thought a moment, trying to find the proper translation. "He was a φωτορεπόρτερ, a fotorepórter. You know, pictures for the magazines."

"A photojournalist?"

"Yes. That is the word."

"So, what was he doing *here*?"

Leo got up, went forward, took a swivel chair next to Erikos, and started a conversation with the older man.

Layna's mouth opened at the rude dismissal, but when she looked at Petras for help, he appeared very involved in his phone conversation.

She closed her mouth and leaned her arm along the side of the boat. The sunlight hit her ring, the lovely ring Leo had given her, the one that had mysteriously appeared in the dream about Jack.

Why was everything so mixed up? She moved her finger so the diamonds glittered like sun on the water. Like the sea. Always changing, forever the same. Skopelos. According to the doctor in Athens, she almost died on Skopelos. The sea and sky faded, and suddenly she heard Jack's voice.

"It's not much," he said. "Someday I'll give you a big old king-size ring that'll knock your socks off, wait and see. We're about to come into a whole lot of money."

"But, a gold band is fine, Jack. It's a symbol. When the swelling goes down in your hand, you can wear yours, too. Millions of men wear a gold band. It's tradition."

"Yeah, tradition," he said, and laughed again. "Well, it's not me."

"Sometimes I think you don't want anyone to know we're married."

"You know what we agreed, Ellie. You said it was okay. I thought you understood. In my business, it's better to let clients think you're single."

"I know. It just seems you're being secretive when there's no need. But I'll stick by the agreement. It's a fine, gold band. I don't need anything fancy. Really."

Layna came to herself in the boat, holding her head while neurons fired away, every memory exacting their price in pain. But beneath the pain, she felt almost giddy. She knew her name. Well, a nickname. *Ellie,* short for Eleanor, right? Or maybe, *Elayna?*

The brightness of the clear sky made her reach for her sunglasses; she stared at the water to focus and remember more. Her mind dredged up a map of the United States, unfolded before her as though conjured up from the ocean depths. Not a vision this time, but a choice. With 50 states to choose from, she went for climate first. Forget Alaska and the upper half of North America. She definitely felt acclimated to a warm climate, like Skopelos. Eyes closed, she merged her mind with the sea.

She remembered a boat, much smaller. The water was blue, but it didn't carry the vibrancy, the depth of color she saw here in the Mediterranean, or more specifically, the Aegean. And the water in her vision didn't resemble the muddy brown of the Gulf that turned blue after Mississippi, right? She opened her eyes behind the glasses. How did she know that?

Okay, she'd obviously been spawned in the South. Maybe the Deep South. Alabama? Georgia? A frown creased her forehead. She opened the door a little wider.

They were in a boat, and the water sparkled with blues and greens. So alive. There was an island. A cave. I was born in a cave? No. You died there.

Her eyes shot open, squinting against the bright white of the sky over the rim of the sunglasses. She took them off, groaned, and shaded her face with her hand, wondering how her mind had shut down so abruptly, like a vault slamming shut with a final thud.

"Layna, you jumped. Are you all right?"

Petras leaned over her, holding the bottle of water she'd dropped.

"Petras, how many caves are there on Skopelos?"

"I don't know, a hundred maybe. Why?"

"I need to find one. Just one."

"There's a computer at the house," he said, giving her a curious look. "Would that help?

She nodded. A quick glance at Leo's narrowed eyes confirmed only his awareness that something had happened. How long had he been watching her? Static voices burst forth from a headpiece looped over his chair, and he turned away. Layna took in the breathtaking scenery of the island of Skopelos, where supposedly it had all begun.

It was certainly the greenest island she had ever seen. Pine trees filled the landscape, which she found surprising in the Aegean. The trip around the island to Skopelos Town on the far side was breathtaking. Petras finished his interrupted phone call and came to sit next to her.

"There are 350 churches on the island," he said, "if you count chapels and monasteries. And many, many caves."

"I'm told all Greek names mean something," Layna said. "Is that true of Skopelos?"

"It means *obstacle.*" Petras followed the remark with a rather skeptical look to see if she caught the double meaning. "It's a rocky island," he said, "difficult for ships to navigate in ancient times. It was originally called *Peparithos*, after the son of Dionysus and Ariadne. But, see for yourself," he said, pointing. "Skopelos Town."

A stunning little city awaited them, beautifully situated at the edge of the sea. To her disappointment, Erikos steered the boat past the town to a large pier with numerous slips. When they finally disembarked, Layna looked around for a taxi, or even another Bentley.

Petras laughed.

"We walk from here," Leo explained. "No automobiles. They try keep natural beauty of the island."

"Of course," she said. "Great idea. Less air pollution. Cleaner streets. Good decision."

After half an hour walking uphill, she no longer felt environmentally correct.

They stopped at a cobblestone street just around the corner from a picturesque market. There, hidden away, surrounded by a flower garden and situated at the end of a winding path of decorated paver stones, lay a modern house of white stone, its exterior shaded from the bright sun by several well-placed trees. Instead of the terracotta tile roofs she'd seen from the boat, this house had a charcoal-gray roof and matching frames on the windows set into the white stone walls. Beds of red geranium borders flanked both windows in the front as well as lining the paved walkway.

Leo opened the door and stood aside for Layna. Beyond the tiled entryway, stairs led immediately up to the second floor. At Leo's shout, a short, robust, dark-haired lady appeared, wiping her hands on an apron.

"Nitsa!" Leo reached down to give the woman a huge hug. They rattled away in Greek, and Layna noticed that Erikos placed their bags inside, then also hugged Nitsa and kissed her cheek in a manner that told her they were a couple.

Leo introduced Layna in Greek to his housekeeper, who nodded a welcome and added a smile. "Nitsa does not speak the English so well like me," he told Layna, "but she is with me many years. Her husband, Erikos, takes care of my boat and the beautiful flowers in the front of the house. Nitsa has big vegetable garden I hope you visit later. She is most proud."

"I'd love to see it," Layna said, allowing Leo to translate as they ascended the stairs.

Two spacious bedrooms took up most of the upstairs, each with a separate bath. Petras placed his bags in the smaller of the bedrooms, which obviously belonged to him. Layna wondered what his family thought about Petras requiring two separate living quarters, but the master bedroom commanded her attention.

She placed her Gucci bag next to Leo's luggage just inside the door and immediately fell in love with the clean, modern lines of the furniture and the color scheme of greens and browns and the colors of the earth. Leo took her hand. Nitsa grinned at them both as she turned to go.

"I show you everything," he said. "Then we eat a small meal, what we bought in market. You will see how we depend on the open market. Not so many frozen things. No dead food."

"Sounds wonderful," Layna said. She couldn't help but notice the king-size bed and the fact that they continued to hold hands.

"I told her you are my wife weeks ago," Leo said, noting her reaction to the bed. "We should appear to be so. It is easier this way. We discuss the arrangements later. There are only the two rooms for the sleeping."

"Yes, of course," Layna said. "It should be fine." She let go of his hand and set her Gucci bag on the bed; it seemed terribly inadequate. "Leo, I was wondering if it would be possible for someone to take me into town tomorrow." She stood facing him, twining her fingers together because she needed his help and she hated asking for it. "The thing is, I need some clothes. This is all I have to wear. And I need makeup, a hairbrush, things like that. The thing is," she said, aware she'd started repeating herself, "well, I have very little money, and I don't know anything about drachmas or euros or how to—"

"Of course," Leo said, laughing. "I am a stupid man who does not think of such things. Someone will go to help with the language, too. If you say what you say to Aleksandra in Athens, I will soon be asked to leave."

Layna blushed and tilted her head at him, squeezing a smile to death between pressed lips, determined not to ever blush again.

"Petras can go with you for the language," Leo said, "perhaps this evening? I give you the money. Is no problem."

Layna smiled, wary of his continued kindness or when he moved close to her and his fingers brushed her hand. She felt torn between backing away and going into his arms. But, he didn't want her in his arms, right?

"You look tired, " he said. "You have traveled far today, no? Come, I will show you the house, then we will eat and rest."

"Would it be okay if I took my shoes off? My feet hurt after walking uphill."

"Please, as you wish," he said. "In fact, I join you in removing the shoes."

He selected a low chest at the end of the bed, and Layna sat on top of the bed. Together, they *oohed* and *aahed* as shoes came off and aching feet rejoiced on cool, tile floors. They laughed in relief, and Layna looked at Leo in a new light, surprised at the change in him since reaching Skopelos. Definitely more relaxed.

Their hands brushed as they walked downstairs together.

The living room, kitchen, and dining room filled up the bottom floor in an open design that made it seem larger than it was. Layna sank into a leather sofa covered with brown, orange, rust, and green cushions that echoed the colors of the area rug beneath the wooden coffee table.

There was a small fireplace in the corner and a blank wall above it, and she wondered why no picture graced such a perfect setting. But Leo was on the move and helped her to her feet. The living room flowed past a dining area and on into a kitchen done in black and natural pine. A round, metal pot-holder hung from the ceiling and polished pine formed the cabinets and dining table, with complementing black appliances. Well-thought out, spacious, surprisingly warm. And terribly expensive.

Such beauty made her heart sing; she couldn't recall ever being in a happier house. And for once, she didn't mind the loss of memory. On impulse, she leaned up and gave Leo a quick kiss on the right side of his face. "It's so very lovely," she whispered.

A moment of confusion followed the compliment during which Leo's lovely tan complexion took on a charming shade of pink. His dark eyes gleamed with pride, and he continued the tour without trusting himself to speak. Of course, it was a small house. Only his office remained.

The room had perhaps been added on or extended out from an opening situated beneath the stairs. A computer and printer sat atop a long desk that flanked a winged-back wooden chair on rollers. Then a filing cabinet, two bookshelves jammed with books, and a communication device, probably ship-to-shore. A map of the Mediterranean adorned the wall while innumerable rolled-up charts lay scattered throughout the room.

Seeing this, Layna knew the Athens house was for show and convenience, but the real work was done right here on Skopelos.

Petras came down the stairs, drawing Leo aside to tell him something. Nitsa came in from the garden directing her husband what to place where. Leo's market bags were emptied, their contents divided, then supplemented with fresh onions, tomatoes, and green bell peppers. Everyone gathered in the dining room, deciding to enjoy a single evening meal instead of waiting until later. In no time at all, food appeared.

Layna sat in wonder and consumed incredibly delicious food while she marveled again at the difference in Leo here in his home. The atmosphere was warm and inviting. Layna listened to the constant stream of laughter and conversation from Nitsa and Erikos, then turned her attention to Leo and Petras for more of the same. It was a delightful picture she'd love to paint, and love even more to be a part of.

Nitsa declined her offer to help clear the table, and Petras signaled a readiness for their shopping trip to Skopelos Town, which carried the same name as the island. Layna, excited to be off, sensed her little adventure would leave Leo time to play catch-up in the office. Besides, she seemed to have found a kindred spirit in *the rock*.

Layna delighted in everything—the little cobblestone streets, the local shops, the people. Petras translated when needed and helped with euros and drachmas. He tried unsuccessfully to explain clothing sizes that came in the same European numbering system that she'd discovered in Aleksandra's closet. It made no sense. Size 34? Good Lord. Was that supposed to be waist, bust, or age?

The one place Petras refused to accompany Layna was into the bra and panty section, remaining outside with his arms folded like a severe, disapproving husband. It took her a while, but she came away with a lot of necessities and a few treasures, like new sandals with extra cushioning for a city with no transportation. She even had some money left from the wad of bank notes Leo had willingly and personally placed in her hands. Her first taste of freedom in a long time proved exhilarating. When they were done, Petras helped carry the bags, leading the way through a maze of little streets.

"Oh, look," she said as they turned the corner. She pointed to a single, scraggly tree with a view of the ocean in the background. Petras waited; the view was one he'd seen many times.

"I've never seen anything so perfectly aligned," Layna said, "like it's been framed by nature! Oh, Petras, it would make a perfect painting. See how the viridian stands out from the pthalo green? It's so vibrant!"

She stopped and frowned.

"Viridian?" Petras leaned back and studied her with raised eyebrows.

It took her a minute. "I have no idea," she mumbled. "Don't even ask."

Leo was hard at work when they returned, and Layna went

upstairs to shower and change. She stood beneath the cascade of soft water and pretended it was a warm, luxurious waterfall. After lotion, perfume, makeup, and Leo's blowdryer, she donned new clothes and felt almost human again. She went downstairs to find Leo, still hard at work in his office. She stationed herself behind him and tried to remain inconspicuous, but he raised his head and paused his hands above the keyboard.

"Your perfume," he said. "What is it called?"

"*Passion*," she answered quietly. Something deep inside her contracted, and everything went hazy. She gripped the back of the chair. Another transition. Oh, God. Not now!

She turned onto her side and reached for him, his face in shadows that swirled.

"Oh, Jack. Why can't you just love me?" she pleaded.

Without waiting for his usual excuses, she lifted her mouth to his. Her arm slid up to the back of his neck. She took hold of his hair and pulled him closer, harder toward her waiting body. The kiss was hungry, powerful. She felt him getting hard beside her, and would have killed to have him inside her, to stop the aching, to stop the nightmare, to help her breathe again.

For a half-second, her eyes flickered open, the fog swirled back and away, and she looked deep into dark, smoldering brown eyes that —oh, God.

She remained frozen in time. The keyboard was silent. Leo's arms rested against the edge of his work table the way some men grace a dining table. He didn't move. As if he knew. Had she said something?

"Yes, it's a fragrance by Elizabeth Taylor—famous movie star? Most beautiful woman in the world? Anyway, it's all I wear. I happened to discover a bottle in a tourist shop in town," Layna said, her voice shaky. "Who'd have thought? It's been around forever, but I was surprised to find it here."

Leo straightened up and resumed typing as if the earth had never trembled.

"It suits you," he said.

Layna glanced over his shoulder, but she couldn't read Greek.

Leo finished what he was typing and hit στ□λνω, obviously the *send* key.

"All done?" She tried to keep her voice level.

"For the moment," he replied. "I needed to leave instructions for Vasili and Malakis, the men who operate my ships. I am much behind in work. Always there are the problems—3,000 miles I must know, and the laws of each country, who will take my cargo, who will not. The sea never dies."

"What an odd saying."

"Not to Greeks. Our lives depend on the sea. It is a very old saying."

"What does it mean?"

"Difficult to translate. You have to feel it, grow up with it. It is a living, breathing thing. Ancient and deep, like truth. Beyond what man does, or nature, or time. We may die, but the sea does not."

"How beautiful," she whispered. Her hand reached out to touch him before her mind could censor the act.

Leo's back stiffened. He took a deep breath and leaned forward, away from her, and pretended to be looking for something beneath the computer stand.

Layna lowered her hand to the hard wood of the chair back. Something was terribly wrong. Why was she so drawn to him? And why did he pull away? Hadn't he been her captor? Was he still? If memories were to be trusted, then at some point in time, she'd been unfaithful to a dead man! Or would be. God, was she losing her mind? Impossible. Been there, done that.

"Leo?" Her voice sounded small. Maybe it was the enclosed space.

"Yes?"

"My name's not Layna. It's Ellie."

He swiveled around and looked at her. There were a million questions in *his* eyes for a change, but she watched him force them back where they came from. Only one surfaced.

"What shall I call you?"

Good question.

"I don't know. I don't feel like Ellie. Not yet. I don't know who she is. Was."

Leo's eyes hadn't left hers for an instant.

"Then I call you Layna, until that time."

She nodded her consent. "Why do you live in two places?" She ignored the waves that still crashed against her heart from the way he'd said her name.

"Are you changing the subject?"

"Absolutely."

"Then I shall humor you, but only because you are young and very beautiful." He paused long enough for his words to make landfall, then continued. "I live on Skopelos because it is my home. Here, I can be who I am. It is more comfortable, more convenient for much of what I do. Not the papers so boring. My ships, they go out of Athens, from Pireaus and Volos. Athens is where I conduct business. It is more accessible for clients. But this is my home. It is quiet here. Not so many tourists."

"You mean all those loud, impossibly rude Americans?"

"Yes, those," he said, and laughed. A deep, natural laugh. Rain on thirsty ground.

"And the shipping business? Do you like it?"

"My grandfather had a small boat. He worked hard and married a Greek girl whose father had much wealth. He bought a ship. My father bought a second ship and a larger boat. I try to keep them going, to honor my father and his father. My country handles one-third of all the shipping in the world. It is a good business, one that has paid for my house on Skopelos."

"That's not what I asked."

Leo turned and looked up at her.

"Then, no," he said. "It is strange. I love the sea, but I do not care for the shipping, or even the fishing. Why do you ask? I was told my business has nothing to do with you."

Layna closed her eyes. "I was angry when I said that."

CHAPTER THIRTEEN

Ο πνιγμένος, από τα μαλλιά του πιάνεται.

A DROWNING MAN GRIPS HIS OWN HAIR.

"And now?"

"Now, I'm curious. You're *different* here. Trouble seems far away."

"And yet, this is where the trouble begins."

Was it? Or was that another lie?

"When you're finished with the computer, would you mind if I use it a while?"

"Take as long as you will like," he said, then turned and studied her face. "You remembered, on the boat."

"Yes. A little."

"I thought so. I wait for you to tell me. Why did you not?"

Layna shook her head. "I need to find Jack first. There, inside the computer."

Leo frowned. "Then I am almost done with emergencies, at least for the day." He finished the last e-mail, sent it, then closed the file and returned the screen to the search engine.

"You are sure you are ready to do?"

"Why do you ask?"

He looked at her, into her. "What if there are things you find you do not wish to know?"

"I've thought of that," Layna said, "but it's getting harder to trust what I remember. What if my dreams are just that? Besides, aren't you curious to meet the real me?"

"I like the person you are become now. Is she not the real you?" Leo turned away and busied himself with papers; he missed the look of surprise on the face of the woman left standing behind him. When he spoke, it was with his back to her. "What you say is logical. It is not as you feel. Sometimes, what you feel is only thing to trust. Only truth. But this is hard thing to know."

"Looks like we'll both have to take a chance," Layna said, her voice quiet, thoughtful.

"Fair enough. I help you." He typed a command—the screen changed from Greek to English. He tried *Jack Taggart,* then *Taggart Photography*. The second one hit. Jack appeared on the screen in living color. There was no reaction from the man at the keyboard.

Layna stared at the face on the screen. It was young and okay-looking, with a devil-may-care grin more reminiscent of a little boy than a grown man. Dark hair, lean face, unremarkable blue eyes, good teeth. Nothing.

No memory.

No attraction.

No remorse.

"So, that's Jack."

"Already you know his face," Leo said. "Surely you know his face."

"Only from the side. In shadows. Nightmares."

She sensed Leo's confusion—he'd have to get in line. "Is there an address?"

"Here, at the bottom. A link to the email." Leo clicked on the contact link.

Nothing happened.

"It's like he doesn't exist," she whispered. "Yet, there he is. Even with a picture, it doesn't tell me anything about him. I wish I could access his personal computer for more information, messages, a bio."

"It is like the email, I think. I doubt anything is there, even if there once was."

"Because he's dead?"

"No," Leo said. "Because people like Boiko and Interpol, they find it by now. Either they leave open to trace incoming messages, like yours, or they remove information and close down. Still, we have option."

"We do?"

"Of course," he said. "We look up you. You have name now. Ellie."

"It could be a nickname, for Helen or even Eleanor."

Leo tried all three. Ellie Taggart. Eleanor Taggart. Helen Taggart. Nothing.

Like Jack, she only existed in the mind of Interpol and here on an island.

"And you are remembering little more each day," Leo said, sensing disappointment.

"Yes," she said. *Like your mouth on mine.*

Leo tried to take her hand, but it slid through his fingers as easily as hope

"I need to lie down for a while," she said, "if that's okay."

"Of course. You need not ask."

She took the stairs like a robot and entered the bedroom. Still light outside, but she felt night coming on.

A foam mattress sank beneath her. She turned on her side to catch the tears in her hands so Leo wouldn't know she'd cried, curling herself into a fetal position like a baby not yet born, a vain attempt to protect her vital organs, or maybe just her heart.

What had she expected to feel, looking at Jack's likeness?

Anything but guilt because she felt nothing. Because she didn't even recognize him. Something about the conversation she'd remembered on the boat still bothered her, but she couldn't weed it out. Was this how it was going to be for the rest of her life? One thread at a time, tangled up with all the others? Thoughts passing her like strangers on the street, but when she turned around to call them by name, they'd turned the corner and were gone.

She didn't know when Leo came to bed and lay down beside her. He was there when she awoke, his arm draped across her body. The clock on the nightstand read 9:00; she'd slept two hours. His rhythmic breathing tickled her ear. She brushed a strand of hair from her eyes, and high up in a corner of the bedroom, a light from a security system blinked yellow.

Leo stirred, reached out with his hand, and ran his fingers along the inside of her arm, sending tingles up and down her spine and through her body.

"You are so beautiful."

His voice sounded deep, hungry. She felt her body stiffen at the unexpected advance, but was it what she wanted? The pull, the undeniable power of the memory of his mouth on hers, whether playful or passionate, had taken residence in her heart and mind. Had they done more than kiss? Everything in her still said no, while her body urged her to turn over, to give in to the attraction, to whatever it was that bound them together, and make the ending a happy one.

You can't satisfy a man. You know that. Why even bother?

Layna's eyes searched the corners of the room, then the corners of her mind. Someone new had intruded into the scheme of things.

A part of her asked the one question she'd already grown weary of asking.

What about Jack? You're a married woman, you know.

Yes, but to which one? To Jack? He's dead. To Leo? He faked it. Who are you?

Ellie, of course.

With her back to him, Layna didn't dare turn over to see Leo's face. She didn't need to. She felt him withdraw before he even moved his hand away. Just like she felt what he left behind—an overpowering presence that covered her like the ocean. Jack was dead. Everything pointed to it. Everyone said it. But she knew better. Jack would never be dead, not until she remembered him. Not until she buried him.

"You will be okay," a familiar voice told her. "Do not cry, my Layna."

Until then, she hadn't realized she was, but the man beside her knew. Somehow, he always knew. What else did he know?

She wiped her eyes, steadied her resolve, and turned around to face those dark, gleaming eyes that knew her far too well. What else did he know?

"Please tell me what happened," she said, laying one hand gingerly on his chest. "Please, Leo, even if you don't want to. I can't go on not knowing."

It didn't help being in such close proximity, especially when he raised himself up on one elbow and studied her face, her mouth. All she had to do was close her eyes and lean into his beautiful body. That one question prevented her from doing so. *What about Jack?*

Layna fought back. *What about Leo? He's been here since the beginning.*

Yeah, well how much do you think he can take of a crazy woman before he turns and walks away? Especially once he gets what he needs to save his precious ships?

Too late, she saw worry, then disappointment flash across his face before he distanced himself, first with his eyes, then with his body. He sat on the bed with his back to her. Had he sensed the battle going on inside her?

"You and Petras have done all you can to protect me," she said finally. "Don't you see—I can't move forward without going back. Until I know what happened, I'm stuck. You're the only one who can help me remember. The only one I can even half-way trust. Please. Help me."

Leo leaned back in the bed and stared at the ceiling. Anger kept his body taut.

"Half-way, eh? No matter. What is it you wish to know?"

Layna flinched at the taunting harshness of his voice. Had he closed himself off entirely?

"Dr. Liatos said you found me on Skopelos," she said. "What was I doing there?"

"I didn't find you," he said, staring at the ceiling. "Petras did. No, that is no correct. A fisherman named Gregorio. He found you. He is second cousin to Petras."

"Go on."

"It is complicate," Leo replied. "Gregorio diving offshore all the time. That day, he see two men place a woman in the water."

"Place? What does that mean?"

"Mm, chomaterí éna sóma. Let me think. In English, it means, maybe, dump?"

Layna gasped, then waited for more.

"The men, they do not see Gregorio. He is submerged except for the face. He has dreams of finding another boy on a dolphin, a most valuable statue. Maybe other treasure. For all his life, he dives. He holds breath a very long time. Then, when the men in the boat pull away, Gregorio swim to find you under the water and bring you up. He gets the water from the lungs as best he can. Then, he calls Petras. He told Petras he reach you in under four minutes. Gregorio prides himself on these things. He even has a special watch—"

"Forget the watch. Who were the men who left me there? Is this what you meant when you said before that they tried to kill me?"

Leo hesitated, somewhere in the darkness. "I do not know for certain. I think they work for Boiko. You witnessed something and you became the problem."

"A problem? What did the police say?"

"It was not convenient."

"Not convenient? They tried to murder me!"

"Summoning the police is not what you do when you find a drowned woman and you maybe know who did it. The police can do nothing against Boiko. It is best not to get involved. Gregorio called Petras, and Petras called me. I call Thurman."

"Thurman? But Gregorio saw who did it! Leo, help me! I think I'm going mad! First I think I died in an automobile accident, then a doctor recognizes me and tells me I drowned, and now you're saying some men tried to murder me?"

"Gregorio only said he see who *might* have done it. He was not sure. He witnessed what happened, but from a distance, for moment. Time was not taken to study the situation; he swam like hell to save your life."

"Yes. Of course. And I'm forever grateful. I am. But he hesitated to get involved, so why did you? Why did Petras? Why did you take me to Dr. Liatos? I can't believe you would have done what you did because of business. You didn't know me."

"This is true. I did not know you," he said, "but I knew Jack."

Layna bolted upright and glared down at him. "You knew my husband? Of course you did! He called you the night he died, right? How could I have forgotten that!"

"No, Layna. I knew your husband before he becomes your husband. At university."

She waited, not taking her eyes away as she digested the information.

Leo began speaking with his hands. "I told you, my father sent me to be educated in the United States. He wants me study maritime law and international shipping. On my second day, I met Jack in boring economics class required if I am to graduate. I study English here in Greece, enough to pass the entrance exam, but I need help with the annoying difficulties of your language—there are more exceptions than the rules. Do you know this? And the technical words that have no Latin roots, they make me crazy. I still get the past and the present mixed together. He offered to help."

Layna smiled at the thought of Leo not excelling at something, anything.

"What he was like?"

"Bored, restless. There was a lake not far from the university, and then the ocean. My father, he rented a small boat for me at the marina. He said it is less money than a room at the dormitory, but I know it was to bring in me a new respect for the water. Imagine, growing up surrounded by the sea with ships that sail all over the world, and I do not care for the water. Not to be in it, at least. It is a source of disappointment to my father. It was."

"So you and Jack were friends?"

"Yes. No. Acquaintances, I think. He understands the economics and loves the water. We shared the boat, the tennis, which I very much enjoy. And one day, he saved my life."

"How?"

"I am standing in the back of the boat, reaching for the rope to tie us off. The boat hit something. I go over the side. I can swim, but the plants along the bottom of the river wrap themselves around my legs. I could not break free. The more I struggle, the harder it is. Jack cut the plants with a knife and he pulled me into the boat. I invite him to visit me in Greece and stay in my house."

"Why did you hesitate to say you were friends?"

"He wanted adventure, the new things. Money. I am some older, serious. I did not know him long before my father became ill."

"So you never saw him again?"

"Only that last summer on the break, when he comes to Greece. I pay for the ticket. We sail, play tennis, eat, drink the good wine. I showed him tourist things. He says he has met someone. I ask him why he did not bring her as well. He said she did not care to travel, that she is busy with school.

"*It was me,*" Layna's eyes are closed so she can visualize her life as Leo recites it.

"Yes, but as Petras say to you, we do not hear your first name."

"So what happened next?"

We spoke on the phone. I asked if he had finished school. He said that, like me, life gets in the way. He mentioned several assignments he could not turn down. That's when he says to me he is getting married. I congratulate him."

"He still didn't mention my name?"

"No. Out of politeness, I did not ask. So I invited him to come and stay with me for the honeymoon. I am thinking this will surely repay my debt to him for saving the life. He says he would enjoy that. So I tell him I would need maybe his help with something."

The images faded to black. "You what?"

"My business. I need someone I will trust."

Instinct told her to stop. Necessity told her to forge ahead. Her voice sounded smaller when it dissipated in the darkened bedroom. "What is it you asked him to do?"

Leo paused a long time before speaking.

"Like Petras say to you, we needed the pictures, proof of the smuggling. It was necessary if I was to put financial and legal problems behind. Jack agreed. He said this will help him get more clients for a his career as investigative journalist. I did not know it would end as it did."

Nothing could stop the mudslide in her soul.

"So, you see, I am the one who bring your husband to Skopelos. I am the reason Jack Taggart is dead."

She must have cried out, because Leo was on his feet in seconds. He walked to the door and turned, his frame silhouetted against the hall light.

Faced with his confession, Layna clawed her way through a cobweb of contradictions while her synapses fired intermittently at nothing.

"You cared for me all this time out of *guilt*?"

"I save your life, because he saved mine."

"I thought you saved my life so I could save your business—which is it? But surely that doesn't matter now, not after we've, I mean, as I see it, I still owe you my life."

"No." He sounded undecided, still in the doorway as if trying to decide which way to go in his own house. "The debt is paid. We owe each other nothing. Not now. Not ever. Típota."

Silence underscored the final verdict as he turned to go.

"Did I grieve for him?"

Leo stopped, started to say something, then didn't.

"Tell me," Layna whispered, staring at nothing.

He stepped reluctantly back into the room. When he spoke, his voice was that of a stranger, filled with anger. He maintained distance between them but lowered his voice.

The pain in that beautiful voice matched the pain in her heart.

"You were sick for a long time," he said, "nearly a month. Delirious, sometimes unconscious, fading in and out, not knowing who you were, where you were. You would get up, eat, even walk around. But you were not there; you were somewhere far away."

"Did I grieve for him?!" Layna rose from the bed and cursed herself for beleaguering the point, but she *had to know.*

Leo almost stepped back, surprised by the force of her demand. "You would cry, even in your sleep. Sometimes like the child, sometimes like the woman. You call his name, weeping, sobbing. You loved him very much."

"And?"

"Sometimes, when things bad, I would get into the bed and hold you, just hold you, until you can breathe deeply again. And sleep. There. I have said it. Now you know."

"Was there ever a night when you comforted me, that you perhaps did more?"

Her words sounded strange, as if a real Layna had spoken them both in hope and in condemnation.

Leo's gasp was barely discernible; there would be no going back. When he spoke, his voice sounded forced, resentful.

"You grieve for him, all right? Just like tonight. I did what I could to comfort you. I found a head trauma specialist in New York City. She told me to play music; I play the music. She told me talk to you; I talk to you. Nothing works! Ask Petras, if you don't believe. He was there! He saw what you were like! I would not dishonor my family name in such a way!"

She rose from the bed to go to him, but Leo stepped back into the hallway, distancing himself even more. There would be nothing between them now. No pity. No prisoners.

He continued talking, unable to stop now that his heart had split open. "I spend days, weeks, months on the computer," he said. "I look up this whatever-you-have, this thing with the name no one

CHAPTER FOURTEEN

Το γινάτι βγάζει μάτι.

ANGER TAKES OUT YOUR EYES:
A BLIND MAN CANNOT SEE.

can say. I read that a person can go through motions of life, but not have the life, okay? It is the brain defending itself. A wounded bird does not know to fight or to fly. I think you still do not know, my Layna."

Layna stared at him, expecting him to leave. Instead, he lingered while his words fled through her brain, seeking a way out. *My Layna*. Twice. No. Three times he'd called her that. Where did *that* come from? Had he called her that in Athens? She sat back down on the bed, confused and defeated. But anger drove Leo forward, and words were all he had left.

"Sometimes I think your life is only real when you dream of your dead husband. Is motion everywhere else, never real, never personal. *No for you*. But I live in real world, so do not talk down to me my business!"

He closed the door hard. The conversation was over, but the pain intensified.

Layna wept from the deepest part of her, but not for Jack

Taggart. She wept for Leo, soul to soul, and for herself. She had no proof of the awful truth that rained down upon her, no evidence to draw upon. But she knew in her heart of hearts. She knew.

So she cried aloud, rocked back and forth, and clutched a pillow to her chest while long-buried guilt spilled over into her life. What it must have taken for Leo to do what he did, holding a woman he desperately needed to survive, a woman he wanted for himself, while she sobbed her heart out for another man. And he could do nothing as long as she was crippled in her mind and vulnerable in her heart.

"Oh, Leo. My poor Leo. I wasn't grieving because I loved him. I was mourning the fact that I never could."

Layna closed her eyes against the world. The ceiling fan turned round and round like her life while the last of her tears trickled down onto crumpled sheets. There were no words left. She turned onto her side and buried her face in the pillow. She had no past to go back to, and the present had just exploded in her face. All she desired in her future was Leo, holding her until she could breathe again, like he'd done so many times before.

But they'd both come up for air, and he'd never hold her like that again.

Leo sat in the dark, one foot on the floor, the other propped against a coffee table. His eyes smoldered at nothing, nothing but Elayna. His wife. Jack's wife. Nobody's wife. Layna. Ellie. Mrs. Jack Taggart. Jack-Shit.

His stomach hurt. He wanted to growl, to hunt, to kill something, maybe punch a hole in the wall. Anything to give him peace, a rare commodity since they'd fished a woman out of the water and Petras had called to tell him Jack Taggart was dead, that his wife would probably be the same by morning. His mind whipped back and forth, then and now, comparing the timeline of events in search of an answer. Either that or absolution, whichever came first.

Waiting had been the most difficult part, until now. Those 48 hours when Dr. Liatos struggled to bring a most important lady back to the land of the living. Watching the doctor cut her shorts off with angry scissors and remove her soaked clothing so he could assess the damage. Like him, Dr. Liatos was always disgusted by unnecessary violence.

Leo remembered the tangled, matted hair, her lips a ghastly blue beneath the oxygen mask, the rope burns on her wrists and ankles. Then, when the doctor turned her onto her side, one slender arm flung itself across her abdomen like a rag doll. For some reason, it struck him in the heart. He found a clean sheet in the cabinet and laid it over her naked form, then brushed a few strands of hair from her face.

Dr. Liatos turned and gave him a curious glance, but their attention was soon diverted to a purplish bruise where a deep cut covered half of her temple into the hairline. These were new, in addition to scratches and cuts covering her arms and legs. Her fingernails still carried traces of blood and sand and flesh. She'd fought back. Hard.

He remembered Liatos shaking his head in companionable sadness over what they both felt for the irreverent death of Jack Taggart's wife.

But she didn't die. She hung on.

One delicate hand escaped the sheet to lay palm up on the table, as if waiting for the doctor to hand her her life back. Euros in exchange for waking up again. Gold coins falling slow-motion through a sleeping mermaid's fingers. This was what that single palm opening slowly up on the exam table had meant to Leo. A life-debt, paid in full.

He'd turned away from the harsh reality of needles, tubes, and pumps that would change her into just another drowning victim. Like Liatos, he'd waited through the night, anxious for her to awaken, alive with answers. But when the miracle happened, she remembered nothing. Worse, her mind had closed itself off. All those things he desperately needed to know remained buried somewhere behind those gray-green eyes.

Leo returned to the present with a snarl and lowered his feet to the living room tile. He bent forward, propped his elbows on his knees, and absentmindedly fingered the knots of a prayer rope from off the coffee table. He barely made it past the first cluster and "Son of the Living God" before he threw it down and watched it slide, discarded, onto the rug.

Where was God in any of this?

He ran his hands through thick hair in a vain attempt to rake her out of his mind. The things he had told her, simply because she had asked! No, that wasn't it. He'd known from the beginning this day would come.

Liatos, who prided himself on his ability with cuts, splints, broken bones, and gunshot wounds, finally admitted he was at a loss. He explained concussions, even threw in a few clinical facts about amnesia and head wounds. But in the end, he admitted the drugs he had used to save her life may have worsened her mental condition, and he recommended a specialist.

At Leo's urging, a German doctor, Ester Hahlberg, whose clinic specialized in head traumas and related disorders, agreed to help. Understandably, she refused to tell him anything without a personal observation. So he flew his Layna to Athens, having already taken her into his house for protection and observation. Dr. Hahlberg spoke English, but no Greek. Leo interpreted what he could for Dr. Liatos, becoming privy to everything said.

Following the consult with Liatos, Hahlberg performed a physical examination before instigating a required 48-hour observation. She watched Layna eat, sleep, bathe, sit in the small garden for hours without moving, and ambulate her way like an Auschwitz survivor for two days and nights. No questions.

"Fascinating," Hahlberg concluded.

Leo tried not to think how much that one-word diagnosis had cost him, but the specialist quickly got down to business.

"And she's been like this since awakening?"

"She has. The first time it happened, I thought she was walking in her sleep," Leo said. "My father did the same thing. But I could not awaken her. And she does not come out of it."

"It's been how long?"

"Three weeks since it happened."

"No one can predict how quickly or slowly the brain heals itself. I would love to observe her for a longer period in a controlled environment. Run a scan—"

"She is not a monkey," Leo said.

"Of course not. She would be well-cared for."

"In Germany? Out of the question. She is safe here."

"Safe from what? You have no surgery facilities, no oxygen tanks or heart pumps. Our facility is clean, modern, easily accessible, and necessary for her continued treatment."

"No, she must stay here if she is to remember."

Dr. Hahlberg gave him a long, hard look.

"I didn't realize," she said. "You said only that she struck her head and drowned. I assumed it was some sort of accident. But she seems to be in danger here, now. What more can you tell me?"

"She may have witnessed her husband's death. She has the nightmares."

Hahlberg's gaze travelled to Layna gazing out the window at nothing.

"Poor child," she whispered. "And you say she has recurring nightmares?"

"She does, but not all the time. And fewer than before. So, knowing this, you can say me how long before she recovers?"

"Well, she is young. Early twenties?"

Leo nodded. He had no idea, but it sounded right.

"That is a good thing," Dr. Hahlberg said. "Amnesia is difficult enough. But complicated with physical and psychological trauma? I cannot say when. No one can. Nor can I say with certainty what her mental state will be when and if she comes out of it. What I *can* tell you is, based on years of experience and my current observations, she definitely presents the classic symptoms of depersonalization disorder, dissociative disorder, trauma, and possibly PTSD."

"I thought only the soldiers get this."

"Not necessarily. I've diagnosed it in secretaries who work in the legal field, drivers of trucks who work with deadlines. Stress is stress. And sometimes, words are more destructive than physical harm. It happens more often when people witness violence too terrible to live with the memory. Tell me, was her husband's death especially brutal?"

"Very."

"Her mind could be struggling to process, uh, understand what happened. It might also be fighting, to keep her from remembering."

"So, even if she wants to remember—?"

"Her mind won't allow it," the doctor said. Leo waited impatiently for some good news, and he wondered what the woman, who struck him as somewhat brutal herself, could be writing in her notebook.

"What can I do to bring her out of it?" he asked.

"Is it so urgent that you do so?"

Leo swallowed and looked away.

Hahlberger took a deep breath, and a moment or two, before responding.

"There are things that may help. Music, for one. Soft music, nothing jarring. And I agree with your decision not to sedate her unless absolutely necessary. To do so could actually prohibit or postpone recovery. The difficulty, of course, lies in remembering."

"What do you mean?"

"How she comes out of her present state is extremely important. I cannot emphasize it enough. Much depends on the inner strength of a person. But there are things you should be prepared for. For example, if she recovers enough to ask questions, talk to her, but do not reveal too much information too quickly. It can create *false memory.*"

"False memory?"

"It's how propaganda works. Recent research into head trauma has shown saying something over and over to someone suffering from a condition like amnesia can actually trick them into believing it happened, when it didn't. Their mind takes what they are told occurred and turns it into a *perceived memory*."

"Even though it isn't real?"

"Precisely. They remember it as being real. I'm not saying she will do this, but you should censor what you tell her to avoid unnecessary confusion when she begins to recall things on her own. From my experience, once she wakes up and is cognizant, she'll feel scattered enough, but she'll want to know what happened. She will ask questions, and get angry if she doesn't receive answers, truthful ones. Very important. Then again, if her memories come crashing in all at once, which has been known to occur, she could go into sensory overload, even shut down all over again."

"Shut down? You mean, go away again? But how can I keep this overload from happening all at once?"

"You can't. Anything could trigger it, from a voice to a simple object, a song, a place, anything." The doctor paused a moment. "I can sense that you care for her, but I'll not pry into the relationship, or why you seem desperate for her memory to return."

"I am."

Hahlberg gave him a once-over with critical eyes. "I need to tell you something. You are a handsome man. I believe she looked lovely before you colored her hair; incidentally, I advise you not to continue using hair dye—the chemicals can harm brain cells. Aside from that, you must be especially careful not to harm her, well, emotionally. She is facing a huge battle, and she must do this on her own. If she finds she must struggle with an unsatisfactory relationship as well, it could prove devastating to her recovery. Do you understand?

"I do."

"And knowing this, are you willing to proceed on your own?"

"I have no choice."

"Then I shall leave you with my contact information and some recommendations for books and internet sites you may find of interest. There is much to consider. And please call me if you have any further questions. I'd like to track this case; it's extremely interesting."

Leo nodded. Petras drove her to the airport, and Leo sat in the back with the good doctor, too stunned for even casual conversation. She smiled and wished him well. On the drive back to Athens, he knew all hope was gone. How the hell was he supposed to understand it all, much less accomplish what the doctor had explained?

All the terms she'd left in her wake and the images they soon overlapped, merging in and out like a kaleidoscope Leo had enjoyed as a child. But the colors weren't simple blues, greens, and reds anymore. They were hidden monsters called false memory, true memory, dissociative disorder, depersonalization, derealization, PTSD, and other things with equally difficult names he really didn't want to have anything to do with.

Leo shifted his focus to the present, to the living room and the dilemma facing him. Had he already made things worse by telling her as much as he had? More than he should? What a mess! And all because of an asshole named Jack Taggart!

He paced back and forth in front of the fireplace, torn by indecision. On the one hand, Layna deserved to know the truth. But how much could he tell her without risking it all? True, Jack Taggart had been an acquaintance at university, but Christos! What a bástardos!

Jack excelled at what he did—taking the pictures, finding the facts, getting the story—but the man flirted like a schoolboy with every woman he saw. He would disappear for hours at a time, while a guest in Leo's home! Not only did he lack basic courtesies, he played at being a third-rate detective. It was all a game to him, with professionalism running a poor second. He drank beer between meals in the face of Greek custom limiting alcohol to dinner, and he ogled women like a third-class sailor. Did he get away with such behavior solely on charm? Or were people simply too polite to punch him in his stupid, grinning face?

And yet, for all of this, women were still attracted to him. Was it his boyish good looks, his lopsided grin, his little bit of knowledge about a great many things? Was that what allowed him to engage an unsuspecting girl in a fun conversation as long as he got what he wanted? But did he? Leo had his doubts from a man's knowledge of the world.

First, he bragged too much about his supposed conquests. In Leo's experience, such behavior, aside from boring and embarrassing to anyone forced to listen, usually indicated a man with issues. Like the man who stares at the women or feels the need to prove himself *the man* in bed. In Leo's experience, such a man, he is usually found to be *insufficient*.

But to think of such a man having such a woman as Layna and not knowing what to do with her? Anger roared through Leo, almost blinding him. The thrill of the chase—this is what Jack Taggart lived for. Flirting with danger. His lack of fear about tomorrow. Only the fool runs headlong into something without thinking twice. And Jack Taggart was a fool. A fool Leo Amratsis hired for just such qualities.

But, damn it! I never thought he would get himself killed!

Leo stalked to the refrigerator, where he struggled with an infuriating plastic lid that refused to twist off the bottled water. He finally pulled a knife from the drawer and mutilated the whole damn bottle, throwing everything in the sink and watching it splash all over the counter, then the floor. He leaned both fists against the counter top and relived Jack's last phone call.

"I've got it! It's the 16th of August," he'd yelled. "That's when it's going down. And listen, I think they're on to me, so I'm doing the honeymoon thing and laying low. Cool, huh? Two birds with one stone! I'll hide it somewhere till I can get it to you. No worries. It's a done deal."

Only it wasn't. Jack's style, or lack of one, always reminded Leo of a B-rated spy movie, and half of what he said on the phone that day made no sense. What was happening on the 16th of August, and where? Who was involved? What proof did he have, and when could Leo get his hands on it? Damn it, he needed proof, not promises! He was under investigation!

But that was Taggart. Everything a game. Life. Death. Marriage. Love. Only Jack would call spending time with an intelligent, sensuous woman like Layna as "doing the honeymoon thing." Leo dared not explore any visuals of such a callous remark, for fear he would go mad.

"Besides, it's none of my fucking business." He flung himself on the sofa. It was what he said every time he went over that last phone conversation to see if he'd missed something. And like all the other times, all he was left with was guilt for getting Jack involved in the first place.

"I didn't even know her then," he muttered. Jack showed him a picture of a blonde-streaked beauty with gorgeous eyes. His first question, to himself of course, was how the hell did Taggart manage to get such a woman to marry him? But the reason showed through in the shy, hopeful way she looked in the camera, her head held down instead of up. Still, an intelligence carried in her face and eyes, and beauty in the innocence of her smile. What a waste.

Christos! He was doing it again!

It was easy enough when Taggart was alive, in and out of his life like a goat in a rainstorm. When his wife was just a picture next to a driver's license. Before Leo saw her naked and dying on an examination, her palm held upward, waiting for life to find her. Before he held her next to him, night after night. Or looked into those gray-green eyes that saw him as he really was. Vulnerable. Before his lips found hers and wanted more. All because a fool named Jack Taggart disappeared, and Gregorio pulled a half-drowned lady from the sea.

Leo got up and poured some whiskey, gulping it down and waiting for the burn. It helped, but it didn't erase the worst of it. When Gregorio told Petras a fisherman he knew had spotted a small motorboat with an odd-looking mast a few kilometers from where they'd found Taggart's wife, they investigated, thinking it odd a motorboat would have a mast. Then, six miles southwest of Amarados, the motorboat lay there, adrift. To everyone's horror, the mast turned out to be the top half of a harpoon, the bottom half of which was buried in Jack Taggart's chest. The amount of blood staggered belief.

Leo took another shot of whiskey.

Jack's murder brought in Thurman, and everyone became a part of the Interpol web.

Leo's phone vibrated. It was the man himself, the weaver of webs in the lives of mortals.

"Leo? Thurman. Sorry to wake you. I think you should take a look at something we found in the ship's manifest."

"*The Golden Voyage*?"

"No. *Prometheus*. Can you come to Volos?"

"Now? Can't you fax it?"

"Too important. It might require action. I'll have a helicopter there, first thing in the morning, out on the hydrofoil landing."

"Fine."

"See you. Oh, is the lady still with us?"

"She is," Leo replied, sorely tempted to smash his phone against the wall, but then he'd have to buy a new one. Instead, he gathered his thoughts and headed upstairs. He woke Petras to tell him where he was going and that he didn't know how long he'd be. Petras nodded, scratched his head, gathered his bedding and pillow, and made a pallet in the hall just outside the door to Leo's bedroom, sliding his gun under his pillow before going back to sleep.

Leo smiled. He started to go inside the bedroom, just to look at her, to check on her, to do something, but he couldn't figure out what, so he didn't. His hand lay on the doorknob, but he heard gut-wrenching sobs, and it broke his heart.

Petras gave him one of his probing looks.

Leo made an exasperated sound and returned to the living room and the waiting sofa. He set the alarm on his phone, plugged it in to recharge, and turned the lights off. His mind wasn't so easy to shut down. It insisted on replaying events he'd rather forget. But love is a ruthless tyrant, especially when everything falls apart.

He hated to hear her crying deep like that. She used to do that whenever she had one of her nightmares. Out of compassion, he lay down beside her one night and held her. She drifted into a peaceful sleep. And he was finally able to do the same. The problem was, he got used to it, to draping his arm across her, to burying his face in her hair, to feeling her body snuggled up against his own.

Then, late one night as he wandered in that strange place between wakefulness and sleep, she turned to face him, then slid her arms up his chest and around his neck.

This can't be happening was his first thought. Normally, she slept on her side facing away from him. Leo wasn't one to turn away from a beautiful woman, but this wasn't just any woman. It was Layna. In her semi-conscious state, there was a sadness about her that kept him from pursuing any thoughts of intimacy. In fact, when it happened, he looked for ways to extract his body from the bed without waking her.

This time, things took a different turn. She moved her arm slowly down his chest until it rested against his heart. One of her slender legs draped innocently over his. Her breath felt hot against his face. Suddenly face-to-face, their mouths almost touching, he gave in to curiosity. He leaned down and kissed her. Her mouth fit perfectly on his, and he lingered, then backed away, fighting the urge to respond, knowing it could go no farther. He removed her hand as gently as he could. She snuggled closer, rubbing against the side of his face like a cat in heat. Part of him responded—definitely not his face.

CHAPTER FIFTEEN

Απ› αγκάθι βγαίνει ρόδο κι από ρόδο βγαίνει αγκάθι.

**FROM A THORN A ROSE EMERGES,
AND FROM A ROSE, A THORN.**

A small revolution broke out in his mind and heart. Which part of him should he obey? His need, or his honor? Suddenly, her hand was back. Slender fingers played lightly across his chest, stopped, and curled slightly. God, she had beautiful hands. She seemed especially attentive to that spot in the center, where a few tiny little hairs had emerged long ago. She sidled up his torso, and he groaned.

Her eyes fluttered open, eyes the color of the sea on a cloudy day, smoky with wanting him. They looked into his, and for half a heartbeat, he could've sworn she saw him *and knew it was him*. That's when he said to hell with honor. It's just the one time.

That's what he told himself.

His fingers buried themselves in her hair and forced her head up and back. He found her mouth and claimed her soul, rejoicing in a delicious, sweet hunger he never expected, and an even sweeter surrender that broke his heart. And he felt another thing. Somewhere, far beneath what he felt and tasted, lay a smoldering volcano more powerful than Vesuvius.

He couldn't do it. It was wrong. Maybe more right than it had ever been. But wrong.

He tore away, cursed himself, and waited for the throbbing to end.

Meanwhile, Layna sighed like she'd downed a double chocolate latté, and fell asleep, her head on his shoulder, perfectly content.

Shit! What just happened?

Now, in Skopelos, on the sofa, Leo stared at nothing, long into the night, Thurman and *The Prometheus* forgotten. It was always the same when he relived his one moment with Layna.

And doubt always followed the joy. Had she mistaken him for Jack? Would she remember what happened? She'd already asked him if he'd done more than hold her. So, she knew, right? What if it happened again? Had he compromised his honor, violated the code of hospitality, the *philoxenia,* by taking advantage of an unconscious female? Would this add to the debt he already owed for what he'd done to her husband? Could he *not* kiss her again?

Maybe. Probably not. God, I hope so. Possibly. Definitely. Doubtful.

It was something they never discussed, but the curious looks she gave him, the playful kisses in the Chevy, the way she studied his mouth, touched him—let him know that, even if she didn't remember, she knew that for one brief moment in time, they were one heart, one soul.

He told himself he should let it go, forget it ever happened.

That's what he told himself.

The raucous cries of gulls woke her. For a moment, she thought she was in Athens again, and her heart pounded in her ears. Then she saw the colors of the earth and remembered where she was and how she'd gotten there. Her eyes hurt, her head throbbed, and her throat felt raw from a night of crying. Still, she got up somehow and stumbled into the bathroom.

It was as bad as she could possibly imagine. Crying always left her eyes swollen and puffy when it came from the deepest part of her. The same thing happened when she was fourteen, and her mother passed away. She remembered sobbing so hard she thought her heart would shatter. And afterwards, she resembled a zombie.

She started to brush her teeth, thinking how some things never change. The electric toothbrush whined away, but her hand paused in time as a door started to open.

The same thing happened when she was fourteen, and her mother passed away.

The one thought repeated itself in her brain even as the elaborate bronze bowl in Leo's bathroom gave way to a white porcelain sink with silver faucet handles. Bathroom tiles wavered and metamorphosed into pale, blue walls. Then, transported onto a manicured lawn, she looked up, sketchbook in hand, at a two-story Victorian house in Tallahassee, Florida.

Ellie had come home.

She remembered her mother, who always floated across the room like a princess-in-waiting, her blonde hair swept up and away from a face that belonged in Hollywood, complete with blue-gray eyes and classic cheekbones. She couldn't recall a single time when her mother had been anything but gracious, soft-spoken and kind; yet, the beauty carried with it an undercurrent of aloofness.

Her father, green-eyed, distinguished and handsome, with or without his mustache, suffered bouts of depression that only worsened when his life-mate succumbed to cancer in her early fifties.

Both parents, terribly in love, had existed in a world of their own that often excluded their late-in-life, only child—a world Ellie was allowed to inhabit on rare occasions when her mother and father had people over. Both men and women would bask in her mother's quiet beauty, ignoring the talking faces who had accompanied them to the party. Ellie preferred looking on, sketching remembrances of how fine the people looked. She was always drawing. People, places, furniture, backgrounds, but mostly people.

At the funeral, she felt like a distant relative. Her father laid his hand on her shoulder, but she wasn't allowed to share his pain any more than she'd been allowed to share his love.

Birthdays and holidays were a blur, a collage of the half-life that defined her growing-up years, an uneventful parade seen from the sidelines. The occasional friend appeared, but, looking back, Ellie had cared little for the latest fashions, remained disinterested in actively recruiting those of the female persuasion due to an acute shyness, and had easily dismissed those with male aptitudes that registered confusion if the conversation encompassed a subject other than sports.

Physically awkward and lacking social skills, she preferred the separate reality of happily-ever-after endings in books and movies, even when Emily Brontë's "Wuthering Heights" tore her soul apart and called to a passion buried deep within her, one she wasn't willing to take on just yet. She googled a picture of what experts believed to be the actual Wuthering Heights, then drew a larger image, with Cathy and Heathcliff walking out the gate and onto the moors, holding hands forever.

Her father, who also preferred a world of his own, taught philosophy and economics at the university. When the house became ghost-ridden in its silence, he started bringing his best and brightest students home with him on Friday nights to fill the void with noise and laughter. When her mother's sister, Aunt Stella, got wind of it, she took her protesting niece into town and bought her "a new frock for the shindig." She even cajoled her into doing "a little something" with her hair, which translated into a full hour at a beauty salon and a hearty lesson in make-up from a jittery cosmetologist.

Ellie first saw Jack Taggart from across a room interspersed with talking faces. Aunt Stella had instructed her to leave the sketchpad upstairs. She was glad; she preferred to watch the boisterous young man work the crowd. She didn't need to draw him. He was smooth, at ease among strangers—everything she was not, a quality she unashamedly envied in others. Then, two things happened. Her father put his arm around her and complimented her on looking especially lovely, like she was suddenly a person, and Jack Taggart sauntered into her life.

It was an easy conquest on his part, even when her father noticed over many Friday nights that young Mr. Taggart had designs on his only daughter. Being a professor, he took her aside and inquired as to her thoughts on the subject.

"He's wonderful," she replied. "Did you notice the way he moves through a room and has something to say to everyone? It's a gift I've never possessed."

"Eleanor, you're a late-bloomer, bless your heart. But you have your mother's grace and posture, her sense of justice. These are no small attributes. And in a few years, when you've reached your potential, I daresay you'll have her beauty as well. But I do hope you shall marry for love, as she and I did. She was always protective of you, in her quiet way."

Her father struggled to continue, a plateau the conversation always reached when he spoke of his lovely wife and their perfect life together. He busied himself filling the bowl of his pipe, then struck a match and produced a fine draw, all with a slightly furrowed brow.

"Why are you worried?" Ellie asked. "You said the best of your students were invited to these Friday night get-togethers."

"I also said the brightest," her father commented. "Not to say he isn't, mind you. What worries me is—look, don't you think he's formed this attachment rather quickly?"

"Maybe." She stiffened. Would he erase her dream before it had even taken shape? And how could her mother have been protective, when she hardly ever touched her or spoke to her?"

Her father shifted in the leather armchair, his eyes seeking confirmation in that other world, as they always did. He rarely made eye contact with people. Even with her mother.

"I'm not saying it's wrong, Eleanor. You've never been interested in anyone before, and now that you are, I feel we should know more about the young man. Granted, he's clever, but he seems to lack direction. When I asked him about his plans for the future, he didn't seem to have any, other than making a great deal of money."

"He's still in school. There's plenty of time for that."

"Time flies by faster than you could imagine, dear. This is an excellent example. I've worked hard a good many years to plan for your future, and it's suddenly upon us. I'm not very good at this sort of thing, not like your mother. She always knew what to do. Promise you'll speak to your Aunt Stella before you rush into anything? You're quite young, barely twenty, and, well, just promise me you'll speak to her. All right?"

"Of course. I'll talk to her tomorrow if you like."

"No hurry."

She watched him sink into himself.

"Father, how old was mother when you first met?"

"Sixteen. Now, I see where you're going with that. We were young, granted. But we were terribly in love. Right from the start. Soulmates, as they say. We just knew."

"What if my soulmate never shows up?"

She never received an answer. Her father started one of his coughing fits and drifted off with his memories.

She left quietly. Glancing back, she cemented the image in her mind for sketching later in her room. The man, the mustache, the glasses, the pipe, the armchair, the lamp, and the walls lined with beloved books, most of which she'd devoured long ago. Still, it was like something out of the 19th century. For some reason, she could never capture her mother on paper. Or Jack.

The next morning, she drove to her aunt's farm, if you can call a fenced-in back yard, two goats, and a henhouse a farm. The area was rural enough to get away with hobby farming. Free eggs kept the neighbors from complaining.

She found her aunt in a corner of the quarter-acre yard, straddling a three-legged stool as she milked a goat with a shiny cowbell around his neck that tinkled at the end of a red ribbon.

"Ellie! What brings you to the hinterlands?"

"Father made me promise to come talk to you about Jack."

Stella gave her niece a raised eyebrow, then finished the task at hand, released the goat, and stood up, removing her work gloves with her teeth.

"Do you love him?"

"He's wonderful."

"I see."

Stella handed Ellie the pail of goat's milk and motioned her towards the house. They worked their way through a gaggle of geese interspersed with free-roaming hens. It was Stella's haphazard idea of heaven.

Once they were seated with glasses of fresh-squeezed orange juice and homemade blueberry muffins, Stella took the initiative.

"My, but you've grown into a fine, young woman," she said. "I was always the rowdy one growing up, but your mother had this quiet beauty I'd have given a lot to get a piece of. I always said she got the class, and I got the carrots. But back to business. I've watched you growing up, so I know you've pretty much been left to your own devices. And that's okay. You had a natural goodness that didn't cause anyone to worry to a great extent, but to my reckoning, it's left some gaps in your learning curve. How many boys would you say you've dated?"

Ellie thought a minute. "Two in high school, three in college."

"Were the three in college in your art class?"

"Well, yeah."

"Okay. The way I see it, you moved from one protected environment into another. I've seen you plowing through books like a farmer turning soil, but life's not anything like what's in those books."

"I know that, Aunt Stella."

"You might know in your head, but you're a sensitive sort, and I'm not so sure you know it in your heart." Aunt Stella looked down and studied the gloves in her lap, then looked up at her only niece. "Now that my dear sister has gone to a better place, it's up to me to keep you on the straight and narrow, if you trust me to do so and won't get offended."

"I trust you," Ellie said.

"Good. Since we've ruled true love out of the picture—it's a rare occurrence—we're left with sex and money."

Ellie blushed. "Since I'm lacking in both departments, I don't see the problem."

"Yes, well thank God for that. I guess. Here, have a muffin. What I'm trying to say is like in that feel-good movie you watch over and over—"

"*Gigi*?"

"The same. The one time you made me suffer through it, I recall a part where her aunt warns Gigi to hold out for the really valuable jewels, not to settle for anything less. Well, that's what I'm saying. Don't give it up till there's a ring on your finger, Ellie. Preferably a diamond, though they're becoming passé. Lower those eyebrows, missy—you're not the only one who knows a little French." Looking satisfied, Stella peeled the paper off her muffin and sank her teeth into it.

"Look, Jack's always behaved like a gentleman. He's flirted a little, and we've kissed a little, but that's it. I like him. As for the money, I have none. So why is everybody suddenly so concerned?"

Caught with a healthy amount of muffin in her mouth, Stella held up a finger until she could swallow and wash it down with juice.

"Because you do have money, and unless I miss my guess, Jack's figured that out some time ago. As for the other, and this is somewhat connected, a man'll lie his ass off to get you in bed. Then it's adios and goodbye."

"What are you saying? And how could I have money? I mean, real money. I hope you're not counting what I make at the art museum! Father doesn't have any. He's always pinching pennies and complaining that the college doesn't pay him near enough."

Stella studied her niece's face, and frowned. "I see he hasn't told you. Okay, then here it is. On your 21st birthday, you stand to inherit your mother's money."

"Mother never even had a job, other than taking care of me."

"But our father did, and his father before him," Stella said. "Your grandfather was an ornery cuss, but he made sure what he'd inherited survived the Crash and two world wars. And on top of that, God forbid, if anything should happen to your father, you're also the direct beneficiary of his hard-earned dollars from all those years at the university."

"How much money are we talking about, Aunt Stella? My mother's money, I mean."

"Oh, your cut would be a little over $200,000."

Ellie stared at her mother's sister a moment longer. "How do you know this?"

"I'm the trustee, dufus. And as such, I'm obliged to remind you you can't touch it until your 21st birthday, though, as trustee, I'm allowed to loan it to you for a good and just reason, Jack Taggart not being either one. Anyway, you'll have to make do, like your father has on what he's getting from teacher retirement, plus his savings, which is nothing to sneeze at."

The two women regarded one another in silence as their relationship of family and friend changed ever so slightly.

Ellie mulled it over. "He said he'd provided for my future," she said. "I thought he meant college. I never thought—this must be why he wanted me to talk to you about Jack."

"Of course. Don't' think he doesn't care about you, Ellie. Not everybody's touchy-feely. I mean, he did voice his concern, right? He probably wanted you to find a true soulmate, but not everyone's that lucky. Anyway, I don't think he had someone like Jack in mind for you. I know I sure didn't. And I can vouch for your mother as well. I think she would've had someone a bit higher on the evolutionary scale."

"Why don't you like Jack? And why did you say Jack knew about my inheritance, when I didn't even know until today."

"Gee, let me see. Only daughter of tenured professor, big Victorian house, paid for, in coveted neighborhood. Excellent market potential. Mother deceased, aging father. Daughter alone and insecure. Led sheltered life, easily managed. Gee, you tell me, honey."

"You make Jack sound like a predator. He's not like that. He's funny and outgoing. This changes everything—we'll have financial security. We'll have a house, raise kids. Jack can get a job in the city—"

Stella snorted. "Granted, I've only met your intended the one time, but I consider myself a good judge of character. And I'm going to tell you what I saw in his eyes the very first time we met. He dismissed me as *not worth his time*. He knew right away I was just an old woman in overalls and a straw hat, in no position to help him financially or otherwise. Because we weren't introduced, he didn't connect me to you or to your father. Don't you see—"

"Aunt Stella, he's not like that. He's full of life."

"He's full of something all right."

"I don't want to stay here if you're just going to tear him down."

"Ellie, I haven't always lived with goats and chickens. I saw how he looked at you, and how he looked at those other two women who were there that night. He ogled them, right in front of you, in front of God, in front of everybody. Then he schmoozed your father. I've seen men like that before. I know how they operate. You're going to be a wealthy woman, and Jack Taggart will go through your money, your mother's money, your father's money, and anybody else's money faster than crap flies through a goose. Mark my words. I love you like you were my own, but there are red lights flashing all over this one."

"You don't understand," Ellie responded with a deep sigh. "Jack's all alone, like me. He's got no one. And he's scared. Sometimes I think I'm the only friend he's got."

"Oh, Ellie," Stella said quietly.

"I'm not entirely stupid," Ellie said, rising to take her leave. "I've seen him work a room, and I've watched him suck up to my father." She blushed. "I must've picked up some straight-talking from you, Aunt Stella. Look, I know Jack's not perfect, but what if the perfect one never comes along? He's my ticket to the real world, and if I don't step up and soon, I'll never get any farther than the pale-blue walls of my bedroom. There's gotta be more out there."

Stella offered a weak, little grin when she capitulated and rose from the chair to give Ellie a hug. "Okay, little one. It's all good. Just keep your eyes open. Remember what your Aunt Stella's told you. I'll be praying for you." Stella looked her niece in the eye. "And I do understand. I just don't like it. I was a lot like you, itching to find out what was out there. And I found out. You've got a great big heart, but you can't adopt every orphan puppy you find on the highway."

"I won't. I promise. And don't worry. Nothing's going to happen to my father, other than he may have to get used to seeing a lot more of Jack."

Stella gave her a final hug, then walked her to the screen door and held it open.

Ellie had always felt more at home in Stella's small, compact house than in the Victorian monstrosity she'd grown up in. Things were where they should be. Casual chic. An economy of effort. Not many things, but what she had was good quality, meant to last. The Victorian house was what her parents had wanted, not what she wanted. She wanted rustic, warm, the colors of the earth, black appliances, a garden, and joy.

Looking back at her aunt, standing in the doorway, Ellie wanted to sketch her like that, in her natural habitat. Outside, in overalls and a straw hat, feeding her chickens. She knew she could never capture the warm kitchen with fresh-squeezed orange juice, blueberry muffins, and a screen door to keep out the flies.

"Be careful climbing out on that tree limb," Aunt Stella yelled after her. "Those wings are still a little wobbly!"

Ellie smiled and waved. She returned home in triumph, with everything according to plan. She looked forward to a fun engagement, a church wedding where her father walked her down the aisle, and a life with Jack traveling the world.

That summer Professor Charles W. Townsend, who always loved a good pipe, suffered a collapsed lung and died on the operating table. Ellie received a letter from the Florida Retirement System stating that, as the beneficiary, she was entitled to $4,232.18 a month for life, unless she preferred a lump sum payment.

A week later, with her father barely in the ground, Jack asked Ellie to marry him. Ellie said she needed time, that they should wait. That's what they said in the novels she'd read. Jack grinned that little-boy, lopsided grin that said he knew it was a done deal.

She went cold inside. She didn't love him, not like in the romance novels. Not like her mother and father had loved one another. Not like she thought it would be. But before, when she'd wanted a husband, a traveling companion, her circumstances had changed to where all she wanted was a friend. Who was going to take care of her, now that both of her parents were gone? Aunt Stella had urged caution, but it was too late. There was only one door to choose from. As for trying her wings, she had a feeling Jack would be the one to push her off the limb all right, and yell fly or die. And laugh. She kept waiting for someone to come and save her, but no one did. And she was far too embarrassed to tell Aunt Stella she'd been right all along. Then again, it could all work out for the best, right? Jack could change.

Why had her parents left her in her own little world so long and done so little to prepare her for life? Her mother left it to her father, her father left it to her mother, and their daughter emerged woefully ignorant. Aunt Stella always seemed to be the one who told her things that mattered, but this was a decision she had to make for herself. Had made for herself.

At least there was someone in her life she could talk to. She wouldn't be alone.

She didn't tell him about the money. The big money. Aunt Stella wouldn't let her deposit it in a bank, not with a joint account on the horizon. Jack went right on being Jack. He wove her fears about the future into the fabric of his marriage proposal, told her things would be a little tight for a while, but they could make it on her father's retirement money. He told her she could borrow it from Aunt Stella. He'd known all along. He told her not to worry. That he'd keep her safe. That he'd always be there for her. She said yes, and sold her soul for safe passage.

Determined to finish her degree in art—the least she could do to honor her father's memory—she stayed behind on Jack's first trip to Greece and immersed her disappointment in colors of the rainbow. Her sketchbook alone told her story, but there was no one to see, admire, encourage, or save. In her pain, she was finally able to sketch her mother and her father in the study. As for the rest, she buried it deep inside. Where Ellie lived.

The marriage, not to mention the courtship, wasn't quite what she'd pictured. Jack failed to show in August, as they'd planned; in fact, he didn't return until late October. He called her and told her to get her passport in order. He'd been working on an assignment for some big-name magazines, and finishing school had to take a back seat. He seemed excited; he said what he was doing was "way more fun" than sitting in a classroom.

He said when she got the next check from her father's retirement, they'd get married and honeymoon in Mexico where things are cheap. He went on and on about a friend from college who'd given him an assignment that could jumpstart his photojournalism and investigative reporting career. It was the chance of a lifetime. That's what he said. He suggested she rent her parents' house out for a year—then, if all the dominoes fell into place, she could sell it. Meanwhile, they'd abroad. It was inconceivable at first; she wondered if Jack was having a manic moment like her father had when surfacing from the throes of depression. In any event, she couldn't touch the principal of her father's money; and she wouldn't receive the inheritance from her mother until her next birthday. She swallowed her pride and called Aunt Stella, who was all for Ellie seeing something of the world, even if some of the money she loaned her would go to Jack as well.

Jack came back to the States. He and Ellie were married by a Justice of the Peace in Tallahassee. Not the wedding of her dreams. No church, no bridal gown, no walking down the aisle, no rice. Just Aunt Stella with a smile on her face and hope in her heart, even if her eyes said otherwise. Ellie grinned when she saw the new hat Stella bought for the occasion.

Do you, Eleanor Townsend, take thee, Jack Taggart?

Can you repeat the question?

The accident happened on the way to the airport for their

CHAPTER SIXTEEN

Το όνειρο πραγματοποιείται εκεί που δεν το περιμένεις.

THE DREAM IS REALIZED
WHERE YOU DO NOT EXPECT IT.

honeymoon in Mexico, also courtesy of Aunt Stella. A pickup ran a stop sign and broadsided their car. The impact slammed Ellie back against the headrest before the airbag deployed. Jack, who always said seatbelts were for sissies, threw up his arms and yelled an obscenity. Both of them ended up in the emergency room. Other than Jack fracturing his wrist, nothing serious came of it. They returned to the house for their wedding night, both on pain medication. Despite his lower arm being in a cast and Ellie suffering from whiplash, he was determined to consummate the marriage.

It was awkward. Since it was her first time, she wasn't sure what went wrong. The books made it sound like something incredible was supposed to happen. It never did.

Jack blamed her. As the days wore on, he accused her of being cold-natured. She recalled being more than adequately affected by the steamy passages in romance novels, so she wasn't sure if it was the headaches and dizziness left over from the accident, or the medications both of them continued to take. Something wasn't working.

Was it her?

He brought home sex tapes; the cheap porn disgusted her, but she endured them to please him. She even danced naked in front of him, blinking back tears of embarrassment. She wore the next-to-nothing lingerie he bought her. Nothing worked. Even kissing became a prelude to the inevitable disappointment that followed. No bonding. No fireworks. Wasn't something supposed to occur on a spiritual plane, like the two of them becoming one?

No matter how hard they tried, they remained two.

It drove a silent wedge between them, and there was no one to ask, even if she could somehow summon the courage to do so. Was it her fault? She felt defective, unable to satisfy a man in bed. That's how they put it in the books.

Maybe she'd read too many books.

After a while, the relationship settled onto a level of friendship they both could live with. They became roommates. Just not lovers. Ellie wondered if a woman can be married and remain a virgin.

Jack adjusted and zoomed ahead, refusing to slow down long enough to focus on anything but the next story. She watched *Gigi* one night, alone, and thought about what Stella had said. Holding out for the real jewels was a line that had always made her laugh, but now it left her in tears.

There had been no getting down on one knee and proposing, or asking permission from her father while he had the chance. Jack just told her there was a surprise in the glovebox. She ran out to the car, all excited, only to find the grand surprise wrapped in a tissue. A gold band, obviously from a pawn shop. Was that what he thought of her? He always seemed to be working. Surely he had the money to get her a solitaire? Well, not today.

No diamonds. No ribbon. Not even a box.

She made excuses. Told herself it was okay. He had student loans. He was just getting started in a career. But a modus operandi list took shape in her mind even then. A to-do list with her name at the top, and Jack, licking the stub of a worn-out pencil.

Engagement ring? Done.
Wedding? Done.
Wedding night? Done.
Next?

The door to the past closed as suddenly as it had opened.

The lady in the mirror took a deep breath, and exhaled all the way to Tallahassee, where a jewel did actually lay hidden among the rocks of remembering. A real jewel.

My name is Eleanor Townsend.

Washing her face did little to improve her morning-after, bloodshot eyes. She showered hurriedly and dressed. Sunglasses hid the worst of the damage.

Where was Leo?

Downstairs, she flew through the kitchen, acknowledged Petras with a wave of her hand, and selected a perfect cucumber from the garden. She felt giddy, like on a first date.

Back in the kitchen, knife in hand, she cut two slices and made her way to the patio. After adjusting the lawn chair, she settled back and arranged the cool, green circles on her swollen eyelids. She was so nervous, one of the slices slid down her face and plopped onto her chest, but she wasn't about to face Leo with eyes that looked like she'd just had lasik surgery. She reached out to rescue the cucumber slice and saw that her hand was shaking. In fact, her whole body was shaking from the inside out. Was she going into shock, or was it just plain old excitement?

Where was Leo?

She recovered her wayward green friend and plastered it back where it belonged. The kitchen door opened and closed. Sandals slapped on the pavers, then stopped. Petras cleared his throat. She waited. Maybe he'd never seen cucumber-eyes before. She removed them, held them in her hands, and looked up.

"You've been crying," he said.

"So much for spa day," she mumbled.

"These are for eating, no? Are you ready for the computer?"

"Where's Leo?""

"Away, on business."

"Petras, what's the matter? You look mad. Have I done something?"

"No," he answered curtly, then turned and walked back in the house.

She shrugged, threw the old-wife remedy in the trash can by the door, and followed Petras inside. Maybe cucumbers only worked on old wives.

CHAPTER SEVENTEEN

Ψάχνεις ψύλλους στ› άχυρα.

YOU ARE SEARCHING FOR FLEAS IN THE STRAW.

"Petras, Leo told me about a specialist who observed me for this depersonalization thing. Did he download the results to the computer?"

"It is possible."

"Can you access his files?"

"Not without his permission."

"Okay. Do you remember the name of the specialist?"

Petras gave a quick nod and changed the screen from Greek to English, then googled Ester Hahlberger, Ph.d.

"Her clinic's in Germany? It must have cost him a fortune."

Petras didn't comment, which meant *subject closed*. She waited, hoping he would tell her what was wrong. Nothing was forthcoming.

She skimmed what she already knew and slowed down over things she didn't. Phrases like *identity confusion*, *PTSD*, and *disorganized attachment* swam before her swollen eyes. She tried to follow, but Petras was a speed-scroller. Either that or he had a disorder of his own. It took several requests to go back before he got the hint and stopped altogether. Layna shook her head. It was all too clinical, irrelevant. "I can't do this," she said quietly.

"Good. We need to find the cave."

A bad feeling settled in her gut. "And if we can't find?"

Damn it, I'm starting to sound like Leo.

"When you remember more, it will come together, like my mother's tzatziki."

"Your mother's what?"

"A most delicious yogurt dish. She mixes things in a big bowl, all kinds of things you would not think go together. When it is done, you are in heaven! It goes on kjöfte, broccoli, pita bread, fried patátes—"

"I get it, Petras."

He scowled and clicked onto a virtual tourist website for Skopelos Island, reading from the screen at breakneck speed. "Skopelos Town, Stafilos Beach, Sedoukia, St. John sto Kastri—"

"Wait. Wait. Go back to that picture of St. John's."

"St. John the Beheaded. Very popular."

"I saw it from a distance, I think. What if I remember it wrong, or I don't recognize it?"

"I am concerned more with what comes after the cave. Bad dogs die hard."

"What?"

"You do not know Boikos. He is not the man to roll over and play dead."

"What an unusual saying. Can you teach me to say it in Greek?"

"Of course. Ta kaká skyliá pethaínoun sklirá."

"Ta kaká skyliá pethaínoun sklirá."

"Are you sure it was a cave?" Petras resumed his speed-scrolling. "Maybe the ruins of a castle or a monastery."

"No, it was a cave. I remember sketching it. I—oh God, hold on. I'll be right back."*I remember sketching it. I remember sketching it.*

Layna scurried up the stairs, dumped out her Gucci bag, retrieved the sketchpad, and raced downstairs. Perched on a stool, she leafed through the drawings, pausing as pictures of her life flipped by, one by one. Her parents' home, the social gathering, her cat, Aunt Stella feeding the chickens, the scene from Wuthering Heights, her father in his study. Her mother, posed beside the fireplace. A lifetime captured on recycled paper. She slowed down.

White-washed homes scaled a mountainside. A roughed-out sketch of St. John the Beheaded Monastery atop the knoll. The usual Greek hillside with boats anchored nearby. An old man leading a donkey laden with jars of olive oil. A cave.

She gasped and handed the picture to Petras, ignoring the twinge of pain that tweaked her left temple.

"I know this," Petras said. She held her breath while he clicked keys, selected pull-down menus, and went through several pictures.

"That's it!" she whispered.

"Velanio Beach," Petras turned to look at her with an odd little half-smile on his face, "where people go to be naked."

"Okay, too much information. We've got to tell Leo! Where is he?"

"With Thurman. He left for Volos early this morning."

She knew now why Petras was angry. He'd been left behind to babysit while Leo met with Interpol.

Leo and Thurman stared at the computer screen. First, they checked out cargo manifests, then skimmed lists of personnel. It didn't add up.

"They went ashore," Leo mumbled, "so they could not have just disappeared. There are records on when and where to take the shore leave."

"How can 19 seamen board a vessel and 27 disembark?" Thurman threw his pencil on the desk. "What are we not finding? They weren't there for a free ride."

"One, maybe. Eight, no." Leo pulled up a different chart. "This cannot be explained by sickness or injury. You're right. We have missed something. All the same, I do not need the PNO on my ass with trade union violations of seamen's rights. Or accusing me of employing the foreign workers, ones I know nothing about! It's not just *who*, but *what.*"

"Or, worst case scenario, both. But we need *proof.*" Thurman straightened up and folded his arms. "Has she remembered *anything?*"

Leo frowned, stepped away from the computer, and reached for his coffee cup.

"Illegal smuggling," he muttered. "Why the hell I am the last to know? And how many are involved? I cannot fire everyone who works for me, but somebody—they are like you say, messing with the figures."

"It has to be what Jack found," Thurman said.

Leo scowled at him. "I don't know. Maybe we never know. But the smuggling, whether it is aliens, drugs, weapons, or people, it is *illegal.* I cannot lose my ships over it. Or go to the jail for it! I may not be Stavros Niarchos or Onassis, but I run a legitimate business." He glanced up at Thurman. "Giannakos, he is with us?"

"He is—he wants to see things first-hand. And he's bringing the rest of the Hellenic Coast Guard. We'd better be damn sure there's something for them to find. We're all taking a chance on this one."

"What about the Port Authority?" Leo switched from cold coffee to bottled water. "They do not like it so much when they are

CHAPTER EIGHTEEN

Ο καθένας για λόγου του κι ο θεός για όλους.

EACH FOR HIS OWN AND GOD FOR ALL.

called out on the blind run." He twisted the top off with a vengeance, drawing a curious glance from Thurman, who responded.

"I know," Thurman said. "Without evidence of some kind, it's going to be hard to justify a raid, even for Giannakos. Customs can open a container, but there damn sure better be something inside."

Leo slid off the stool. "Where's Giannokos?"

Thurman scowled. "Coast Guard's catching smugglers off Lesbos. Waste of a good man, chasing refugees in rubber rafts. He promised he'd be here, ready to go."

"I just hope *we* are," Leo muttered.

"You didn't answer my question," Thurman said. "Has she remembered anything?"

Leo gave Thurman a dark look. "No. Too many people know too much already. It won't be long. She starts to remember, then she does not. I think she needs little more time."

"Don't we all. Tomorrow's August 16th and we're no closer to figuring it out than we were a month ago. Do you still think Aleksandra's involved?"

Leo gave a half-laugh. "Don't you?"

Thurman's forehead wrinkled. "We're tailing her, but not much has happened. We still can't figure out where the payoff's going down or who's handling the money. It's coming from somewhere. She's smart, Leo. My boys have questioned her. She knows what she's doing."

"Yes," Leo replied, his thoughts returning to Layna and how beautiful she was since she got rid of the black hair. "Have you thought of putting a woman in?"

"In where?"

"The hair salon."

"What do you mean? André's all set up. Nothing's happened."

Leo's eyes narrowed. "Aleksandra is street smart. Not intelligent, not educated. She will keep the things simple. Never will she put her hands up and go quiet. She will run, and maybe take someone with her, too."

"You mean, kill somebody? It might be a good idea after all, having a female on the inside, just in case. I've got someone in mind. She's damn good. Let me make a phone call."

"She must be very, very good, or my wicked stepmother, she will spot her."

"Got it. Do you want the helicopter to take you back?"

"No." Leo laughed as he left the office. Aleksandra wouldn't think twice about kicking a man where it hurts. Or a woman? He pulled out his cell phone on the way to the hydrofoil to check in with Petras and see if anything had happened in his absence. He'd been gone a while, and wondered if their house guest was still safe within the confines of his home.

There was no answer.

Maybe they went to the marketplace, or Petras left his cell phone upstairs, or downstairs. No need to worry. There could be a hundred reasons why no one answered. He could be charging the phone. He could be leaping off the cliff.

Leo broke into a full trot back to the office to tell Thurman he'd changed his mind, and could he hurry.

With any luck, they would make Skopelos in 45 minutes.

Nitsa went to market in the early afternoon, before the shops closed.

Layna sat on the bed and stared at her sketchpad, chewing on her pencil to keep from going mad while she examined her work over the past hour. Leo smiling. Leo in the back seat of a Chevy looking sternly out the car window. Leo looking down at her, his eyes glittering. Petras at the computer. Nitsa in the garden. Leo laughing. Damn.

She didn't know what else to do, now that she knew where the cave was. Would Velanio hold the answers they were looking for? If it did, then what? If it didn't, then what?

Where was Leo?!

She wanted to explain everything, to make him understand. Would he even listen, or had anger killed any hope for compassion? He felt so guilty about Jack, he was on the defensive, fighting any kind of attraction he may have felt. Okay, maybe they were right to pull away. If nurses form attachments for patients, and patients toward caregivers, could that explain the weird bond between them? It happened with Leo's father.

You're overthinking it.

I know, but I can't stop!

She veered away from viewing Leo in the role of caregiver and looked at it from another perspective, the bond between patient and psychiatrist. He had certainly never tried to diagnosis her, that she knew of, but had she become emotionally dependent on him?

Enough. He only wants what's in your head.

I know. I know.

What about the emotional detachment she'd experienced with her parents? Could it have contributed to the problems of intimacy with Jack? Could the same thing happen with Leo?

Okay, way too much to deal with.

She heard Petras come upstairs and go into his bedroom, so she slipped her sandals on, grabbed a bottle of water, and escaped to the patio for some mind-numbing sun. It was hot enough, almost 2:00

o'clock. With the mid-morning breeze gone, the markets would be closing up, everyone disappearing indoors for a nap until evening. She'd been in a darkened room too long. With a glorious sigh, she lifted her face to the sun and closed her eyes.

Footsteps sounded softly. She thought Petras had come to join her, until she caught the unmistakable click of a gun way too close to her right ear. She froze, eyes open.

"Do not turn around."

She obeyed, her eyes the only thing moving—a quick glance down revealed a man's shadow next to her own.

When Petras walked calmly out the kitchen door, Layna turned, slowly. Her protector wore a tight expression on his face and sported a bruise on his forehead, his hands raised in a half-ass manner, his shoulder holster empty. When he returned her look of panic, Layna saw something she'd never seen before on the mighty Petras—a look of embarrassment. His simple babysitting assignment had proven not so simple after all.

The gunman behind him held a weapon with a silencer in one hand and Petras' Beretta 9mm in his left hand.

A voice behind Layna barked an order in Greek. Cold metal pressed into her skin.

The thug took Petras' gun, ejected the magazine, then tossed the empty weapon into a pot of geraniums. He laughed, slipped the magazine in his pocket, and resumed his watch.

The first gunman growled something in Greek, and his partner turned to obey. She assumed he'd been ordered to search the house.

Petras snorted. The second gunman, already at the kitchen door, turned around.

"Something funny, sheep-shit?"

"Your name, *Balios,*" Petras said. "I find it humorous you are named after a horse."

Balios took two strides and struck him across the mouth, then left to search the house for God knew what.

The first gunman chuckled and turned to Layna.

"So, wife of Taggart, you have something to say to me, yes?"

"I have nothing of value. No jewels or money. Nothing."

"Don't be stupid," Petras said to him. "She doesn't know anything."

A sinister smile crossed the gunman's face.

"You like to turn other cheek, as they say?"

Petras looked away.

"Do not worry. We are not the merciless killers. We keep her alive, yes? We shoot first the arm, then the leg, then the face, but only if we must. It is a very pretty face."

She went cold inside. Petras glowered at their captor.

The gunman's black eyes glittered back. He shrugged. "One bullet, her. But maybe I save two for you, before you can to reach me." Even in broken English, he got his message across.

Balios flung the kitchen door open, Layna's sketchpad in his hand. He showed it to Rhouben, then both men grew animated, laughing and speaking rapidly in their native language.

"Balios just told Rhouben he *found it,*" Petras whispered to Layna. "Rhouben shot the computer."

"What? But I didn't—"

Balios threw her sketchpad to the concrete. Rhouben pointed his weapon directly at her face and ended any communication with Petras. She noted the silencer on the end of the gun; it looked bigger up close. Her hopes sank. Either one of them could shoot them right here on the patio, and no one would hear. No one would ever know.

"We go," Rhouben snarled, "to the place you cannot remember." His partner joined him in vicious laughter and slid his gun into his pants.

Rhouben moved his gun into his jacket pocket, keeping his finger on the trigger. They left through the side gate that connected the back of the house.

Layna knew the alleyway led to the cobblestone streets and eventually to the landing. They had timed the abduction well. The market was closed; few people lingered. Layna glanced longingly back

CHAPTER NINETEEN

Φασούλι το φασούλι γεμίζει το σακούλι.

BEAN BY BEAN, THE SACK GETS FULL.

at the house, thankful at least that Nitsa had escaped. But, they had known that, hadn't they? And planned accordingly. No witnesses.

Why hadn't the security alarm gone off? They'd disabled it. No surprises, no complications. Layna knew if she tried to run, they would shoot Petras, and if Petras tried to escape, they would shoot her. He'd saved her life; she'd do whatever she could to save his.

A few vendors, just closing up, gave the group a curious glance then looked away. The four of them reached the landing without incident. Petras and Layna were propelled into a canopied motorboat painted aqua with orange trim like so many others. Kidnapped in plain sight, and she didn't dare scream.

Rhouben cradled his weapon on his chest while Balios maneuvered them to open water. As soon as they were out of the sight of the town, Balios jerked Petras' hands behind him and bound them with plastic ties. Rhouben bound Layna's hands in front, then pulled out a short rope and ran it through a heavy bolt on the side of the boat, jerking it taut where she couldn't move. She had to strain her neck in order to see Petras behind her and to her right.

Her captor leaned over and tugged Leo's ring off her finger so quickly, it was done before she realized what he was doing.

"That's mine!" she yelled, struggling against the plastic ties.

Rhouben sneered and slipped the diamond ring into his jacket pocket.

"And now, is mine."

Balios snorted and chuckled behind her. He continued to steer the boat, but with a gun in his right hand.

Rhouben raised his weapon to within a foot of Petras' head, and leered at Layna.

"There is something you wish to say, Taggart's wife?"

She tried to get a breath while panic threatened another hyperventilation. "I don't know anything! What do you want me to say?"

Rhouben used his free hand to strike her across the cheek, then pushed the barrel of the automatic closer to Petras, flush with his skull. She gasped from the blow, and talked.

"I don't know where it is. I haven't been there in a long time."

Rhouben put his hand to his ear and bent his head down.

"I won't know until we get there!" She screamed it over the sound of the motor, while she prayed with every part of her that her words would prove true, even though it didn't really matter. Whatever the outcome, they were going to die.

The two men shared a smile. Layna bent down and wiped the blood from her cheek where Rhouben had struck her. She twisted and pulled until she could see Petras, who winked at her. Seriously. She could have sworn—but he turned away, and she remained tied to the boat as it skimmed and bumped its way toward an unknown destination.

Besides losing Petras, who had become a friend as well as a protector, tears gathered in her frightened eyes at the thought of losing Leo as well. It had started so slowly and happened so fast—like a train gathering momentum in the distance, then failing to stop as it flies past, so wild and dangerous, so unexpected, you catch your breath and forget to wonder why love didn't stop and let you get on board. Now, it was too late. The train was gone.

She would die, never having told Leo Amratsis she loved him.

The helicopter arrived on time. Leo and Thurman ran up the paved streets to the house. Leo fumbled for his keys, then saw the door was ajar. He burst through, calling for Petras, Layna, Nitsa. Thurman did the same up the stairs, two at a time.

Nitsa ran in from the kitchen straight into Leo's arms. She buried her face in his chest, sobbing and sputtering while she gestured toward the patio. Thurman came downstairs, shook his head that he hadn't found her, then followed Leo out the back door. A quick search turned up Petras' gun in the geraniums.

"No magazine," Leo mumbled, and slipped the gun in his jacket pocket. Layna's discarded sketch pad lay on the pavers next to the chaise lounge. A bottle of water, unopened, lay on its side next to the empty lounger.

They went back inside.

"He'd never leave his weapon unless he was outnumbered, or hurt." Leo said. "There were more than one, or Petras, he would have taken him. If they have Layna first, then he can do nothing. His phone is in his room beside the bed."

"It wouldn't help," Thurman said.

"His phone was in his room beside the bed," Thurman muttered. Leo nodded. Thurman motioned for them to return to the patio. Neither man mentioned that Petras might not be able to answer his phone.

"I never feel so fucking useless!" Leo turned, grabbed a clay pot, and smashed it against the fence. He stood with hands on his hips, teeth clamped together, his insides shaking.

"Leo." Thurman's quiet voice breached the wall.

He half-turned and saw Thurman studying the patio. "What?"

"Something's not right." Thurman walked over and sat on the lounge, then looked down at Layna's sketch pad and picked it up. "There are no pencils," he said, giving the patio a cursory inspection. "It's an incomplete crime scene. If she was sketching, there would be pencils. Those black ones she likes. I remember finding them scattered all over Jack's room when we searched it. They were

CHAPTER TWENTY

Κακό σκυλί, ψόφο δεν έχει.

BAD DOGS DIE HARD.

everywhere. I put them in the bag with her clothes. But here, no pencils."

Leo strode over, took the sketchpad from Thurman, and thumbed through it, then shook his head. "She maybe took them with her, in her purse or something." He noted there were no pictures of Jack, but several of him. He didn't recall posing for any drawings; he felt almost violated by the emotions she'd captured deep inside him, in his eyes, how he held his head.

"I saw her bag on the bed upstairs," Thurman said quietly, "and two pencils."

Leo glanced at Thurman. He searched the other sketches, twisting his neck to the side until he heard the creak he needed. With his body wound up like a trigger on a bomb, he studied the people and places from Layna's past life, then several that were more recent. Tingles told him the answer lay there. Thurman came alongside and peered over his shoulder.

"What about St. John's?" Thurman asked.

Leo shook his head. "The location is all the wrong," he muttered. "See? Too many tourists. Boiko's men would choose something with not so many people."

"I think you're right," Thurman said. "What about this one? Do you recognize it?"

"Not really," Leo muttered. "It is Layna in the foreground, but it could be any cave, on any island, anywhere." He dropped the sketch pad onto the lounge chair, then stopped. "Wait a minute," he said. "Petras gave me a hard time about being left behind. He was pissed off because Layna wanted some help on the computer!"

Both men rushed inside and stumbled over one another to get to the office, only to find what was left of the monitor—a bullet hole through the heart of the screen.

"Damn it!" Leo slammed his fist into the wall, then straightened up, gave Thurman a perplexing look, raced up the stairs, and came back with Petras' laptop. Thurman grinned, fidgeted with the wires, and hooked it into the hard drive. Leo paced until the monitor came to life; he pulled up the last sites searched. The list encompassed depersonalization disorders, a German doctor, tourist sites, and caves.

"Thurman, the sketchpad!" Leo gritted his teeth.

Thurman returned in record time. Together, they scanned the entries. Leo held the sketch up and compared it to the images on the screen.

"There!" Thurman said. "That's it!"

"Velanio Beach? Are you sure?"

"Positive. It's just a different angle. See? There's that huge rock just outside the entrance. It's close enough."

"For bocce ball maybe. We talking people's lives."

"At this point, it's all we've got." Thurman said.

Leo stared at Layna's rendering of the cave, the water, the boat. "I think you are right, Thurman. That is the same boat Jack was in, or one like it. Shit, I don't like the feeling I am feeling."

"Look, we've never known the exact spot where Jack was killed, right? But Boiko's men have known all along 'cause they're the ones who killed him?"

Leo frowned. "But if they know, and this is the cave, then they search already. So what do they expect to find? And even if she sketched it, does not mean she remembers what happens there?" His face darkened. "Boiko's men are only interested in the evidence. If she cannot provide, or even if she can—"

"Don't go there," Thurman said. "What's the nearest place we can touch down without letting them know we're there? I'll get my men on it while we're in the air."

Leo clicked a lever beneath the desk, and a secret drawer slid out. He grabbed a Sig Sauer .45 and slid it into his jeans at the waist.

The two men talked strategy as they ran to the helicopter. Thurman retrieved his Glock 34 from an overhead compartment and activated the copter's GPS as the rotor blades reached full spin. By the time the pilot lifted them into the air, the screen was up and running. Thurman punched in the information, and three maps appeared.

"Agriosikia is closest," Leo said, "but there is—how you say—ακρωτήριο?"

"Promontory. Yes, I see it," Thurman said, "there between Stafylos and Velanio."

"I think maybe we cross from Stafylos, through the trees."

"Perfect. We can get a boat from there. They'd hear a 'copter a mile away."

"Do it!" Leo shouted as they left Skopelos behind. He stared out the window as land and water flew by, and prayed they'd be in time.

The closer they got to Velanio, the more nervous she became. How would she ever find the cave? What if she'd remembered it wrong? Didn't Petras say there were a hundred caves? Her eyes ached from sunlight reflected on water.

Horse-face didn't slow down, but Velanio couldn't be far. Another ten minutes, and the boat's engine lowered to a sputter. Then, it was suddenly upon them, growing larger as they approached. She knew it immediately and wanted no part of it. Her body shivered. She struggled against the plastic binders that prevented her from cradling her head in her hands.

Rhouben grinned when she squirmed, ogling the way her breasts squeezed together with her wrists tied in front. Layna saw the animal lust blaze in his eyes and looked away, disgusted and terrified.

They moved in as close as they dared to the rocks. Rhouben released her from the side of the boat, but kept the lead rope attached to the binders. He pulled her like a slave, and she was forced to follow. Stumbling on the slippery rocks, she fell to her knees in the water. He yanked her back up and tugged even harder on the rope.

"*Bástardos,*" Petras muttered under his breath.

Balios heard and shoved his elbow into his ribs. Petras grunted and doubled up. His captor pushed him over the side of the boat into the water, then took equal pleasure in dragging him over the rocks onto dry land, where he dumped him on the sand. Petras coughed up sea water and made it to a sitting position. Balios grinned and knocked him down again.

"Please, don't hurt him," Layna begged.

Rhouben laughed, leering at her nipples through her wet blouse.

Fear and the sea water she'd swallowed made it hard to breathe. She coughed and wheezed. Afraid she'd fall or pass out, she leaned against a large rock that led to the entrance. Rhouben watched her face, made a disgusted sound, and stopped tugging on the rope, but he held it taut. She took shallow gasps until breaths came normally again. She noted Petras had managed to make it to his knees, and that he'd been allowed to stay in that position.

Her gaze took in the outcropping she'd stumbled over and the slope of shells and sand. It seemed familiar, but when she tried to match it with a memory, it blurred like a picture out of focus. The mouth of the cave yawned before her. She felt a yank on the rope. Rhouben grinned and urged her on.

When she glanced back at the stone where she'd rested for a moment, she visualized Jack taking her picture in the sun. The cliffs blocked the sun's harsh rays and left cool shadows, but she definitely knew this place.

Petras whispered behind her. *"Bad dogs die hard."*

She turned just as Balios yanked her friend by the arm so they could keep up with Rhouben. Even so, Petras had blessed her with hope and a half-grin from a split lip.

She hesitated as they entered the cave, fear settling into her spine and up between her shoulder blades, fear she'd die here. Rhouben sensed her hesitation and took sadistic pleasure in tugging on the rope, forcing her farther inside where she peered at walls and a ceiling made smooth by endless tides and currents. A large, craggy boulder, nearly as tall as a man, held court in the shadows at the back of the cave. When they reached it, Rhouben jerked the lead especially hard to bring her to her knees, then flung the rope in her face and growled his command.

"We do not have all the day! We have other things to do...you and me."

She ripped her mind apart, frantic for something, anything remotely familiar. A place where sunlight bathed the floor of the cave meant something, but what? She scrambled to it on hands and knees, running her fingers across the dirt like a blind man reading Braille, desperate to keep them from shooting Petras. Memories came like vague, haphazard things to taunt her.

Rhouben growled at Petras in Greek. Balios raised his gun, determined.

"If you shoot him, I'll never tell you!"

Rhouben was there in two steps and wrenched her wrist to pull her to her feet. She stared at his death grip on her wrist and screamed and screamed and screamed—long, piercing sounds that echoed in the enclosed space before being swallowed up by dirt and sand.

Rhouben had already dropped the rope and backed away.

Thoughts and images inundated her brain in swells and eddies. She grunted and swayed, struggling against the binders. It was difficult to distinguish between the voices in the cave, now muffled and distant, and the new ones forming in her mind. As the vortex of remembering sucked her in, she no longer cared about life or death. All her energy focused on the huge rip in time opening up in front of her, taking her down into the maelstrom that was her mind. She tasted terror, and steadied herself to meet it head-on.

The kidnappers stepped back at first, unsure of what was happening. They struggled to understand the tangled words she spewed from her mouth like a madwoman. At first, they made no sense, but Petras caught on immediately. He wondered if Boiko's thugs even knew what was happening.

"It's lovely here, Jack," she said, only her voice sounded much younger. "Why can't we stay a little while longer? You don't have to turn the pictures in until Wednesday, right?"

"Pictures?"

Rhouben and Balios glanced at one another to confirm what they'd heard and strained to understand the jumbled dialogue that seemed to fly past them.

"We can come back tomorrow, right Jack? Jack, what is it?"

"What is he doing?" Balios asked.

"Restless," Layna responded, "like when he's on to a good story. No, something else."

She moved toward the large boulder. "It's fear," she whispered, then looked down at the floor of the cave. "Where did that come from?"

"What? What do you see?" Rhouben prompted her.

"Jack, rummaging in my purse. Where did that flash drive come from? What are you doing with my camera? It's not funny, Jack."

"Flash drive!" Balios yelled, moving forward.

"No!" Rhouben said, holding his partner back. "First we learn where it is!"

Layna pulled away from a ghost and sank to her knees next to the rock. She turned away. "No, I won't. Not in a filthy cave."

Rhouben looked to Balios for help, then to Layna. "What is he doing?"

"Playing games. Love games."

"With the flash drive!" Rhouben yelled.

"He's sealing it in a bag, only it's difficult. His hands are shaking, like he's digging a grave. Wipe it smooth, he says. Why is he so scared? He covers it with seaweed and ignores me. Up tight, out of sight. That's what he says. Words to a song. Silly, stupid words."

"Where is the bag?!" Balios yelled.

But Layna, oblivious, lifted her face up, closed her eyes, and smiled. "You never kissed me like that before, on my eyelids." Then, she frowned and opened her eyes. "What do you mean, your only friend? Is that all I'll ever be to you? Jack? What's wrong?"

"Bah! She makes no sense," Balios grumbled, making universal crazy-person signs with his finger and forehead. Rhouben shushed him.

Layna stood up and moved to an open spot on the cave floor, where she made digging motions with her hands.

"Layna, what are you doing?"

She stopped and looked around; her eyes settled on Petras. "I know you," she said, smiling. A look of puzzlement came across her tilted head.

"What you doing?" Rhouben repeated, trying to copy Petras' voice.

"Burying the past," she said, matter-of-factly. "I'm burying my camera. But we're coming back for it. He promised." She sat back and stopped digging, talking to someone who wasn't there. "No. Please. They're the only pictures I have of the honeymoon."

Her words were laced with sadness and watered with swallowed

CHAPTER TWENTY-ONE

Μια ζωή χρωστάμε όλοι μας.

ALL WE OWE TO US IS OUR LIFE.

tears.

Petras glanced at their captors, both so captivated by the crazy woman, they didn't see him slide a knife from the inside of his boot and begin to slice through the plastic tie, a strategy made all the easier on his knees with his hands tied behind his back.

Layna started digging again, then pretended to bury something invisible. Her hands smoothed it over. She made motions like she was picking things up and placing them on top the burial site. "No cross," she mumbled. "There should be a cross. The rocks and pebbles will just get swept away like everything else." She stood up, a puzzled expression on her childlike face.

Rhouben and Balios were so caught up in the drama, they didn't hear the quiet snap of Petras' knife as he cut through the plastic tie.

"Run? Run where?" Layna tilted her head. "No, of course I won't forget, Jack. Why would you say that? No, wait! That's my purse!" She turned around, halted, then whipped back in place and froze. Color left her face.

"What happened?" Balios muttered to Rhouben, but Rhouben was equally confused.

"He walked away," Layna whispered, "He walked into the sun."

Layna took a lurching step toward the opening of the cave and listened. She ducked to one side as though dodging something that had barely missed her. Her eyes seemed locked in place, searching the universe beyond the cave for answers. "Jack? What was that crunching sound? Something just flew by me. I wonder—"

She turned, frozen in place, then screamed and screamed. Her eyes widened in disbelief, staring at something no one could see on the floor of the cave. "Oh, God." She fell to her knees and struggled to reach her husband, made all the more difficult because of the plastic wrist tie. She fell over twice and scrabbled up again to reach his side, taking his hand in hers and kissing it, tears pouring from her aching eyes. Then the comforting changed to struggling as though she were being held.

"No! Jack, let go! I can't run if you don't let go! How can I get it out? I can't leave you, Jack! If I do that, you'll bleed to death! Tell me what to do! No! Let go, Jack. Jack!"

In the silence of the cave, then and now, she ceased to struggle. Her shoulders sank inward. Tired eyes studied her hands, her clothing.

"I'm sorry, Jack. There's nothing I can do. The—the harpoon—it's in too deep. Don't you see, if I pull it out, you'll bleed to death for sure. I don't know what to do, Jack. I'm sorry. I'm so sorry."

The two men and Petras continued to watch the conversation between a crazy woman and her dead husband.

"So much blood," she said quietly. "What am I'm supposed to do with all this blood? And words, words I don't understand. So many words. So much blood." With a great deal of effort, she rose slowly to her feet. Mumbling the same things over and over, Layna moved like a sleepwalker toward Rhouben and the opening of the cave. She shielded her eyes, presumably against a bright sun. Then, something happened.

"Voices shouting! Too many voices! No, I've got to go for help! Let me go! Please, you've got to help my husband!"

She screamed, grabbed her left temple, and crumpled to the ground like a puppet when the strings are let go all at the same time.

Rhouben, apparently tired of the drama, grabbed her, yanked her to her knees, and shook her. "The flash drive! Where is the flash drive?!"

It was like she couldn't hear him. Her head sank onto her chest.

"I will have the truth!" Rhouben shouted, taking hold of her arms and shaking her so hard, her head flopped back and forth. When Rhouben stopped, she lifted half-dead eyes to his face. Her shoulders flexed, her voice stronger.

"Wait, I know you," she said, "You hit me and tied me up. The humming noise went on and on. In the boat. I remember the boat. I begged you to help Jack, and you laughed. I begged you, and you just threw me into the water. The water—so cold I couldn't breathe. That was you!"

Tears streamed down her face. Her body shook. She stared at her bound wrists, then at Rhouben, zeroing in on his soul. She shrieked in his face like a banshee and threw herself at him, fingernails out, determined to claw him to death for what he'd done.

Rhouben cried out.

Caught off guard, Rhouben grappled with Layna and tried to shake her off or catch hold of the rope so he could pull her down. He yelled in Greek. She pummeled his neck with her bound fists and kicked him everywhere she could. He slapped her face, hard. She reeled from the blow. Balios grabbed her by the hair.

"Pictures!" he yelled, his words spitting in her face. "Where are the fucking pictures?!"

She gasped when he pulled her head back and twisted her arm.

"Give us the flash drive, NOW!"

Layna screamed at him and struggled, opening a window of opportunity for Petras to throw off the plastic ties, scramble to his feet, and head for the nearest bad dog, Balios. He jump-kicked *horse-face* in the chest. Balios dropped his gun and bowled over. Petras kicked it away, then delivered an upper cut that connected with both chin and nose. Balios roared, but amazingly wasn't down for the count. He came up swinging, wondering what had happened.

Rhouben tried to get a shot off at Petras while Layna scratched at his face like a mad woman and pummeled his face with both her bound hands. When Rhouben finally fired, the bullet meant for Petras zipped past Layna's left ear and ricocheted off a rock. Layna, oblivious to anything but revenge, ripped at Rhouben's clothes while slamming her foot down on his instep. Rhouben, who sorely wanted to forget the contract and shoot the woman instead, tried to push her away so he could try and bring Petras down, who was still trading blows with Balios.

Suddenly, Leo was there! He landed a blow across Rhouben's jaw; Layna heard the gun go off seconds before Michael Thurman appeared out of nowhere, grabbed her, and dragged her down onto the floor of the cave where she lay, stunned, her shoulder numb from the impact. A second later, Thurman raced to help Leo with Rhouben.

Every part of her hurt, but there, amid the chaos and dirt, with bullets and fighting all around her, Layna felt her mind begin to clear. Layers of gossamer retreated, one at a time, until only truth was left. The painful, horrible truth of what had happened to Jack. She groaned from the horror and a feeling of deep regret that swept over her. Rising above it all, she forced her body to action and pulled herself up to see what was happening.

Petras grappled with Balios over his weapon, both men gripping it while they fought for control. Balios tried to kick him in the groin, then Petras elbowed *horse-face* in the side. The gun went flying and slid almost to within reach of Layna, then it got caught up in Leo's scuffle with Rhouben where it was kicked around quite a bit. Layna watched Balios slam Petras up against the cave wall, where he crumpled and slid to the ground. When *horse-face* looked around for his gun, Layna saw her chance to enter the fray.

She scuttled across the floor of the cave like an attack crab and retrieved the weapon without getting stepped on or accidentally kicked. Balios roared at her, but Layna raised the gun as fast as she could and fired twice. Her first shot missed. She clamped her lips tight and told herself to focus. Her second shot grazed his leg. He turned and made for the mouth of the cave in an awkward, limping gait.

She held the weapon with both hands, held her breath, and fired again. Balios grabbed his left arm, stopped, and raised both hands, or tried to. Leo spotted him and yelled at Thurman, who was trying to revive Petras so they could take on Rhouben. Layna watched as Leo jerked his head in Balios' direction—and got jaw-punched by the leader of the pack.

She tried to shoot Rhouben, too, but Leo was in the way. When Thurman yelled at him to distract him, the brute whipped around, weapon raised, and fired. Leo reached for the gun and managed to knock it out of Rhouben's hand, but too late—he'd already fired. Thurman grabbed his side, and Layna raced to help him. With Thurman's arm across Layna's slender shoulders, they made it to the side of the cave away from Rhouben and Leo.

"Fucking asshole!" Thurman squeezed his eyes hard against the pain, then half-opened them. "What are you doing shooting at people? You were supposed to stay down!"

"It's my fight too, you know."

Thurman rolled his eyes.

Layna's attention flew back to Leo, who had whirled and sucker-punched Rhouben. In retaliation, the man growled and came at him like a grizzly. Layna could hardly breathe, seeing the two men matched in height and strength. Her hands were shaking so badly, she didn't dare fire a shot at the scuffling duo. When Leo landed a heavy blow to Rhouben's temple, the man reeled back, stumbled, decided he'd had enough, and tried to run. Leo yanked his Sig Sauer from his pants and took aim, but his hands were as shaky as Layna's.

"To hell with it," he grumbled, and fired.

Rhouben yelled as a piece of his shirt exploded from the upper shoulder. He gripped his shoulder and shouted obscenities in his native tongue, kicking Leo viciously in the knee. Layna could tell the blow to his knee knocked the breath out of him; Leo staggered back in pain. But Petras recovered enough to hold Rhouben's arms while Thurman limped over and cuffed him.

It was at that point that Layna remembered Balios and glanced around to make sure everything was okay.

It wasn't.

"*Leo*!" Thurman shouted.

Both men switched their focus to *horse-face*. Even Rhouben.

"*Christos,*" Leo whispered.

With everyone's attention elsewhere, Balios had gotten hold of a hand grenade. Maybe he'd limped to the boat and back. Maybe he kept one in his trousers. In any event, with a demonic grin, he removed the pin and lofted it into the cave.

Rhouben screamed. With his hands cuffed behind him, there was nothing he could do.

Layna watched in awe as Special Agent Michael Thurman took three steps, leaped into the air like it was fourth quarter and final down. He caught the grenade, shouted "One!" and crumpled in a heap a few feet away. Then, immediately, miraculously, he struggled to his knees and threw the grenade back where it came from in a perfect arc.

"*Two*," he gasped, and collapsed.

Behind her, Layna heard a sound like someone letting the air out of a cushion.

It was Leo, wrestling Rhouben to the ground while he shouted to Petras to take care of Layna, which he did. He grabbed her by the arm and shielded her on the floor of the cave with his body. She buried her face in the dirt with her still-bound hands.

"*Three*!" Petras tried to yell, but his voice came out muffled and was interrupted by a blast that rushed through the cave with the amplified sound of a small cannon. Pieces of shrapnel echoed off the walls and made spitting sounds in the dirt, throwing it up into half-buried faces and pinging off rocks.

Layna bit her lip to keep from crying out. The ringing in her ears, painful at first, slowly diminished in sound and substance.

She would learn later that Balios was so shocked to see the grenade being lofted right back to him, he actually caught the thing. He flung his arm back, determined to complete his mission, and that's when the clock ran down.

Petras was right. He'd said once that Boikos didn't hire men based on their intelligence.

When the ringing in her ears subsided, she turned over. Petras was on the ground next to her, not moving. Lying on her side, she reached out and placed her fingers against his neck for a pulse. God is merciful, she thought, finding a strong one coursing through the veins of the indestructible bodyguard and friend.

She shook his shoulder, gently, whispering his name. His breathing changed, and he began to stir, groaning, reluctant to break the surface of his sleep. Layna definitely related. When she saw his bleeding lip and all the cuts and bruises he'd taken on her behalf, she started trembling and couldn't stop.

Petras opened his eyes, blinking several times until he could focus. He turned his head and looked at her.

Layna leaned down and kissed his forehead. "Thank you," she said. "Again."

Petras smiled, then slowly turned his head to the other side. Layna knew he was looking for his friend.

"Leo?" Layna called out, surprised by her new voice—dry and dusty.

Leo got up, a bit unsteadily and favoring one leg. He pulled out a short-bladed knife, and made his way to her, leaning down to cut through the plastic ties that bound her wrists. She noticed how he held the injured leg straight out and pressed his lips together for the pain. When she was done, he handed her his Sig Sauer and motioned at Rhouben, who sat cross-legged on the dirt floor.

"Can you keep the eye on this *bástardo* without shooting him?"

She looked into his eyes. Leo's heart leaped. It was the smile of a woman, fully grown.

"Fysiká nai. Ta kaká skyliá pethaínoun sklirá."

"You speak Greek well," Leo said, his dark eyes registering first shock, then approval.

Layna sighed and pointed the weapon at her captor's manhood. She was far too weary to grin, though the thought occurred to her.

Rhouben curled his lip into a snarl. "Is true I die hard," he growled, "but you are dog, too. You are *bitch*!"

Beside her, she heard Leo urging Petras to try and sit up if he could.

"See, I knew you come through. There were only two of them, eh?"

"Feels more like twenty," Petras said, "and my hearing's not so good."

"Everything will be taken care of, my friend."

Leo made his way across the floor of the cave, picking his way among the debris to check on Thurman, leaning against the wall.

When he grunted, Layna glanced up. She watched him remove his shirt and pull his t-shirt up over his head. Thurman took the undershirt, folded it into a compress, and held it next to the wound in his side. As tired as she was, the sight of Leo, muscled and bare-chested, was enough to give her pause. Rhouben shifted positions, and she pointed the gun at his face without even looking. This particular bástardo wasn't going anywhere except to prison.

A rustle of material, another grunt, and Leo replaced his shirt but didn't bother buttoning it up. She watched as he slipped one arm around the Interpol agent and headed for the entrance.

"Let's see if Balios is still a major concern," he said.

"Doubtful."

Leo and Thurman weren't gone long. When they returned, both limping, Thurman hauled Rhouben to his feet, and Leo walked directly to Layna. "Are you ready to surrender your weapon, Miss? It is the evidence." His smile was a weak one, but offered with unspoken gratitude.

She gave up the gun, which Leo passed to Thurman, who placed it in a zippered plastic bag and slipped it into his jacket pocket.

Leo took both of Layna's hands in his, gently inspecting her arms, wrists, and hands. His eyes scanned her face as he checked for bruises and turned her head to one side so he could see her now-swollen jaw. "Do you need the doctor?"

"No, but there's something I need to do."

Leo helped her to stand. Layna walked over to Rhouben, ripped open his jacket pocket and grabbed the ring, putting it back where it belonged, on her finger. Rhouben, defenseless with his wrists tied in back, leaned back at the murderous look on her face.

"Is *mine*," she said, then turned and walked into Leo's arms.

"He's dead," she whispered. "Jack's really dead."

"I know," Leo said. "I know." He placed his hands on her shoulders, but she could tell it was not to comfort her.

"God, it was so awful," she cried, sobbing and trying to talk past the awful pain that poured out of her, now that it was over. "They put him in the boat with me, and the harpoon, it was still in him, and his eyes were staring at me, and the harpoon stood straight up and they wouldn't take it out, and they just left him like that. They just left him like that! And they took everything we had on us, and they tied me up and tried to drown me and—"

"I know, Layna. I know." Leo stroked her hair, but she could tell there was something else, something more, and she didn't want to ask. But part of her, the new her, had to know.

"What?" she said, her voice shaking as hard as her bones.

"Do not let it go, my Layna. Not yet."

"No! It's over!" She yelled, struggling to make it so, to go back to that place where he was holding her close to him, but he kept her at arm's length, and she hated him for it.

"Jack's dead," he said, "but we are alive. You have remembered so much. So much! But I need you remember one more thing, please Layna. One last time. I promise. I know you don't want to. If it was not important, I would not ask. I need to know everything Jack told you. Is most important."

"He didn't tell me anything," she said. "That's what I was trying to tell *them*!" Tears gathered in her eyes like a storm coming on. Why wouldn't he hold her? Why wouldn't he let it be over?

"Could you walk us through it, Layna? One last time?" Petras' gentle voice reached her.

"Whatever you remember," Thurman said. "It won't truly be over, not for the rest of us or for you, until you remember it to the end."

"I can't. Not again. Can't you see? It *hurts* to remember."

"Layna, I'm sorry we were late," Leo said. "We did not hear what you tell the others. I am sorry, but I need you do this for me." He stated it as a fact, with no ulterior motive.

Oh, how she wished for just one ulterior motive. Just one. But not the immovable Leo.

She took a few ragged breaths.

"Nothing made any sense," she began. "He didn't say or do anything that would change the world." She moved slowly around the cave, massaging her wrists, as she spoke and wiping dirty tear tracks from her face. "We talked, he rummaged through my purse, made a

CHAPTER TWENTY-TWO

Κάλλιο γαϊδουρόδενε, παρά γαϊδουρογύρευε.

IT'S BETTER TO TIE YOUR DONKEY THAN TO GO SEARCHING FOR IT AFTERWARDS.

big game of everything, lied about it, and buried a flash drive."

"A flash drive?" Leo looked as though he would leap out of his skin.

Petras perked up as well. "That's right! I remember! You said something about Jack burying a flash drive behind a rock."

"Yes. He dug a hole behind that boulder, the large one."

"Which side?" Leo took her arm. "Can you show me?"

Layna led him to the right side of a six-foot slab near the rear of the cave. Leo started to squeeze behind the rock, but gasped when he scraped his side.

Thurman came up behind them, bleeding a little through Leo's undershirt. "Here, let me try. Keep talking, Layna. What else happened?"

"Nothing. He acted very strange. He buried the plastic bag and covered it with rocks and pebbles, like to commemorate the spot. But you can't even see it from here. And everything would have washed away by morning tide, right? It made no sense."

No one appeared to be listening.

"Petras, your knife," Thurman said. "The blade's longer than mine."

Petras handed it over. Thurman leaned back as far as he could. He blinked, straining to find something, anything. Layna could see him sweating with the effort.

"Thurman, don't strain yourself; you're wounded. Here, let me do it."

Knife in hand, she squeezed between the rock and the wall of the cave, feeling around until the cold steel struck something. She worked the blade, pushing and shoving until she could work it slowly up the side of the massive rock and into Thurman's hand.

Petras and Leo both crowded in to view the zipper bag containing a small, black case. And inside the case, a flash drive.

"Got it!" Leo yelled, kissing Layna on the mouth.

She was too tired to be excited about anything. "I'd like to get my camera while we're here," she said quietly. "It's buried about two feet in front of the rock."

Leo turned to her with narrowed eyes. "Why did you bury a camera? What is in it?"

She shrugged. "Vacation pictures, mostly, but there are some of my Aunt Stella and pictures of Florida I'd like to have."

"Of course," Leo said, his voice gentle now. "Show me where."

Layna moved quietly to the nondescript place where, in a trance, she'd dug frantically in imaginary sand. Still holding Petras' knife, she knelt down and tested the soil until she located it. Another plastic zip bag. Holding it to her chest, Layna returned the knife to Petras and thanked him, then turned and walked slowly out of the cave and into the sun.

Petras followed, helping Thurman with his sulky prisoner. Then Leo with the flash drive. Everyone moved slowly, in varying degrees of pain.

Just beyond the cave entrance, from the corner of her eye, Layna thought she glimpsed a hand among the broken rocks, a hand that had once belonged to Balios. She caught her breath, but after reliving death by harpooning, it seemed irrelevant. Besides, it would disappear by morning. Interpol would do damage control. She envisioned men in white who come in the night to have it clean by morning. Sounded like a song. For some reason, the image brought a smile to her tired face. It was finally over. But in her heart of hearts, she wondered if she'd ever get the image of a harpoon high against the night sky out of her head.

Thurman helped her into the boat and sat next to her, easing onto the hard seat while Leo took the helm. Petras dumped Rhouben unceremoniously in the gunmen's canopied boat. Slowly, both boats made their way to Stafylos, to a waiting helicopter, a waiting car, and safe harbor.

Then, God willing, home, to Skopelos.

By the time they got back to Leo's house, they all showed signs of fatigue. Layna looked longingly at the sofa and thought how perfectly lovely it would be to hug a pillow to her chest and maybe take a little nap. But the men shoved weariness aside, rummaged up a pot of hot coffee, and gathered around the dining room table. Petras patched up Thurman's side, declaring it a flesh wound, while Leo inserted the flash drive into his laptop, and though she struggled to stay awake, Layna found herself drifting away. Finally, she stumbled to the sofa and collapsed.

After eliciting a promise from Leo to wake her the moment they found anything, and drinking the shot of whiskey he handed her, she drifted off. The drone of voices faded in the distance, and the last thing she recalled was Petras calling Dr. Liatos—something about Leo's knee and getting a shot—and Leo saying there wasn't time. She drifted awake when Thurman covered her with a throw and a look of immense gratitude, then gave in to the sandman.

At some point, the voices stopped and silence hung in the air so heavy, it woke her. The men, still crowded around the laptop, were quiet. Something was wrong.

"Great pictures of Athens," Thurman said.

"Spectacular," Petras said, "just what we needed. Tourist snapshots."

Leo pulled the flash drive out of its slot and threw it on the table.

Layna rubbed her eyes and tried to awaken herself to at least a functioning level. Across the room, Leo leaned over, his arms braced against the wood, and lowered his weary head in defeat. It tore at her soul. They'd been through so much. What had gone wrong?

She thought back through the confusion in the cave and Jack's meaningless, ridiculous games. Step by step, she rehashed what happened. After burying his flash drive, he'd gone through her purse, rattling on about doing the same to her digital camera. There had been no point to it at the time, but she'd gone along, even though it had angered her. She'd wanted those pictures of their so-called honeymoon, the still shots of scenes of Greek life she longed to resurrect on canvas when they got back to Florida. A single picture of the two of them from an obliging tourist. They were important, but only to her. Why would he want to bury them?

Layna reached down and retrieved the zippered bag from her purse, wrapped the throw around her, and stumbled to the table. Petras and Thurman smiled, but Leo's head was lowered in defeat. She slid her arm through his. He raised his head, looking like he'd lost his best friend, or his worst battle.

"I think Jack did something to my camera," she said, "in the cave." She handed the plastic bag to Leo. "I'm not sure. His back was to me, and I couldn't see." Still groggy, she stumbled over the words.

"What are you saying?" Leo asked. He pulled out a chair so she could sit down.

"In college, we spent a whole semester on digital cameras and flash drives. You know, going back and forth with a computer, transferring pictures and drawings, photoshop, pixels, you name it. Jack was into photography, and he'd taken the same classes the year before I did. Well, what if Jack downloaded something into my camera?"

Thurman tilted his head in amazement; his tired, blinking eyes showed signs of life again, and he turned to Leo. "If you don't kiss her, I will."

Leo obliged, kissing Layna on the forehead and regarding her as if she were the best thing since baklava. He took the camera.

Awake now, she propped her chin on both hands, determined to see it through, to stay a part of the group. Her friends.

When she awoke, she was back on the sofa under a warm, cuddly throw, and it was morning. Nitsa-type sounds creaked and banged from the direction of the kitchen. A glance at the dining room table revealed no evidence of a midnight meeting the night before. The dining table held a fresh flower arrangement. That was the only difference.

She checked her purse. Her camera lay inside the flap. A smile played along her lips like she'd broken a secret code.

"Nitsa!"

The little woman rushed in.

"Where is everybody? What happened? Where are Leo and Petras?"

The housekeeper pleaded ignorance and seemed more concerned about Layna's bruised and battered face than the fact that the men had disappeared. She retrieved a jar with a picture of a coconut on the label from the kitchen and immediately began applying it to all her cuts.

"Is good, yes?" Nitsa asked.

"Nitsa, you speak English!" Layna grinned, though it hurt to do so. She'd forgotten about her jaw.

The woman blushed and skittered back to her domain. Layna explored her abrasions and gently flexed her jaw, or attempted to. She'd slept soundly for however many hours allotted her and felt renewed. Part of her had died on Skopelos, and somebody else had arisen—like the Phoenix, Greece's national bird—and even if that someone else was seriously bruised and battered, she was itching to test her wings. She needed to move, to upset the prevailing silence and insert newness of life.

But damn it! She'd meant to stay awake and be part of it!

She went upstairs, noting Leo's bed had been slept in. A check of Petras' tangled sheets across the hall confirmed the same. So they'd caught at least a few hours of sleep, then what?

Her aching body commanded she mull it over in a tub filled to the brim with hot, soapy water. In the bathroom, she found a note taped to the mirror above the sink.

It was decided to let sleep. We have what we need. You are marvelous. We will return soon.

Leo

She dropped her head and shook it from side to side.

How could one crazy-ass Greek with broken English grab her heart one minute and treat her like a second-class citizen the next? She knew it was probably the effects of after-shock, but she teared up and grabbed a towel. Then, just as suddenly, she went from being misty-eyed to being angry. His note told her absolutely nothing. She accused herself in the mirror; there was no one else in the room.

You idiot! You don't have any information! You don't even have a cell phone! And even if you did, how could you call them? You don't have their numbers!

She forced rebellious muscles into soothing, just-hot-enough water while a recalcitrant mind stubbornly pursued the what-ifs. What had the guys discovered on the flash drive, and where had they gone? They must have grabbed what sleep they could and left at daybreak—and left her sleeping! She tried to do the math. Damn it, he promised to wake her if they found something! Wait. Had she actually asked him to do that? God, she'd been so out of it.

As steamed as her bath water, she soaked in the tub until the worst of the horrors of the cave gurgled down the drain with the dirty water and the majority of her aches receded. Nitsa's coconut oil had been washed away, so she re-moisturized, brushed her teeth oh-so-carefully, applied light makeup, and told herself that when the swelling went down someday, she might be mistaken for a human being.

Fresh clothes awaited her in the master bedroom, neatly folded on the ottoman. She made a mental note to give Nitsa a hug. Wait. Wouldn't Nitsa have some way to get hold of Leo? Of course! And Nitsa already thought of her as—okay, maybe not his wife, but fiancée maybe?—and treated her as such. Finally, bathed and perfumed, she found herself sitting on the bed with no place to go.

Okay, girl. Let's get it in gear. You sit around all day, and you'll go bonkers.

The aroma of bacon and coffee brought a smile to her face, but only for a second.

Remind me not to grin.

Downstairs, she found a glass of her favorite, freshly-squeezed orange juice waited. She took her time with breakfast, chewing slowly on the side that didn't hurt. It kept her occupied, but once

Nitsa had cleared away the dishes, a sense of restlessness returned. She attempted to drill the housekeeper for information, acting out punching a number on a smart phone, then holding it to her ear and talking and saying, "Leo? Leo?"

Nitsa shook her head. But she did it in a way that let Layna know that someone had already been there and had told her to *act* like she didn't understand. So much for charades.

"Okay," Layna said and thought it through. Maybe food will do the trick. What was that cucumber dish Petras raved about? She grabbed a wooden spoon and gestured accordingly, pretending to beat something in a bowl. Nitsa's eyebrows knitted together. Was she just being difficult, or what?

"We...make...tzat-zi-ki?" Layna said, raising her eyebrows for effect.

"Ahhhhhh!" Nitsa smiled, nodded, and walked away. But she soon returned from the garden with three giant cucumbers. She started pulling things from the cabinets as though preparing for war. Under her tutelage, Layna peeled, deseeded, depulped, sliced, diced, and otherwise mutilated her green friends.

Next came yogurt made from goat's milk, lemon juice, olive oil, minced garlic, a lot of salt, and a ton of mint flakes. It looked, well, interesting. Different. Nitsa inhaled, smiled, covered the bowl, and whisked it into the fridge. No taste test?

Layna told herself she wasn't making tzatziki to win Leo's heart—after all, she was leaving. It was a farewell dinner. That's it. A farewell dinner to thank Leo, Petras, and Thurman for saving her life.

That's what she told herself.

When Nitsa grabbed her bag for the market, Layna saw her big chance. She slipped on her sandals, donned sunglasses and a floppy hat to hide the worst of her injuries, and joined the housekeeper at the front door. To her surprise, Nitsa welcomed the company, floppy hat and all.

Layna hoped by the time they returned, Leo and Petras would be there, waiting. And the problems with Leo's business would all

CHAPTΣR TWΣΠTY-THRΣΣ

Τώρα έφαγες το βόδι, θ›αφήσεις την ουρά;

NOW THAT YOU'VE EATEN THE BULL, WILL YOU THEN LEAVE THE TAIL?

be over. And she wouldn't have to go back to Florida and bury Jack.

Yeah, right. That's what Stella would say. Stella!

Layna stumbled over a cattywampus cobblestone. Her favorite aunt, only friend, and adopted godmother didn't even know what had happened! How long had she been absent in mind and body? Could she plead an extended honeymoon? How could she tell Stella what happened, when it wasn't over yet? Or was it?

Layna smiled. That kind, sweet housekeeper could be downright aggressive when it came to melons. And yet, with the purchases completed, a happy Nitsa accompanied Layna to the shops off the beaten path. Like chums on a shopping spree, they exclaimed over jewelry, woven baskets, statues, and flowers of all sizes and colors. Layna hoped the hat and sunglasses would keep her from being identified as yet another tourist. She'd read it was rampant in countries like Greece.

With money left over from her adventure with Petras, she stayed in the background while Nitsa navigated currencies on her behalf. Her first treasure was for Leo. A beautiful man's necklace made of gold with amber beads spaced intermittently on a strip of brown leather and a wooden cross at the bottom. The perfect going-away present for a man like Leo. Something he could get for himself, but wouldn't.

And what do you get for someone who saved your life three times and counting? A polished piece of agate that shone in the sun. Perfect for a man whose name meant *the rock.*

Next, a fashionable straw hat for Stella, who wore one faithfully, every day while she tended her vegetable patch and fed the chickens. *Oh Stella, how I miss you!*

Last, a lovely scarf for Nitsa, which caused much laughter, feeble protests, and great joy.

Oops. Out of money. J. Michael Thurman would have to settle for a kiss on the cheek and a dynamite dinner. Somehow, she didn't think he'd mind too much.

Leaving the market, Layna spied the largest, most beautiful strawberries she'd ever seen. Just for grins, she started haggling as best she could with hand gestures she had learned from Nitsa. The housekeeper laughed and joined in the fun. And paid for the strawberries.

On returning to Leo's house, Nitsa ran into the garden to show her husband the beautiful scarf Layna had given her. Layna followed and selected a flower.

Upstairs, a necklace was laid lovingly on Leo's pillow. Across the hall, a polished rock and a flower adorned Petras' pillow. Stella's oversized gardening hat waited atop Layna's packed belongings, while Layna, returning downstairs to see what Nitsa had planned for the rest of the afternoon, found herself commandeered as kitchen help.

She smiled. Rule number three. Never volunteer. It bore repeating when, hands-deep in ground beef, rice, parsley, and cumin, she gained an appreciation of the immense effort that went into Greek meatballs. The pain in both wrists were brutal reminders of the plastic ties and her captor's perverted gazes. But that was another place and time.

Layna had a great time rolling some not-so-perfect meatballs in flour before browning them in olive oil and setting them on paper towels to drain. Nitsa, by now confident that her protégé was on a roll, instructed the pretty American in the finer arts of a Greek salad with feta cheese and black olives. It looked like enough to feed an army.

Speaking of army, where were the guys?

Layna tried once again to glean knowledge of their whereabouts from Leo's loyal housekeeper. No luck. So she scowled and fidgeted, her mouth salivated with hunger, her mind echoing with the incessant ringing of a dinner bell.

Where was everybody?

Like everyone else, Leo's blood was running high. With Aleksandra out of the picture, everyone had gathered at the house in Athens—it was located closer to the ports of interest. Commander Giannakos of the Hellenic Coast Guard had just arrived smoking a cigarillo, his short, stocky body far more agile than the starched uniform let on. Seeing the other three men looking the worse for wear, he took over.

"Assuming Jack Taggart spoke the truth, today is the day," he said, glancing around. They'd printed everything Taggart had copied onto Layna's camera, and Commander Giannakos had yet to view it.

"So, what do we know that we did not?" His tone conveyed a command rather than a question.

"We know *who*," Leo said. "We have compared Thurman's list of known terrorists with Taggart's list of photos and we know six of the ten."

"Again, the how." Giannakos scanned the print-outs.

"Toilets," Leo said, almost like he was spitting the word out. "Two 22-foot containers of ceramic toilets, loaded in Turkey at the Port of Izmir. Doors shut, standard mechanical seals applied, numbers recorded. In this picture, you see the truck driver, he makes the detour into alley with loading dock."

This is where the switch takes place?"

"It is," Leo said. "The driver backs up to the warehouse, the workers remove the hinges on one of the doors, then open the sealed container and make room for the men. They know what they do. The weight remains the same, but the cargo has been replaced. Taggart caught many faces on his film, but not everyone obliged."

"How do we find out what's inside?" Giannakos asked.

"We cannot, not at Volos. Wait. There is more."

Leo pulled back to a full screen image. The scent of tobacco hung in the air while everyone watched sixteen terrorists, head-wrapped and carrying automatic rifles, walk single file into the container.

Giannakos rubbed the stubble on his chin. "This—not what I expected," he muttered. "The seal, it remains intact?"

"It does," Leo said. "It is smart. Simple."

"And what is this?" Giannakos pointed to a man on the screen; the picture was slightly out of focus, but it looked like one of his legs appeared larger than the other.

Petras speaks up from behind Thurman. "A guard with an automatic rifle. You can see by the way he holds it straight down beside his body."

"And the reason I am here?" The Coast Guard commander set his face to unreadable as he squinted at the screen.

"There," Leo said, pointing. "The two men, they strain to carry a single metal container. Is different in shape from weapons carriers. Too heavy for drugs or bullets, yet the men are especially careful, almost as if afraid."

The next group of photos showed the other two men coming back—the ones who had broken the seal. Each frame, each stillshot showed step-by-step how they set about to repair the damage to the doors. There was a photo of a third man in black holding what looked like a new seal, laser-printed and ready to go. In the next picture, Jack had zoomed in and captured the container numbers. Leo almost felt sorry for the bad things he'd said about him. Almost.

The last picture showed a fourth man drilling a hole into the side of the container, high up, where it wouldn't be noticed.

"Breathing holes!" The commmander raked a hand through his thinning hair. "They think of everything we do not!"

Petras stated what the others were thinking. "They've been planning this a long time."

Leo nodded. "Once they're loaded on *Prometheus,* they are transshipped anywhere—Syria, Italy, Israel, France. With seal replaced, it will not be open until journey's end."

"So, what we do?" Giannokos asked. He leaned against the edge of the table.

Leo glanced up at his long-time friend. "I'm afraid *The Prometheus* will have to be mysteriously diverted," he said, "to Piraeus."

Giannokos glanced up, a gleam of approval in his pale, blue

CHAPTER TWENTY-FOUR

Πήρες πολύ ψηλά τον αμανέ.

YOU ARE SINGING THE SONG TOO HIGH.

eyes. "The RDM? Is true. They have a radiation detection monitor. This is good thinking. But we cannot move forward until *after* they pass through. Even then, we need Port Authority's help. Unless customs—"

"Not a good situation," Leo admitted.

"So far," Thurman added, "the men we've identified are Al Quaida."

"Is there no way to detect it after this point?"

"Not after Piraeus," Leo said. "They fasten the door again and conceal evidence showing doors ever opened. Containers, they load onto Prometheus, then shipped to other port, then other port. Like I say, detour can be anywhere once it leaves Greek port."

Thurman turned and addressed Giannakos. "The container we're tracking now originated from a trusted company in Nicosia, the Greek side, just like the one Taggart caught on film. You are familiar with these things—won't the shipment be inspected by a customs inspector?"

"Weights, papers. These are always checked, but once sealed? No. Will not be opened until it reaches destination." Giannakos looked at Leo. "The same process, it is the same at journey's end, but in the reverse?"

Leo nodded, anger like fire in his eyes. "They are using my ships for maybe global supply chain. My ships! And I can do nothing!"

Giannakos grunted. "We cannot know how far the connection stretches, why so many men, they are concealed. Bah! I do not like going into such a thing the blind man."

Leo nodded in agreement. "A lack of the evidence. This is only thing so far. It is why we must take cargo through Piraeus."

Thurman broke into the conversation. "Are you saying there's a device there that looks *inside* a container? This I have to see!"

"Let us hope we find more than toilets," Giannakos said. "Still, if we isolate container, we will have their asses either way!" He ended the thought with a malicious grin.

"I should advise Interpol," Thurman said, then frowned. "Though we won't know what they're carrying until the last second."

Giannakos harrumphed, laying his hand on Thurman's shoulder. "Then that is when we advise."

"We'll need vests," Petras said.

Thurman exhaled and turned a worried countenance in Leo's direction. "I hope you realize how far I'm stepping out on a limb for you," he said. "If you go down, I go down. And maybe we don't get up again."

Giannakos appeared offended. "I vouch for Amratsis! Would I let two civilians on major raid if I do not trust? It is my ass on line, same as yours!"

Thurman backed away, even while he stood his ground. "I'm just saying I damned well better not live to regret this."

"The same for us all," Petras replied. He stood a little taller, his voice calm as he looked around the room. "It may be none of us lives to regret this day or any other," he said, "but if a bullet finds us, let it not be one of ours."

Thurman scowled, but Leo could tell the matter was settled.

Everyone began checking phones, watches, weapons, and bullet-proof vests, knowing time was against them. Then, Petras made the situation worse.

"We'll be making a slight detour," he said, directing his words at Leo and Thurman. "I've done what I could, but if we don't get ourselves in better shape and fast, we'll endanger the mission."

"What are you saying?" Leo scowled, knowing the answer.

"I made a call earlier. Liatos will meet us at his office." Petras said. "He said 20 minutes. Tape, cortisone, and B12 should do it."

Leo caught a look of concern on Giannakos' face, but he made no comment as all four men piled into the Bentley and headed for Athens.

Special Agent Christina Panopoulos presented her slender fingers to the manicurist with a modicum of disdain, in full character, knowing that one either walked into *The Athenia Hair Salon* with an attitude of wealth, or went elsewhere. She'd been selected for the one-time back-up assignment because of her ability to present herself in a variety of personalities, her fluency in four languages, a certain history with J. Michael Thurman, and a reputation at being very, very good at what she did. The fact that she was attractive didn't hurt, though she often downplayed her appearance when the assignment required it.

Aleksandra Amratsis's cursory glance found nothing particularly useful in the woman, and she moved on. The *Athenia* did not cater to just anyone off the street. They were a full-service salon offering a spa, massage, manicures, pedicures, facials, stone therapy, aroma therapy, eyebrow-tattooing, and gossip. Agent Panopoulos had signed up for the whole treatment—why not, since the department was paying. She had already taken note of the oversized Gucci shopping bag on the floor next to Aleksandra, hidden in plain sight.

Christina Panopoulos looked around, appeared bored, closed her eyes, and waited, having seen all she needed to see of her target.

The manner in which her target swept the entire salon in a casual glance told her Aleksandra Amratsis bided her time and guarded her privacy—that she probably thought she'd worked too many years to secure her position to endanger it now. She'd gotten away with every euro she could squeeze from her husband's will and was enjoying a healthy influx of wealth from her current venture, and that's what Panopoulos counted on—that Aleksandra had grown overly-confident and would make mistakes.

André, the owner of the salon, finished discussing hair coloring with a well-endowed customer in a low-cut blouse, and he came over to do his bit. Agent Panopoulos knew he'd been rehearsed and knew the deception must be complete. She also knew, being a woman, that an arrest in his salon would not be devastating to his clientele. On the contrary, it would bring in even more customers to hear the details first-hand. But before, during, and immediately after such an event, André must maintain his innocence; he must appear as shocked as the ladies, if not more.

"André, you busy."

"Always, my dear Aleksandra. I do not see you for many weeks."

While her target name-dropped recent vacation spots and celebrities she may or may not have encountered, Agent Panopoulos took note of André's polished smile and the charming way he bent down for the appropriate greeting on each cheek, lightly squeezing the woman's shoulder in an almost intimate gesture. *Good job, André. Don't overdo it.* Before turning away, she caught a look in Aleksandra's face, like a shark that hadn't been fed in a while. *Run, André. You've planted the listening device, now get the hell away.*

But the salon owner, obviously relishing his role in a covert operation, stayed in character, complementing his high-maintenance, client.

"Ah! I see you still indulge in your favorite pastime. You have always loved the shopping, no? Your Gucci bag overflows! A successful afternoon, no doubt."

Damn it, André.

Aleksandra's eyes flew to the bag in mid-laugh, but she covered herself as best she could with even more fake laughter. The salon owner played his part to the very end as he turned and raised his hand in answer to a call from the dark-haired lady of the low-cut blouse, soon to be a blonde. Agent Panopoulos grudgingly admitted that André's talents might be wasted in a salon; his transfer of attention to another client proved perfectly natural and gave Aleksandra time to come up with a reply.

"Oh, these not Gucci," she said, in a voice just loud enough for all to hear, "they just things I give my friend Raisa in back of store. She no make much money. I help."

"Oh yes, Raisa. Excellent worker. But am I not generous as well, when many have no work? I think perhaps she is most fortunate to work in such an illustrious salon, no?"

Let it go, André. Move on.

"No, I not say that. Is hard for many, these times."

"How true. And it is generous of you to help her," André said. "Raisa is most fortunate, both in her friends and in her place of employment."

"Yes, of course. Ah, my nails—they done. Maybe I give her now."

Aleksandra gathered her belongings. A look of alarm swept over André's face for an instant, but he responded with a casual nod and a condescending smile.

That was close.

"They say he is a gay," the lady next to her whispered with a nod in André's direction.

Agent Panopoulos stayed in character and played along as any woman might, giving the matter her full attention before replying with a deliciously wicked smile.

"Trust me. He is not."

The lady formed a silent, delicious "oooooh" with her plumped-up lips before chuckling and returning to her magazine.

As if to emphasize the fun lie she'd just told, Panopoulos caught Aleksandra's glance at the departing André's buttocks before the woman rose to deliver her offering of cast-off designer clothes to her friend in the back. She didn't blame her. André had it together in one scrumptious package—distinguished, rich, and easy on the eyes. And you don't get a body like that without working out, especially when you're older. The interest was all on Aleksandra's part, though. André would never enter into any kind of relationship with someone as coarse as Leo's stepmother. And Thurman's people wouldn't have enlisted his help if there'd been any question of a romantic involvement.

Her internal alarm clock went off and Panopoulos rose to inquire discreetly after the ladies' room. Aleksandra may have allowed a moment's appreciation for André's tight ass, but Panopoulos knew the woman had more important things on her mind, if Thurman's hunch was on target and the deal in the back room went down.

Aleksandra's background had confirmed her single-minded focus on money, that the only time she multi-tasked was in a shoe store.

Once in the restroom, Panopoulos locked the door, checked both stalls, then removed the toe separators. There would be no pedicure today, damn it.

Outside, André moved calmly among his customers while preparing himself for whatever may come. He'd never been particularly fond of Aleksandra, but she'd been a loyal customer for many years.

In the ladies room, Panopoulos whispered into a hidden microphone.

"It's on. Watch the front and back. Listening device active, any of three languages possible. Be alert."

She looked around at the room the size of a closet. Mysterious whisperings into her blouse lapel while seated on a toilet in a room painted lavender seemed more than ridiculous, though it didn't come close to the time she'd run a sting operation while riding a donkey. The fact remained they'd explored every other possibility of a drop site, and the salon pushed every button. Panopoulos slipped her gun free of her thigh holster and checked the magazine.

Ready or not.

In a much larger room in the other end of the shop, Aleksandra and her friend Raisa, both older women with dark hair and even darker minds, whispered conspiratorially in a supply cupboard. Raisa verified the payoff information Aleksandra had delivered to an Afghan terrorist through her uncle—shipping dates and times, container assignments, and ports of destination, delivered as requested.

"We have done well," Raisa said. "Maybe now I quit this shit job and open my own place. You use Leo's private plane to bring the five kilos from Cyprus, no? I envy you."

"I know," Aleksandra said, oblivious to the sarcasm. "I told you long ago I outsmart that bastard stepson. I take his business, too. You wait and see. Maybe I get rid his smartass wife."

Raisa shook her head at the hatred her old friend held toward life in general. Still, it was none of her affair. Aleksandra lifted a hefty package hidden beneath a designer evening dress in her bag and set it on the table. Raisa slit it open and tasted a tiny amount on her little finger.

"Is okay," she said, "but €100,000? Depends."

"On what?"

"The market!"

"Fuck market. You know I only bring best," Aleksandra argued. "You try screw me, you stupid. When I get paid?"

Raisa got out her kit for the final test. "Money is there, in cooler behind basket," she said, indicating with her free hand. "If okay, I give €100,000 information on *Prometheus,* €80,000 for heroin. "

"I tell you don't screw! I get more in Pakistan!"

"Then go Pakistan!"

Aleksandra, already on her feet, growled and opened the cooler where the beautiful stacks of bank notes awaited her. She reached in just as the door burst open.

"Federal officers! Raisa Muhtar, Aleksandra Amratsis, you're under arrest for—"

Raisa grabbed a gun off the table. Panopoulos got off a shot that grazed her hand and gave Aleksandra the two seconds she needed to plow the two officers like an ox run amok and head for the door leading to the outside, where a third armed agent waited. Unprepared for an older woman with no compulsions about slugging him in the jaw, the man ended up on the ground holding his vitals while his attacker disappeared through a side door.

When Aleksandra headed for the alley, Panopoulos fired a warning shot in the air, which did nothing to slow the fleeing woman. But Aleksandra Amratsis was ill prepared for an agent who had lettered in track and scored high in kickboxing. Panopoulos grabbed a hunk of shoulder, slammed her against a building, and brought her elbow into the hollow of the woman's bejeweled throat. Aleksandra spit in her face. Panopoulos grinned and cuffed her, despite the many obscenities the spewed forth from the woman's snarling mouth.

Meanwhile, the not-so-efficient Raisa sat in custody with a

CHAPTER TWENTY-FIVE

Την προδοσία πολλοί αγάπησαν, το προδότη κανείς.

MANY LOVE TREASON; NO ONE LOVES THE TRAITOR.

bandaged hand, moaning her lot in life while the hair salon erupted in chaos. When the first gunshot, muffled as it was in the supply room, finally gave way to belief, André appeared, appropriately aghast. He muttered expletives, flitted back and forth, then barked commands of deepest apology mingled with abject fear to his clientele. Before echoes of the second shot had died away, ladies streamed from the salon like bees from a smashed hive, which the agents had counted on happening. The fewer customers in the way, the better. They hadn't dared empty the salon for fear it would've given everything away.

Now, women flew into the street, some still with their hair in rollers, green masques on their faces, colored separators between their toes, and pastel robes flying in the wind.

André laughed so hard he had to cover his face with a makeup towel and hide behind a coat rack while he wiped away the tears. Then, realizing a good prop when he saw one, he kept the towel and used it to accentuate his horror when stunned customers peeked out from the doorways of other businesses or hid behind ancient fountains, waiting for the all-clear.

As proprietor, he did his part to assure them—along with the curious onlookers—that nothing like this had ever happened before and would never occur again. And no, he had no idea what it was all about, but he would do his utmost to find out.

Meanwhile, he moved and gestured so they wouldn't see his stomach shaking with restrained laughter. Apart from the gossip, the salon business was pretty boring. But this? Why, it was even better than the time the angry husband stalked through the place in a tirade, waving a large knife and vowing revenge because he'd caught his wife with a fisherman.

Oh, yes. This was definitely better.

Still shaking his head, André wondered what people in the adjoining buildings must be thinking, and he knew by the end of business and possibly through tomorrow, his place of business would be overrun with policemen and Interpol people searching every nook and cranny for evidence. But after that, when the dust had settled, he'd make a fortune off of Aleksandra's downfall. Maybe the front page of the local paper, unless Interpol hushed it up. Everyone would ask to visit the infamous back room, and he would be the center of attention.

He rose, put on a most serious face, and held the door open for all the ladies who returned, one by one, as they realized what they looked like and that the danger was over.

Together, they watched Agent Christina Panopoulos help a very angry customer, knocked down during Aleksandra's attempted escape, into a local ambulance that had mysteriously appeared.

Two men came and went, lugging a Gucci bag and sacks filled with bank notes and brown parcels of white powder. Other men in gray suits arrived to help customers finish their hair colorings and nail polishings under tight scrutiny, then helped them gather their belongings, search them thoroughly, and see them out the front door. During which André produced two bottles of Retsina wine and a box of wine glasses he'd been saving for a holiday, allowing that, because "they had all narrowly escaped death," everyone deserved a drink. They applauded.

He smiled, knowing he could now replace grumbling, old Raisa with a happier, younger woman. The fact that he'd never see Aleksandra Amratsis again was of little consequence.

Silently congratulating himself on a job well done, he felt quite sure that if he was ever in deep shit again, Interpol would remember his unwavering cooperation.

And, in the end, wasn't that what mattered?

They reached the port at Piraeus an hour and a half before *Prometheus* was due, and they got to work. With the number of the container, they could locate it, isolate it, and set it up for the radiation portal monitor. A small, on-site shed became their center of operations.

Thanks to the good doctor and an agonizing needle directly in the kneecap, Leo was ambulatory, but he noticed Thurman still favoring his right side. Dr. Liatos had warned the Interpol agent there was only so much gauze and tape could do. Leo felt like the B12 shots would carry them for a while. Petras appeared in good form again, having received similar treatment despite his objections. Hopefully they were no longer a threat to the operation and could pull their own weight.

"There are other agents at Interpol, you know. All it takes is a phone call," he told Leo.

"I know," Leo replied, "but they would just form the committee and hold the webinar on illegal trafficking. We have not the time. They will have to miss the fun this time."

The Hellenic Coast Guard was already in port with ten of Giannakos' best men, along with the five agents Thurman had been able to summon on short notice. For appearances' sake, Thurman's men were immediately put to work, posing as workmen hosing down several containers and hauling boxes from one of the containers into a storage facility—they'd be called in at the last moment. Satisfied that everything appeared normal, Giannakos accompanied Thurman to the office of the port authorities to alert them as to what to expect. Two Coast Guard men were left there, in case anyone got the idea of sounding an alert and earning a few drachmas on the side.

Leo made a mental note of everything, hoping Interpol *and* the Coast Guard would be enough to deter any idiots from trying to spoil their game plan. He pulled two sets of binoculars from his backpack and checked his Glock 22 for a full magazine, as well as the extra mag in his jeans pocket. He'd left his beloved Sig Sauer behind, opting for a lighter weapon. In a sheath against his back, he carried a Glock Feldmesser FM78 field knife, just in case.

He glanced at Petras' weapon, a Browning 9/19mm Hi-Power GP35 and entertained the fleeting thought that there was really no need to get his cousin and friend involved in a gun fight on a pier, but the look in his cousin's eyes warned him not to go there.

Thurman, a Glock .34 resting in one hand, brought up the subject of protocol once again, especially now that the moment was at hand. "I still say I could get into a whole mess of trouble letting civilians tag along on a sting operation."

"You can always say you needed us for identification purposes," Petras said, then grinned.

"It is my ship," Leo argued. "I am responsible for the cargo. I don't care if you are the St. Nicholas, you still need my permission."

Thurman rolled his eyes. "Just don't do anything stupid, like die, or I swear I'll disavow all knowledge. Hell, I'll disavow all knowledge either way."

"It works for me," Leo said.

Petras held his Browning pointed up just a little. "Want me to hold a gun to your head so you can say, in all honesty—"

Giannakos, who'd been listening to the exchange, laughed while balancing a stainless steel Smith & Wesson 40 Tactical with a woodgrain handle.

Leo noted the look of envy on several faces in the room including his own. Even so, his stomach tightened. He was nervous, but hell, they all were, or should be. He'd give a fistful of euros to know if anything radioactive lay in that crate without having to open it. His wristwatch beeped. Grabbing the binoculars, he swept the area until he located the *Prometheus* at the inspection dock—the crane was being lowered in order to swing it over the platform.

Thurman mumbled an expletive. "Why can't we just drop the thing in the water and drown the bastards?"

"No," Giannakos said. "We must be sure who and what is inside. If it's a bomb—"

"Time to go," Leo said.

The four men quickly made their way to the inspection dock office, where they crowded around the port's large-screen RPM. At a signal from Thurman, his Interpol agents gathered around as well. Though no room remained, Giannakos squeezed in as many of his men as he could; most of them either stood up on tiptoe or leaned this way and that to get a look at the target.

They only saw stacks of cartons at first, hundreds of toilets. Then, shadows of over a dozen men floated amid rows of weapons carriers like ghostly images. Some of them stood; others crouched on top of, next to, and in between the cartons, all waiting to reach their destination, all waiting for the doors to open. The monitor focused on a smaller crate, seemingly impervious to detection.

"Switch to a radioisotopic identifier," the port technician muttered.

Nothing.

Leo watched a band of sweat trickle down the technician's face.

"It's shielded," the technician said, "probably lead-lined. Usually means radioactivity. I'll let YPEKA know. They're standing by."

"No, you won't," Giannakos said.

The technician eyes moved up and to the side to the commander's face. "Then you'll have to go in with a hand-held," he said quietly. He reached down and held up what looked like a space-age gun from a sci-fi comic. "It uses spectroscopic monitoring based on sodium iodine. It's a passive system, which means the detector itself doesn't emit radiation; it just detects things that do."

"*Things that do*," Leo whispered.

Exchanging glances, they watched as a crane hoisted the container up to swing it off the inspection pad back onto the landing. Leo imagined the terrorist congratulating themselves for passing the usual inspection.

Giannakos gave a hand signal. Two men stepped aside, stationing themselves against the wall to make sure nobody gave a warning; the others rushed out the door, where they scattered and began their approach to the container. Some carried tools they needed to open the doors; other carried AK47s to shoot whoever was inside. They used hand signals to communicate. No one wanted to warn the terrorists or learn first-hand what was in the box they carried. Silently, they slipped on mini gas masks. Thurman's team readied the tear gas bombs.

Leo fought to keep his breathing steady. He knew the perpetrators inside the container could do nothing until it was lowered onto the dock, but if the container stayed immobile too long, they'd get suspicious, if they weren't already. Hadn't they noted the difference in time between Volos and Piraeus?

Giannakos closed in and centered himself at one end of the container with a huge pair of bolt cutters in his hands. Six or seven of his men positioned themselves around him, armed with various weapons. Thurman and his men stood closer to the door, a little to the right, with tear gas bombs in one hand and an automatic rifle in the other. Everyone stood ready to run, either to or away from—depending on what happened.

Leo went to the left and got down on his good knee, his weapon aimed at the container doors.

Petras crouched on the ground in firing position.

Giannakos counted to three on his fingers where everyone could see and count along with him. On three, with three quick steps, he clipped the seals on both doors and they yanked open with a sudden grating noise. Thurman's men tossed in two tear gas bombs from either side of the container.

Sounds of coughing quickly changed to that of machine guns and revolvers. One of the terrorists threw the tear gas bombs back out the door and leaped onto the ground, where he rolled to one side and came up firing.

Shouts of "Allahu Akbar!" rang in the air as others followed, shooting, leaping, rolling, and running. Some tried to swing the doors back for cover, despite tears and coughing. Others used their headwraps for makeshift shields against the gas. The ones who made it out sought protection behind whatever they could find—stacks of pallets and materials awaiting shipment.

Someone got the leader in the arm, but not the arm that held the automatic rifle. Leo heard men crying out all around him; he didn't stop to wonder who'd been hit. He fired, hitting one of the terrorists in the chest.

Meanwhile, others in black holding various weapons leaped to the ground and came up shooting. One of them fired at Leo. The wood on the crate in front of him splintered. Pain seared his scalp. His eyes watered, and he wiped them clear and and fired.

He spotted four Coast Guard men on their knees, firing. Two of them went down along with one of the terrorists, spinning around and gurgling from a bullet in his neck. When he could, he glanced around for Thurman or Giannakos. He spotted Petras following the trajectory of someone running, winging him in the leg. Another maniac in black came staggering out from the far side of the container, and Petras took him out while Leo watched, helpless, as Thurman half-ran, half-limped for cover behind the crane on the pier.

Two shots split the air. One ricocheted off a crane with a ping; the other grazed Leo's shoulder. He gasped and looked up. A dark shape on top of the container confirmed his worst suspicions.

"Petras! Cover me!" His friend returned fire while Leo took off, scrambling in between boxes, lumber, and debris scattered along the pier, hoping to get closer.

Giannakos appeared at the opposite end of the container and worked his way along the side. One of his men leaped in front of the just-opened doors and shot several times into the interior. A figure jumped out and took him down, fighting and kicking. Giannakos got him with an upper cut, then struck him on the head with the butt of the assassin's own rifle.

Leo saw movement in the shadows around him, but he focused on the gunman on top of the container. He found an advantage point and fired four times, but the pings and more return fire told him he'd missed. Petras' 9mm rang out, and the gunman fell, crashing through an empty crate. Then a final shot from one of Giannakos' men, an answering groan, a splintering sound, and silence.

Leo waited, counted to five, and ran to Petras. Automatic rifle bullets tracked him all the way to his friend, then stopped.

"Got him!" Thurman yelled.

Leo made his way cautiously into the open to see what was what and who was left. The other men did the same, appearing one at a time to account for a total of 16 terrorists—twelve dead and four alive but wounded. A closer inspection of the area nearer the water began, including a body count of their fallen warriors.

Thurman gave the all clear to several ambulances on standby that arrived in a matter of minutes, then to radioactive units that soon appeared in huge, elongated, shielded trucks—men suited hand-to-foot emerged and entered the cavity of the container. Only then did Thurman glance down at a bloody, swollen left ankle and notice a stinging cut along his cheek.

Giannakos was in worse shape. He grasped his left arm and limped forward. Blood stained his trousers from his right thigh down past his knee. Once he knew the fighting was truly over, he collapsed where he stood. Thurman, unable to walk, sat down on a wooden crate and yelled at Leo to help.

But Leo, wounded in one shoulder, was using his good shoulder to assist a struggling Coast Guard officer wounded in the face, who still clutched the assault rifle he'd taken from the terrorist commando. A Russian AK-47. They had indeed been fortunate.

Two more of Giannakos' men emerged, both hurt, from the other side of the container, one with a tight grip on his right elbow to halt the trickle of blood, the other bent over and barely able to walk, his left side stained with blood. Petras appeared and helped both men to one of the ambulances where one of the Interpol men was being treated for a throat wound. Others with less serious complaints leaned against the vehicles, waiting. The whirring of a Coast Guard transport helicopter spelled hope for the critically wounded. Paramedics loaded three men in the transport and watched it rise into the air before returning to the task at hand.

Those unscathed in the battle assisted others in carrying dead bodies dressed in black to an unmarked van. The wounded terrorists were transported under heavy guard, strapped down in one of the ambulances. No sirens.

Eventually, the area cleared. Onlookers gathered along the outer perimeter, and Leo groaned inside as he realized the shitload of questions and yelling that awaited not just him, but Petras. Interpol would not be pleased they had "gone along for the ride." And they'd be equally pissed at the reams of paperwork made necessary by their actions. This time, there were too many bodies, too many contingencies for Thurman to work his magic. Damage control would take a very long time.

Leo held a gauze bandage on the gash in his forehead. Both shoulders ached, as well as his knee as it came back to life. A medic worked on a large, open wound across the right side of Petras' neck requiring a great many stitches. Leo put a call through to Dr. Liatos, then started to put in a call for a helicopter before deciding against it. Athens was only a half-hour away.

He cringed inside when three men in hazmat suits cautiously approached the interior of the container while a fourth man, also suited, passed a Geiger counter over each and every man there, dead or alive. Then two men emerged from the container with the sealed crate between them and lowered it gently into the armored van. Everyone breathed a collective sigh of relief, including Giannakos, still somewhat conscious.

"Well, old friend," Leo said and offered his hand. "You've done it. No doubt your name will go down in the histories." Giannakos managed a smile before being helped into a second ambulance, along with two of his men.

Leo found Thurman in the third ambulance, sitting in the back with his legs dangling while a paramedic tended his ankle. Leo joined him.

"Looks like I won't be dancing for a while," Thurman said, his

CHAPTER TWENTY-SIX

Θέλω να είμαι το πιο δύσκολο αντίο σου.

I WANT TO BE YOUR HARDEST GOODBYE.

face drenched in sweat. "After the x-rays, I may get that two weeks of rest and relaxation with pay in a location of my choosing—the one I've always dreamed of taking. They may even make it *permanent*."

"Without the pay, I think," Leo said. "Surely they will know we have saved thousands of lives in exchange for a few good men?"

Petras joined them, reaching into the medic's emergency kit and retrieving a large bandage for a deep cut on his right hand. He winced in pain, which immediately aroused his cousin's suspicions.

"Off with the jacket," Leo said. He brushed aside the medic who was attempting to examine his head wound.

"It is nothing," Petras said. "I have had women who have done much worse."

"We both know this is the lie," Leo said, "or your lovely Demetra would weep."

Petras grinned. "A man does not speak of such things."

"Ah! What has happened here?"

"The edge of a shipping container," Petras admitted. "It is steel, you know."

"Yes, I know," Leo said, shaking his head. "So, AK-47's weren't bad enough? You had to find some other way to hurt yourself?"

"You didn't tell me you did that on a container," the medic said, leaning over to examine it yet again. "You'll need a tetanus shot."

Petras winced. "I think maybe our friend should go to the hospital," he said, hoping to distract the medic. "The ankle does not look so good."

"I'm sure Liatos, he will be glad to give you the tetanus," Leo said.

"Damn." Petras frowned and raised his face to the darkening sky. As soon as the medic had tended the slash on his back, he got to his feet, refusing Leo's offer of assistance. Thurman joined them for the ride back to Athens, groaning aloud and squeezing his eyes against the pain.

"We'll drop you off at hospital," Leo told Thurman. "I think Petras is right. That may be beyond Liatos' experience. If you are still among the living after, then you are welcome to come to the island. My stomach, it is rumbling, and I believe the night requires much wine. If there is nothing on the table, we will find something."

Thurman grumbled, then agreed.

Leo's head hurt, but he was ravenous. Had they not eaten since yesterday? He wondered if Nitsa had gone home. Then, for the first time in several hours, he thought about Layna. He glanced at his friends, wondering if he looked as hideous as they did, or as weary. Unable to endure the silence or his deep concern for them both, he talked to stay awake.

"What do you think they will find when they open the crate?" He grabbed a handhold as the ambulance hit several ruts in the road.

"Something deadly," Thurman mumbled.

"A nuclear six-pack?" Petras asked.

Leo laughed. Thurman did not.

"Plutonium's difficult, too dangerous to transport," Thurman said. "It's easier to make at the source. The same with uranium. My money says it's a *dirty bomb* of some kind."

"Biological, like anthrax?" Petras asked.

"I don't think so," Thurman said. "It wouldn't have been sealed in lead. No need. I mean, it would have been sealed, but the detection monitor would have been able to see inside the crate. No, my money's on a dirty bomb."

"A weapon of mass destruction?" Petras looked surprised.

"More like mass *disruption*," Thurman said. "A dirty bomb can cripple a city, but something biological can wipe out thousands in a matter of days."

"I think I will trade with the Chinese from now on," Leo said, looking out the back window at nothing. "At least you know before the wine is served they will try to screw you. No clean bomb, dirty bomb. You know they are the enemy. So, Thurman, you think maybe they buy my freighters?"

"You'd sell your father's ships?"

"I am not my father, and these are not my father's times," Leo said with a sigh. "I am too old for this shit."

The ambulance hit a pothole, and they all cursed.

Petras, with one hand on his neck, looked around. "Where's the bottled water?"

Leo laughed and leaned his aching head against the insufficient headrest, wondering if he would ever make it home again. And if someone would be there, waiting, if he did.

What straggled in the front door that night was scary. First Leo with his head bandaged, limping badly. Then Petras with a white bandage on his hand, a gauze bandage on his neck, and bent over slightly, like either his back or his chest wasn't quite working. And finally Thurman, on crutches and sporting an orthopedic shoe, which he banged into every piece of furniture he encountered. None of them looked like they'd bathed or slept, yet between them they carried a sense of camaraderie and a hint of victory.

Layna completely forgot how mad she'd been when no one had showed up to eat the food she'd spent all day preparing, and Nitsa carried on unphased, as if this sort of thing occurred on a daily basis.

"You come," she said, touching Layna's arm. "We get food now."

"But they're exhausted!" Layna said. "Look at them!"

Nitsa rolled her eyes and spoke to the men. They looked at her like she was crazy.

Leo gave his bossy housekeeper a tired, little smile. "Come on, Petras."

Layna watched the two men climb upward, slowly and painfully, to wash up—or so she surmised by Nitsa's hand gestures. Thurman opted for the kitchen sink in lieu of the stairs, pointing to his orthopedic shoe. Just as Layna and Nitsa placed the last dish on the table, Leo came downstairs with Petras not far behind. They looked reborn with scrubbed faces, sparkling teeth, and fresh clothes.

Leo wore his new necklace. He walked up to Layna and brushed a kiss across her forehead, his hand at the small of her back. "It is beautiful," he whispered. "It is good to be home."

Petras thanked her as well, minus the kiss. "I'm going to ask Demetra to make my agate into a necklace or wristband. She is expert in such things."

They joined Thurman at the table, which seated six. Leo motioned for Nitsa to join them, which apparently occurred often enough for her not to be surprised or embarrassed. Then, the housekeeper proceeded to point out every dish Layna had either prepared herself or helped Nitsa prepare. The gleam of pride in Leo's eyes—that Layna wanted to become a part of his life, even in a small way—did something wonderful to the pit of his stomach.

Leo uncorked the wine, and the meal began. The table seated six, so Nitsa took a chair along with everyone else; she still managed to serve the food, supervise, and take part in the conversation.

Layna discovered she'd developed a love of Greek salad and feta cheese. Even the cucumber yogurt dip Petras had raved about, which she thought a bit heavy on the garlic, was consumed wholeheartedly by all present. The meatballs were gone by the second passing, and what she'd thought enough to feed an army disappeared between excited snippets of AK47's and talk of battle scars.

"What were they smuggling?" Layna asked.

Thurman looked around the table. "I don't think we can get into that without breaking five or six laws on confidentiality, need-to-know, and the involvement of innocent civilians."

"Don't you think it's a little late to be concerned with what I know or don't know? It sounds like you just involved two civilians in an Interpol sting operation, or did I miss something?" Layna studied each man's face for the verdict and settled on Leo.

"They used one of your ships to smuggle something major connected with terrorists, and since Aleksandra is missing in action and no one's even mentioned that fact, I take it she's involved somehow. And all of you were able to do what you did because of the information Jack obtained and I delivered. So give it up. After Rhouben and the cave, I think I'm entitled."

"Weapons of mass destruction," Leo said, "on the *Prometheus*."

"A routine operation," Thurman added.

"Oh, I think not," Layna said, glancing around the table. "You're all beaming through your bandages—a blatant display of pride well-deserved if these men you mentioned were Al Qaeda." Her gaze centered on Leo again. "Was there much damage to the ship?"

"No. But it doesn't matter one way or the other," Leo said quietly. "I'm selling the *Prometheus.*"

"What?" Layna's mouth abruptly closed.

"Over one operation?" Thurman gestured with open palms.

"You were serious, what you said in the ambulance?" Petras tilted his head and regarded his friend and cousin.

Leo leaned over and laid his hand on Petras' shoulder. "What if it happens again, my friend, and we are on our own? I consider this for some time. Things have changed. Shipping, it is not as it once was. But now? Besides all the bribes, the taxes, the insurance—which is enough to purchase small country? What I see in the future is spending fortune covering our asses by sending every container through the detection monitor at Piraeus. And while we do this, what will escape through the ports at Volos? No. I am done. I no longer enjoy."

"What's a detection monitor?" Layna asked.

"You don't need to know," Thurman muttered. He gave Leo a warning look.

Layna pulled away from their talk of terrorists and smuggling. How had her world grown smaller in one afternoon? She looked around the table at the brave men she had come to know, struggling to survive in an environment that had apparently become unsupportable. A world vastly different from the one she had known in Tallahassee—or had she simply not seen it, not cared enough to look.

Her life as Ellie, secluded and protected, seemed a lifetime ago. As Layna, she'd survived things she never thought possible. She felt a sudden urge to talk to someone who'd known her in that other life, the one before Leo, before Skopelos. Aunt Stella came to mind—she'd tried to tell her before, but Ellie didn't want to hear it. Layna was ready to listen.

"Thurman, I need a phone."

"Sure thing." He stretched out his good leg and struggled to reach into his jeans pocket.

"No, I meant a phone of my own. I don't seem to have one. And I'd prefer to make the call in private. I need to let them know I'm alive."

"Oh. God, I'm sorry. I didn't even think of it. If it's an emergency—"

"Someone from before?" Leo's voice sounded quiet, gentle, wary.

"Yes," Layna said, warming to her subject. "She wears overalls and a gardening hat and talks to chickens. You'd love her."

"Over-alls?" Petras asked.

"Jeans with a top attached."

"Ahhh."

"Tomorrow okay for the phone?" Thurman made a note to himself.

"Perfect. Thanks."

"No problem." Thurman gave his favorite amnesia victim a tired smile. "Now, if there's nothing else, as much as I'd love to stay and chat while the blood coagulates in my lower leg, I'm overdue to elevate. And hopefully take enough meds to sleep till noon." Thurman looked around for his crutches, and Leo rose to help his Interpol friend.

"And then, Leo," Thurman said, taking his crutches in hand, "I'm going to talk you out of this stupid idea of getting out of the shipping business. I mean, we won! The bad guys know we're on to them. They won't try anything for a while."

"My point exactly," Leo replied, helping Thurman to a standing position. "Next time, they'll be smarter."

"Not necessarily. Oh, speaking of smarter, I meant to tell you—and Petras here. That phone call I got right before we left for Piraeus? Aleksandra won't be bothering you for a very long time. We got everything on tape. Took her out before she could walk off with the bank notes. We're tracing them to the source. I'll let you know what happens."

"Does this mean I'm not pregnant anymore, and I can go back to Tallahassee?"

Everyone turned to Layna. Leo and Petras looked at one another.

Thurman sat back down.

"Apparently we missed something at the cave. Leo and I arrived a bit late, so we could make an entrance. Mind filling us in?"

Layna took a deep breath and feigned innocence. "I don't know.

It's pretty confidential. On a need-to-know basis."

Leo and Petras laughed. Nitsa had left the table. Thurman's eyebrow went up.

"Okay, I deserved that," he said. "But if I'm going to help you, it *is* a need-to-know."

Layna bowed her head in agreement. "Then here it is. My name is Eleanor Townsend. I grew up in Tallahasee, Florida. My parents are no longer living, but I have a crazy aunt named Stella."

"Who wears over-alls," Petras said.

"And likes chickens," Leo said.

Thurman laughed and motioned for more. She acquiesced.

"From what I recall, I led a quiet, unassuming life in a huge Victorian house, until I vacationed in Greece and became embroiled in smuggling, kidnapping, and murder."

More laughter.

I'm socializing! I'm funny! I can do this! Okay, on to the hard stuff.

Layna turned to the man with the gorgeous necklace and bedroom eyes. "There's something I've wanted to ask you for some time," she said, her voice suddenly quiet. "Once and for all, am I married to you, or am I not?"

Silence slid down like the curtain on a bad play—in complete silence.

"Thurman?" Leo said, finally.

After clearing his throat, Thurman inched his way forward mentally, wincing against the pain in his ankle and foot. "I thought you explained it to her."

"Thurman!" Leo growled.

"As I'm sure you realize by now, you needed protecting," Thurman said. "We couldn't put you into a WITSEC program—I mean, we could—but we didn't want you waking up in Wisconsin or Alaska and going into shock. Did you see that movie, *The Long Kiss Goodnight* with Samuel Jackson and Geena Davis? No? Well, you should've. Then again, maybe not."

"The *marriage*, Thurman."

"I'm getting there, Amratsis, lay off." He turned back to Layna. "Let me know if I'm repeating myself or anyone else in the room who shall remain nameless. Anyway, like I was saying, we needed to keep an eye on you until you got well. A hospital afforded little or no supervision. Anyone dressed as a doctor or nurse could just walk in and—do whatever. A private sanitarium posed the same problems. More difficult, but still possible. Military bases and detention centers held more proportional risks than advantages, because we needed to know the moment you came back to the world of the living."

Layna motioned with her hands for Thurman to get to the point.

"We studied our options and decided the only way for you to be both *housed* and *protected* was to disguise you and hide you in a place no one suspected, but where someone would be readily available at all times. The one criteria was it had to be someone familiar with what really happened. We changed your appearance as best we could and did what we thought appropriate at the time, which included the added protection of being married to a well-known shipping magnate with a bodyguard whose house could be kept under constant surveillance."

"You dyed my hair black and bribed a priest."

Leo noted how Layna's voice had gone cold. At another time and place, such a retort might have been considered humorous.

"I see your point, though at the time it didn't seem ludicrous," he said. "If you became seriously ill, and we had to rush you to a hospital—you get the picture. The decision was a difficult one for all concerned. We had to act quickly—the nurse was one of our people. You were in no danger there."

"And the marriage?" Layna asked.

"We didn't bribe anyone. We simply found an Orthodox priest, fully ordained, who understood the seriousness of the situation and was willing to sign the necessary papers."

Layna followed the thought to the end, and came up empty.

"I'll reword it. Last time—is the marriage valid or not?"

Leo looked at Thurman. Petras pressed his lips together and

glanced at Layna through lowered eyelashes, then at Leo. Thurman regarded them both.

"If the marriage wasn't legal," Layna said, "then neither am I, not here in Greece. It might not mean a lot to you, but it's my life we're talking about."

Thurman rushed in to smooth out the situation. "You're right, of course. And we can get you into the WITSEC program now. You can begin again in another city, another country. It's up to you. Or you can stay in Tallahassee."

She smiled at the man who'd once tipped his hat to her in the moonlight. "Spoken like a true INTERPOL operative, Thurman. You tell me much and say nothing at all." Her fingers played with the wooden grooves in the table. "So, to capitulate, my choices are: (a) get a falsified birth certificate, passport, and driver's license to go along with the falsified wedding certificate and raise goats on a rocky mountain on the northern slopes of a foreign country; or (b) get all of said documents in my real name, live in my parents' house, and continue to look over my shoulder for a terrorist dressed in black the rest of my life. How am I doing so far?"

"Good," Thurman said. "A bit harsh, but hey. If it's the marriage you're worried about, we can get you annulled the same way we got you married. It's just another document, right? And the Al Qaeda thing's over. I doubt they even know you exist. We have what we need; there's no reason for them to bother with you anymore. In fact, you're—"

"Expendable? Superfluous? Dead meat?"

"I was going to say free to go. And as my *partner in crime*, I'm sure Leo won't mind putting you up until you've reached a decision concerning your future. Right, Leo?"

"Of course. Whatever it is needed." His voice was hoarse; he cleared his throat.

"What I need to arrange is a life," Layna said quietly. "But first I need to take my husband's body to Florida for a proper burial, unless—I don't even know where he is—his body, I mean." She turned

CHAPTER TWENTY-SEVEN

Αμαρτία εξομολογημένη, η μισή συγχωρεμένη.

A CONFESSED SIN IS HALF A SIN.

to Thurman. “Has it already been taken care of?”

“He’s in Athens,” Thurman said, “in a morgue. By law, nothing can be done without the permission of a family member, so we were waiting until you—until you were ready.”

“Then, as Mrs. Taggart, I can ship him back to the States for burial?”

“Absolutely. I’ll cover the cost of shipping, your ticket, the works. About the plot—if you let me know where—”

“Thank you,” she whispered. “And can you guarantee that, as Mrs. Taggart, my life will no longer be in jeopardy? That my involvement ended at the cave?”

“Absolutely.” Thurman nodded.

“But not my involvement with you, and Leo, and Petras, and Nitsa.” Layna lowered her eyes and stared at the table, then sat up straight and took a deep breath. “I’d like everything done as soon as possible, please. I’m thinking two or three days. Thurman, can you arrange things by then?” Her eyes glittered with tears, but her voice was quiet and even.

"No problem," Thurman said. "As you may or may not know, Interpol doesn't normally handle this end of things, but I'll pull in some help from another department and get it done."

"Thank you." Her focus turned to Leo. "It's rather late for a hotel. It seems I must accept your kind offer to sleep on your sofa a day or two longer."

"Don't be ridiculous. You can have the bed. I will sleep on the sofa."

"No, it's your house. I'm your guest. I'll take the sofa."

"Before you two start duking it out," Thurman said, "I'm going to hobble my way home." Thurman rose from the table and looked at Leo. "It'll take me a while to get to the pier, where I hope to find a helicopter waiting. In case I don't—"

"Then I shall drive you," Petras said, picking up Thurman's backpack and equipment.

"Oh, one more thing. You'll need a passport." Thurman started to set one of his crutches to the side. "If you could step into the light—"

"Of course." She stood by the fireplace.

"I'll take it," Leo said suddenly.

"Okay. Now, Layna, you don't have to smile, but it would be nice if you did, maybe one last time?"

"For my friends? Of course." Her shoulders relaxed, and her face softened into a lovely, thoughtful pose that stopped the hearts of every man in the room. Thurman openly admired her while Leo and Petras clicked away.

"Thanks," Thurman said for them all. He cleared his throat. "Don't know about you, but I feel like I've been through a war. Petras, be sure and thank Nitsa for a great meal—she seems to have disappeared. I don't blame her. Mrs. Taggart, I'll take care of everything we discussed, possibly before my head hits the pillow. Or first thing in the morning."

"Perfect." Layna turned away to capture a runaway tear with her fingers.

So now I'm Mrs. Taggart. When did I stop being Layna?

Petras opened the front door and stepped through to wait outside. Layna put both hands against Thurman's chest and gave him the kiss on the cheek he so richly deserved. He was, after all, family. He sighed and smiled, then hobbled away on his crutches.

Layna claimed the sofa before Leo could, glad it was finally over, that nobody would be trying to kill her. She sighed to think that, after everything she'd been through, the most difficult part still lay ahead.

Endréus Leonidas Amratsis.

It was late afternoon, almost evening.

Leo busied himself in his office and started the paperwork necessitated by the assault on the shipping container. He'd promised Thurman to help, but his attention lay elsewhere. He walked into the kitchen for bottled water, but it was an excuse to stand next to the open window so he could hear Layna's voice one more time. She sounded quiet but confident. What would happen once she saw Jack's coffin and became familiar with her old life?

Layna paced back and forth on the paver stones, her voice interjected with pauses. "And you can get me a passport both as Eleanor Townsend and as Layna Amratsis before I leave for Florida? Perfect. You'll have them delivered here? I'll look for them. Yes. Yes. And thanks, Thurman. I appreciate it. Yes. You, too."

Leo sighed and returned to the office. He accessed the section on cargo insurance that would hopefully explain, in words a mortal could understand, what he was covered for in the event of espionage. Would they call it an Act of God? He cursed and rifled through the desk drawers looking for papers.

Nitsa fixed moussaka and salad for dinner. Layna had wine to try and lift her spirits. She heard Petras on the phone with his wife, promising he would be home soon.

If I leave now, I'll never get to meet Demetra and their four lovely children.

She heard Leo telling Nitsa he would eat later—he needed to check something at the cabin cruiser.

If I leave now, I'll never ride in his boat again and watch the wind in his hair.

She took over the computer and played catch-up on what had happened in the world outside while she'd been occupied with kidnappers and smuggling. She settled for international news on a British station. Nothing had changed much in her absence. Crime, taxes, interest rates, and inflation up, terrorist attacks in the Middle East, anti-Semitism rising, crooked politicians, thousands starving in Africa, ongoing battles over health care and education, a new strain of contagious virus, and political unrest worldwide. Greed remained a universal constant.

She turned it off and helped Nitsa with the dishes, listening for Leo's return, though not much could be heard over the clatter of plates, the hum of the dishwasher, and Nitsa's constant chattering in Greek. Finally, she trudged upstairs to pack her meager belongings in the suitcase Petras had resurrected from a closet. It was a bit travel-worn, but so was she.

It tore at her heart to see things she'd purchased during outings with Petras and Nitsa, things that found a final resting place in a canvas bag. Her sketch pad and pencils went in next. When she began removing her bottles of lotion and perfume from their coveted place atop the counter next to Leo's aftershave and cologne, she couldn't do it without crying. Their things belonged together, side by side. Last came her floppy hat and sunglasses. She looked out the window through the trees and into the heart of a halo moon. Night approached with a sense of urgency—it was her last on Skopelos.

She fled downstairs, through the kitchen, and onto a patio awash in translucent blue, an otherworldly stage of such beauty, she breathed it in like a soul dying, seeking the best of sea and sky before the end. A wistful smile played across her lips.

Moon over Skopelos. Every woman's dream or a damned good song title. Take you pick.

She reclined onto a lounge chair and stared into the heavens, dreading the dawn. So much to take in, to remember. So many people and places, all waiting to be painted. She reveled in the recurring urge to open a shop in Skopelos Town and sell her paintings to locals and tourists. She could learn to speak fluent Greek and wait until the customer had his or her hand on the doorknob before yelling, "Y'all come back now, hear?"

Laughter came as freely as the sudden breeze that caressed her like a promise. When had she gone from recluse to rebel? She felt giddy, impatient to explore the cracks and crevices of her new life.

The kitchen door opened. Petras joined her, straddling a chair and breathing in the night air. I'm surprised," he said. "I thought you would not like the patio, after what happened here."

"Things seem different now," she said.

"Yes." Petras studied the paved stones glowing in moonlight. "Have you decided what you will do?"

"Try and tie up the loose ends of my life, I suppose. Florida is an option. There are things I must do. I've learned there are no guarantees. You can get stalked by assassins or get run over by a bus. Is it true what Thurman said, that they won't bother with me now?"

"All they wanted was the flash drive."

They sat a while longer in shared silence. She pondered the question Thurman had put on the table, and now Petras. What would she do?

"It's funny," she said. "I can't think beyond Florida. Not yet. What I really want to do is find a Greek restaurant, dance the scarf dance to the bouzouki, drink Retsina wine, and watch the hasapiko. I'm probably mispronouncing everything, but I don't care. I want to see a real live belly dancer and smash a plate on the ground."

"You say the words fine," he said, laughing. "You are a strong woman. I pity the plates."

"And more than that, I want to see a dance I saw in a movie with Anthony Quinn and Jacqueline Bissett."

Petras rolled his eyes. "Not the one where he is supposed to be the great Onassis!"

Layna squealed with delight. "That's the one!" Petras laughed, but she sensed a restlessness in him that matched her own, like he was waiting for something. Then finally it happened.

"I would ask you something," he said, ducking his head. "No, it is not my business."

"After Velanio, you can ask me anything."

"Then I will ask, because he will not. "Do you love my cousin?"

Layna looked at the moon and the faraway pinpoints of light.

"I have offended you?"

"No, not at all. You are concerned about him. I understand that."

"Like you, I cannot see what the future holds."

"You mean if he sells the *Prometheus*?"

"It is only a ship."

"What are you saying, Petras?"

"I look out for my friend. When you have wealth and power, you attract the women like flies to shit. I am careful that my friend isn't treated like the shit."

Layna laughed. "That's a horrible comparison and a ridiculous concern. I have money of my own. But even if I didn't—I mean, if I wanted Leo just for his money, then why would I be leaving? He could be penniless, and I would still want to be with him every day for the rest of my life."

"So you will bury your husband and come back."

"If it were only that simple."

"Is it not? It is either philos or agápē. Erotica we will set aside."

"What?"

Petras got up, turned the chair around, moved it closer, and sat back down.

"Philos, the love between friends, and agápē, the—how you say—*unconditional* love. It is sometimes used to explain the spiritual love between God and man, but I think this also happens between a man and a woman. For some, the agápē is too much. This is why it's reserved for God. You understand?"

"I think I do. It's like a bond between two souls, right? In America, it's called *soulmates*."

"Yes, that is how a love should be."

"And have you ever felt it, this agápē?"

"I have," Petras said. "There was someone, when I was very young. I could not live without her."

"What happened?"

"I married her."

"Demetra?"

"Yes. She is my soul-to-soul," he said. "Have you been as fortunate?"

A period of silence passed. "Not until now," she said, listening to the wind in the trees.

Petras scooted closer. "I do not understand. I was there in Athens when you mourned for your husband. This was not agápē?"

Layna's throat tightened. The words struggled to get out.

"I will tell you the awful truth, my friend," she said, "but only because you *are* my friend and I owe you my life. But first, you must promise never to tell Leo. It's too painful."

Petras nodded in the moonlight.

"In Athens," she said softly, "Jack's death invaded my dreams. His real death. But it was so horrible, I pushed it beyond where it could hurt me, and locked it away. Yet, somewhere in my muddled mind, I knew he was dead. Do you understand?"

Petras waited.

"I'm sorry. I don't know how to say the rest. Anyway, in Athens a terrible sadness reached into me when Jack died, and I grieved. Continually. Every waking hour. Even in my sleep. But it wasn't because I loved my husband." She paused, forcing herself to say the words aloud. "It was because I couldn't love him, no matter how hard I'd tried. And that, dear Petras, makes me a horrible, unfeeling person who deserves no happiness, no pity, and no Leo."

Petras studied the ground, then slowly shook his head.

"I disagree. I remember how it was in the cave, what you said. You cried hard and deep. I don't think this would happen just from guilt. Only a truly good person would regret an inability to love. No, it is not a failure on your part. If the love is not there, you cannot make it be so."

"Thank you for that," Layna whispered. Her voice broke, and she looked away.

"I am not a priest," Petras said, "but you would not be stoned for such an offense. Not even in Greece."

Layna raised her eyes to his, unsure whether to laugh or to listen.

"It is more common than you think," Petras said. "Marriages have been arranged here for centuries—in other countries as well.

CHAPTER TWENTY-EIGHT

Που πας ξυπόλητος στ› αγκάθια;

HOW IS IT YOU ARE WALKING BAREFOOT ON THORNS?

But the husband and the wife understand this from the beginning. They do not expect the agápē. You did. And it was not there."

Layna returned her hands to her lap, fighting the urge to wring them until nothing was left that hurt. The two sat in mutual silence a while longer before Petras spoke again.

"I have seen you together," Petras said suddenly. "It is in your eyes. It is agápē."

"I'm afraid so," she whispered.

"Afraid?"

"Yes. It goes so deep, it scares me. That's why I must leave and soon."

"But if there is love in your heart, why must you say goodbye?"

"I have not been asked to stay."

"Leo is Greek and very rich," Petras said with humorous indignation. "He does not ask."

"I am American and very poor," Layna replied, with the hint of a smile. "I do not beg."

"Ah. Now I see the difficulty." Petras shook his head in disbelief. Another silence fell before he spoke again. "But this is not the only reason you leave, I think."

"No. I need to bury my husband. There's no one else, and it's the right thing to do. Even if it's just a graveside service, he deserves at least that. Then, there's the house in Florida my parents left. I need to decide what to do with it. And I miss Aunt Stella. She's the only family I have left."

"Family I understand. But the rest? These are just *things*."

"You're right." Layna sighed and looked away, "but there's something else I must do, something that goes much deeper. I don't know if you'll understand this, but I need to find Ellie and make peace with her. There's a battle going on inside me between who I was and who I am now. I don't know what caused the thing that happened. Well, I do—but, what if it happens again? What if something small or insignificant triggers this thing inside me? I can't do that to Leo, or me, or anyone else. Not again."

"Yes. These are things to consider," Petras said, "but you and I have faced death together, and Leo is more than family, more than friend to me. Do not put so many miles between you. What you have, it can wither and die if it is not fed."

"Thank you, Petras. I'd give anything just to know he feels the same about me as I do about him, but maybe by going away and getting well, then looking back, we'll both see things more clearly. Oh Petras, I put him through so much because of what I was going through. And now, I'm going through something different. In a matter of months, I went from being Ellie Taggart to being Layna Amrsatsis, and now I'm supposed to be Eleanor Townsend. I don't know who I am anymore."

"I still think you're making a mistake. And I think you will miss us very much."

"I already do."

"Is there nothing I can do, Elayna?"

"There is! You can tell me what that means. Don't names mean things?"

"They do. In Greek, this name means *Truth.*"

She could only stare at him as he got up and returned to the house. A short time later, in the smaller hours of morning, on the sofa beneath a throw, Truth cried herself to sleep.

Once awake, Layna felt a restlessness to get what had to be done, done. A special delivery envelope awaited her on the dining room table. Inside—a new passport, another envelope with several hundred US dollars, a cell phone with a charger, and a note from Thurman letting her know she had 1000 minutes of talk and text, and not to use them all at once.

When Nitsa walked past the table, she saw the items all laid out. She stopped. "Why passaporté? You leave, you break Mr. Leo heart. Why you do? You make tzatziki. We make together. You sleep in bed. Why you go?" Nitsa fled to the kitchen on the verge of tears.

Layna took a deep breath and folded the blanket, then left it on the sofa with the pillow on top. She went upstairs to change—grateful for something to occupy her hands and mind—when the bathroom door opened and Leo appeared. A glance told her he was well-rested, and she was glad. But it also showed her all the cuts and scrapes and bruises he'd endured.

"You stare at me," he said.

"I—thought you were gone," she said.

"No. It is not the time." He looked like he wanted to say more, but didn't.

God, he smelled good.

She grabbed her clothes, went in hurriedly, and closed the bathroom door. The musky scent of his cologne hung in the air from a bottle he'd left open on the counter. She inhaled once, then replaced the lid to keep her knees from trembling. Leo's voice reached her from the bedroom.

"Then it is your turn for the shower, no? Do you require help?"

She took off her clothes and tried not to think that moments before, he'd stood where she was standing now, naked, ringlets of water making their way over every inch of his body. She braced herself and changed the hot water to lukewarm, then to cold.

After showering, she brushed her teeth and gargled—looking in the mirror brought back the day she'd finally remembered, here in this very spot. Something about her 14th birthday. Would she ever wake up again and not know who she was? Shaking away the mess in her mind, she dressed, taking care with her hair and cosmetics, then grabbed her perfume and spritzed her neck and wrists.

All dressed up and no place to go.

She opened the door to an empty bedroom.

Disgruntled, she packed what she might need on the plane in Aleksandra's Gucci bag and felt displaced. Maybe it was the full moon. Maybe it was her life, scattered over two continents. At least her life was her own again, maybe for the first time. She itched to put it back together.

When she went downstairs, the clicking of a keyboard caught her attention. Leo seemed totally occupied at the computer, so she followed the scent of bacon into the kitchen and fixed herself a plate of bacon and eggs, toast, and juice. She sat at the kitchen table and waited.

Leo finally came into the kitchen for coffee. She drank some juice, trying to ignore the sexy, confident way he had of walking and how just watching him walk excited her. By the time he sat down at the table, her mind went blank. He waited, then began.

"Nitsa told me you received a package," he said.

"I did," she said. "Passport, money, cell phone."

"You go to Florida then?"

"Yes."

"What day?"

"I'm not sure."

"Do you wait still on Thurman?"

"I do. As soon as the, uh, transport can be arranged. A few days maybe? I know you must be anxious to have your life back, now that all the excitement is over. How long do these things take? Are there people to bribe?"

"There are always people to bribe," he said, smiling. "If we do these things ourselves, it takes weeks, not days. But this is how is done in my country. Thurman will see to everything."

"Right."

"So Layna," he said, then, "Ellie. What will you do?"

"I've considered finishing my master's degree in art. Did Petras tell you I'm an artist? No? Well, it's what I do, I mean did. After a while, I'd like to come back to the Greek Isles and paint."

"You are good. I see your sketchbook."

Her stomach clenched. "You looked at my sketchbook?"

"Of course. It is how we find you."

"Oh." Layna couldn't stop the heat rising up into her eyes. "Maybe I'll study law. Can you see me as a lawyer?"

"No," he said. "I do not think you care much for the law. I don't say you would not be good, but there is much corruption, much prejudice, little justice. There are still men who do not want the woman to be intelligent."

"You're kidding. Still?"

"For some, always."

"Speaking of lawyers, I suppose we should look into—I mean, well, have you thought about an annulment?"

Leo's dark eyes flashed. He rose from the table, then turned.

"Why you say *superfluous?*"

"What?"

"When Thurman is here, you say you are superfluous, unwanted, unneeded. Why do you say? You go 5,765 fucking miles away thinking *this?*"

Layna grinned. "You checked the mileage charts?"

Leo just looked at her.

She searched for a more suitable reply and found none, failing in her struggle to remember the context of what she'd said or how to get out of the now-impossible situation. From Petras, the question would have been a natural part of the conversation. From Thurman, perhaps a show of genuine concern. Coming from Leo, it sounded suspicious, forced.

He waited, mind and body tensed. She focused on his chest, just above the second button on his shirt where, beneath, there beat the heart of a lion.

"You stare at me," he said, his eyes unreadable, "again."

"You're right," Layna said, miffed that she was affected and he was not.

He walked out.

Okay, that didn't go over well. Putting Leo on the spot like wasn't on my to-do list, but damn it, there are things that need to be taken care of.

She sat at the table, misplaced in time, remembering the day Leo had told her they were married in order to protect her, but she didn't need protecting anymore. She was better now. So why did he get so angry? And why did she feel nervous and sweaty after a nice, cool shower? So far, she'd embarrassed Petras and offended Leo, and Nitsa didn't speak English. Would that make it 0 for 3, or 3 for 3?

For a moment, she considered finding a USA news station on the big screen in the living room, just to assure herself she wasn't invading a foreign country. After all, she'd been gone a long time. And here on Skopelos, it had proven difficult to imagine a world outside. But she was on her own now, or soon would be.

She took a deep breath and raised her eyes to the ceiling to exhale. If things were this difficult, maybe she should get a room in a hotel until she left. Only Florida didn't feel like home anymore. And now, she didn't feel so welcome here, either. She gave up and went upstairs.

The room was cool and dark from the shade trees all around the house. She saw the bedroom curtains were open to the breeze coming in over the king-size bed. Odd, not noticing that before. When she walked to the window and looked out, her eyes were drawn immediately to the patio directly below. And the two empty lawn chairs.

She could hear the leaves scuttering over the paving stones.

From Leo's bedroom window, on a quiet moonlit night, a person could see and hear everything taking place on the patio below. She groaned inside. How could she have been so stupid? He must have heard every word she'd said in her *mea culpa* to Petras. *Dear God.*

Fighting back useless tears, she raised her eyes to the world beyond, to the town and the water in the distance. It still took her breath away, the stark beauty of Skopelos, this little piece of heaven. She could stay here. She could stay here and paint. No, it was too much and not enough and no good. They'd just clashed over a culture thing, a misunderstanding, a word flung out because of her stupid pride. Her heart ached at the thought of leaving, and tears stung her eyes. Maybe Petras was right. Maybe agápē's too hard for ordinary mortals.

She heard the door open and close. Leo. She felt his presence with each step that brought him closer, closer. In a matter of seconds, he was behind her, their bodies not quite touching.

"The window," she said, almost in a whisper, "was it open *all night?*"

He waited a minute or two, then answered, almost apologetically, "Yes."

"Then, you heard."

Leo remained silent, but she knew. *Oh God, I've got to get out of here.*

"Why do you do this, when you belong here, with me?"

A hot flush pushed upward, ever upward, like she was catching fire. She half-turned, but with Leo directly behind her, the bed to her right, and the dresser to her left, she endured a fight-or-flight moment Leo seemed to sense. He placed his hand on her arm to keep her there until he'd said what he needed to say.

"You love me," he said. Then he leaned over and whispered it again in her ear, his heart in every word, his voice steady, sure, like he was stating a truth everyone knew except the one person who needed to say it aloud. "It is important to listen when the heart speaks," he whispered. "Are you listening, my Layna?"

His hand left her shoulder and slid down her arm. The earth shook. Or was it her body?

The essence of the sun and sea washed over her.

"Do not regret," he said. His words were measured and quiet.

"You should not have listened! It was a private conversation!"

"That does not change the truth."

"You could have closed the window."

"No, I could not."

He moved his other hand to her waist, where it resided, quiet and respectful like an uninvited guest. He leaned over and spoke next to her ear in a hot whisper.

"Do you not hear? You are my breath," he said, caressing her arm as he spoke. "I want so to hear you say the words. Do not regret speaking them aloud. If you stay silent now, it is from pride. Listen to your heart, my Layna."

Her soul cried for the beauty of his words, but another voice rose inside her.

Remember what happened with Jack!

CHAPTER TWENTY-NINE

Το μυστικό της αλλαγής είναι να εστιάσετε όλες τις ικανότητές σας, όχι στην καταπολέμηση της παλιάς, αλλά στην οικοδόμηση της νέας.

THE SECRET OF CHANGE IS TO FOCUS ALL OF YOUR ABILITY, NOT ON FIGHTING THE OLD, BUT ON BUILDING THE NEW.

Fear flooded her mind and body, a torrent of things she hadn't confessed and never could—the horrible knowledge deep inside her that she could never satisfy a man in bed. What could be worse? She already knew the answer—to love a man with her whole being for the rest of her life and never have him, never make him truly happy. Would he make love to her and find out what Jack had said was true, over and over? Would he give up and send her back to the nothingness of her life in Florida, carrying pieces of her heart in a broken-down suitcase?

Run. Now.

"*I—have—to—go.*"

He kissed her neck, found a nerve somewhere on the path to her shoulder, and sank his teeth into it. Electrical charges shot up her spine and into her brain. When she leaned back against his chest, her body rejoiced in the surrender.

"*Betrayed,*" she whispered. Hot tears fell from her closed lids.

"Do not say no," he whispered, kissing her neck, his breath hot, demanding. The palms of his hands spread across her abdomen and slid downward.

She wasn't aware she moaned until he turned her around, and his mouth found hers, his hand against the small of her back, pressing her body into his. Her hands took on a life of their own, sliding up his shirt to encircle his neck. Never had she felt such power, such a joining of mind and body. Vast and strong like the sea.

"Leo, no. You don't understand." She stammered, barely able to get the words from mind to mouth and out. Don't you see—I could go to bed tonight one person, make love to you, and wake up somebody else in the morning, like Athens! I can't put you through that! I won't!"

It was enough.

Leo paused at the resolve in her voice, the sudden stiffness in her shoulders. His hand left her arm and hung at his side. He didn't speak for a while. He could make her; he knew how. But he would not. One day, he would make her to weep from joy, not regret. She must come to him on her own, and surrender. It was the only way.

He willed his hand to return to her shoulder, where it rested.

Sensing every move, she waited. For a moment, she thought he would lean into her and will her to submit, and she would. But they remained, with an ocean between them, as time and all its possibilities sank into the afternoon sun.

"If you go," he said in a husky voice, "you do not come back."

Her mind searched frantically for what he meant. Was he stating a fear or asking a question? Was he telling her not to come back if she left him?

Leo waited for her to deny what he'd said, to say the words he hoped to hear, even as Layna struggled to understand them.

She sighed. It didn't matter. *Truth,* come what may, was the name he had given her. "There are times," she said, "when I never want to leave you." Tears blinded her, and he released her.

For a moment, she couldn't even open her eyes. When she did, it was to his own, blazing with desire, filled with questions and a terrible sadness, a hunger that matched her own, and a pain she couldn't face.

Lowering her eyes, she stepped away and slipped the wedding ring from her finger, holding it out to him.

"You are mine! How can you leave? Do you still not know I love you?"

"Oh, Leo, how can you? I don't know who I am, and neither do you!"

Words, whispered before, now lashed out in anger and demanded a response. Layna's hand moved automatically to his chest, to the spot where the heart resides. That's when she withdrew from him, much as a spirit departs the body. It was true what they said, that love is one body inhabited by two souls.

"I don't know how long I'll be gone—"

He closed his hand around hers with the ring still inside her trembling fingers, then held her, brushed his lips across forehead, and let her go. When he spoke, his voice was gruff, unyielding, unloving.

"Go home," he said. "Bury your husband." He walked out of the bedroom and down the stairs; the front door opened, then closed.

She knew he wouldn't be back until she'd left for good. The irony was that now, she couldn't bear to stay there either. She'd ask Petras to find her a hotel for the night, and she'd get in touch with Thurman in the morning.

It didn't matter if things were ready or not. It was time to go.

Leo leaned back in the chair, a bottle of ouzo and a shot glass on the round table in front of him. The smoke-filled room and sad music from the bouzouki suited his mood, even when a firm hand gripped his shoulder. He growled at the interruption, but smiled when he gazed up at a familiar face.

"Petras, come. Drink with me!"

His cousin noted the bottle was still three-quarters full. Good.

"You are serious?" he asked, pulling up a chair. "Ouzo? In the afternoon?"

"I am always serious with the ouzo," Leo said, "but it is not yet serious with me. There is still the anise, some clove. I still taste it. This tells me I am sober. I want to get drunk, but I'm—"

"Too old for this shit," Petras said. He grinned. "I think it is a good thing. They do not call it *the dry hammer* for no reason. Ouzo can turn from a blessing to a curse."

"You are too late, my friend. I am already cursed. Layna and I have said our goodbyes."

"Leo, why not go home? Nitsa will make you a wonderful meal. It's quiet there."

Leo glided his forefinger along the rim of his glass. The crystal hummed. He was surprised they had crystal. It was not the best of clubs. "It is the quiet which bothers me," he mumbled. "I do not wish to see her face all around me, to smell her perfume on the stairs, to hear her voice. No, my friend. Not tonight."

"Layna's gone," Petras said in a quiet voice. "She's staying the night at the Melrose, five blocks over. Her plane is scheduled around mid-morning tomorrow. Thurman will see her off."

Leo stared at his glass for the time it took him to digest the information. "I wonder if Onassis had such trouble with Jackie Kennedy."

Petras laughed.

Leo looked around and sighed. "She burns hot, then cold, and forces me to do the same."

"She is leaving," Petras said. "Is one night all you want her to remember of her last night in Skopelos?"

CHAPTER THIRTY

Eísai i anapnoí mou

YOU ARE MY BREATH.

"I would take it, my friend. But I know it would not be enough. We are of one soul. Of that there is no question. And yet, she will not have me."

"The first year was difficult for Demetra. She was a daughter, then a wife, then a mother. And still very young. It was not easy, bringing these things together in her heart and mind."

"Shit, I know she is troubled," Leo said, "and that she needs time. But I need her."

Petras laid his hand on Leo's shoulder. "If it is not to be—making the love, I mean—at least send her away with good memories of her last night on Skopelos, no?"

"I am not the one who sends her away," Leo said, "but what do you say? And why must I take the advice from someone too young to know?" His eyes flashed with renewed humor.

"Make it a happy goodbye, as much as you can. Give her the flowers. Buy her a dress. Take her to a fancy restaurant. Do what you would do for any young woman. *Dikastírio tis.*"

"Court her?"

Petras tilted his head and grinned. "The same as if she lived with her father and you were a young man wishing to marry—unless it has been too long and you have forgotten how."

Leo burst out laughing. "Careful, my friend. It has only been a while since I wished to do so. This does not say I have forgotten how! But you are not listening. She wants nothing to do with me!"

"And you accept this? You heard what she said. She listed all of the things she wanted to remember of Skopelos and her time with us."

"Every word is carved in my heart. But that was then. If I ask now, she will say no."

"Den archidia?"

"Fuck you! I have the balls! I also have the sense not to beat them against the bricks!"

"All right. All right," Petras said. He propped his chin with his fists and thought. An obvious solution came quickly to mind.

"Would Layna say no to—Demetra?"

Leo gave his conniving cousin a second look. A plan began to form. He felt rock sober now. "Do you remember what size she takes, the time you took her to the market?"

"I do."

"And shoes?"

"Aiyee! Seven, I think. I cannot remember everything!"

"I will take care of the flowers," Leo said, his eyes and mind racing. "You will make the reservation, at that new restaurant that just opened." He stopped and held up his hand. "Wait. What do I say? No. You are on holiday. This is your time with Demetra. I cannot ask you to give up your time together."

"Do you not think the evening will pass more smoothly if there are four, rather than two? If you do not mind, we will come with you. Demetra's mother will watch the children. It will be a dipló rantevoú. The double date!"

"You are certain?"

Petras slapped his cousin on the back. "Trust me. Demetra will thank me many times, in many wonderful ways, if I should take her to a nice restaurant with music and dancing."

Leo laughed long and loud, considering the possibilities.

"So?" Petras said, pulling his chair back. "Reservations for four?"

"A *date*. Yes." He gave a half-laugh, stood up, and pulled his jacket from off the chair. "It pisses me off that I didn't think of it first!"

"Think of it as a way to make it really hard for her to say goodbye," Petras said. "Oh, and I'll need your credit card."

Leo rolled his eyes and threw some bills on the table for the ouzo he couldn't drink.

"Let's get out of this shit-hole."

She got off the international call with Stella after a very long chat; she was glad Thurman said he'd foot the bill for the hotel room.

When she told her aunt the official version according to Interpol—that Jack Taggart had died in a boating accident while working as a photojournalist—she heard silence on the other end, then words of sympathy so genuine, Layna felt bad about lying her ass off.

It was a tale more readily believed than one involving espionage or murder by harpoon. Then again, anyone who'd known Jack might not have been that surprised by the grisly explanation or the fact that it involved terrorists and drug-smuggling.

After letting her know she was returning to Florida in a matter of days, Layna had closed by telling her aunt she was fine. Yes. Okay. Liar, liar, pants on fire.

All was forgotten when she answered the door and saw Petras with a shopping bag and a lovely, dark-haired woman at his side—a woman who smiled and held out her hand in greeting.

"I am pleased to meet you," she said in a shy voice. "I am Demetra, wife of Petras."

"Demetra! Of course! Come in!" Layna showed Demetria to the sumptuous sofa. Petras took the armchair so the two women could sit together.

"I've heard so much about you," Layna said, taking in the hazel eyes and flawless olive complexion, then the dark blue sheath and the diamond pendant that graced it. And matching earrings. Wow. And Petras, sporting a dark navy jacket and designer jeans. His cream-colored shirt looked silky, costly, and un-Petrasy. But then, she hadn't seen him off-duty before.

"What's going on?" She asked. "Both of you look so beautiful, so handsome."

Petras grinned and handed her the bag.

The first thing she removed was wrapped in soft, brown paper and tied with twine. Whatever it was, it hadn't come from a tourist shop or a market stall. When she undid the bow, the paper fell away to reveal a backless halter dress in shades of blue and green, a silky material that flowed through her fingers when she held it up in amazement. Next came a pair of three-inch lace-up heels in gold lamé, individually wrapped. The last offering was a gorgeous, open-weave shawl with four feet of fringe that pulled the entire, costly outfit together. That, and a pair of gold earrings in a small box. Two circles. A small blue circle in the middle, surrounded by a golden circle on the outside.

"This is all so beautiful," Layna whispered. "Why—"

"They are from Leo," Petras said, "for this evening. He knew you had not the time to purchase them. Also, he worries the shoes will not fit. Can you try on?"

Layna laughed and complied. The shoes fit.

"How did he ever find all of this in one afternoon?"

"Let us say he had help," Petras admitted, glancing at his wife for confirmation.

"It is all good?" Demetra blushed. "Then, we are here to ask you for the date."

Layna laughed and gave them a strange look.

"It will be the four of us, together," Petras said, coming to the rescue. "My cousin desires to take you on a date to a nice restaurant, and lacks the courage to ask. But do not say I tell you."

Demetra intervened. "There will be food, wine, dancing—everything to make your last evening on Skopelos a joyous one."

"This is incredible."

"Then, you will go?" Petras asked.

"Of course I'll go."

Petras breathed a sigh of relief.

"I am glad," Demetra said, reaching over to hug Layna. "If it is all right, we wait for you to dress. Then, we meet Leo in the lobby."

Layna hurried to the bathroom and did what she could in the short time allotted. The dress slid onto her body like it was designed for her. She leaned over and brushed her hair upside down. When she stood up, it cascaded, thick and luxurious, well past her shoulders. She enhanced her makeup. Her hands were shaking. A real date! With Leo!

She laced up her heels, loving the added height. She didn't want to bother with a purse, so she took the card for the hotel room and started to slip it into her bra, only to remember she wasn't wearing one. Not with a backless, halter dress. Oh well, Leo could keep it for her.

Draping the shawl off-shoulder, she noted that it helped conceal at least a tiny portion of the outrageously low vee in the back that showed way too much skin. She looked in the mirror one last time, added an extra spritz of *Passion*, and told herself she was ready.

The three of them rode the elevator down. Leo stood a moment, admiring his handiwork on the lady in question before walking over. Layna caught her breath. Dark jeans hugged his thighs. His white shirt opened at the collar, revealing the necklace she'd bought him, and a gray jacket completed the outfit. Casual rich and drop-dead gorgeous were words that came to mind. All of which took second place to the sexiest walk of any man she'd ever seen, on-screen or off.

He handed her a single, long-stemmed, crimson rose surrounded in baby's breath and enclosed in green paper, with a matching crimson ribbon. Leaning over, he kissed her softly on the cheek right next to her ear.

"I breathe again," he whispered.

Her intake of breath told him she didn't know what to do or say, which was good.

And she didn't. The last time they were together, he'd slammed out the door. Now, he was bringing her flowers, buying her gifts, taking her out?

"Could you keep this for me?" she asked, and handed him the room key card. "I don't seem to have anywhere to put it."

Leo's gaze flickered briefly to her cleavage and back again, which evoked a decidedly wicked gleam. Layna overlooked it, gave him a brilliant smile, and took his arm.

Outside, Petras and Demetra joined hands. Leo and Layna did

the same. Together, the two couples made their way through the heart of Skopelos Town, two streets over and three streets down. Gulls cried against the setting sun. Shadows lengthened where boys played soccer on cobbled pavements. Mothers called to them, saying it was time to go home. Lovely aromas wafted on the air from open restaurants. Other couples passed and nodded in greeting, some their age, some younger. Old people smiled and passed them by with knowing glances. Mediterranean music and a lovely sea breeze made the evening perfect.

Some vendors had closed down for the evening, while others remained open to catch the late-night crowd. There were no automobiles to honk or zip past them, no gears to grind or doors to slam. And no tourist buses to threaten the pedestrians. People strolled happily along.

Petras laughed at a braying donkey that refused to get off his rear; the owner paced back and forth, threw his hands in the air, cursed vehemently, and pushed the animal from behind. The donkey finally gave in, or gave out.

Several eateries had the standard blue chairs and round tables outside for casual dining beneath the stars, but the double doors they eventually faced required a dress code and a reservation.

Leo and Petras had dined in restaurants of all levels of class and condition, but for Layna and Demetra, the white tablecloths, huge dance floor, and crystal chandeliers represented a new world. Layna recalled the little restaurant she'd fled to after escaping the embassy so long ago— so vastly different than what she now witnessed. Yet, Leo seemed at home in both.

They were shown to a small, intimate table advantageously situated at the edge of the polished, wooden dance floor. They were seated and given menus, but not before Leo had asked the maître d most discreetly to move Layna's chair six inches closer to his own.

Satisfied with the proximity, Leo laid his arm along the wooden back of the chair in question with a casual air of self-confidence that told every man there she was his. Layna, mesmerized by the chandelier and trying to remember to sit up straight, took little note of either the protection or the assumed ownership.

Balalaika music played, but Layna observed a bouzouki as well. Music accompanied a lively discussion of which dishes to order from a menu which was printed in both English and Greek. Layna, already starving, was soon confused by too many options. With Leo's help, she chose the lamb. He did the same, and ordered for them both, adding Assyritiko wine for its black-cherry flavor. Petras and Demetra ordered Shrimp Saganaki with a white wine called Agiorgitiko.

Layna and Demetra took in the sights and sounds around them, while Leo, when not called upon to answer a million questions, feasted instead on his date—how the silky material of the dress he'd chosen draped her breasts perfectly, leaving just enough to his very active imagination. He noted, too, how the colors played against her eyes and complemented her dark-blonde hair. She looked so beautiful, he couldn't even conjure up the image of her half-dead body beneath the fluorescent lights of the doctor's examining room. Nor did he wish to.

Later, when she accompanied Demetra to the ladies room, he admired her from the back as well. Her Venus de Milo shoulders, slender neck, and flawless skin. The sexy swishing of the fringe across her lower body. And what her new high heels did for her legs, her ass? My God.

"*Beautiful*," he whispered, then realized he had said it aloud. He glanced at his cousin, almost embarrassed. But Petras agreed.

"We are the most fortunate of men," Petras said. "Look at them. A ravishing blonde and a dark-haired beauty. The two most beautiful creatures in the restaurant."

"In all of Skopelos!" Leo declared. The cousins laughed together, perfectly content in knowing that every male in the building envied them their good fortune. As they should.

When the ladies returned, chatting quietly as they approached the table, Leo struggled to keep his admiration to himself and failed. He leaned over.

"You are pleased with the gift?" he asked. His eyes roamed her breasts and more as he spoke. "The dress does much for what is here. The color, for your eyes, your hair. But you have not yet thanked me."

Layna gave a little gasp. "I was so excited about seeing you again, I forgot!" She stopped, realizing she'd admitted what the rule books said not to. But one look at his grin said it had been the right thing to say.

"How did you guess my size?" she asked. "Everything fits so perfectly."

Leo paused to find what he wanted to say. Her perfume was intoxicating.

"I never *guess* where love is concerned," he said. His hand moved her hair away from her face as he spoke, brushing it back from her neck. In doing so, he stroked the hills and valleys of naked skin. She shivered, as he knew she would.

"As for the size," he said, continuing to play with a strand of her hair, "I wish to say I have imagined holding you. But I cannot. You are more than fantasy. You are Truth. So I admit to having excellent advice from a friend."

Layna's heart pounded at his seductive words and the way he touched her hair. A furtive glance at Petras confirmed that *the friend* had heard and approved.

When Layna's shawl slipped down onto the chair, Leo rescued it. But he took his time retracing the highway home. Beneath the basket weave, hiding from curious eyes, his fingers whispered across her skin from the lowest part of her spine up, up, and up to the back of her neck. Layna's shoulders responded to the maddening tingles with almost imperceptible jerks. Her intake of breath did things to Leo's insides that he very much wanted repeated.

Layna longed to flirt back, but she'd never really done that, certainly not with Jack. When she'd tried, it always ended in abject failure. But she recalled something from a book she'd read. Leaning over, she removed a petal from the rose atop the table, brought it to her mouth, closed her eyes, and breathed in the aroma. She played with it, moving the soft color across her slightly open lips while pretending to listen to Petras' conversation. Finally, she slid the rose petal seductively down the side of her throat, almost absentmindedly, before returning it to the table.

Leo stared at her throat, thinking of other places he'd love to explore with rose petals. He had hoped to impress the woman he loved, and now, she was flirting back, alerting his senses in the process. If he could only control the passion that raged through him and remain a gentleman. And yet, he was enjoying this attention very much.

The food arrived. Throughout the meal, the two couples laughed and talked. Leo continued to keep possession of Layna's hand, while Demetra and Petras acted more like newlyweds than a married couple with children. Leo had long witnessed their devotion and continued attraction for one another, but Layna had not. Now, she considered them the perfect role model for lovers.

She took note of the way Petras ran the tips of his fingers slowly up Demetra's arm, or the way Demetra leaned into her husband's space to whisper things that always seemed to delight him. She lived for his smile. He lived for her touch. Demetra may have been shy, but when she looked into the eyes of her husband, Layna could swear she saw proof of fire. They continually held hands, both above and below the table. Even the manner in which they genuinely listened to each other's words, confirmed to any but the legally blind that Demetra and Petras were soul-to-soul.

Layna noticed they didn't bring up their children in conversation. Rather, they focused on each other, taking full advantage of their date night. She wondered how many nights like this they had had since Petras started working for Leo. Few and far between, she wagered.

She gingerly felt her way around questions that developed in her mind, unable to comprehend the fact that Leo wanted her enough to entice her. She hadn't seen him in public, but she would have imagined him to be proud, even severe. How old was he, anyway? He hadn't offered the information, but he'd mentioned starting graduate school later than most. What did that mean?

While Leo engaged in a lively discussion with Petras regarding the man playing the bouzoki now, Layna attempted to guess his age. She decided mid-thirties. A very young, very handsome mid-thirties. And since she would turn twenty-five in a matter of months, that would amount to what? Baby Bear's porridge. *Just right.*

Leo turned to her to explain the difference in strings and sounds between a balalaika and a bouzoki, and while Layna appreciated his bringing her into the conversation, it went way beyond a need to know. He realized that fact and grinned.

"You are right," he said. "The music, it is not to dissect like the frog. It is to hear with the heart, no?"

It amazed Layna how funny Leo could be. He laughed openly, freely. And he caused her to do the same. Together, the two of them discovered little things they didn't know about each other, like their tastes in wine. Or the admission on Layna's part to a partiality for tequila, though she confessed to an appreciation-in-progress for the black cherry wine Leo had ordered.

After which Demetra related a story of a favorite uncle, rolled home in a wheelbarrow from a local bar by two friends, equally drunk. The aunt was awakened by laughter and the flashing lights from several cell phones. The uncle's grown children, watching from the window, laughed till tears fell from their eyes. The aunt was not amused.

Throughout the meal, no mention of ships, kidnapping, memory loss, or leaving.

Layna reached over and took Leo's hand. It was so natural, he didn't even pause in his conversation with Demetra describing how his mother used to make lobster stew. Not for the first time, Layna could almost swear that Leo was the one who hadn't been out in a while.

The dishes were cleared away and a new bottle of wine presented.

CHAPTER THIRTY-ONE

Το βόδι έχει μια σκέψη, ο άλλος ο άλλος.

THE OX HAS ONE THOUGHT, THE PLOWMAN ANOTHER.

When the waiter left, Leo sighed, reluctant to let go of Layna's hand even for Retsina. Besides, too much wine might interfere with his plans for later that night. His attention turned to the two men walking toward the center of the dance floor, where they linked arms. Layna turned as well, and her face lit up. She glanced at Petras. "The hasapiko?"

Leo's cousin nodded and grinned. Leo remembered as well, having set to memory every word she'd spoken on the patio that night. This was one thing on Layna's wish list about to come true. Her winning smile and enthusiastic applause at the end of the performance sealed it.

The scarf dance came next. Men and women rose from the audience to form a long line on the dance floor. Layna looked at Leo, expectation scribbled across her young face. But Leo shifted his arm on the back of her chair and merely sighed.

"Don't you know this one?" she asked.

"Of course I know. It is just...I do not to dance in the public."

"Even Onassis dance in the public," she said, teasing him with his broken English.

"What is this with Onassis?" Leo shifted his weight in the chair. "For now, I am content to watch. And to hold your hand."

Layna couldn't find any fault with such a romantic sentiment. She gave up and followed the line of dancers, the leaps, the intricate footwork, and the unity of rhythm. The person at the front of the line danced what his spirit demanded before passing the scarf to the next person, the line weaving in and out and around.

After a brief intermission, the lights dimmed. A veiled belly dancer swirled onto the stage in full costume and posed with arms held high. When the violin began, a slow clinking of her finger cymbals, or zils, began their hypnotic rhythm that spoke of ancient ruins and Bedouins in tents in the desert. Layna watched, amazed by the ripple and flow of the woman's body.

Demetra reached over and touched her arm.

"Is not so difficult," she whispered. *"I teach."*

Layna glanced at Leo. His countenance brought her to a standstill. He had distanced himself from everything but the performance and the performer. His glittering, burnt-umber eyes never left the dancer's gleaming black ones that flashed at him from above the veil. And yet, Layna could swear he saw every move of her body. After stepping side to side with a jerk of the hips, the woman twirled and jerked her way to within two feet of their table.

Layna threw a plea for backup in Demetra's direction, but Petras and his wife were busy critiquing the dancer's expertise as well. Left to her own devices, Layna swallowed in disbelief as Leo's gaze finally shifted. He grazed up and down her body, slowly, respectfully, while the dark eyes flashed and cymbals clanged in Layna's brain.

Reaching out, Layna placed her hand firmly on Leo's. The woman shimmied her shoulders ever so lightly, causing other parts of her to do the same, and Layna dug her fingernails into the skin on the back of Leo's hand. A brief flicker of the eyes was his only reaction before he smiled with a barely perceptible nod of his head.

The woman caught his meaning, glanced at Layna, lowered her head ever so slightly, and jingled her way to the next man, the next table, all without missing a beat.

The second man proved more appreciative. He ogled her to his heart's content and buried a €100 banknote in her costume, just north of you-can't-go-there. The woman smiled and returned to the center of the floor to end the dance. Following polite applause, Layna wondered if Demetra could ever teach her to dance like that. Then she remembered. After tomorrow, she wouldn't be here. She felt homesick, but for which country?

She jumped when Leo leaned over and spoke to her.

"I tell you, I am well-known in Skopelos," he said. Laughter tugged at his lips. "I have done this many times. But I have never seen a dancer dismissed by the laying on of the hands!"

Demetra and Petras laughed quietly.

Leo held up the back of his hand. "I have the scars to prove!"

Petras' wife clapped her hands and laughed aloud. Petras shook his head in disbelief.

Leo addressed those present. "Only a woman in love would be so jealous. I think it was the color of the face that frightened the dancer away, when it turn pink and then red like a pomegranate. Or maybe the eyes, when they are green fire?"

Leo continued to chuckle over the entire episode. Layna wanted to smack him.

Demetra had the good manners to cover her mouth, but Petras laughed aloud. What made Layna's blood boil was that what Leo had said was true. At one point, she could have easily set fire to the tablecloth with sparks from those same green-fire eyes. Or ripped the zils from the woman's fingers and clanged her to death on the wooden floor!

Blushing horribly, Layna mumbled an apology and made for the ladies room.

Demetra looked at Leo, then Petras, then followed her.

Layna leaned against the long counter, facing away from the dreaded mirror. She knew her face was still red, and if she gave in to the overwhelming compulsion to cry, then her eyes would match.

What the hell just happened?

Demetra came in and quietly joined her, leaning against the counter with her back to the mirror. She waited. They stared in companionable silence at the gray-tiled wall, its sealed beauty marred by an automatic hot-air hand-drying machine. Layna wondered if it worked on damp hearts. She felt as though she were drowning all over again, but this time in humiliation. Yet another culture thing.

"I must be out of my mind," Layna whispered. "I thought it would be different with Leo. I thought what we had—"

"What you have is beautiful," Demetra said, "You only did what he wished you to do."

Layna turned to face her, hoping to read her lovely face and discover what she meant by such an odd remark.

"When you think and move as one," Demetra said, "then what you have is truly beautiful. With the belly dancer, Leo think one thing and you another. He could have said no to her right away. I have seen him do so many times before."

"Then why—"

"Like you, he wishes you to fight for him. And you did." Demetra smiled while Layna chewed the inside of her mouth.

"Did it never occur to you that he would wish the same?"

"No," Layna replied. "He's strong, confident."

Demetra sighed. "Love takes strength," she said. "But I think you know this." She turned around and washed her hands in one of the sunken sinks, then dried them beneath the machine.

Layna sighed and studied her shoes.

Demetra touched her arm. "You are right to be angry. It was not right, what he did. You are not used to our customs, and he use this to make you jealous. Have you never been with him with other women?"

"I've never seen Leo interacting with anyone other than Nitsa."

Demetra laughed at the thought. Layna did the same.

Layna was surprised when Demetra took her hand.

"Men live to make the sex," she said quietly, "and women live to make the man. To make him to hold her, to say it is all right. Always it is so. No matter the money, the power. It is only when two move as one, like the oxen and the farmer, that both come together and make a field ripe and golden. You see?"

Layna nodded her head. "I made a fool of myself," she said.

"You claimed him as your man," Demetra said. Her eyes sparkled. "Come. We go back. Leo honors you. He will make the amends. You will see. You must forgive him as well."

"Forgive him? For what?"

"He worked hard and spent much for you this night. Do not take that from his heart."

Layna allowed Demetra to escort her back to the table, where Leo rose to help her with her chair. He poured a small portion of the black cherry wine in her glass, his hand lingering over hers, his eyes no longer laughing. Recalling Demetra's words, Layna forgave him, knowing her over-reaction came from years of being ridiculed for being different. And from her entire youth spent in another country where they had no clue how to really play the game. But Demetra was right—Leo had no right to use her ignorance of their customs just to get a rise out of her.

Layna reached over and kissed Leo on the side of his face and saw relief fill his lovely, dark eyes. He brought her hand to his lips to make the amends, as Demetra had predicted, and Layna allowed her fingers to linger a while next to his lips.

Petras watched and waited, wondering what his wife had told Layna in the ladies' room. He knew his wife to be the wisest of women, despite her young age.

Leo wavered between relief and anger. What he'd wanted to happen had happened. But somehow, it had come back into his face. He had tried to pull Layna from her dream world where a man waits forever for a woman to make up her mind. To get a reaction from her, to get her jealous. And did she ever! Now, he wondered if he had ruined their special night.

He leaned over and whispered in her ear. "I am to apologize," he said. "I love you too much."

Layna closed her eyes against the sudden tears. Leo made her emotions continually run hot and cold between joy and rage. Would it always be so?

She slowly turned to face him, words of forgiveness on her lips, but the high-pitched chords from a violinist caused both of them to jump and shift their attention to the couple approaching the center of the dance floor.

Leo immediately recognized the music from that movie Layna loved so much, though he would never admit to having watched it. The one with Jacqueline Bissett playing Jacqueline Kennedy Onassis. *The Greek Tycoon.* He'd known what it was the moment she'd described it to Petras that night on the patio. He'd never admit to it, because he knew Anthony Quinn was Mexican, but the man did a pretty good job. Now, his heart lurched at the thought of seeing anyone dance this way with his Layna. No, he must someday dance it with her. Yes. But for now, he took her hand, breathed deeply, settled his shoulders, and waited for the dance with no name to begin.

Layna dared not look at him. She could practically feel the wheels churning in his head about something or other. She looked at Petras instead. This was the dance she'd told him about on the patio that night. But Petras had laid his hand on Demetra's shoulder, both of them focused solely on the dance floor as the lights went down. A softer light illuminated the couple on the dance floor who faced one another, arms out straight, eyes together.

They began to sway, but in opposite directions. The man moved fluidly to his right, passing the woman as she swayed just as gracefully the other way. Again and again, side to side, never coming together, yet never apart. Riveting, teasing, determined, and proud. The music changed slightly as other instruments were added. With his arm now linked in hers, they circled one another, adoring, challenging, their eyes still locked. Layna remembered to breathe. More than anything she'd seen or heard, this was the dance that said *love is the life*.

The tempo increased, along with the tension. The woman whirled and positioned herself in front of the man, facing away from him, her long, black hair swaying across his chest. Arms straight out, they stepped to the side, back and forth, as one, bodies touching. The music changed yet again and grew even faster, separating them. Hands held high, they celebrated their own independence, the freedom of being themselves, the joy of life. As they laughed and twirled, Layna did the same in her mind, her senses heightened.

Then, the violin made the woman sway like a reed in a gentle breeze as she reclaimed her position in her lover's arms, her back against his chest. He leaned over with her and worshiped her breasts with his eyes. She smiled knowingly, and stretched her arms up and out in a gesture of surrender, acceptance, weaving love through the air with delicate fingers that made the air come alive around them, or recalled her dance of freedom moments before.

As if it was the last time they would be as one, the man reached out and covered her hands with his own, then lowered them both, swaying ever so slowly, ever so sexually, to gently enfold her. The woman turned her face to one side, with a sad, triumphant smile. They were together, but for how long before the music began again? The man buried his face in her hair, and the music slowly ended. The lights dimmed. Everything stopped.

Thunderous applause brought Layna back to reality. Stunned, she felt the trickling of tears on her face and the agonizing grip of Leo's hand on her own. She turned to him, knowing from his smoldering eyes he was so far inside her head, she didn't have to speak. He reached over with a napkin and brushed the tears away. He didn't let go of her hand again, until dessert was served with tiny cups of coffee so strong she knew she'd never sleep again.

When Leo left the table for a moment, Layna thought about the things Demetra had said in the ladies room. For the first time, she saw how women's eyes followed him—tall, straight-backed, confident—even with their escorts or spouses sitting next to them. With some, it was merely a glance, with others a second look. But in every case, they withdrew, a little sadly, as if they knew they wouldn't stand a chance winning such a man for themselves.

Layna understood perfectly. Leo was daunting, self-confident, and not interested—all of which assured a woman's interest. Not to mention his way of walking which was just shy of arrogant. But Leo would always have that effect on women, even if he was standing still.

Okay, maybe she was prejudiced. And maybe her pride had been hurt because she'd been laughed at. But if his strategy had been to alert her to these facts, then he'd succeeded. It had caused her to think twice about going thousands of miles away and leaving him alone in a world of lonely, unfulfilled women where the hunter could so easily become the hunted. Good-looking *and* wealthy? God help him.

The object of her thoughts returned to the table just as the chandeliers dimmed and tiny colored lights played across the ceiling. The balalaika started with the theme song "Somewhere, My Love" from the movie *Dr. Zhivago*. With such a double dose of romantic, and after an evening with way too much wine, Layna didn't expect any survivors.

Leo stood and held out his hand. Petras did the same with Demetra.

"I thought you do not to dance in public," Layna whispered as he took her hand.

"I do not, usually," he replied. "But tonight, with you, I make the exception. It is maybe the last dance. I want to remember."

Leo took her in his arms and everything stopped. The breadth of his shoulders, the fabric of his jacket beneath her fingers, the heat emanating from his hand at the base of her spine as he floated her effortlessly across the floor—these things were real, like his breath hot against her cheek, his eyes boring into hers. These, too, were

CHAPTΣR THIRTY-TWO

**Εάν δεν μπορείτε να πιάσετε ένα ψάρι,
μην κατηγορήσετε τη θάλασσα**

**IF YOU CANNOT CATCH A FISH,
DO NOT BLAME THE SEA.**

real. But not the silence that faded everything to black, to another place where snowflakes filtered down from towering pines and the smell of winter coming took her breath.

She couldn't break away. It would be like dying. They danced, together, forever. Until the music's end. And they slowly returned to a restaurant on Skopelos.

Layna was amazed. For not dancing in public, Leo literally floated across the dance floor, allowing her to do the same.

The night of magic drew to a close, and two couples soon made their way back to the hotel under starlit skies and a breeze from the sea that teased the pines.

Petras and Demetra hugged Layna goodbye. She whispered her thanks to them both for such a wonderful evening. Demetra squeezed her hand and smiled.

Leo saw Layna to her room on the second floor, his hand still holding hers. She couldn't find any words. He drew the card from his pocket and paused a moment to study her hair, her face, her body, her eyes.

He leaned over and clicked the door open, then drew her inside, where he cradled her face in his hands. She heard the door click shut again, but Leo was so far into her mind and heart, she didn't care who saw the tears. He kissed them away, before his mouth found hers. A gentle whisper of a sad goodbye became a probing, urgent hunger for them both. His hands slid to her waist, then gripped her buttocks with his fierce hands, forcing her against his already hard body forming a rhythm as ancient as the oceans.

She ached for him, and he knew. He always knew.

One hand moved up to untie the strings of her halter dress, and his phone rang. He ignored it, kissing her face, her neck, her eyes, trying to get the damn knots out of the halter top.

His phone rang again; it continued to ring. He cursed and jerked it from his pocket. It was Giannokos. Two tries with no message meant something going down. He gripped Layna's hand, but turned away from the question he knew he would see in her eyes.

She slid her hand up and down his arm, driving him insane. He could feel her wanting to do the same with her legs against his thighs. She was ready, and more than willing.

He tried hard to focus on what the man was saying.

Layna half-listened to Leo's arguments while blood thundered in her ears. None of the words made sense. None of the pauses between the words told her what was happening.

Yes... Are you sure?... No... No, I can't... Not now, damn it!... I can't help that...Yes... You're sure.. Okay.. I know... I know!...Yes... I'll be there... As soon as I can.

He ended the call and stared down at the carpet, still gripping the phone in one hand, Layna's hand in the other, not moving.

"Leo? What is it? What's wrong?"

"I have to go," he said. He pulled her to him so powerfully she could hardly breathe, and held her there while their hearts counted down the minutes through a long, hard kiss.

She pulled away. "I'm coming with you," she said, reaching for her purse on the sofa.

"No," he said, pushing her away. "You'll leave in the morning, as planned."

"I can't leave! Not now!"

"Bury your husband," he growled the words while his eyes devoured her soul. "But do not forget this night. Or me."

"Leonidas?"

It was the first time she'd called him by name.

"The *Prometheus* is on fire." His eyes glittered with frustrated tears as he turned, let go of her hand, and walked briskly to the exit sign that led to the stairs. He didn't look back.

"I love you," she whispered to an empty hallway. It was the rest of what she'd meant to say. But he already knew.

She closed the door, exhausted and confused. Sobs wracked her body as she wobbled toward the bed and sat down, still breathing hard with wanting him. Still throbbing inside with no remedy in sight. So close. Dear God, so very close. But of course he had to go. And she understood. Of course she understood.

And she had to go. Of course he didn't understand. Of course he didn't.

Layna bent down and unlaced her shoes, then crawled in between the cold sheets. After a brief sigh, she got back up and exchanged her new dress for a nightshirt recently purchased that said *Opa*! in huge, blue letters against a white background.

She got in bed again and curled her still-aching body into a fetal position.

Her wake-up call was for 7:00 a.m. A helicopter would take her to Skiathos, and from there, to Athens. And from there, home.

No arms to keep her warm at night.

No colors in her world.

No Skopelos.

No Leo.

Only Ellie Townsend, waiting for her in Tallahassee.

Leo hit the street running. He whipped out his phone to call Petras, decided against it, and found the number for Heliline instead, the helicopter service for Skopelos. It would be faster than going by water. The call had been from Giannokos at Volos. There'd been an explosion on the ship berthed next to *Prometheus.* If they couldn't contain the fire, his ship could be next!

He cursed as the helicopter took off, and got Giannokos back on his phone, straining to hear him above the cabin noise and the whir of the blades.

"What's happening?" Leo yelled into the headset.

"We're trying to contain it," Giannokos said, shouting from his end, where Leo could hear alarms and sirens. "We've got two fire boats. One's already on the *Heleentje,* but there's a moored vessel we can't—ιερό σκατά!"

Leo heard the explosion as well, the one right before Giannokos yelled *holy shit*. Now, he listened with his heart in his throat as the Coast Guard commander turned away from the phone to shout things he couldn't make out.

"Giannokos! What is it?!"

"A secondary fire on the *Heleentje!*" Giannokos yelled, struggling a second time with the Dutch *hay-lay-ntye* pronunciation. "She's spewing shit all over the place. We've been able to put out two small fires on the *Prometheus,* but a larger one got through the hull. Where are you?!"

"Five, six miles out," Leo said, his heart racing. "Get my ship out of there!"

"We're trying!" the commander yelled back, and hung up.

Leo scanned the darkness to the north, and saw what was happening. First, the black smoke that obscured the stars. Then, the billowing flames. Ironically, the *Heleentje,* which meant *Torch of Fire,* was living up to its namesake in a tragic way. As it lit up the night sky, he saw a smaller fire billow upward from the *Prometheus.*

Flames reflected in his eyes as he took it all in, including the two ships moored in the harbor effectively blocking the pathway to freedom. It was little comfort to see the second fire boat finally chug its way into position and begin to shower his father's ship. He watched in horror from the cockpit as the helicopter veered into a landing pattern. Giannokos was there, barking orders to people and sweating profusely though the night was cool.

"Thank God," the commander said with a hurried embrace. His words scattered like the night. "They were discharging cargo when it happened. Several wounded, two dead."

"On *Prometheus*?"

"No, no, the other one. The *Heleentje* out of Belgium," Giannokos said. "No, your crew is fine. We were able to evacuate them. But there's another problem. Come. See. "

But Leo stayed where he was, staring at the arc of water that reached into the sky, then down onto the deck of *Prometheus*, oblivious to the life-flight helicopter that hovered overhead like a vulture, or the ambulance sirens, or the constant whooping sounds of the dock's alarm systems. His heart sank, while his mind reached out to Layna and their perfect night ruined by disaster. Dedication to his business. Love, divided by necessity. To hell with Onassis.

Giannokos tugged at his arm.

"Tell me what happened." Leo forced himself from numbness to reality.

"We don't know. It could be anything—faulty electrical, overheated engine, fuel spill—I just found out the *Heleentje* was hauling 16 tons of calcium hypochlorite!"

"That is over limit!"

"I know! Vasilis called me as soon as he could," Giannokos said. "There was an explosion on *Heleentje* there on the right. It sustained the most damage, but incidental fire spread to your ship and caused another explosion there, below deck, before we could pump CO2 in or segregate the unit. What was *Prometheus* hauling?"

"Uh, bamboo and rubber," Leo said, struggling to dredge it up from memory. "Sixteen containers."

"No wonder," Giannokos said, leading him toward the outside

perimeter. "The larger fire burned through before we could get to it. We're having a hell of a time putting it out. The bamboo would have combusted in no time; the rubber accounts for the dark smoke and nasty smell and why it just keeps smouldering."

"Exactly," Leo replied. "Centimeters of steel don't mean shit when it burns from the inside."

The commander nodded. "All we've been able to determine is that something destroyed several containers on the side of *Heleentje* closest to *Prometheus*."

"The hypochlorite?"

"Probably. We won't know until the fire's put down, but that could be 48 hours or more. Sorry about the call. I thought you'd want to know."

Leo waved off the apology. They cleared the second gate and were walking back toward the first one. Giannokos stopped at a tarp. It covered what turned out to be the dead body of a dock worker, his throat slit, his dock pass missing.

Leo shook his head. Both men bent down to examine the body.

"Access?" The commander put it forward.

Leo nodded, then gave him a questioning look. "Boiko?"

"Or his men. Although Boiko has an alibi for the time in question."

"Which is?" Leo asked, not wanting to hear the answer.

"When the explosion occurred, he was being arrested for human trafficking," he said. "I don't think he'll see daylight before he's too old to piss."

"Fine by me," Leo said, standing back up. Nervous energy had replaced the initial shock. Now, he wanted desperately to do something. To make the nightmare stop. He hurried back to the billowing smoke and lazy arcs of water that said *Prometheus* was a wounded ship, though it had only been hit with incidental fire. It had been enough to do a hell of a lot of damage. The Coast Guard commander's stocky body easily kept up with the leaner Leo, who desperately needed an outlet for his anger.

"All they're doing is maintaining," he growled. "We've got to put it out!"

"My friend, they are doing all they can," Giannokos muttered.

"My father gave me that ship," Leo said. "He entrusted it to me. And now it's gone. Even if they salvage the biggest part, it will never be the same. How can I give it up?"

If Layna gives up her past for you, will you give up your future for her?

The thought surprised him. He took a last look at his father's ship, then stumbled through his thanks and a brief goodbye to Giannokos, who promised an hourly status report. Leo climbed into the helicopter that had brought him. It was well past midnight, and he had much to do before he made the airport in Athens. He considered returning to Layna's hotel room and waking her up. God, he needed to talk to her.

He decided against it. They both had too much going on.

Since he didn't know when he'd be coming back, he needed the Bentley. He relegated the image of *Prometheus* burning to the outside lanes of his racing mind and had the copter pilot take him to Skopelos Town instead. He had a lot of thinking to do, and he didn't want the hassle of a rental car. He should call Petras. No, it could wait. His insides were shaking.

After a quick shower and change of clothes, he filled a thermos with hot coffee and packed an overnight bag. He walked to the landing and took his cabin cruiser to Volos, where he picked up his car to begin the three-hour drive to Athens. Plenty of time to consider his options, if he could stay awake. He told himself he could sleep later, after she'd gone. After he'd decided what to do about *Prometheus*. That's what he told himself.

It surprised him to admit he was tired of his business dictating when and where he did things. He had given Layna an evening to remember, not counting his abrupt departure with no more than a hurried explanation. Now, he meant to be there when she got on the plane. He had decided, and it would be so. And if Thurman showed up, they could talk. Leo could tell him about his ship, probably going up for auction once the paperwork was complete.

So, you've already decided. Not yet. Not yet.

Still moving on adrenalin, Leo thought about the weeks and months to come as he pulled onto the highway. Selling *Prometheus* would be like selling his brother, but it helped him see Layna's predicament in a new light. What had she already had to say goodbye to? Leo thought of his father, and how it was always assumed he'd take over the family business. No one ever asked him if it was what he wanted to do. Just like no one had ever asked a young Ellie Townsend what she wanted to do for her twenty-first birthday.

He thought again of stopping at her hotel room, then let it go. At this point in time, they were doing the right thing. They both had some hard decisions to make about the future, things they needed to learn about themselves that they couldn't learn from one another.

His revolved around an ugly container ship in the harbor at Volos.

The business part of his brain automatically calculated the figures involved. A new container ship could cost $40 million, but a damaged one? Accounting for depreciation, and subtracting what he would be losing every day once he sold it, then altering the estimate to accommodate the current, staggering inflation rate in Greece—he threw up his hands, then immediately grabbed the wheel again. Thank God for the nearly nonexistent highway traffic in the wee hours of the morning.

It was too much to deal with. Was this what Layna meant by *overwhelmed*? No wonder she went trelós. He reworded it. No wonder she *thought* herself crazy. Which led him to the episode in her hotel room before he was called away, but he forced it back down. The last thing he needed on a three-hour drive was to get καβλωμένος —what is the slang word? Horny?

Instead of how her lips tasted on his, he focused on what she would or wouldn't do once she found herself in Florida. And if she would ever forgive him for bringing her husband into the middle of something he was incapable of surviving. A second tangent zeroed in on the argument they'd had before he'd slammed the door. She'd said things—a lot of things—that stuck in his heart like a splinter that is hard to find, impossible to remove.

"I could go to bed tonight one person, make love to you, and wake up somebody else in the morning, like Athens! I can't put you through that! I won't!"

Was she right? Could it really happen again, without anything to bring it about?

If something or someone took her back to that place where no one could reach her, could either of them survive it a second time? Frustrated, he slammed the steering wheel with the palm of his hand and slowed down for the turn from A12 onto A1, and a straight shot to Athens.

"I don't know who I am, and neither do you!"

That was another splinter in his heart. He tried to extract it, to somehow work it into what Petras had said about Demetra. The caffeine kicked in, and Leo's mind opened a second before his mouth, following the thought to an undesired conclusion.

"So the battle is with herself? Shit! Then what am I? The εγγύηση —what was the word? The *collateral* damage? It is what ships leave behind!"

He took the curve too fast and made himself slow down, wishing he didn't have to wait for answers from words that swam in his mind like barracudas.

"Bah! I have never been good at the waiting," he mumbled, then smiled. "But I am a great date." *Not counting the part where he walked away when she needed him the most.*

He reached for more coffee. The full meal and the wine had taken their toll. Though he was alert at the moment, he needed to stay awake long enough to make Athens.

"I will court her, as Petras said. I will not leave her alone in Florida to forget me," he told himself. "I will write her letters of much love. And flowers. Maybe one phone call, so she remembers the sound of my voice."

She could still be his, was his. When she came back to him, he would make her to weep for joy. For now, he would take flowers for their farewell at the airport.

"You are the idiot," he grumbled. "You do not take flowers to a woman standing beside her dead husband's coffin! I do not wish to see her *there*." He still felt the sense of responsibility for Jack's death that he couldn't shake, no matter how he rationalized it. Yet, even dead, Jack was going with her when *he* could not! No. No flowers. He would take Thurman's place and walk with her into the plane.

Unwise. Same thing could happen. She could link him with her husband's dead body, or with Thurman. If the subject hadn't been so macabre, Leo would have relished the thought, even smiled, knowing Thurman had long desired her. But Thurman desired many women. And he, Leo, wanted only the one. He focused on how to court a grieving widow.

"Hell, if Onassis did it, I can, too." The words sounded small when he said them aloud in the car. A sigh escaped his lips. Another goodbye. This time, he was letting her go. Willingly. That's what he told himself while he put a call in to Thurman.

After a helicopter ride from Skopelos to Skiathos, and a delayed flight to Athens, Layna sat slumped on an uncomfortable bench beneath an overcast morning sky at Venizelos Aerodrómio in Athens. Thurman sat beside her, his orthopedic shoe stretched out in front and a heavy-duty cane perched against the back of the bench. Early morning, but it already felt like the end of a long day. Storm clouds grumbled nearby.

"Thanks for taking care of everything." Despite a pounding headache, Layna managed a lovely smile.

"You're welcome," Thurman said. "I feel like makarónia."

"Does it hurt terribly? Your ankle?"

"Only when I'm on it," he said. "I was thinking more about life, you know? Yours, mine. Life is a lot like pasta."

"Are you on meds?" Layna asked. Laughter quivered in her voice. She leaned over, but she couldn't see his pupils through the sunglasses.

"Big time," he said, with a wandering smile, "but I know what I'm talking about. I saw them make it one time, you know. The dough is stretched over and over. Then they cut it. If they cut one way, it's rigatoni. Another way, and a lot more stretching, and it's spaghetti. If they make a mistake, they punch it in the stomach and start all over again. Egg noodles."

Layna sighed. "Okay, I'm starting to relate. Can we talk about something else?"

"Like why you're leaving?"

She looked at dark clouds in the distance.

Thurman shifted his weight on the bench and glanced around like he was waiting for someone.

"Petras has a cure for your predicament, you know," he said, turning back to Layna. "He told me on the way to the landing last night. Wisdom from a would-be thief."

"You have no proof of that," Layna said.

"Then how did the three of you get into the Athens house? Care to discuss crime scenes?"

Layna looked away. "That's breaking and entering, not theft—exactly."

"Well, the not-exactly-a-thief predicts you'll have two, maybe three children."

Layna frowned. "Don't make fun. And I don't see Petras saying that at all."

"Of course, I was rather out of it at the time. From the pain, not the meds."

Layna rubbed her brow with her fingers. Her head was pounding from the change in air pressure on the ground. Or too much wine and not enough sleep. Or both. Anyway, a storm was coming. She dreaded to think what a 16–hour flight in a pressurized cabin would do to her sinuses. She just wanted the whole thing to be over, but that wasn't Thurman's fault.

"I'm glad you're here," she said, working through the pain behind her eyes. "There's no way I could've done this alone. You handled everything. Outstanding job."

Thurman grinned. He wondered if Layna was going to bail on him mentally. She didn't look too good. Then again, neither did he. Where the hell was Leo?

"There is a point," he said. "And I'm looking for it as we speak."

CHAPTER THIRTY-THREE

**Τώρα που ζω, θέλω να γδω τα πιθυμάω κι ορίζω, κι άμα, σα φύγω να με κλαίς,
χάρη δε στο γνωρίζω.**

NOW THAT I AM ALIVE, I WANT TO SEE, TO WISH AND OWN; WHEN I'M GONE AND YOU CRY FOR ME, I WON'T KNOW.

Layna considered her doped-up friend behind the Foster Grants, along with the dilated pupils she just glimpsed when he lowered his head and peeked over them. "I seriously hope someone's driving you home after this," she said.

Thurman chuckled.

Layna took his arm so he'd know they were still friends.

"You were explaining how all my problems would be solved by giving birth."

"Oh, right. It's Greek logic, of course. Not as reliable as Vulcan, but—"

"Thurman, I don't have a lot of time. If you were coming to America with me, it would be a different story."

"I could be."

"I don't think so. You need to stay here and take care of Leo."

Thurman imitated a look of petulance. "You're right. Okay. Petras said if you have a family, you raise the children, cook the meals, clean the house, go to the market, visit the friends, and sleep with the husband. His words, not mine. You have no time to grow problems into the mountains. Again, his words. And you are happy to share your bed in the arms of your husband when the day is through."

"Which leads to more children."

"Yes, well, Petras says Demetra is *the wisest of women.*"

"That sounds like Petras. But Demetra is about as far from a household drudge as a woman can be."

"You met her?"

"Mmmm. Leo took me on a date. A double date, actually, with Petras and his wife."

Shocked, Thurman turned to her just as the sky burst open. With Layna's help, he made it inside the airport. Together, they watched rivulets of rain blur the panes of glass that covered the front of the building. A huge plane taxied in. The wait was over.

She turned to Thurman for their last goodbye.

"I have no intention of having many *childrens,*" she said. "but I'll never forget that spectacular catch you made in the cave, or the many things that brought us to this moment."

Thurman smiled and kissed her on one cheek, then the other, European style. She kissed him back the same way.

"Find what you're looking for," he whispered, and handed her a piece of paper.

"What's this?"

"Private telephone numbers—as hard to come by as fours in Yahtzee. Me, Petras, Leo. In case you're ever in the neighborhood."

"Thanks, Thurman," she said, taking his hand for a moment before letting go of it again.

"Good. Let's get this over with so I can go home and get drunk."

"On meds? Wouldn't advise it." *Although she could definitely use a margarita.*

Thurman opened the door and leaned into the rain that had lessened into a light sprinkle. He motioned to an officer under a tarp, standing solemnly beside a casket. Layna felt her heart go south, then back again. She hadn't even noticed them.

"Jackson will take it from here," he said. "Take care."

The hallway that led outside seemed twice as long as it looked. Jackson joined her there, provided an umbrella, and escorted her to the plane where he supervised the loading of the coffin into the belly of the transport. He ran the papers past the necessary people before handing them back to Layna. Finally, he escorted her safely into the plane and seated her at the window. In first class, with a minimum of fellow travelers.

Layna thanked the assistant and looked through the thick glass until she located Thurman, leaning into his cane just inside the terminal, waiting.

"Way to go, Thurman," she whispered. He had taken care of things, as promised. It would be a long time before she got this kind of preferential treatment again. Restless, she gazed out at the foggy airport and looked again. "Leo?"

Through the glass, just for a moment, she thought she saw him standing alone in the rain. Her heart came into her throat. Her hand pressed hard against the pane. She tried to wipe the condensation away, frantic for one more glimpse.

The door closed. The engines roared into life. The air came on.

The glass cleared. She found him again. A man in jeans and a jacket, standing beneath the overhang. He could have been just another person in the crowd. But she knew him. His build, his mannerisms. She'd seen his eyes dance, heard every cadence of his voice, felt the hardness of his body against her own. And now, just as surely, she knew something was wrong by the way his shoulders pressed inward ever so slightly. The way he stared without seeing. So close.

Of course. Thurman must have given him clearance outside the gate. That was why he kept looking around when they were on the bench. But, why didn't Leo kiss her goodbye or let her know he was there? She knew, but she didn't want to take it out and acknowledge it.

Leo fought the sense of urgency that threatened to overtake him. He clenched his fists so tightly, the muscles in his forearms tensed and held. The same powerless rage coursed through him that he had felt while watching the *Prometheus* burn. Then, as now, there was nothing he could do. He kept telling himself he was letting her go. That it was better this way.

The plane began to turn. Layna's heart lurched and threatened to explode. She held her breath. Leo studied the ground for a moment, then something broke his concentration. He looked up. Thurman had joined him. They spoke hurriedly. Layna watched, stretching and turning in her seat as the plane moved farther away.

She saw them walk away together, then stop. Leo said something that made Thurman put his arm around him. Tears blurred her vision. She pressed harder against the glass, thinking surely Leo would feel, would know, would turn and say goodbye!

The plane taxied, lifted its wings, and strained against the sky like a bird too heavy to ride the wind.

Ellie Townsend walked off the plane through the disembarking tunnel, then into the main terminal. After two stopovers, endless delays, and jagged hours of hit-or-miss sleep high above the earth, passport control and customs was a breeze.

The official story behind Jack's death was now a *boating accident.* Thurman called it "a tale more readily believed than one involving undercover espionage," though anyone who had known Jack wouldn't have been surprised by either. She wondered if he had any relatives hidden away, like a grandmother in Mississippi she'd never heard of. As Stella had often remarked, Jack was *always a bit secretive.* Would that be irony, or sarcasm?

"Ellie!"

She turned, beaming with joy as her dearest friend and confidant shrieked and swept her into her arms next to the luggage carousel. Aunt Stella, come to meet her, in an old pair of jeans, a short-sleeved shirt, and a gardening hat. She'd always insisted on being called Stella; she considered herself too young to be someone's aunt. Though her tendency towards brashness often threw people off their guard, her niece had always sensed the kindest of hearts beneath that rough exterior.

Neither of them wanted to let go.

"Girl, I didn't know if I was ever going to see you again!" Stella said, wiping tears from her eyes. "I must've called every American embassy in the whole of Greece looking for you!"

"I didn't know!" Layna cried, stealing Stella's handkerchief while her aunt took command of the luggage carrier.

"That's what this guy Thurman told me when he called and briefed me, like they do in the movies." She lowered her voice as they walked toward the exit. "Ellie, when you phoned me from that hotel room in Athens, you weren't exactly telling me the truth. Now how the hell did you ever get mixed up with Interpol? When he called you a material witness, I nearly died!"

"Well, there's a lot I couldn't tell you over the phone," Layna said, taking some papers out of her shoulder bag, "but first I need to take care of Jack." She noted her aunt's curious glance that seemed to ask, "why are you so calm when you should be devastated?" But, to her relief, Stella said nothing; she merely smiled and accompanied her while she confirmed the arrangements for the body to be delivered to a local funeral home for burial in two days' time.

The image at the Athens airport of Thurman and Leo huddled together flashed before her for the hundredth time. What had happened to the *Prometheus*? Was Leo all right? She needed to be with him, not thousands of miles away. Then she thought of Jack and Stella, and knew she needed to be here as well.

Stella drove, while Ellie regaled her aunt with a follow-up story, adding to what she'd told her from the hotel room before leaving Athens for the States. Conversation halted when they drove up the circular driveway and stopped in front of the old, Victorian house. Ellie stared up at the second story, her old bedroom, remembering the day in Skopelos when her memories had all came flooding back. And now, she was here.

"I had this made for you," Stella said, handing her a key. "The Interpol guy said everything you had was stolen when those men tried to kill you." Her voice broke. She leaned her face down against the steering wheel. "I can't believe what you've been through," she said, close to tears.

"Gosh," Layna said, "I haven't even gotten to the good stuff yet."

Stella raised her eyes and studied her niece's face. "How can you make light of it?" she asked. "You've changed."

"Yes, and I'm not making light of it," Layna said. "Trust me. I get terrified all over again, just thinking about it. But you're right. I've changed. Let's get the suitcases in. And something to eat. I'm starved!"

"Say no more," Stella replied, hoisting a shopping bag from the back seat. Once everything was inside the house, she set the bag on the kitchen table and opened it up to reveal a plastic container of orange juice and a huge carrier filled with blueberry muffins.

"I come bearing gifts," Stella said with a laugh. "Sorry. Couldn't resist the Trojan Horse thing."

"Perfect!" Layna said, delighted. The aroma of blueberry muffins and the splash of cold orange juice took some of the jet lag away, but she knew the bulk of it would hit, and soon.

"Ellie, I haven't begun to take in what you've told me, but I have the feeling there's a shitload more."

Layna quietly selected a muffin and took a seat.

As the sun shifted overhead, moving silently toward the horizon into evening, she filled in details, added information, and finally unpacked her sketchbook to show Stella some of what she'd seen and done. Quite a few drawings had been added on the flight back. Her hands paused over each drawing as she was taken back to Skopelos. Talking kept her hands and body occupied through three blueberry muffins and two glasses of juice.

Stella listened, sitting back in the chair with hands folded. At times, she would comment or occasionally nod, but mostly she tapped one forefinger against the other. When Layna told her what happened in the cave, Stella cried. She stared at each picture in her niece's sketchbook as they were explained, wishing she had been there to protect her. When the story was done, she sat back, astonished.

"And you kept a pistol leveled at his privates?" Stella said.

"I did."

"Is this the child who hid in Little Jack Horner's corner?" she asked. "Who never could quite get the correct placement of silver down, or why clothes mattered? Lordy, no wonder you seem different. But poor Jack." Stella looked away for a moment. "What a ghastly way to die!" She turned to Layna and leaned forward, resting her elbows on the table.

"I'm glad you brought him home," Stella said. "Lord knows I wasn't thrilled when you married him, but he had a certain way about him. He was nice to me all those times I came to visit. You did the right thing, Ellie. Yes sir, the right thing. And you know, I think maybe he was trying to tell you, there in the cave, that he loved you the only way he could. Some men just don't have it in 'em." She reached over and placed her hand on top of her niece's. "But that's over now. And we'll see to it that he gets a nice send-off."

Layna shuddered inside at the term. "One thing I owe Jack is that he got me all the way across the Atlantic. And you helped. I owe you for that advance on my trust money."

"Well, you needed a vacation. Though it wasn't the kind to write home about."

"Anyway," Layna said, "I've got my 25th coming up, so I can finally pay you back."

"No rush," Stella said, leaning forward. "Why do I think you're all tensed up? Is it coming back to the old place?"

"It feels like what you said—an old place. It's like that song grandpa used to sing about Paris. Do you remember?"

Stella laughed. "How 'Ya Gonna Keep 'Em Down On The Farm (After They've Seen Paree)?"

"That's the one!" Layna pictured her grandfather's framed poster depicting The Great War, relegated to the attic when she was still a girl. His die-cast metal toys would be worth a fortune in today's market, but she wanted to hold onto them, along with his rocking chair.

"Is the old rocker in the attic?" she asked.

"Sure is," Stella said. "Your mother never forgave him for shortening your name to Ellie. He always thought the name Eleanor was too old and stuffy for a little girl with big dreams. If you were a dreamer back then, it didn't show. But looking at the new you, I'm thinking he could see into the future."

Ellie sat up straight in her chair, slipping into another era as easily as she slipped in and out of Layna's mind. Stella touched her on the arm.

"Ellie, what is it?"

"I think the jet lag's catching up with me," she whispered.

"Don't you worry," Stella said. "I'm spending the night with you. I don't care for the idea of you being all alone in this big, old house, just coming back and all."

Gratitude washed over her niece's face. Stella took the dishes to the sink and helped Layna carry her things upstairs. Then, she went to the car and brought in a change of clothes she'd packed beforehand, just in case.

Later, Layna slowly descended the stairs in a t-shirt and pajama shorts. She carried a pillow and some covers under one arm.

"What is it, darlin'?" Stella asked. "There's no need for that. I can sleep in the guest room upstairs."

"These are for me," Layna said, her voice strangely tired. "I can't sleep in Ellie's room."

Stella gave her niece a curious look, but chalked her strange words up to jet lag. It did weird things to your mind and body. That's what she'd always heard. Still, she hung around downstairs until Layna had crashed on the sofa into a deep sleep. Only then did Stella go upstairs to the guest room, a frown creasing her forehead and deep concern spilling from her heart. But it had been a long day, and her eyes refused to remain opened for long.

In the morning, she was gone at first light to feed her chickens. The note was on the fridge. Layna saw it, poured the last of the juice into a glass, and looked around the kitchen, picturing every room in the house and wondering how she'd ever endured it.

"You were cared for," Ellie said.

"Like a monkey in a cage," was Layna's response.

The strangeness of coming home made her realize what an isolated life she'd led until Jack had entered the picture, and even after. The stark emptiness helped drive that fact home. Stella had filled the void that should have been filled by girls her own age. But Ellie hadn't formed that circle of acquaintances most girls cultivate in high school and college. Her parents' exclusive need for one another had overshadowed the life she might have had. Instead of rebelling at being ignored, she'd quietly withdrawn.

As Ellie, she'd learned to be content at being forgotten, adjusting to a life of loneliness and social stupidity. She'd drifted along, leaving her parents' life for Jack Taggart's life. Now Leo wanted her in *his* life. What about *her* life?

As Layna, she wondered at the unfamiliarity of a world where three generations of Townsends had lived and worked. After knowing Leo, it was like a world gone gray. It reminded her of Emily Bronte's poem, "Remembrance"—"Once drinking deep of that divinest anguish, how could I seek the empty world again?"

And empty it was, without the pulsating vibrancy of her parents' love for each other. The vacancy filled her with regret. No, what was that word from her French class? She smiled at the image of Jean-Claude facing his students on a Monday morning with his jacket slightly off one shoulder, like Napoleon.

God bless the French.

Ennui! That was it! Listless, dissatisfied, lethargic, depressive.

Like Ellie, the house had faded into the pale blues, creams, and beiges that filled every major room. Strange, she'd never noticed that before. The kitchen's greens and browns were mildly restorative, yet fell short of the rich earth tones she'd discovered in Leo's house.

A wistful little smile played along her lips. Leo's beautiful home on Skopelos. The window in the bedroom. The patio where she and Petras were kidnapped. The little office where they'd discovered Velanio Beach, where Jack had been harpooned. Layna turned away.

Her parents' bedroom in pale beige with cream-colored furniture led her to the bathrooms, pale blue downstairs, pale lavender upstairs. Everything pale, understated, lifeless.

Layna surfaced with a violent urge to incorporate a huge splash of vermilion or fuchsia on the table in the foyer, or a deep, vibrant purple—something to shake up the lackluster palette of yesteryear. Could she redo everything putting her artistic talent to use? After all, she'd inherit a great deal of money in a matter of weeks.

Then again, what good would it do, if Ellie's ghost still roamed the halls?

Stella returned with two bags of groceries.

"I don't want you spending money on me," Layna said.

Stella ignored her and proceeded to fix eggs and bacon.

Layna transferred food to the fridge.

"So, what do you think you'll do now?" Stella asked. The grease popped and sizzled.

"I'm working on it," Layna replied, "and having difficulty. I think and think, but I keep going in circles. The major decisions in my life were always made by someone else. This thing is huge, with too many unknowns."

"Understandable," Stella said, nodding. "Like you said, if you're not sure you're over that *depersonal* thing, maybe now's not the time to look at a relationship logically. It sounds like you barely escaped being in a coma for the rest of your life. Jesus, that's scary. Are you sure you don't want to sell this monstrosity and live with me?"

Ellie rebelled. It came across as a slight twinge in Layna's left eye.

"I appreciate the offer," Layna said, her voice oddly level, "but it wouldn't solve the problem, would it? I've got to make a decision, or two or three. And soon."

"Just don't overthink it," Stella warned. "Your father had a tendency to do that."

Ellie warmed inside her. Layna pushed on.

"I'm trying not to, but you're right. The thought of waking up with amnesia terrifies me. Just the possibility of it—well, it was one of the reasons I left. I was scared I would see or hear something that would send me back into that dissociative disorder. I won't go through that again, or put Leo through it."

"You think you're safer here? That there's less chance of it happening?"

"Well, it makes sense, doesn't it? I know. I'm not a doctor. I wish I could get in touch with a real doctor like the one in Germany."

"Why can't you?"

"You think she'd talk to me about it?"

"Darlin', she'd jump through hoops! Just stay far enough away so she doesn't put you in a cage and start charging admission, calling you her great success story. Google her, but promise you won't hop

CHAPTΣR THIRTY-FOUR

Κάθε θαύμα τρείς μέρες, το μεγάλο τέσσερις.

**EACH MIRACLE TAKES THREE DAYS:
A GREAT ONE TAKES FOUR.**

a plane to the fatherland."

"I promise," Layna said with a laugh.

"Relationships are usually about facts versus feelings," Stella said. "Why don't we start with the facts, where you are at this moment in time? Remember, this is war. No prisoners."

Layna sat up straight, then seemed almost to shrink.

"I don't know. Maybe I shouldn't take chances like moving to another country. What do you think?"

Stella gave her a second look. Her niece's voice had changed to something hesitant, shy.

"Girl, what's going on in that brain of yours?" she asked in a stern voice.

Her niece flexed her shoulders and crooked her neck, stared at the floor for a moment, then spoke in a confident manner, head held high. "My husband is dead, I have a house I don't want and a mental condition nobody understands, including me. My dearest friends, present company excluded, are thousands of miles away in a macho culture I don't get. I'm not Ellie anymore, but I'm not fully Layna. In fact, just now, part of me argued against contacting the doctor, while another part of me voted full-steam ahead." She looked her aunt in the eyes. "Straight down the middle. And that's where I'm at."

"Interesting," her aunt said, nodding. "I think I just witnessed that, but I'm not sure. You know, I don't think I've ever heard you talk like this. I like it. You're laying all your cards on the table. Hell, the girl you used to be'd still be in that room in Athens in a fetal position! But what about you? How do you feel inside?"

"Afraid."

Stella waited, curious at the little-girl voice that kept surfacing. Her niece had lowered her eyes, but then looked up again, determined.

"When he kissed me like that—you know, when we said goodbye—I felt more in that one kiss than in all my time with Jack. I felt it every time, not just that once."

A part of her realized what she'd just said, and she blushed. Why? Something inside her shuddered. Ellie?

"Don't you blush speaking the God's honest truth." Stella's admonition spilled into her thoughts. "I have to admit, I always wondered about that part of it. 'Course, I never said anything. You were so God-awful shy. I practically raised you, like you were my own, you know. Jack shouldn't have said those awful things to you. You do realize they're not true."

"I'm starting to. But back then? I was really stupid, and Jack was the first one, the only one. What if Leo and I do more than kiss, and I—I know he wants all of me, but that all of me is still in pieces? Does that make any sense? And he's Greek. You know. *Opa*, and all that."

"I don't doubt it," Aunt Stella replied, her eyes twinkling. "He's a real hunk."

"Stella!" Layna said, grinning.

"Hey, I'm old, not dead. I've seen the renderings in that sketchbook. Nice eyes. Here I am with all the know-how, and there you are with all the hormones. There's no justice."

"So, what am I going to do about the sex thing? Or the culture thing?"

"I don't know about the culture thing, but I have plenty to say about the sex thing. The plain old fact, despite women's lib and all the burned bras, a woman's body is built to respond to a man's touch. Biological, proven fact. Sounds to me like you're already responding all over the place. Before you know it, you'll be instigating as well. Don't look at me like that. It'll come later in its own time. No, I think you've got a real man on your hands. A real man will respect the difference and make you respond like there's no tomorrow. You're just sabotaging your own heart. Happens to the best of us."

Layna fidgeted with a napkin, then realized it was something Ellie would do, had done.

"Sabotaging my heart," she repeated. "Finding something to stop the machinery from working as it should."

"You got it," Stella said.

"It couldn't be that simple," Layna argued. "Though it does kind of explain the split-down-the-middle thing," she said.

"That sounds serious." Stella saw a frown flicker across her niece's face.

Layna smiled. It lacked conviction.

"Ellie? What is it?"

"It's *that,*" she said, "that *name*. Every time you call me Ellie, I cringe inside. And the house. I feel like it's sucking me in. Whoever I was, died on Skopelos. But that part of me is still here. I can feel it. Maybe that's what's really bothering me. I felt like the real me when I was being Layna."

"God, I didn't realize. Layna it is. That'll take some getting used to. But, there's still only one question, for whatever you're facing. Even the split down the middle."

"And that would be?"

"Do you love him?"

Layna closed her eyes, exhaled, and lowered her head in defeat.

"He's everywhere," she whispered. "His face, his voice. He's part of me."

"And there you have it, folks!" Stella snorted, stood up, and took a bow. "Don't forget to send me a postcard!"

Layna laughed and swatted at her, motioning her back into her seat, wondering how Stella ever got to be so wildly unpredictable. She knew Stella was her mother's sister, but the two women were planets apart. Both were intelligent, but Stella was street smart. What she said made sense but more than anything else, it had helped to talk it out, even if the end result was what Petras had said all along—to follow her heart. She wondered what they were doing, her Greek friends. She glanced at the wall clock, figuring in the seven-hour time difference. It was 7:00 p.m. there, tomorrow night. She pictured the four of them together around the dining room table, laughing, talking. Was Leo alone? She could almost feel his arms around her.

She looked around at the only home she'd ever known and knew it wasn't home anymore. After devouring the last slice of bacon, she carried the plates to the sink, got out her phone, and called a realtor. Whether she returned to Greece or not, there was no way she was living in a haunted house.

As the thought took shape, so did a fluttery convulsion in some part of her brain that made her pause. It had happened before. Even then, she had known, somehow, it would happen again. A coldness settled in her chest. A tiny something in her temporal lobe spasmed in brief rebellion. She pressed her fingers into the side of her face and leaned against the sink. A sharp whimper and a deep inhale escaped her lips.

Stella half-rose from the chair.

"Ellie?"

Something in her aunt's voice led Layna to turn her face to the side. She gave Stella a wretched look, then nodded ever so slightly.

Aunt Stella was right, calling her by that name.

It was Ellie, wanting her life back.

The funeral was a quiet, graveside affair with a sealed casket, a bereaved widow, her favorite aunt, and a priest. The widow wept quietly in a dignified manner, thinking *what a waste* till sadness turned to tears.

White roses and her first letter from Leo came the day the realtor stopped by to look at the house. The woman told her the timing was perfect, that a married couple were looking for a Victorian close to the college. Ellie warned her not to sell it, that nothing in life was certain. She told Ellie to fuck off, then sat beneath an oak tree, heart trembling, to read her letter from Leo.

My Layna,

I wonder where you are in this moment. What you are doing. I wish to share the wisdom of a man called Socrates, also Greek. He said healing is a matter of time, but also a matter of opportunity. I hope you see truth of this and find what you search for. My business is going through a change. I am in Athens more than in Skopelos, but Nitsa sends her greeting, and Petras. Thurman is putting his foot up and enjoying much-needed rest, but says there is something that may take him soon to Istanbul. I also think maybe he likes the Demerol too much.

Petras enjoyed a long time away from me, and Demetra has thanked me many times. They are expecting another child. When I was driving to Athens, I wondered if you would ever forgive me. When I am in Skopelos, I remember our words. You are everywhere.

Leonidas

Layna read it again, especially the part about seeing her everywhere. But why did he still need her forgiveness? Leo was a proud man. He would only seek absolution for one thing—her husband's death. She thought of how to word her response.

She went inside and pulled some stationery from one of the boxes headed for storage. She lit a candle that purported to carry an ocean scent, and stared out the window at trees and sky until the vision gave way to the sights and smells of Skopelos. It took a while to get his name on paper, only to have her eyes mist up. She stood up, shook her hands, then her whole body, then sat down and tried again.

Dearest Leo,

I miss you and Petras and Nitsa. Even Thurman, but don't tell him. I'm glad he's finally elevating his ankle. I've put the house up for sale, and there's a buyer. Soon, I'll be able to decide what to do next. Everything is in boxes except my oils and brushes. I'm ready to paint again, and scared I've forgotten how.

There was a scene I wanted to paint there on Skopelos, looking out from the street that leads to your house. The sea is in the distance, and there's a wonderful, scraggly tree on the left, in the foreground...

She stopped and crumpled the stupid letter into a tight little wad. The last thing she wanted to talk about was Jack, but wasn't that why she was writing the letter? She began again, and found herself falling into a natural cadence, the way Leo talked.

Leonidas,

I should have said this before, but there was much noise and we couldn't hear each other's words. Also, my heart was too broken to speak, but I'm quieter now.

Jack was put to rest at a lovely graveside service. It's over. Do not carry the blame for his death. Once he knew the assignment was dangerous, you could not have prevented what happened next. He lived for the next adventure. He agreed to help you, knowing the dice were loaded. You didn't force him. He put his money down, and he took his chances like the rest of us. If not a job for you, it would have been an equally dangerous assignment for someone else. No one could have known it would end as it did.

I'm healing, slowly. I take long walks and remember more and more. There are patterns to life, and I'm finding such patterns in everything that led me to Athens and you.

I have emailed the doctor in Germany to see if she can help. I need to know I won't lose myself again. She seems eager to talk to me, so maybe there is hope. My greatest fear is waking up in your arms unable to recall your mouth on mine, the sound of your voice, and how you smell of the sun and the sea.

My heart is filled with you. You've awakened things in me I've never

CHAPTER THIRTY-FIVE

Αν πιαστείς στο χορό θα χορέψεις.

IF YOU JOIN THE CIRCLE OF DANCERS, YOU DANCE.

felt before, but against that fear stands a love I'll carry with me the rest of my life.

My love to Petras and Nitsa. And Thurman.

With all my heart.

Layna

Writing proved a lovely respite, counterbalanced by Stella who showed up to help with minor repairs like mowing and edging while Layna put a fresh coat of paint on the front porch. They worked out an arrangement for Stella to take temporary custody of Grandpa's rocker until Layna got settled.

The couple who put down their earnest money didn't have much furniture of their own, so they negotiated with the realtor, and everyone came away happy. They were to close in three weeks' time, barring any holdups. The realtor had suggested possibly renting the house out, or leasing it, but Layna knew it had to be a clean break. Now, with Jack dead and buried—it still sounded cold when she said it, even to herself—and her questionable marriage to Leo an ocean away, Layna felt free, solvent, and on her own.

She couldn't have done it without Aunt Stella's help. The woman helped her downsize, go through every truck in the attic, donate goods, and start the machine turning regarding the trust money. A date was set to meet with the lawyer and make it legal.

After salvaging her drawing pad and pencils, Layna purchased acrylic paint, a few extra brushes, and several canvases. She spent afternoons painting. No more quiet landscapes in muted colors. Now her brush spoke with boldness and passion. Images came alive as never before. She painted Volos, the cave where they fought the kidnappers, the open market of Skopelos Town, Nitsa in the garden watering her cucumbers and tomatoes, Petras grinning from behind the wheel of a beat-up Chevy, and Leo. His was a simple portrait that included a self-portrait of Layna standing next to him, his arm over her right shoulder.

On a wild impulse one night after more than one margarita, Layna packed up the painting and arranged to have it shipped priority mail to Skopelos with a note that read, "for over the fireplace—love, Layna."

She blamed Jose Cuervo for making her do it.

Later, she pulled out more stationery from one of the boxes headed to storage at Stella's and whipped out her favorite, extra-fine, expensive, black-ink pen. After lighting a candle, she stared out an open window until the song of the wind in the trees transported her all 5,683 miles across the ocean to a beautiful island. It took a while, but she got his name on the paper, and the words poured from her heart like never before.

Dearest Leo,

I know you were listening when I told Petras the truth about my time with Jack. You may think me weak, but my father had just passed away, and I had no one. I hadn't been raised to be strong, not like I am now after Skopelos. I married him, but I didn't love him. I think it was the same for Jack, a kind of disappointment both of us learned to live with. My Aunt Stella has hinted that he was after my trust money, but I hate to think that of anyone. So, when he died, I grieved more for a wasted life than for a beloved husband. I had no idea what true love meant or felt, other than what I had read in books, and I had my doubts about that after a while. I was afraid to tell you because I thought (and still do) that you would think badly of me, that I was somehow disloyal, or uncaring. I couldn't bear a look of disapproval in your eyes, so I said nothing. Not even when I began to realize what love really was, what it felt like, and how much it hurt.

I thought something happened between us, but you were so focused on saving your business I started to think you'd taken care of me just to get at what was in my head, and being attracted to me was just something that happened. I can understand that. I couldn't tell you how I truly felt, or how you truly felt about me until that last time when you kissed me.

On the patio, Petras said you would not ask me to stay because you are Greek, and I told him I would not beg you to let me stay because I am American. So, in a way, I see that as why we are here, an ocean apart. You see, my father taught at the university, and I've met students from many countries. I'm familiar with the problems some of them faced when they became interested in an American woman or man. Merging two cultures can be difficult, sometimes impossible.

I have put the house up for sale. Ellie Townsend is not who I am anymore, so I walk and think, and try to merge the past into the present. I try to stay away from the future, but, like you said, wherever I look, you are there.

Thank you for saving my life, for holding me when I cried at night, for making me laugh, for bringing color back into my life. For taking a bullet for me. For loving me.

Hug Petras and Nitsa. And Thurman, if you should see him.

With all my heart.

Layna

She copied his address and made a note to go to a UPS store first thing in the morning.

Then, her task complete, she reached for the tequila.

"That should twist his little knickers," she muttered, then drew her head back in surprise. Where did that come from? Probably Stella. She wished her old friend was there, so they could high-five. But Stella wasn't there. Nobody was there.

She looked around at the boxes, the empty fridge, and the silence.

"God, what have I done?"

Dr. Hahlberg had scheduled a Skype meeting for the following day via e-mail. Layna asked her aunt if she would like to sit in. Stella gave her a beautiful leather handbag for her birthday and mumbled something about wild horses not keeping her away.

The woman on the computer screen seemed formidable at first. Dr. Hahlberg had been there in the very beginning of a frightening reality, but the doctor soon put her at ease.

"I'm thrilled to see for myself how the woman I observed in Athens has metamorphosed into a lovely young lady, normal and healthy to all appearances."

The doctor asked permission to record the session.

After introducing Stella and making sure it was all right if she sat in on their talk, Layna thanked the doctor for her time.

They spoke at first of Dr. Hahlberg's visit to the house in Athens, and her impressions at the onset of Layna's condition. Being well-aware of what she looked like, Layna was horrified to learn of her behavior, how truly "out of it" she really was. She thought of what Leo must have endured to take care of her. And she heard intakes of breath from her aunt sitting beside her.

Layna related bits and pieces of memory that had come to her before everything crashed down on her in the cave, when her memory spontaneously returned.

"How did you feel, physically?" the doctor asked.

"It was an outpouring, like an erupting volcano or an explosion," Layna said. "I thought my head would crack like a fissure in hard ground."

Dr. Hahlberg smiled, nodding slowly as she considered her words. "Perfectly normal when the memory comes all at once instead of over a period of time. You are fortunate. For some, it is so traumatic, their minds draw back in horror and that is where they remain. But tell me, dear, has your memory returned in full?"

"I can recall as far back as kindergarten," Layna said. "I would say at least 90% has been recovered. But I have questions after googling all the things you referred to in my initial diagnosis."

"Yes?"

"I couldn't find anything to tell me if it would happen again. I mean, without being hit on the head or witnessing a death."

"You have also read my articles on predisposition to dissociative disorders?"

"I have."

"What did you find of interest there?"

"The things you mentioned —being clumsy and withdrawn, ignored by parents, insufficiently prepared for the real world—everything rang true. I admit, I was shocked when you related it to high-functioning autism. Then I realized that's my past. What does it mean for my future?"

"The symptoms you identified with only mean you were predisposed to some kind of dissociative disorder," the doctor said. "Many people experience these things without suffering a specific, traumatic event. It is like high-functioning autism being the *new normal*, as they say. Half a million people can check off every symptom, but most of them will never know they have any kind of disability."

"But will it happen again?" Layna asked. "I don't think I can move forward until I know one way or the other."

The doctor thought a moment before continuing. "Do you feel like it could recur?"

"No, but that's not what I asked. Please, doctor."

"Because it happened before does not mean it will occur again of its own choice. After seeing you and speaking with you, I would say you've outgrown the predisposition, put it behind you, as it were. You appear stronger mentally than the majority of my patients who have survived conditions similar to your own and worse."

With tears in her eyes, Layna cleared her throat and stared at the face on the screen. She felt Stella's reassuring hand on her shoulder.

"Still," the doctor continued, "I cannot project into the future based on a casual session done by computer. So I cannot say something may or may not trigger an onset of amnesia in the future. I must see you in person and observe you. Would you be amenable to this?"

"Yes, of course," Layna said. "I could even come to Germany to see you when it's time."

"That would be wonderful!" the doctor said. "I had wanted to do so in the beginning, but your young man was most adamant that you stay in his protection."

"Leo?"

"Yes, I believe that was his name. Is he still your guardian and protector?"

"He is," Layna said. "He was one of the men in the cave who saved my life."

"Ah. Your voice softened. Do I detect a romantic interest?"

"You bet your bippy," Stella commented in the background. Layna shushed her.

"Which is why I'm anxious to put this matter to rest," Layna interjected. "But I'm having difficulty doing so. What do I do with the person I was before I was Layna?"

Dr. Hahlberg tilted her head and narrowed her eyes for a moment. "You're speaking in the third person, past tense. I'm not following. Could you be more specific?"

"I need to know whether I must live with who I once was. Ellie isn't who I am today."

"Are you implying an entirely new personality?"

"Not really," Layna began, her voice hesitant.

"Yes, really," Stella said over her shoulder.

The doctor appeared confused, but interested.

"Before I woke up in Athens," Layna said, "I was Eleanor Townsend from Tallahassee, Florida, married to Jack Taggart. You said Leo told you how I witnessed my husband's death, right? But now I'm Layna, the name Leo gave me, the one you know me by. And she's different. I mean, I'm different."

"Clear as mud," Stella added.

Layna waved her hand at her to be quiet while the doctor continued.

"Have you taken on this Layna personality only since the accident?"

"Yes, since waking up in Athens. I mean, really waking up. But there have been several occasions when I feel Ellie—Eleanor—pulling me back into the past. I've lived in Florida most of my life, but I can't relate to anything anymore, other than a favorite aunt—the one I introduced you to—the one who keeps interrupting. Everything else seems alien. Ellie's clothes, her room, her life. In fact, I'm selling the house. I don't understand why the person I used to be keeps surfacing. It feels almost like I have a split personality."

"It is a diverging personality and a fascinating transference. But if you're asking if there's some way to get rid of this Ellie, then my answer must be no. Who you were will always be a part of you. Yes, I can see how this would be discomforting. However, there are ways to reach a compromise."

"A compromise? How?"

"My dear, you've already begun, acknowledging who you were before. Everyone wants attention, even the many people we carry inside us every day. The wife wants attention as a wife, but she is also a mother, a daughter, perhaps a child. These can all be inside us in one mind, one personality. Normally, this is done without thinking of it. In your case, you must consciously merge these two personalities into one. It would perhaps be simpler to return to being Ellie, but that would be returning to the past. Yes. An interesting dilemma."

"Do I have to go on being both?"

"You've had no time to assimilate," the doctor said. "I can understand why you would wish to move forward. From what you've told me, you are more comfortable with the Layna personality, true?

"Definitely."

"Then continue towards that destination. You are in a unique position to change where you live, where you work, the people you know who still think of you as that person. These things will help the transformation. This phenomenon is common among trauma

CHAPTER THIRTY-SIX

Μάτια που δε βλέπονται, γρήγορα λησμονιούνται.

EYES THAT DO NOT SEE EACH OTHER,
THEY SOON FORGET.

patients coming out of amnesia into a new world. It is extremely difficult for those already married, who emerge as a different person, or those returning from a war who present another personality altogether. In time, Ellie will fade into the background, into the past where she belongs, but she is your only link to your former life. I would not advise you sever the connection; rather, allow it to die a quiet death on its own."

"Are you saying I have to placate that part of me until it happens?"

"I'm saying I applaud your determination to be the person you feel called to be. The part of you that is Ellie knows her time of prominence is at an end. She only wants to be included, else she would not be fighting so hard, yes?"

Layna buried her face in her hands and sobbed from relief and apprehension. She was free, but Ellie would always be there in some form or other.

Stella put on hand on Layna's arm. "Honey, I knew Ellie most of her life. She was a sweet girl. Smart, brave. You could do worse."

Deep inside, Layna and Ellie agreed to disagree, realizing Dr. Hahlberg had just made both their lives possible. It was a truce, not a surrender. Layna knew it wasn't over, that there would be a few more battles, but there would be peace talks, too.

"Doctor, how can I ever thank you?" she asked.

"By staying strong," Dr. Hahlberg said, herself a little misty-eyed. "And by realizing this is not a cure. It is a process. Please, leave me your e-mail address. I'll send you my schedule, a list of my fees, and a paper I would ask you to sign and return."

"A paper?" Layna asked, wiping tears from her face.

"If you would be so kind," the doctor said, smiling, "I am working on a book covering exactly what you have survived. I plan to call it *Coming Out of Darkness*, and I would very much like permission to include your story as one of the chapters. I would use only a case number, not your name. It could help others facing what you have gone through. Would you do this?"

"Yes, of course," Layna said. "And I'll remember what you said, that it's not over yet. We can meet once a month by computer then, until I can get to Germany?"

"I look forward to it. I am curious to see how the Ellie situation resolves itself. If you have any concerns between our sessions, please call me at once. Agreed?"

Layna nodded.

The doctor chuckled. "I usually warn those emerging from a suppressed past not to go on any new adventures, or do something wild and crazy to make up for lost time. But somehow, I think you have already had your adventure—and quite possibly are planning another?"

"I have, and am," she said.

Stella snorted in the background.

The doctor laughed. "The main thing," she said, "is to enjoy the dance." And she signed off the zoom meet.

Layna turned the computer off and watched the screen fade to black, along with many of her fears and misgivings. That night, after long months of turmoil, she slept peacefully, deeply, surrounded by the fragrance of white roses whispering her name.

The Greek name. Not the other one.

Stella had arranged for a letter of credit with the bank so the money in her trust fund was now available even in a foreign country, either as Ellie Townsend or Layna Amratsis, thanks to the two passports and a Marriage Certificate. Stella said it was amazing what artists and writers get away with. Layna's first act was to transfer a hefty sum over to her aunt's account as payback for funding her Mediterranean adventure at the beginning. Now, she could look for a smaller, more comfortable place. Rent an apartment. Start her own art studio. Buy an airplane ticket. Go crazy.

After weeks of waiting, a second letter arrived from Skopelos.

My Layna,

Your letter was most welcome. It adds the warmth to my heart. Your painting, it is above the fireplace now. It belongs.

Can you tell me what Dr. Hahlberg says to you? I am most anxious to know.

Your words for your husband took my guilt away and let me see your compassion. I ask if you are willing to do as you suggested, to roll the dice where we are concerned. You are a beautiful woman. Not just on the outside. A man wants what is outside. He loves what is inside, if it is also beautiful. If God wills it for us, then it will be.

I want you in my bed. I will make you happy. It is my job, my pleasure to do so. Know that I did not want to leave you that night at the hotel. I had to. Like everything else that interrupts my life, it had to do with my business. I will explain later, in the bed.

For now, I leave you another quote from Socrates. He said "Painting is silent poetry, and poetry is painting that speaks." I think maybe you will understand this because you are an artist. I was at university two years and observed many women, American and others. I saw women who could not get the man because they became like the man for the power. I am not so good with the words. Please understand. A woman who is loved for who

CHAPTER THIRTY-SEVEN

Γυναίκα που δε θέλει να ζυμώσει, πέντε μέρες κοσκινίζει.

THE WOMAN WHO DOESN'T WISH TO BAKE BREAD, SPENDS FIVE DAYS SIFTING THE FLOUR.

she is already has the power. It is sad few women understand this. American, that is. Women in other countries know this from a young age.

I wanted you, yes. I love you now on the inside. A beautiful bird that can only fly on the wind, you do not put in a cage. Do not worry, little bird. I know you have the heart of an eagle. Like my ships, we will plow the waters as we come to them.

I think of you always.

Leonidas

Emotions ran the gamut in her heart and mind, and she wished he'd explained what was happening with his business now, not later. Still, she had to smile at his Socrates quote. She'd been painting for weeks—and not just the living room walls.

Leo sat at his desk, his left hand shading his eyes even though no sun coursed through the French windows. Everything in his study had been repaired or replaced. He'd decided to keep his father's desk after filling in the bullet holes and refinishing the surface, despite the excellent advice from the furniture restorer to let him handle the entire thing.

The busted French windows had been replaced, and all evidence of Aleksandra's presence had been boxed up and mailed to her uncle's house. End of story. Even Thurman assured him the book was closed on Aleksandra.

But Leo's mind wasn't on his recently-convicted stepmother, or on Layna, though she was a part of every day. His business was in jeopardy. He refused to run guns, trade in illegal contraband, or traffic in drugs. And in his country's failing economy, that meant an end to any kind of profit. Between piracy, graft, and growing concerns over environmental issues and climate change, Piraeus was fast becoming the last stanchion of Greek shipping. Should he move his ships through Piraeus instead of Volos?

It was difficult enough dealing with the dissimilar mentalities, changing currencies, and cultural differences since joining the EU. Now, with the influx of refugees pouring in from all directions into an already struggling economy, the older shipping families were struggling to support themselves and remain the bulwark of a nation dependent on the shipping industry.

He felt in his heart the "Greek adventure" would continue as it had for thousands of years, though he was hard-pressed to come up with any valid reasons. He let out a long sigh and looked over his accountant's report yet again before calling it a night.

Maybe he should sell real estate.

He'd given Petras a well-deserved vacation so his friend could reacquaint himself with his wife and children, but his cousin's absence left a strangely quiet void Leo hadn't experienced before. Background music helped, but when he unhooked his MP3 or turned off the CD player, silence crept back in like a reluctant thief.

Before moving back into the master bedroom, he replaced the old-fashioned canopy bed with a more modern memory-foam mattress on a riser. Instead of a headboard, he found a print by someone named Richard Franklin. He hadn't paid much attention to art before, but this one had tugged at his heart until he felt compelled to purchase it, even though it lacked a title and cost a fortune. It depicted the old adage that "love is blind."

Even now, Leo looked at it, entranced by the faces of two lovers standing next to one another, their eyes contemplating other worlds, yet seeing nothing. It was painful, yet beautiful. He knew the artist was born in the United States; he'd looked him up in the computer. But he didn't understand how his work could seem so ancient, and yet, so modern until he read even further. The man had studied in Europe and the Middle East. He wondered if Layna knew about Richard Franklin.

Layna, who had lost her mind and then her heart. And then had left.

Leo stood half-naked in his bedroom and allowed himself the luxury of sorrow and regret. How could he not, when everything reminded him of her presence, her absence, and their time together. Raising his eyes once more to the painting, he turned the light off and felt the cool sheets embrace him. He stretched out, then automatically turned onto his side, draping his arm over a body pillow and closing his mind to the thunderous silence.

Above him, two lovers, content to be in one another's presence, stared off and down at nothing in particular, oblivious to the world.

Layna awoke with a throbbing head. She vaguely remembered trying to belly dance, but her fingers had somehow gotten tangled up in the zils. Maybe it was the discounted CD of Greek music she'd found at a media store. She'd tried shouting "Opa!" and gyrating her hips, but her heart just wasn't in it, or her hips for that matter. Not to mention not having enough on top to shimmy. In the end, she decided if Petras' wife intended to teach her to belly dance, she'd definitely have her work cut out for her.

Finally, she crumpled in a heap on the hardwood floor, sobbing. Animal sounds dissolved into intermittent tears, interrupted by her cell phone vibrating in an obscene manner. Wiping one eye clear, she saw the caller ID. Stella.

"Ellie? Are you there?" Her aunt's voice could normally be heard over lawn mowers.

"Stella! You've got to help me!"

"Ellie, what's wrong?"

"Stop calling me that!"

"Sorry. I forgot," Stella said. "Stay where you are. Wait. You're at the house, right?"

"Yeah."

"Well, stay there. Don't go anywhere. Okay?"

"Uh-huh."

"I'll be there in 25 minutes. Hear me? Ellie, Layna, whoever…say something."

"I'm tired of dancing alone."

"That's not what I meant, but it'll do," Stella said with a slight chuckle. "But right now, I need for you to focus. And keep talking. I'm on my way."

"Okay. Bye, Stella."

"Bye? Nononononono. Don't end the call," Stella yelled. "Keep talking. Understand?"

"Uh-huh. G'bye."

Stella heard the click at the other end.

"Damn it, girl."

Layna remembered ending the call and stretching out on the nice, cool floor, thinking everything would be all right now. Aunt Stella would make everything okay again.

That's where her memory faded to black.

Now, waking up to the smell of cinnamon and nutmeg, she wondered why everything was way too bright, and why she was sleeping all alone in someone's twin-size bed in a strange house with a gazillion windows. And why she felt like she was going to throw up.

How convenient.

Someone had left a lined trash can right beside the bed.

Much, much later, she raised up and wiped her face on her shirtsleeve. She opened the door, stumbling into what looked an awful lot like Stella's kitchen. And look, there was Stella, grinning and shaking her head. If it was a dream, it was pretty damned realistic. And in color. She made her way to the table with four chairs and slumped down in one of the empties.

Stella's voice sounded past the fuzzy barricade. "Has it ever occurred to you that you shouldn't drink if you can't hold your liquor?"

"It wasn't my fault," Layna grumbled. "It was José. We had this huge send-off for Evil Ellie. Gone for good."

"I see," Stella said. "No more split personality?"

"Nope. No personality *whatsoever*. Promise." Layna looked up at her friend with sad, quiet eyes. Eyes that were thinking clearly. Even through the morning-after haze, it showed.

"Damn, you *are* better," Stella said. "I wondered when your mother would finally surface."

"My mother?"

"Yeah, I was getting tired of Ellie looking like Layna and trying to sound like Stella when we're all as different as fudge and turtle soup.

You were just starting to find your way out of Pubertyville when you married Jack, but he kinda put a damper on things. I'm thinking the real you is out at last. You don't drink, darlin'—you never have. At least, you've never done it well. And you sure as hell don't say *shit* or *fuck*. Takes a certain flair to curse and do it right, and you ain't got it. Sorry. Out of character. So, *Layna*, what do you have in mind, other than buying a new wardrobe and an airline ticket?"

"Shit, how did you know?" She hiccupped. "Sorry. You're absolutely right. Last night I asked myself why I was looking for a smaller house. Do I *really* see myself living in Tallahassee the rest of my life?"

"And what did you and José decide?"

Layna undid the clasp of the silver chain necklace she had worn since returning to Florida. She pulled the chain from her neck, held it up, and heard the ping of the diamond ring as it hit the wooden floor, where it flashed back and forth until it settled.

Layna leaned over to retrieve it and deeply regretted the decision when the room tilted. She put out her hand so she wouldn't keep going forward, and finally succeeded in picking up the ring. Once upright, she held it in her palm, marveling at how it reflected the light, how perfectly beautiful it was, like the man who'd given it to her.

Stella gasped and took it from her.

"Jesus! It appears you haven't told me absolutely everything after all."

"I confess," Layna said, stumbling while her tongue tried to work properly. "This, dearest auntie, is the one I would pick out if I had all the rings in the world to choose from."

"Wasn't that a line from a Meg Ryan movie?"

"Probably."

"It is!" Stella yelled.

Layna jumped.

"*Sleepless in Seattle*, right? Before she dumps the guy she's with to meet a stranger on top of the Empire State Building! What? I thought you loved romantic comedies."

"*Ellie* liked them."

"Touché. So when you told me about the ring, I assumed you gave it back to him. You failed to mention you *kept* it!"

"He wouldn't take it back."

"He wouldn't—girl, what are you doing *here* when you should be *there*!"

"I'm taking care of business."

Layna's raised palms started pumping air, totally out of character, as she boogied up and down and sang, or tried to.

"Taking care of business. Whooooo! Taking care of business. Whooooo!"

"Oh Lordy, you're still snockered," Stella said, grinning. "You need coffee and plenty of it. And I can do without Bachman Turner Overdrive, not to mention the seventies." Stella rolled her eyes, made her way to the counter, and came back with coffee for her favorite, only niece.

"Now, why are you still here?" she asked, resuming her seat.

"Stalling for time till I could put myself together again, all the little pieces that made no sense. Burying my husband. Selling my house. Getting ready to do a really crazy-ass thing, and I got that from you so don't shake your head at me. Oh, and I needed money."

"Not any more," Stella said. She slid an envelope across the table. "This, my dear, is your going-away gift."

"I can't take your money," Layna said, pushing it halfway back.

"It's *your* money," Stella said quietly. "Remember? Twenty-five? The magic birthday?"

Stella grinned, went to the cupboard, and came back with a small box. She slid it across the table to Layna, who grinned a little-girl grin and opened it up. Inside, there was a gorgeous antique diamond necklace with matching dangling earrings.

"Happy birthday, darlin'," Stella said. "It was your mom's. Your father bought that for her on their first anniversary."

"Stella, it's beautiful."

Her aunt sat back, assessing the situation in between heartbeats.

As much as she loved her niece, she knew she'd have to push her off the branch, or Little Ellie would stay in Florida the rest of her lonely life. And the kind of love the kid felt for Leo only came along once in a lifetime. She'd have to act quickly, while Layna was still only slightly woozy.

"And my present to you," she said, "is an appointment with a hair stylist, a manicurist, and a day spa. You can't go to Greece lookin' like that."

"Wow," Layna whispered. "I feel like Cinderella at the end of the story. And you're saying that, on top of all this, I get money, too? To do whatever I want?"

"The whole enchilada, from the trust your father set up. The one I told you about."

Even with tequila-brain, Layna remembered. She tilted her head until her eyes cleared, then took a swig of hot coffee and opened the envelope. It was a letter of credit from the Tallahassee bank her father had used for years. She could have sworn it said she had $513,566.22 available funds in U.S. currency. Stella grinned big and wide.

"See? You can do any crazy-ass thing your little heart desires," she said.

"I think... I'm already...losing my resolve," Layna said, swallowing hard. "Must be the shock." She drank more coffee.

"Hell, we can't let that happen." Stella got up and started imitating her niece, both palms pumping air while she attempted to bump and grind parts of her that remembered how but weren't quite up to it.

Layna erupted in a cascade of laughter, like pearls floating over a waterfall. Stella stopped and sat down again, wiping happy-tears away with her shirt sleeve.

"That laugh was your mother all over again," Stella said "pure and sweet and ladylike."

Layna took a deep breath and sipped her coffee, made a face at the lack of sugar and cream, which she finally noticed, and rose

CHAPTER THIRTY-EIGHT

Ή μικρός παντρέψου, ή μικρός καλογερέψου.

EITHER MARRY EARLY, OR BECOME A MONK.

to rectify the situation, even as her mind moved upward and out, spreading those wings, or trying to.

"So, what's the worst that could happen?" Layna asked. "That I make an utter fool of myself, after which he says thanks but no thanks?"

"In which case," Stella said, "you open an art studio and paint your ass off. But, whether you're here or there, you're gonna go right on loving him, right?" Stella pointed to Layna's hand. "There's really only one decision, and it looks like you already made it."

Layna followed her aunt's line of vision. She'd placed Leo's ring back on her finger. A part of her deep inside was calm. Of course, the rest of her could have jumped out the window of a very tall building. She'd gone all the way there and back again, full circle. The only thing still standing in her way was one tiny little problem. He hadn't asked her to come back yet. Then again, he'd asked her not to leave.

Should she take a leap of faith, and land on her butt in a foreign country?

Ever since her plane had landed in Tallahassee, and all through the funeral fiasco, in the back of her mind there had always been the question of *how long is long enough?* What if she waited too long? What if she went back too soon, and wasn't really ready? And what was he going through that wove its way in between his words but never made a complete sentence? Even if she wasn't ready, she knew he needed her just like she needed him.

She looked at Stella, who was taking sausage-and-egg biscuits out of the oven.

"Stella, Leo said maybe we should just go for it, though not in those words. You know, lay our cards on the table and roll the dice, like Jack did, that we don't really know what's going to happen. I mean about my coma thing."

"That's true about anything. It's the fun part of being in love. From what you've told me, I think this Leo of yours is a once in a lifetime, darlin'. And when he takes to you bed, you don't be afraid or embarrassed. My money says he knows a thing or two."

Layna acknowledged the comment with a coy smile and slathered homemade strawberry on her sausage biscuit in wild anticipation, before the scent of pork assaulted her nostrils and her stomach rebelled. Stella laughed and put some bread in the toaster.

Meanwhile, Layna thought about Nitsa and Petras and Thurman and everyone she'd left behind, people who meant more to her than anyone she'd ever known in the States, except dear, sweet, lovable Stella. Doubts descended like a torrential downpour. He said *the sea never dies*. Maybe, just maybe, for some people it was true. But the only way to know was to dive in.

Stella handed her a slice of dry toast and waited.

"It's a big gamble," Layna said.

"Love always is," Stella replied. "So, where are you headed?"

"I'm going home," Layna said, "to Leo."

Stella let out a very unladylike rebel yell and gathered Layna into her arms, speed-talking as she pushed her through the front door.

"First, we go shopping. You are not going to see Leo dressed in anything but new and classy. By noon, you should be done. Then on to the spa. Meanwhile, we go on the internet, book your flight, and reserve a room, just in case. Don't look at me like that, girl. Always plan for contingencies, even with a sure thing."

All went according to plan, almost. Reservations were made, but the last of the boxes had to be stored at Stella's. And shopping took way longer than either of them expected. The four outfits Layna decided on may not have been designer, but they reeked of quiet class. Stella kept her on schedule for the hair salon and manicurist, then the spa treatment. When it was over, Layna felt as though every part of her body glowed.

She ate a healthy meal, and Stella gave her a supplement to help her sleep. Her last, stomach-churning night in the United States of America. Until Stella's herbal concoction kicked in, and she awoke to sunshine and cackling chickens.

Finally, armed with a purse, a carry-on and two humongous suitcases asleep in the belly of the plane, she said a tearful goodbye to Stella, which involved a great many hugs and even more promises to call and write.

Chewing her lip, she presented the passport Thurman had acquired for her.

The Greek one. Not the American one.

She boarded a United headed for Atlanta, then a Lufthansa over the Atlantic. Final destination, Athens. The last time she saw Leo, it was goodbye. This time, it would be hello.

She closed her eyes, and the plane flew into the sun.

Nearly eighteen hours later, including a five-hour flight from London, a tired Aegean airplane descended through a light, mid-morning drizzle onto a runway in Athens. Even with Greece being seven hours ahead of Florida, Layna had still somehow managed to lose an entire day. She'd booked a room at the Electra for four days and nights, since she anticipated much sightseeing, but she continued to ponder the mysteries of time zones all the way through customs, declarations, and some stranger rifling through her underwear. Five clocks, staring at her from an otherwise blank wall, didn't help.

Finally, she escaped into the real world and hailed a cab, fairly certain she'd be overcharged—even after a crash course on Greek currency.

Aunt Stella had assured her she needn't worry about looking for bargains any more, but Layna's newfound wealth was going to take some getting used to. Her zoned-out mind pondered the point, but only for a moment. She grabbed the oh-shit handle as a taxi driver careened down narrow streets. She grinned. It felt good to be home.

Her hotel room was spacious and inviting, with a living/dining area and a separate bedroom/bath. After a hot shower, she ventured to a nearby restaurant for a salad. She declined a side dish of calamari but opted for moussaka. It seemed strange to be enjoying a famous city by herself—everywhere she looked, she saw couples, out on the town. Jet lag settled around her like London fog, and she returned to the hotel where she crawled into her pajamas and beneath cold sheets, hoping the fatigue would pass.

When she awoke ten hours later feeling sufficiently recovered, she ordered a chicken salad from room service. It was 4:30 p.m., and presumably Friday, though it could've been Saturday in China for all she knew.

Standing beneath pelting water from the showerhead helped clear away the last of the misfiring synapses to where she could think again. The heat from the hair wand seemed to seal the split ends in her head as well. After slipping into a sweater and slacks and saying to hell with either sandals or a bra, she realized she needed a strategy. She was here, in Greece, but where was Leo? She sat on the bed, realizing it could take several days to track him down.

She'd explored a hundred imagined scenarios during her awake moments on the plane, but no ideas had come to mind, other than sexual ones. The same thing happened now. She'd never chased a man across the world to a strange country or anywhere else. But even now, when she pictured him in her mind, she couldn't breathe.

She drew back the drapes and opened sliding doors that led onto a small balcony. Being on the second floor, she felt relatively safe in doing so. She breathed in the sea, wondering what on earth she thought she was doing. It wasn't just Leo she'd missed. A gal from Tallahassee had fallen in love with the people and places of Greece.

The sights and sounds of people and traffic, slightly muffled, calmed her mind but provided no answers to her dilemma. But what should she do next?

Let him know you're here. Duh.

With a wishful smile, and one more deep inhalation of a sea breeze, Layna came back inside, picked up her phone and lay across the queen-size bed, inputting one of the numbers Thurman had given her when she'd departed Greece on that awful rainy day. The sun's rays were low in the sky, and her fingers were a little shaky, but what the hell.

The number came up on the screen. *Simple enough to press the button.* But the thought of hearing Leo's voice made her stomach clench in anticipation. She realized the memory of Jack and their disastrous sex life still hung on her mind, trying to mess with reality.

She got up and checked her makeup in the mirror—it's easier to sound sexy when you look the part, right? A few sips of bottled water did little to quench the butterflies in her heart.

Back on the bed, she played for time, pressing her lips together and rocking herself back and forth. The screen on her phone had gone dark. Exasperated, and before she had time to think about it, she clicked the Home button and put the call through.

There.

Done.

Petras the speed-scroller would be proud.

She waited, holding her breath while her stomach turned somersaults.

Someone answered in Greek. It wasn't Leo; it was the speed-scroller himself.

She stood.

Her heart lurched into her throat.

"Petras?" Her voice sounded small and terrified, not at all the devil-may-care, aggressive one she'd intended to use. In her nervousness, she'd entered the wrong number!

"Layna?"

"Yes. It's...Layna."

Of course it's Layna! Ellie wouldn't have made it to the plane. And Eleanor would never have considered carrying out such a foolhardy adventure. No, only Layna would make an utter fool of herself!

"How are you? And Demetra ? And your lovely children?"

"I am fine. Demetra is beautiful. My children are strong and healthy," he said.

Layna could tell he was grinning.

"What's wrong?" Petras asked. "Where are you?"

"I'm-I'm-I'm in Athens, actually. At the Electra."

"Did you say Athens? You are in Greece? Does Leo know!"

She held the phone away from her ear. "No, no, no. I just called to let you know I'm here," Layna said. "You know, on vacation, kind of." *Liar, liar, pants on fire.* "I'm at the Electra. Oh, I said that. I'm not sure why. I mean, why I'm calling, not why I—"

"Much has happened," Petra said. "I am in Skopelos, but Leo is in Athens, not far from where you are. I know he would like to see you. I will call him."

"I—I—"

"I will call him," Petras repeated. "He will be so happy."

"Okay. Okay. Thank you. God bless you. And Demetra.

Goodbye—and Nitsa. Petras!"

But Petras had hung up to call his cousin.

"And Thurman," Layna sighed. She always put him last on the list. She didn't know why. Or why she flopped back on the bed, exhausted.

Oh God, what have I done?

She scrambled off the bed, her heart thumping. She hadn't expected things to move so quickly! A race to her luggage provided a cream-colored silk blouse and gold gabardine slacks. Thank God she'd taken a shower and fixed her hair! She still hit the bathroom running in order to change, fumbling over the buttons and checking herself in the mirror. Finally, she searched the room for tequila. Realizing she was going to have to do this cold turkey, she started talking to herself, out loud—never a good sign.

"All good. We are good to go. Houston, we have lift-off. Okay. Now, what? I wait, right? Leo's in Athens, but where? How far away? Do I have time for a nervous breakdown? Why is Jose Cuervo never around when you need him? Why am I rushing around? He's probably too busy to call! Maybe he's changed his mind and doesn't want to call!"

Her phone rang. Her pacing ended at the bed, where the phone rang a second time.

Don't ever appear anxious.

Her brain screamed in defiance to protocol and she grabbed the phone.

"Hello?" she said, her voice sounding more like a wounded frog than a sexy female.

"Layna?"

She closed her eyes in wonder at his husky voice and what it did to her when he said her name, the lovely name he'd given her. Her heart sang.

"Yes. I'm here."

"I am very near," Leo said. "Twenty minutes only. Do not go away, yes?"

"You're coming over *now?*"

"Yes, of course, unless you do not wish me to. Say you wait for me?"

"*Se peremino*. I wait for you."

A pause lingered in the air around her.

"*You say it well,*" Leo whispered.

The phone call ended on his end, then on hers.

In a daze, she brushed her teeth, again. Not an easy task when your hands are shaking.

She checked the time, again. Glanced in the mirror one last time.

"Sorry, Ellie. This is where we part company."

She sprayed Passion on her wrists and neck, reapplied her makeup, fluffed her hair, lotioned her elbows, and cursed the fact there were no candles. Who cares if they're a fire hazard? Not being accustomed to staying in hotels, it finally dawned on her to dim the lights.

A knock on the door. Already?

She made it there without hyperventilating.

His dark-lashed eyes gleamed with indescribable joy.

She could only mouth his name, soundless and speechless at the sight of him in a black polo shirt and black slacks, wearing the necklace she'd given him.

God, he's so gorgeous.

Leo stepped into the room and framed her face with both hands, running his fingers into her thick hair as his mouth covered hers. The kiss was long and deep. At one point, she felt him move his leg, and she heard the door close with a click, then Leo's hands slid down her back to press her slender body against his muscled one.

"*Layna,*" he whispered, "*you are so beautiful like I remember, but more now. My heart, it is full of love for you. Do not tell me no.*" He kissed her neck, sinking his teeth gently into a place where her shoulder began, sending chills up and down her spine and into her mind so that she couldn't think for wanting him, needing him.

She slid her hands up his hard-muscled arms and encircled his neck, answering his question mouth-to-mouth and heart-to-heart. He lifted her up, causing her face to rise a little higher than his own and continued kissing her, her hair cascading down around them as he turned slowly around and around all the way to the bedroom. Finally, he lowered her down, ever so gently, until they stood face-to-face. He pried off his loafer-style shoes with apparently no socks to bother with; his bare feet touching hers felt strangely exciting.

A smile blessed the corners of his perfect mouth, and Layna reached up to brush his hair back, sinking her fingers into his thick hair, reveling once again in the sure knowledge they belonged together forever.

In the quiet, Leo ran his fingers along her back and teased her with half-kisses as he undid each and every button, brushing her blouse off her shoulders and onto the floor while Layna returned the favor by slipping his shirt up over his head, where it got stuck for a moment, causing nervous laughter from them both.

Leo's curious fingers undid the button to her slacks and slowly, seductively unzipped the zipper, lowering them down over her hips and letting them drop to the carpet, leaving her in nothing but laced bikini panties. She trembled as Leo lowered them carefully onto the carpet at her feet. A cool evening breeze caught her nipples and brought them up taut, while the noises of Athens in the streets below and restless stars across the night sky incensed her to reach up and grab the hair on the back of her lover's neck, drawing him into a fiery kiss.

Leo swallowed his surprise; the old Layna would never have been so openly seductive, or as playful. He was even more surprised when she started to unbuckle the belt on his jeans, but he stopped her from going any further.

"I am too excited to see you," he said with an embarrassed grin. "If you touch, I could die. I will do, this time." He pulled his black slacks off, then his terribly sexy, midnight blue, retro briefs. In two swift moves, he stood naked as well.

Layna couldn't help a short intake of breath at his muscled thighs, along with other aspects that in her artist's mind made him appear like something close to a Greek god bathed in moonlight. Then she caught the gleam of hunger in Leo's eyes and knew he'd devoured her assets as well. Feeling suddenly small and vulnerable, she looked up at her captor of long ago and felt under his power still, or again. Behind her, the huge bed yawned wide and terrible like the cave.

"Leo—"

But he'd sensed what was wrong and held her, feeling her soft breasts pressed against his chest and exercising supreme control until he knew she was ready. Something had happened to throw out the moment, but he knew with all his heart it was meant to be.

He lifted Layna in his arms, laid her on the bed, and looked at her, at all of her, in the moonlight that poured through the open drapes. With gentle fingers, he traced the contours of her lovely body while he kissed her face, her hair, her throat, her nipples.

"Leo, I don't—"

"Shhh. I wait long time to do this."

His hands roamed her body, teasingly up and down her back and spine, tracing the hills and valleys, running curious fingers up and down her inner thighs. When she trembled, his mouth found hers, and he claimed her with all the power at his command. His tongue teased her senses and halted her objections while his hand tormented her nipples until she arched her back. His hand slid down to the source of her agony and brought her to the point of wanting him so badly that she moaned and made sounds like begging. Only then did he move on top of her, and enter her, suddenly, powerfully, completely, covering her mouth with his and torturing her nipples until she dug her fingernails into his back.

Together, they rode the waves, her gasps and sighs carrying him deeper and harder. He lifted her buttocks with both hands and plowed her hard and fast until she gave out with a long cry. Her body shuddered as Leo groaned and joined her in a blinding release.

She cried. He smiled, knowing they were tears of joy and wonder, knowing that what she had spoken to Petras was the truth.

"I will love you always," Leo whispered, *"and you will never want another."* He leaned up and kissed her eyes, her mouth, her hair, her breasts. *"S'agapo."* His voice was husky and passionate, and Layna loved him more than she ever thought possible.

Leo lay back, perfectly content, and studied the ceiling with glistening eyes. When he pulled Layna to him, she placed her slender hand on his chest and cried quietly, her tears spilling past her quivering smile to trickle onto the crumpled sheets beneath their bodies. He took a deep breath. He had made her weep for joy, as he'd promised to do. He leaned over and kissed her face, still damp with her tears.

"My Layna," he said. "I see us in future. We grow old together, very happy. And we have two, maybe three childrens."

Layna's heart sang at his words. She laughed and cried in wonder.

He showered her with kisses. Her eyes, her mouth, her hair, the side of her face, as her breathing quieted and tears gave way to sighs.

He lay beside her, content. More so than he'd been in a very long time. *My God,* he thought to himself. *My God.*

"Layna?"

"Yes?" She turned toward him and nestled her face on his shoulder.

"We marry now, I think. If you want."

"Again?" she asked in a teasing tone. "Will there be a real priest this time?"

"There is beautiful chapel on St. John's, the *Agios Ioannis*—of course a real priest!" He feigned indignation, but she saw him smiling in the half-light of a full moon over Athens that streamed through the glass. "If you had not annulled, you would still be my wife."

"I thought *you* had the marriage annulled."

"No, Thurman, he give the papers to you," Leo said, then, "I do not wish to annul."

They paused a moment, looked at each other, and burst into laughter. They were still married, kind of.

Leo grabbed a handful of dark, golden hair in his excitement. So soft, so thick. "You are too beautiful," he whispered. "You drive me mad in the bed."

Layna closed her eyes to halt the tears of absolution, acquittal, deliverance.

She turned to Leo. "Is there a way to change my name to Layna? Legally, I mean?"

Leo pulled back and looked her in the face. "You are sure?"

"I'm sure."

"Then we find the way," he said, laying back. "And you will have the wedding dress. We buy in Athens. And a real priest. Everyone will come." He sighed. "But tonight, I am too happy. I sleep with the woman I love, and do not become a monk."

Layna clamped her lips together, but couldn't suppress the laughter. "A monk? Where did *that* come from? I *cannot* picture you in brown burlap with a rope around your middle!"

"It is an old saying. If you do not marry young, you become a monk. I would be a very young monk, of course. A very young, very handsome monk."

"I thought monks were celibate," she teased. With Leo distracted over *celibate*, she slid her hand shyly up his thigh and brought everything back to life. He had to laugh when he saw the surprise on Layna's face. If she could do that by accident, God help him when she learned how to do it on purpose!

As their souls grew quiet, they turned to look out the opened door, where the sounds of Athens, still a collage of vehicles and people, seemed more real to Layna than any part of Tallahassee she'd ever visited.

Leo turned to study her face. He could not get enough of her. His palm rested ever so lightly on her abdomen again. Her flat stomach and perfect little breasts turned his mind to what beautiful children they would make together. Maybe a daughter? Maybe a son! It was something he'd never thought possible until now.

Layna smiled and placed her hand on his.

He leaned over to kiss her. God, he loved kissing her.

He started to pull away, but she stopped him, wrapping her legs around him and pulling him in for more. Leo buried his face in her hair and held her for a long time, thinking of the many nights they would share in the bed, learning how to please one another and themselves.

There would be time enough to tell her about the fire, or that he'd sold *The Prometheus* and had purchased a hotel in Athens. There would be time enough for all the words later. For now, he would sleep with his Layna.

"I am thinking I finish business tomorrow and we go home."

"To Skopelos?"

"To Skopelos," he said, his face buried in her cascading hair when she threw her arms around his neck. He marveled at her laughter, so light and lovely—it filled him with the purest joy he'd ever known.

In the back of his mind, he began selecting names for two, maybe three children. He frowned. They could use Petras' room for the first

Thank you for reading "To Die on Skopelos." If you enjoyed reading it as much as I enjoyed writing it, please take a moment to post a review—I covet your feedback! Also, visit my website at www.cadenstclaire.com for interesting things I discovered in my research and incorporated into the book. Sometimes I select photos off the internet as visual representatives of how I see each character in my mind. While you're there, check out some free short stories and several poems. You're also welcome to leave comments and suggestions there as well—I'd love to know which scenes spoke to your heart! If you like historical romantic suspense, I've posted two chapters from The Ellington Hall Trilogy (1898 Devonshire, England) to peak your interest under a drop-down menu "Ellis in New York!" as well as blogs on writing and life in general. Have fun!

Thanks again for allowing me to take you far, far away.

Caden St. Claire

one, but what about the second one? Maybe he would build a villa, or enlarge his home. Their home. Yes, he liked that. *Their home.* Hell, he owned an entire hotel now!

He felt Layna's fingers tracing his mouth ever so lightly before she leaned up and kissed him. After a long, most delicious tarrying, he felt her hand wander across his chest, stopping near where the heart resides. She drew little circles with her polished fingernail lightly on his skin.

"Leo, you've seen my sketches, right?"

"I have. They are very good. Tell me, do you know Richard Franklin the artist?"

"I don't know him personally, but I love his work!"

"Good, then I have a wedding present for you at the house in Athens."

Layna gave him a curious glance. "Speaking of paintings, I've been thinking of setting up a shop in Skopelos Town where I could sketch and paint—I started to tell you before, but we were having a fight at the time. I did a lot of painting and sketching while I was in Tallahassee, and I'd like to sell my work to local people and to tourists. Will this be a problem for you?"

Leo kissed her hand. "Once you understand the customs, I think is a good idea. Do as you like. I have watched you struggle to find who you are, so if this is who you are, I would feel bad to say no. We will navigate the waters like the ships that plow the seas. You and I, we are the safe harbors."

"And the sea never dies," Layna said.

Leo's mouth covered hers tenderly in a drawn-out kiss.

Layna took a deep, easy breath in the quiet that followed. "Actually, I've always like the name Nicholas," she said, pretending to study the ceiling, "for a boy, I mean. *If you want.*"

His hand went up to rest itself alongside her lovely face.

"*My God, how I love you,*" he whispered.

She smiled, like the sun on water, even as her hand tripped playfully southward.

ACKNOWLEDGMENTS

My heartfelt gratitude to Mark Phillips with The Final Twist Writer's Society for his continued expertise at editing. As always, kudos aplenty to my beloved Beta reader, Jaime Welsh-Kovars, whose lovely eyes have found tiny little errors hiding in all the nooks and crannies and brought them into the light! I must also thank my writer's group, WriteMinded, for their patience and diligence in critiquing a very rough draft of Skopelos (Nessa, Chelsea-Buns, Steve, MJ, Gina, Ernie – you guys are above and beyond!) Special thanks to Greg Rupel of Enchanted Ink Publishing for his continued patience and artistic renderings, along with my special shipping container guru, Robert Hokanson, for his expert advice. Last but not least, a shout-out to Tasha Storfer for her artistic flair in taking a premade cover design and bringing it to life.

Caden St. Claire

CADEN ST. CLAIRE is a pseudonym for C. J. Sweet, a native Texan who graduated cum laude from the University of Houston with a degree in Communication (Radio/TV). She worked in the legal field for many years and taught English as a Second Language in public high school. She currently lives northwest of Houston with her gaming son, Cereal Masticator, and her orange & white verbal feline companion, Hemingway.

Made in the USA
Coppell, TX
20 May 2022

78007239R00188